Asher's Assignment

Wagner Brigade

Book Five

Ashley A Quinn

TCA Publishing LLC

ISBN: 978-1-959943-29-7

ONE

Days like today were ones where Esther Campbell questioned her life choices. Rain pelted the window to her classroom, doing little to drown out the sounds of the twenty kindergartners busy at their desks. No one was screaming, so she took a moment to glare at the weather. She had to drive in it soon. And not to her house, which was only a few minutes away. No, she'd picked up a tutoring job and now she had to drive across the city in this weather.

At least it wasn't snowing. She very much disliked driving in the rain, but she despised the snow more.

The shrill screech of one of her students turned her head. A moment later, Zoey stomped toward her. The girl held up two ends of a crayon, a fierce frown on her face. If kindergarteners could have a murder face, it would be the look on Zoey's.

"Evan broked my favorite blue crayon."

Esther glanced up, looking for the boy. He sat at his desk, tongue poked into the corner of his mouth while he concentrated on his work. He didn't look like he'd been causing trouble. But with a classroom full of five- and six-year-olds, she didn't always see everything.

"Let's go talk to him." She put two fingers on the girl's shoulder and turned her around.

The little girl marched over to Evan's desk and slammed the two pieces of crayon onto the tan surface. "You're in trouble now!"

"Zoey." Esther waited for the girl to look at her. "Let's be calm and polite, okay?"

The frown on the little girl's face deepened. "He broked my favorite blue crayon," she said, like that explained it all.

"I didn't do it on purpose!" Evan yelled. "It fell!"

Esther patted the air. "We need to keep our voices on the indoor setting. No one needs to yell." She looked at Zoey. "Is that true? Did it fall off the table?"

She nodded. "It rolled off, then he stepped on it."

"Not on purpose!" Evan glared at her, then looked up at Esther. "Zoey's always tattling. I didn't do nothing."

Esther counted to ten. These two had been bickering all day.

"Zoey, I'm sure Evan is sorry he stepped on your crayon. Right, Evan?" She cast a quick look at the boy.

He nodded. "I didn't mean to break it, Zoey."

"See? Now, what do you need to say to Evan?"

The girl's bottom lip popped out. "Sorry," she grumbled, then held up the pieces of crayon. "What about this?" That bottom lip started to quiver. "I liked this one. It colored nice."

"Come here." She took Zoey's hand and led her over to the cabinet, where she kept all the art supplies. Opening the door, she pulled out the bin that held all the blue crayons. "How about you pick a brand-new one?"

Zoey handed her the broken pieces of the one she held, drama forgotten, as her eyes widened at the sight of all the fresh crayons. She peered into the bin and picked one.

"You think that one will work?"

"Yep!" She scampered away. "Thanks, Miss Campbell!"

Esther sighed and put the bin back, shutting the cabinet door. Sometimes, all a girl needed was a sharp crayon.

The last thirty minutes of her day passed without incident. Once the kids were packed up, Esther led them down to the dismissal area, where they were split into car rider and bus rider groups. She was on car rider line duty today, so she stayed with those kids from her class.

"Yuck!"

Esther looked down at Zoey, who'd come up to her side. The girl stared out at the rain, her nose wrinkled.

"I agree, Zoey. I'm ready for some sunshine." They'd had several days of rain. Sometimes it was no more than a drizzle. Other times, it was a deluge. But it hadn't stopped since it started Monday morning. Right now, it was somewhere in between.

An image of a pristine beach, soft waves, and warm sunshine popped into her mind. It was hard to believe two months ago, she'd been sipping cocktails on a beach in Costa Rica with her sister, Edie, for Edie's vow renewal. Her sister was living it up, surfing every day, and walking in the soft sand with her sexy husband. All while Esther was stuck here, mitigating arguments over broken crayons and contemplating how fast she could run to her car in her high-heeled boots.

The radio in Esther's hand crackled to life, pulling her from her daydream. The teacher outside, reading off the names on the placards in the parents' vehicles, called Zoey's name.

"Bye, Miss Campbell!" The girl ran out the door before Esther could even lift a hand in farewell.

Esther chuckled. She might not be on a beach with a drop-dead gorgeous man, but she liked her life. Kids were great.

Once the car riders were all on their way home, Esther

hurried back to her classroom to gather all her things and head to the Tylers' house. She wished she could go home, but tickets to Costa Rica weren't cheap, and she intended to visit Edie and Jordan as often as possible.

Hitting the lights, she looped her big purse over her shoulder and left the building. Water dripped down the sides of her face as she got into her little white compact SUV. Esther swiped at her face and started the car. Digging into her oversize purse, she unearthed her digital thermometer and took her temperature, checking to make sure she was safe to visit Leah. An illness could be deadly for the little girl.

The thermometer beeped and showed a temperature well within the normal range. Satisfied she was well, Esther stowed the thermometer, buckled her seatbelt, and put the car in gear. With her windshield wipers swishing away the rain, she rolled out of the parking lot.

The steady downpour gave way to a drizzle as she reached the other side of town. She was glad. This family was a little... judgmental, and she didn't want to walk into their house looking like a drowned rat. They already didn't like the fact that the state made them have a teacher come into their home every day. But their daughter couldn't go to school. She'd had a heart transplant a couple of months prior and was still recuperating. Honestly, Esther didn't understand why her parents didn't submit the documentation to the district that would allow them to homeschool the girl. But until they did, she would continue to show up with a smile and keep Leah caught up so that one day she could return to school.

After parking at the curb, Esther walked up the crumbling porch steps, then knocked on the door. She heard the family's Chiweenie set off a howl inside and smiled. The parents might be rude, but the dog was sweet. So was the kid.

The inner door opened and Leah's father, Rob, frowned at her through the screen door.

"Good afternoon, Mr. Tyler." She pasted a bright smile on her face.

He grunted and pushed open the storm door. "Leah's in the kitchen."

Esther stepped inside and hurried past him. She felt his eyes on her as she walked through the living room to the small kitchen at the back of the house. He wasn't someone she'd want to be alone with. Everywhere she went, his twitchy gaze followed. The only respite she got was when she and Leah sat in the kitchen. Sometimes, though, he'd sit in on the couch, which gave him a direct line of sight through the kitchen doorway. Those days, she tried to turn her back to him or sit on the other side of the table, out of view. The moment she stepped out of the kitchen to leave, however, his gaze was on her, raking over her body and lingering on the places that made her the most uncomfortable. Today was no exception.

Buster, the family's dog, ran over and sniffed her feet as she walked. She smiled and greeted the dog, but didn't stop. Rob didn't like it when she lingered.

The flooring changed from faded carpet to faded linoleum as she entered the kitchen. "Hi, Leah." Esther's smile turned genuine as she spotted Leah sitting at the small table pushed up against the cream-colored wall. At nine, the girl was the size of a six-year-old thanks to her long battle with myocarditis. She was a sharp cookie, though.

"Hi, Miss Campbell." The girl's voice came out quiet—quieter than usual.

Esther frowned and lowered herself into the chair next to Leah. "Everything okay?"

Leah pursed her lips and shrugged.

"Are you feeling all right? Should I get your dad?" She glanced over her shoulder toward the living room.

"No. I'm okay. My mom's sick, so I'm not allowed to see her right now."

"Oh. I'm sorry, honey." Esther's curiosity piqued. She'd never met Mrs. Tyler. She'd always been at work when Esther arrived. Rob Tyler was Leah's caregiver. Leah said her mom's job paid better and had better insurance, so her dad had quit his to take care of her.

"I hate this. I'm ready to be normal, but I know I'll never be."

"Eventually, you'll get to a point where it won't be so dangerous for you to get sick." Esther hastily rethought her lesson plan for today. She'd brought some worksheets for them to go over for math, but she thought a game might be better. It might help lift Leah's spirits.

"I know, but I miss my mom. She seemed fine last night, but dad said she's running a fever. She hasn't come out of her room all day."

That didn't sound good. "Well, how about we play a math game, then I'll help you design a get-well card for her? Does that sound fun?"

Again, Leah shrugged. "I guess so."

"Okay. I need to run back out to my car for a minute to get supplies for all of that." She kept a supply tub in the cargo area of her vehicle with all the materials she thought she'd need for Leah's home visits. That kit included a bag of candy. The girl loved M&M's.

Esther pushed to her feet and retreated from the kitchen. Rob looked up from the motor sports magazine in his hands as she entered the living room.

"Where are you going?"

"I need something from my car. Leah's a little upset she can't see her mom right now, so I'm changing things up today."

"Don't baby the girl. She's fine."

Esther balled her fists but forced her voice to remain neutral. "It won't hurt for her to have some fun."

"You're not here for fun. You're here to teach her."

"I know. And I promise she'll learn from this."

The skeptical arch to his eyebrow told her he thought otherwise, but he didn't stop her as she left the house.

Outside, she opened her SUV's rear hatch and popped the lid of the clear plastic tote. The candy was on top. She grabbed the bag and a few art supplies, then closed the car. Arms loaded, she turned to head inside.

Movement at the side of the house caught her attention. She paused and squinted through the drizzle that was rapidly turning to fog.

A shadow shifted, too tall to be an animal. Someone was there.

Not in the best neighborhood, she hurried up the walkway. She doubted Rob would help if someone tried to do something to her. He might give her the creeps, but being inside with him was preferable to being outside around someone with nefarious intent.

Heels clacking on the concrete as she slowly walked toward the door, she squinted into the fog to get a better look. She caught a glimpse of a figure, but nothing else.

Esther frowned, pausing at the base of the steps. Who was that? With the fog and the growing darkness, she couldn't even tell if it was a man or a woman. Who would be walking up their driveway?

Rob pushed the door open. "You coming?"

Her gaze swung to his. "Huh? Oh. Yes. Yes, I'm coming." She gave him a tight smile and stepped inside. "Thank you."

His dark eyes latched onto her as she walked past him. Esther kept her gaze forward and said nothing else. She crossed the kitchen threshold and pasted on another smile for Leah's benefit. "Okay, kiddo. Let's have some fun."

The next hour flew by while they played some fun multiplication games and made a pretty card for Leah's mom. When their time was up, Leah had a smile on her face.

Esther gathered up all her supplies and picked up her bag. "I'll see you tomorrow. I hope your mom feels better soon."

"Me too. Thanks, Miss Campbell." Some of the melancholy came back to Leah's face.

It was all Esther could do not to hug the girl. Rob would not like that, though. Instead, she laid a hand on Leah's shoulder for a moment. "You're welcome. Have a good evening." With a quick wave, she walked out of the kitchen.

Eyes followed her as she moved through the living room. "Have a good night, Mr. Tyler. I hope your wife feels better."

He grunted from his chair, not bothering to get up and see her out. Esther opened the door and immediately breathed a sigh of relief when it closed behind her. She picked her way down the brittle stairs and hurried to her car. It beeped as she unlocked it.

A hooded figure emerged from the fog across the road, highlighted by the streetlamp. It was a man, about six feet tall, and thin. His baggy gray sweatshirt and dark jeans hung on his frame. He paused in the glow, facing her. She couldn't see his face, but she could feel his eyes watching her every move.

Freaked out, Esther didn't bother putting her things in the tote in the back. She yanked on the passenger door handle and tossed everything onto the seat. It could be sorted and put away when she got home. Where she felt safe.

Rounding the hood and keeping one eye on the stranger, she got in and pushed the lock button as soon as the door shut. From the corner of her eye, she could see the man still standing there. For the first time, she questioned whether the extra money was worth it. This was a rough neighborhood. The nights were growing darker sooner. Before long, she'd be leaving the Tylers' home in total darkness.

But if she didn't tutor Leah, who would? The girl's education would lapse while the district tried to find someone to fill her place. Esther couldn't let that happen. Maybe she'd talk to Edie about the best kind of pepper spray to buy. Or a taser. Something to help her feel safer.

Two

Esther's stomach growled as she rinsed the rice for her dinner. She'd forgotten to cook it when she cooked the shrimp and vegetables, so now she was doubly hungry. After she ate, she was going to sink into a bath with some wine and hopefully relax. Her brain was so scattered.

The phone rang across the kitchen. She glanced over her shoulder, but couldn't see who was calling from where she stood.

Picking up the saucepan, Esther held the dripping strainer over it while she took a few steps back to look at the phone where it sat on the opposite counter. Her sister's face lit up the screen. She set the strainer in the pot, then swiped the screen to answer and put the call on speaker. "Hi, Edie. I'm cooking dinner."

"Oh, yum. What are you having?"

"Nothing special. Stir fry. What's up? It's not movie night."

"Can't a sister call to talk?"

"Sure. But you usually have a reason. Is everything okay?"

"It's fine."

Something in Edie's tone told her otherwise. She put the rice pot down and waited, knowing her sister would tell her what was wrong when she was ready.

Edie groaned. "Technically, everything is fine. I'm just— I'm just not—" She stopped again and huffed. "I'm pregnant."

Esther sagged into the counter. "You're what?" she squeaked.

"Pregnant. And I'm not sure how I feel about it. I mean, I'm happy," she hastened to add, "but I'm—scared? Nervous. Nervous is a better word."

"Does Jordan know?"

"About the baby? Yes. He figured it out before I did. When we sparred the other morning, I just didn't have the same energy I usually do. Then we made breakfast afterward, and I told him the bacon smelled rancid. After we ate, he disappeared for a bit, claiming he had an errand to run." A snort came over the line. "His errand was to the drugstore. He came back with a pregnancy test."

Esther laughed. That sounded like him. She also wasn't surprised that he'd picked up on the changes in her sister. Jordan was a perceptive man, and he adored Edie. "So, does he know you're nervous?"

"Probably. I haven't said as much, but obviously, he can read me like a book, so..." Edie blew out a breath. "I just wanted to talk to someone without any stake in things, you know? You always give it to me straight. Help convince me everything will be okay, Essy. Because I don't know how to be a mom."

Esther pushed away from the counter and picked up her saucepot. "Sure you do. You had a great example. Mom's going to be thrilled, by the way. And you better tell her soon. If you keep this from her like you did your marriage, she's liable to fly down there and skin you." She dumped the water out, then tipped the rice from the strainer into the pot.

"Hey, I had a good reason for keeping Jordan a secret at the time. I came clean as soon as it was safe."

Esther turned on the water and added some to the rice. "Maybe so, but you know you could have told us before. We wouldn't have said anything to anyone." The entire family had been a little hurt when Edie broke the news of her nuptials. She claimed it had been to keep them safe from the person terrorizing Jordan, but Esther had a feeling she'd also done it so she didn't have to deal with the emotions involved. Edie only had so much emotional bandwidth.

"Well, you know now. And yes, I promise I will tell Mom and Dad soon. I just need to get a handle on it myself. It's only been a couple of days."

"How far along are you?" Esther shut the water off and set the pot on the stove, turning on the burner.

"We figure about seven weeks. With all the chaos around here lately, I haven't paid that close attention to my cycle."

"Chaos?"

"Margot and the twins officially moved down. Her divorce went through, and she finally got her house sold. We've been busy getting them settled."

"Hey, that's great. Hopefully, she can move on now." Margot's story was a complicated one. Her husband left with no warning, leaving her to raise twin toddlers on her own. Thankfully, Edie's friends had stepped up to help. She wasn't alone, and the girls would grow up with an amazing group of role models around them.

"Yeah. She already looks more relaxed. I've been watching Em and Lily a couple times a week so she and Annabeth can work on the clinic. Their goal is to open right after the new year. I know the locals are ready for them to open. There just aren't enough doctors here, especially pedi-atricians."

"Well, that will be one less thing you'll have to worry

about when your baby comes. There will be two doctors close by."

"True." She groaned again. "This is nuts."

Esther laughed. "You'll be fine. You've done some wild and crazy things in your life, Edie. And you've overcome even more. A baby is nothing compared to that."

Edie scoffed. "Hardly. Because this isn't only about me. I just found out about this kid and I'm already worried about everything that could happen. Not just in the delivery, but as he or she gets older. Like, what if they're born with some sort of congenital disorder or they get really, really sick some time?"

Leah flashed through Esther's mind. That would be rough, definitely. But her sister was the strongest person she knew. "You'll be fine. And you're not alone. Jordan will be there through it all."

"I suppose that's true." She sighed. "I'm being a worry-wart. That's new too. I don't fret like this. I'm a mess."

"Welcome to pregnancy." Esther grinned. Her brother-in-law was going to have his hands full over the next few months.

Edie moaned. "Okay, let's talk about something else. How's your week going?"

"Fine." She glanced out the window. The fog had only grown in density since she arrived home. "Wet."

"It's the Pacific Northwest. That's a given."

"I know. I wish I was down there, though."

"Uh-oh. I know that tone. What happened?"

"Nothing." She leaned her palms on the counter and stared at the phone. "I'm just in a bit of a funk, I guess." Truthfully, she had been since Edie got married. It had high-lighted how far she was from having the family she craved. Hearing Edie's baby news didn't help. She was thrilled for her sister, but she was also a little jealous. Esther had always wanted to be a mom.

"It's too bad you don't have a break until Thanksgiving.

I'd tell you to come down here for a little getaway. I could use an in-person movie night."

"Me too."

The bubbling of the rice pot drew her attention. She turned the burner down and put a lid on the pan.

"You need to shake things up," Edie said.

"I don't have time to shake things up."

"I'm not talking anything crazy. Go on a date."

Esther snorted. "With whom?"

"I don't know. Aren't there any cute, single teachers at your school?"

"Single, yes. Cute—well, if you like baby men, sure." There was a second-grade teacher fresh out of college who was easy on the eyes. But she didn't want to date a guy so much younger. She was twenty-eight, but Mark was only twenty-three. The only other single male teachers at her school were forty-something divorced dads. That was too far in the other direction for her. And as much as she wanted to be a mom, it would take a special man for her to consider starting that part of her life with teenagers already in the mix. None of her colleagues fit that bill.

"It's too bad Jordan doesn't have a brother," Esther quipped. Jordan MacDowell was a catch. Handsome, successful, kind—he treated her sister like a queen.

"No, but I have some friends..."

Esther could hear the smile in Edie's voice.

"Asher's single. So is Max," Edie said.

"Max is not single. He and Margot just refuse to admit it."

Edie chuckled. "He's too old for you, anyway."

"Margot's only a few years older."

"Yeah, but that woman's got life experience coming out her ears. But you're in luck. Asher's still available."

Dark hair, laughing brown eyes, and a bright smile beneath a full beard flashed through Esther's mind. That man was sex on a stick. And he knew it. He was also *so* not her type. "Asher would drive me crazy inside of a week."

"Eh, maybe. He's not as nutty as he first seems."

Esther raised an eyebrow but said nothing. If that were true, she hadn't seen it on her trip down there. He'd been the life of the party at every gathering.

"I think Asher uses his humor to protect his feelings. The man's a genius, and it's hard for him to connect with people sometimes."

"Well, in any case, it wouldn't work. He's there and I'm here."

"Love finds a way, dear sister. That's something I've learned in the last year. It doesn't matter who you are or where you live. Love finds a way."

"Well, I wish it would find its way here."

"Maybe I'll send him your way. He could use a vacation."

"Edith, don't you dare!"

Edie laughed.

"I'm serious. You won't have to worry about Mom skinning you. I'll do it for her."

Edie continued to laugh. "I'll hold off for now. Maybe I'll ask you again in a few months."

"The answer won't change."

"We'll see. So what's got you in a funk? Other than the weather."

She wasn't about to admit she was jealous of her sister's life. Edie didn't need that burden, because it wasn't her fault.

"I've been thinking about my job."

"Your job? You love your job. Don't you?"

"I do." And that was true. "I adore my students. Kindergarteners are the best. And it's not really school that's bothering me. It's the home tutor job I took on."

"It's not going well?"

"The kiddo is great. Leah's bright and funny. Eager to

learn. But her family—I've never met her mother. She's always at work. And her dad gives me the creeps."

"Has he tried something?" Edie's voice turned hard.

A small smile toyed with Esther's lips. Her big sister would be on the next plane, pregnancy or no pregnancy, ready to beat someone if Esther said yes. "No. He just stares at me and grunts when I ask him questions. They don't live in a great neighborhood, either. I was going to ask when we had movie night on Friday, what's a good kind of pepper spray or taser to carry?" It wasn't just Rob who creeped her out. So did Hoodie Man.

Silence came over the line. It lasted so long, Esther frowned and looked at the phone to make sure the call hadn't dropped. "Edie?"

"We'll come up with a different way to pay for your plane tickets down here. You're a decent artist. Maybe Brooke will—"

"No. We're not exploiting your friends. I'll be fine."

Edie huffed. "I won't have to ask. If Brooke gets wind about any of this, she'll be the first to offer her help. All I was going to suggest was for you to paint a few pictures of the area down here and see if she liked them enough to buy them for the resort."

Esther hummed. She might. She had enough photographs to get her started. And it would give her some new material to work with. Lately, she'd been struggling to find any inspiration. Nothing sparked her desire to paint.

"In any case, I think you need to quit that second job. Let the district send in a man."

"We'll see. I might broach the subject of quitting the home tutor position with my principal. Tell her to start looking for a replacement. I can't leave Leah in the lurch, though. That girl's already been through a lot."

Edie went quiet again for a long moment. "Fine," she eventually growled. "But if you feel more unsafe—"

"Don't worry. I will quit if I feel truly threatened."

"I'm still going to worry about you."

"I know. That's what sisters do. I'm going to worry about you too. And pity Jordan." Esther chuckled. So did Edie.

"Yeah, he's in for it. I'm all over the place. All right. I guess that's all I can ask for without flying up there and becoming your shadow."

"No shadowing is necessary. Do you feel calmer now?"

"I'm certainly distracted."

"Well, at least my problems are good for something."

Edie laughed softly. "I guess so. Okay, well, are we still on for Friday night?"

"Wouldn't miss it."

"Great. I'll talk to you then. Love you, sis."

"Love you too. Bye."

"Bye."

Esther touched the end call button and pushed away from the counter. Well, damn. That was a twist she wasn't expecting.

A slow smile spread over her face. Excitement pushed out the melancholy. She was going to be an aunt.

THREE

A low buzzing drew Asher Horn's attention away from his computer screen. He glanced toward the sound, which came from the security monitor to his left that showed his front door. Edie stood on the stoop.

He pushed away from his desk and got up to answer. His smile of greeting dimmed when he took in the slight frown that marred her forehead. "Hey." He stepped back so she could come inside. "What's up? Everything okay?"

"It's okay enough, but—" She stopped and wrung her hands together. "Can you do a little digging into some people for me? I'm a little worried about my sister."

Asher shut the door and his frown deepened at her words. "Esther? Why?" He couldn't imagine what trouble the soft-spoken kindergartner teacher could get into. Edie, sure. But her younger sister? The two women were polar opposites. If they didn't look so much alike, he'd question whether they were actually sisters.

"So, she took on an extra job as a home tutor for an immunocompromised child in her district. I guess the family lives in a rough area, and the dad's a little creepy. I'm quoting there. I just want to know she's not walking into some viper's den or something. Could you run some background checks on the parents?"

"Sure. Come back to my lair. It shouldn't take long to do a cursory check." He motioned for her to follow, then led her through the house to the room he'd outfitted for his computers.

"Thanks, Ash. I appreciate it."

"Not a problem." He sank into his chair and spun another one out for her. "Have a seat."

She dropped down next to him and looked at the wall of monitors.

"Okay, what are their names?" Asher focused on a screen and pulled up the database he normally used for background searches, ready to type, but silence answered his question. Frowning, he glanced at Edie. She had her lip between her teeth and an apologetic look in her eyes.

Asher sighed. "You don't know, do you?"

She shook her head, a chagrined smile forming. "I know the kid's name. Does that help?"

"Maybe. What is it?"

"Leah Tyler. She's nine. And she had a heart transplant a couple of months ago."

Asher let out a low whistle. "Poor kid." Fingers flying, he pulled up a different database and typed in the child's name. This one checked news stories. "What city does she live in?"

"Heron Ridge, Oregon. It's near Coos Bay."

He added that to his search. "Let's see what we can find." With all the information entered, he hit return. They were at the mercy of his internet connection now.

Thankfully, today it was fairly quick. Several results popped up within a few seconds. Asher clicked on the first one. "This is for the local elementary's honor roll. Her name is on it." He clicked away and picked the next one, which looked more promising. It was a quick write-up in the local paper for a fundraiser, benefitting the girl.

"There." Edie pointed at the screen. "Rob and Connie Tyler."

Asher pulled up the background screen and ran the dad first, using the wife and daughter's names to narrow the possibilities. He found one result and clicked on it, wincing when a rap sheet for several burglaries and some drug use came up.

"I knew it!" Edie leaned closer, reading.

"These are years old, though. His last conviction was seven years ago." Asher read through the list. "It looks like he was picked up for some meth use. Nothing after that."

"Or he just got smarter about it."

"Or"—he cast a quick glance at her from the side of his eyes—"he realized he needed to be there for his sick kid and kicked the habit."

Edie pressed her lips together. "Perhaps. Run the mom now." She pointed at the monitor.

Asher went back to the previous screen and put the mom's name in. She came up clean.

"Well, that's something, at least."

He hummed, switching to a different monitor. The spidey sense that never steered him wrong had reared its head.

"What?" Edie tipped her head. "It's never good when you make that noise. What are you thinking?"

"That it's weird for a woman with absolutely no criminal history, not even a sealed juvie record, to marry a man with his past. Especially since he was still committing burglaries and using long after their daughter was born. She'd have been two when he was convicted the last time."

"Can you access their marriage license?"

He moved the cursor back to the first monitor and clicked

on the tab at the bottom that said, "Other records," then on their marriage license.

"There you go." He turned back to the other monitor.

"Huh," she said after a moment.

Asher glanced over. "What did you find?"

"They've only been married five years."

He rolled closer. That was an interesting coincidence. Rob Tyler's last conviction gave him a two-year sentence. He'd have gotten out of jail around the same time he and Connie were married.

"Click on that." She pointed at Leah's birth certificate.

He did, and they both read over the document that appeared.

"It has both their names on it," Edie said.

He hummed again, the date of her birth pinging something in his brain. Moving down the screen, he went back to the bottom tab, then looked up their address history.

"What are you doing?"

"Checking dates." He scrolled down the list of addresses for Rob until he found the year Leah was born.

"Okay, that's weird," Edie said. "He didn't live anywhere near her when Leah was born. Or the year before."

Asher nodded. "No, he didn't. And actually"—he switched screens again to Rob's rap sheet, checking another date—"he was in jail when Leah would have been conceived."

Edie's eyes grew round. "What does that mean? Other than they lied about Leah's father. Why would they?"

"I don't know. Maybe Leah's real dad isn't a good man?"

"Worse than that?" Edie gestured at the screen, eyebrows winging upward.

"There are a lot of worse crimes than those, Edie."

She huffed. "I know that. But why would she pick Rob? Instead of someone with a clean record? When she has a clean one herself? It just doesn't make sense."

"It doesn't. But people do a lot of strange things when they're desperate. If she thought she and her baby were in danger, she might have turned to the first person she could for support. We don't know what her life was like at that time. Or whether she had any family to turn to."

"But he was in jail. How is that support?"

Asher's jaw worked, and he looked at the screen, thinking. She had a point. "I'm not sure. Look, I'll keep digging, okay? I don't think Esther is in any immediate danger. He either got suddenly really smart about his drug use, or he really did quit. I'll see what I can find out about Connie before she married Rob. I'm not sure I'll be able to find Leah's biological father, though. Not without talking to people Connie knew back then."

"That's okay. I just want to be sure Esther is safe. If Leah's bio dad hasn't interfered in the nine years the girl's been alive, he probably won't now. And I don't want to stir up trouble and possibly make it an issue for her. Whatever you can find online and through official records is fine."

He nodded once. "I'll see what I can do." He tipped his head, studying her. She seemed extra worried. Anxious. "Is everything okay?"

She glanced at him with a frown. "What do you mean?"

"You just seem more anxious than usual. I mean, I know you love your sister, but I've never seen you like this."

She sighed and looked heavenward. "Jordan's going to kill me for telling everyone, but apparently, I can't hide it." She turned her bright blue eyes on him. "I'm a little hormonal at the moment." Shoulders squaring, she sucked in a breath through her nose. "I'm pregnant."

Asher's eyes widened. "Holy crap." He looked away for a second, trying to wrap his head around that. Edie was the last person he expected to say that. Especially so soon after getting married. But then again, it didn't completely surprise him.

She'd done a lot of growing up in the last few months. Gone was the woman who'd run from her feelings. Now she embraced them. And change. She opened her arms to that too. "That's—that's great."

"You don't sound like it's great."

"No, it is. You just took me by surprise." A genuine smile formed on his face, crinkling his eyes. "I'm happy for you."

She returned his smile. "Thank you. We're excited. Nervous. Very nervous. But excited. It's a whole new world now."

That was no lie. So much had changed for their little group in the last year. Ford was married now. So were Audra and Sam. Dean's wedding was in just a couple of months. Max was the only other single one. Though Asher wouldn't call him unattached. The moment Margot and her twin tornadoes arrived, Max had given his heart away. Now that Margot's divorce was final, and she was living in Costa Rica full time, he expected Max to make a move soon. It was a lot, and Asher would be lying if he said he wasn't reeling a little from it all. He was happy for his friends, but it was also a tad lonely now.

"You'll do great, Edie." He laid a hand on her shoulder briefly.

She gave him a tremulous smile. "I know we'll do our best." She puffed out her cheeks as she blew out a breath, then pushed away from the desk. "I'll let you do your thing. Thank you for checking into this. It helps put my mind at ease to know you're on it."

"You're welcome. If there's anything else I can do, let me know." He started to rise to show her out, but she waved him down.

"Stay. I know how to find the door."

He sank back into his seat.

"See you later." With a smile, she left.

Asher spun around to stare at his screens, pushing his

personal thoughts and feelings aside so he could focus on Esther's problem. His eyes raked over the information he and Edie had uncovered in their brief search, and his brain catalogued it, filing it into neat sections. Something about the couple had his radar up and working. He didn't know what it was, but he was missing something.

Four

ot damn. Esther laid a hand on her chest and stared at the television screen with wide eyes. "Oh, my."

"Right?" Edie said from the laptop screen. "That was hot."

Esther agreed. They were watching *The Lost Husband* and were at the scene where James grabbed Libby at the farmer's market and kissed her in front of the bitchy patrons.

"I need to come up for a visit and bring Jordan with me. We can go to the coffeeshop where all the snooty girls from high school hang out and he can do that. Mmm-mmm, yes, please." She fanned her face.

Esther chuckled. "That's your hormones talking."

"Considering all I've wanted to do for the last couple of days is sleep and puke, I'll take it. Sex has been the furthest thing from my mind."

"At least you have the option." Esther grimaced. "Sorry. I'm being all melancholy again."

"You're fine. I can still send Asher up." Edie sent her a naughty grin.

"No." Esther rolled her eyes. "Stop pimping out your friends."

Edie chuckled. "I'm not. I actually think the man needs a vacation. He spends too much time in his lair, staring at computer screens. Oregon might be good for him."

Humming, Esther stared at the TV screen. "So would Texas. Or California. Or—"

"Okay, I get it."

A soft chuckle escaped Esther's lips. "Do you, really?"

"Oh, hush and watch the movie."

Laughing now, Esther glanced at her sister, who smiled back. She couldn't wait for them to do this in person when Esther flew down for Thanksgiving. They still had fun on their long-distance movie nights, but it was so much better when they were together.

When the movie finished a little over an hour later, Esther shut off the TV, then picked up the laptop and carried it with her as she went to the kitchen to put her dirty dishes in the dishwasher.

"I liked that one," Edie said, doing the same thing.

"Me too. So, what are we watching next week? It's your turn to pick?"

Edie sighed. "I was going to say an action flick, but now I'm running that actor's film list through my head. You know, he was in a TV series a few years back. About cops. We could watch that. I hear it was funny."

"Sure." Esther set the computer down on the counter next to the sink. "I like—" She broke off and leaned closer to the window, peering out at the darkened street, as a hooded figure under the streetlight caught her eye.

"Essy? Everything okay?"

"I'm not sure. There's a man on the sidewalk. Just standing there."

"Is he watching you?"

"I can't tell." Sweat dampened Esther's palms. She couldn't see the man's face, but he was facing her house. "His face is hidden by a hood."

"Let me see."

Esther picked up the laptop and clicked the button to switch to the front-facing camera. Edie leaned closer to the screen.

"What's he wearing? A hoodie?"

"Yes." Esther's heart rate quickened. He was still there. Just standing and staring.

"Close the blinds and call the police."

"What?" She reached for the stick to close the blinds. "Why should I call the police? He hasn't done anything."

"He's a peeping tom. You don't want him to think it's okay to keep hanging around. Call the cops, Essy."

With a huff, Esther set the computer down. "Fine." She pushed away from the counter to go get her phone.

"Turn me around so I can see you again."

Backtracking, she clicked the button to return to the other camera. "I have to get my phone." She spun away. "I still think you're being a bit ridiculous. He's not even on my property. The cops are going to laugh at me."

"You can still call and report a prowler. Give a description. They can keep an eye out. It's better to be safe than sorry."

"When did you turn into such a worrywart?" she called as she left the kitchen.

"You're my little sister. I always worry about you," Edie yelled back.

Esther sighed as she picked up her phone. Jordan wasn't the only one who would have his hands full during Edie's pregnancy. Her sister was a doer by nature, but she rarely worried. It was probably driving her up the wall that she couldn't be here to charge outside and confront the man. Essy wasn't defenseless. She'd bought pepper spray yesterday, and she had some rudimentary self-defense skills—something their dad had insisted both girls learn as teenagers. But she wasn't the fighter Edie was. And she didn't like confrontation. She preferred to either let others handle things or to let the other person cool off and put some distance between them for a bit. In this situation, she'd much prefer to just shut her blinds and forget the man was out there.

A sharp knock sounded on her door.

"What was that?" Edie yelled from the kitchen.

Esther froze. Why would someone knock on her door at this hour? It was almost ten o'clock.

She forced her feet to work and went back to the kitchen.

"Essy, what was that noise?"

"Someone knocked on the front door."

"Is that guy still lurking outside your window?"

Esther pulled a blind slat down and looked out at the sidewalk. "No."

"Call the police. Don't you dare answer it."

"Don't worry. I won't." With trembling fingers, she called 9-1-1.

In two rings, a dispatcher picked up. "Coos County Emergency."

"Hi, um, I'm not sure if this is an emergency or even what to call it, but there's a man on the sidewalk outside, and he was staring at me through the window. And just now, someone's knocked on my door." Saying it out loud made Esther feel really stupid and like a big chicken. "I'm sorry. I know I sound a little loony, but he freaked me out. He had a hood up and I couldn't see his face—"

"It's not a problem. Could you tell me your address, please?"

Esther relayed the information.

"I'll alert the officers in your area to keep an eye out," the dispatcher said. "Are you able to see who's at your door without opening it?"

"No. I mean, I can peek out my front windows, but I'll only be able to see someone if they're walking away."

"Go do that and tell me if you see anyone."

"Okay." Esther glanced at Edie and held up a finger, then walked away.

In the living room, she shifted the sheer curtains to the side and peeked through the blinds. The area in front of her house was empty. "No one's there," she told the dispatcher.

"What about outside the window where you first saw him? Is he there?"

"I don't think so. He wasn't when I called."

"Look again."

Esther backtracked to the kitchen.

"What's going on?" Edie asked.

Holding up a finger again, Esther turned the stick for the blinds and looked out. "He's gone."

"Okay. Just make sure all your doors and windows are locked. I'll alert patrol. If you have any other issues, please call us back."

"I will." Esther frowned and assessed the world outside. Her neighborhood was generally quiet, but this late, nothing moved.

"Have a good evening."

"You too. Thank you."

"You're welcome. Goodnight."

"Bye." Grimacing, Esther hung up.

"Well?" Edie asked.

"She's alerting patrol. And told me to make sure my doors and windows are all locked."

"Good advice. Are they?"

"They should be. I'll check again."

"I'm hanging up and calling you on your phone." Edie's hand moved toward the camera.

"You don't need to do that, Edie. I'm fine. I'll go check the locks, then I'll probably take a shower and read for a while." She'd been ready to go to bed after the movie, having been up since six-thirty. But she was too keyed up now to fall asleep.

"Es—"

"I'm *fine*. Put your pregnancy hormones away and stop worrying. I'll keep my phone and my pepper spray close tonight. I'll even lock my bedroom door if it'll make you feel better."

"It would."

"Then I will."

Edie let out a long sigh, then a soft growl. "Fine. I can't promise I won't still worry, but I'll stay off of an airplane."

Esther chuckled. "Good. Our parents do live just a few miles away. I can always call them, you know."

"It's not the same."

Esther's laughter rang louder. "I think I like this side of you. It's slightly unhinged, which is wholly unlike you and fun to watch."

"Laugh it up. One day, it'll be you. And trust me, I will return the favor."

"I know." Esther grinned. "Now, I'm going to take myself upstairs and try to shake off this excitement so I can sleep. You should do the same. Your baby needs the rest."

Edie rolled her eyes. "Then maybe he or she should stop waking me up to pee every five minutes. I swear, it's like someone flipped a switch. Since I took that test the other day and found out I was pregnant, all the symptoms have come out to play."

"Maybe you're just recognizing them now."

"Could be." Edie shrugged. "All right. I'll talk to you tomorrow. If anything weird happens—"

"I will call the police."

"Good. Be careful, little sister."

"Yep. Love you, Edie."

"Love you too."

Esther waved and disconnected the call. Closing the lid, she frowned and peeked outside again. It would be more than "excitement" she shook off upstairs. That entire situation had given her a serious case of the willies.

FIVE

Asher rubbed at his eyes, trying to bring some moisture back to them. He'd been in front of his computer screen far too long today. But after he finished his normal work for the day, he'd attacked Edie's sister's case again. He still couldn't find Leah Tyler's real father. All he'd learned was that Connie Tyler didn't exist before Leah was born. Whoever she was, she'd covered her tracks well.

He hadn't told Edie that yet. Until he had more information, he didn't want to worry her. Stress wasn't good for pregnant women. And with the way she'd been acting Wednesday, he wouldn't put it past her to get on a plane and fly home to Oregon. She needed to stay here, out of danger.

A low buzz filled the room. Asher blinked, then frowned as the noise penetrated his thoughts. One quick look at his security monitors revealed Edie standing on his doorstep again. This time, Jordan was with her.

Disquiet unfurled in his belly. He glanced at his watch. It was late. Something must have happened.

Pushing away from his desk, he hurried to answer the door.

It only took a quick glimpse at her face for the disquiet to sink into unease. "What happened?"

"Something weird is going on up there." Edie pushed past him and entered the house.

Jordan chewed on the corner of his lip, his hands stuffed in his pockets, and gave Asher a look of concern as he followed his wife inside.

"Weird how?" Asher shut the door.

"Some guy was standing outside her house this evening, staring at her."

Asher frowned, his gaze going to Jordan, who nodded, then back to Edie. "What? Did she call the police?"

"Yes, but they can't do anything, because nothing actually happened."

"Okay, start from the beginning. What *did* happen?"

Edie sank onto the tan couch that faced the windows overlooking the backyard. "We had movie night tonight, like we always do on Fridays. After it was over, she carried the laptop into the kitchen while she cleaned up her dishes; we were still talking. She looked out the window and saw someone in a hoodie standing on the sidewalk, staring at her house. I made her show me. It was creepy, Asher. The guy had on a black hoodie and jeans, and he just stood there, under the streetlight, facing her house. We couldn't see his face because of the angle of the light and the hood. It was like a black void." Her mouth twisted as she recalled the event. "Anyway, she closed the blinds, and I encouraged her to call the police and report him as a peeping tom. We argued about it, then someone knocked on her door."

"Edie pretty much forced her to call the cops at that point," Jordan said.

"Fat lot of good it did." Edie's expression darkened, and she glared. "They said they'd inform patrol."

"Did she answer the door?"

"No." Edie shook her head. "The dispatcher advised her to check her door and window locks, so that's what she did. Then she kicked me off the call so she could shower and read."

Jordan snorted. "She did not kick you off. You mutually agreed to hang up."

Edie directed her glare at her husband. "You're supposed to indulge your pregnant wife."

"Not when you lie."

"I'm not lying. I'm just... stretching the truth. I'm worried about her, and I want answers."

Asher crossed his arms. "I don't know what I can tell you. Are there cameras I can hack into?"

"No." Edie got up and paced to the window, staring out into the blackness. "I'm just frustrated. My gut tells me something is wrong, that she's in danger, but at the same time, my head is a mess, so I don't completely trust my gut." She turned back to him. "Have you uncovered anything that can give us a clue about what's going on?"

Again, Asher shot Jordan a quick look. He didn't want to upset Edie, but now that she'd asked, he didn't want to lie to her, either.

"What? Don't look at him for permission to tell me. I'm not an invalid now that I'm pregnant. Tell me."

Asher sucked in a breath. She was right. He couldn't coddle her just because of her condition. Edie could handle a lot, even when she felt scatterbrained. "Connie Tyler didn't exist before Leah was born."

"Hell," Jordan muttered. He crossed an arm over his chest and rested his other elbow on it, pinching the bridge of his nose.

"So, who is she, then?" Edie walked closer.

"I don't know. I haven't been able to figure that out. She hid her tracks well."

"Dammit." Edie paced to the window again, then spun

back. "I knew something was off." She pointed at Jordan. "I told you something about this whole thing bugged me."

He dropped his arms. "That doesn't mean the weird guy outside her house tonight and the Tylers are connected, babe."

"So, there are two dangers circling my sister? That makes it better?"

Jordan tipped his head back and looked at the ceiling. "That's not what I said."

Asher waved his arms, coming to a quick decision. "Before you come to blows over semantics, how about I take a trip up there? I can put some cameras up at her house, maybe do a little surveillance on the Tylers."

"Good luck with that," Jordan said. "Essy's quieter than Edie, but she's no less stubborn."

"Hey!" Edie propped her hands on her hips.

Jordan showed his palms. "I'm just telling the truth, honey. You know it's true."

She flattened her lips and narrowed her eyes. "It doesn't mean you say it out loud." Her expression cleared some as she turned to Asher. "But he's not wrong. Esther is just as stubborn."

One side of Asher's mouth lifted. "I can be rather charming and persuasive."

Edie blinked twice. "Asher, I hate to break it to you, but Esther's had your number from day one."

That didn't surprise him. Her quietness didn't mean she wasn't engaged; she was just observing as life went on around her.

He wagged a finger. "Maybe so, but that doesn't mean persistence won't wear her down. And I think someone needs to be there to convince her to put in cameras. I doubt she'll do it on her own. Right?"

"Yeah. She'll drag her feet." Edie crossed her arms and

glanced at Jordan. "I could call Mom and Dad. Dad would make sure she did it and would help her put them up."

"No, I'll go. Being there might be the only way I can find out who Connie Tyler really is. It might come down to me talking to people." Asher held up a hand. "I don't plan to talk to anyone as of now. Like you said, we don't want to create problems for her if she's hiding from someone. But if Esther is in danger because of Mrs. Tyler, I won't hesitate to out her."

Edie studied him for a long moment. "Are you sure, Asher? You're not normally in the field. That's more Dean's thing."

"I'm sure." The more he thought about it, the more he liked the idea. He could use a change of scenery.

"I think it's a great idea." Jordan glanced at his wife. "It keeps you here and out of trouble, but it still gives Essy a layer of security that should make you happy."

Edie huffed. "Fine. But for the record, I don't like being sidelined. Even if it is for a good reason."

Jordan walked closer and took her hand, tugging her into him. "Duly noted, babe."

She rolled her eyes. "Keep it up, Jordie. I'll make sure you change *all* the nasty blowout diapers."

He scrunched his nose in disgust. "I'm sure I'll get my fair share, anyway."

Asher mimicked Jordan's face. The thought didn't appeal to him, either. "I'll go book a flight. I should be able to get on the early flight to San José, then from there to LAX, and then Portland."

Edie nodded. "Ford needs to find a friend who can fly and recruit him to our merry band. Then he can chauffeur us all around on a whim when we need him to."

"We have Ezra," Asher pointed out.

"I know, but the planes aren't his. Brooke probably wouldn't mind, but if we're going to keep doing it, we need to pay her for fuel. Plus, it takes him away from his family. On short notice, I mean. We need someone who's able to drop everything quickly."

Tongue in cheek, Asher nodded, giving Jordan a look. Edie's mind was like a tilt-a-whirl. Pregnancy hormones had hit her hard. "I'll get on that."

She rolled her eyes again. "Stop humoring me." She pushed back from Jordan but kept hold of his hand. "Come on, Jordie. Let's leave him alone so he can pack."

Asher turned, smiling, as she pulled Jordan to the door. "I'll keep you posted on things."

"Yes, you will." She glanced at him as she reached the front door. "Or I *will* be on a plane to Portland, and you won't like me when I get there." She speared him with a fierce look. "Keep my sister safe, Asher." A vulnerable note he'd never heard from her before entered her voice. "Please."

His smile faded away. "I will, Edie. You have my word."

SIX

Music blasted through Esther's earbuds, and she hummed along, wiggling her hips to the beat as she vacuumed the gray rug covering part of her living room floor. The song crescendoed, and she raised the wad of cord in her hand, using it like a microphone to belt out the last of the lyrics. As the last notes faded, the sound of the doorbell pealing through the house filtered into her ears. With a quick touch, she turned off the vacuum and turned toward the front door, pausing her music.

The memory of last night echoed through her mind. She'd peeked outside earlier to get her mail. Her mysterious knocker hadn't left any presents, for which she was grateful. But the lack of gifts or notes just left her wondering. Why had the person knocked? What did they want?

Cautiously, she crept toward the window. She didn't know what she expected to see; if someone was ringing her doorbell, she'd never see them. But maybe they'd given up by now and were walking away. It wasn't quite as late as last night —only a little after seven—but it wasn't normal visiting hours, either. And the pizza she ordered for dinner shouldn't be here for at least another ten to fifteen minutes.

The bell pealed again, then whoever it was knocked. Esther backed away from the glass and debated whether to answer. It could be a neighbor. Or her parents. Though they would probably call or text first, so she'd know they were coming.

"Esther?"

The deep voice on the other side of the steel door sounded familiar, but she couldn't place it.

"Esther!" He knocked again. "It's Asher. Open up."

Her anxiety morphed to surprise. What was he doing here?

She strode the last few steps to the door and flipped the locks, throwing it open.

The bright smile he bestowed on her showed off his straight, perfect white teeth. "Hi, Essy. Can I come in?"

Not for the first time, she was struck by just how handsome he was. If Asher were to show up at a modeling agency looking for a job, they'd sign him on sight. Between the perfect smile and the dimples, *and the damn beard*, the man looked like he'd been carved by one of the sculpting masters.

And what he had hidden under his clothes—at least the top half—was just as perfect as his face.

"Asher, what are you doing here?"

"I'll gladly explain. Inside. May I come in?" He glanced at the sky and the softly falling rain.

Esther cocked a hip and propped a hand on it. "Edie sent you, didn't she?"

"No."

"No?" She raised an eyebrow, not believing him. "Why else would you be here?"

"I came on my own. She knows I'm here, but she didn't ask. Can we continue this conversation inside?" He swirled a finger, pointing at the rain that had soaked the shoulders of his jacket. "I've been out here knocking and ringing your bell for over a minute."

"Sorry, I was vacuuming." Esther huffed and backed away from the door. He stepped in, and she pushed it closed. "Why are you here?"

He leaned around her and locked the door, getting much too close. She could smell the mix of rain, detergent from his clothes, and the spicy scent of man coming off of him. Esther clenched her teeth and tried not to sniff his neck. He shouldn't smell that good. Not after traveling all day. It wasn't fair.

Straightening, Asher stood there for several moments, raking his dark brown gaze over her. A smile toyed with his lips as his gaze lingered on her hair. "You look cute."

Her face reddened. What he likely meant was she looked like a child. She'd donned an old college t-shirt that was two sizes too big, a pair of running shorts, and tossed her hair into a horribly messy bun on top of her head. There was a sheen of sweat coating her skin too. She hadn't exactly been cleaning like a grandma. Esther took the opportunity to turn her weekly house cleaning into a workout.

Giving him another eye roll, she spun away and marched into the living room. The rest of the living room carpet beckoned, but she knew she wouldn't get it done now. "So, if Edie didn't send you, why are you here?" She picked up the vacuum cord and pulled it from the plug, then started winding it around the hooks on the machine.

"Your sister is worried about your safety. I'm here to keep her from being so stressed. I also think it's a good idea for you to at least put up a doorbell camera."

"I can get one of those on my own, you know." She crossed her arms and hitched her hip to the side.

"But would you?" He mimicked her pose.

Esther poked her tongue into her cheek and glanced away. He might have a point. But it didn't change the fact that she didn't need him here.

"Look, I know you don't want me here, but even if you kick me out, I'm parking outside your house and camping in my rental. Has Edie told you any of what I found out about the Tylers?"

Esther dropped her arms; surprise straightened her spine. "Edie asked you to look into the Tylers?"

He muttered a soft curse. "She didn't tell you that?"

"No." She shouldn't be surprised, though. Her sister didn't like being in the dark. If she wanted information, she was going to get it by any means necessary. And with Asher Horn around, she could get a lot of info.

"Okay." He rubbed his fingers over his forehead, thinking. "Have you had dinner? I haven't. We could talk while we eat. Because it might take a while."

"I ordered pizza just before I started vacuuming. It should be here in about ten minutes or so."

"Perfect. Do you mind if I impose on you? I can always run out and get something, though." He hooked a thumb toward the door.

"No, it's fine. So long as you don't mind peppers, onions, and olives on your pizza."

"Is there pepperoni? Or sausage? I haven't eaten much today, so some protein would be nice."

"It has both." She liked the supreme pizza.

"Awesome."

Esther fiddled with the vacuum cord, standing there awkwardly staring at him. If they weren't going to talk about why he was here, she didn't know what to say.

After a moment, she glanced away and cleared her throat. "I'm going to put this away and change."

Once again, those brown eyes raked over her body. A

cocky smile lifted one side of his mouth. "Don't change on my account. I kinda like the look. It's real, you know?"

Her insides warmed as his rakish smile turned more genuine. Ducking her head, she nodded. "Well, I'm sweaty and have been cleaning most of the afternoon. I'll be right back." She gave the vacuum a push and rolled it away.

Out of sight in the hallway, she paused and closed her eyes, drawing in a steadying breath. Mr. Hot Stuff needed to leave. She knew she'd told Edie he would drive her nuts rather quickly, but it wasn't because of his gilded tongue. It was that damn smile. It did things to her insides.

But isn't that what you wanted?

Esther clenched her teeth and told her inner voice to shut up. Asher was not the man she wanted. She didn't know who she wanted, but it wasn't one who lived thousands of miles away.

With a nod of affirmation to herself, she gave the vacuum a firm push toward the hall closet.

SEVEN

Asher took off his sodden jacket and laid it over the back of a dining chair. Running a hand over his hair, water droplets sprayed, dotting his light blue long-sleeved shirt. He wiped his hand on his jeans and glanced around.

Esther's house wasn't large, but it was homey. From the front door, the living room was to his right. A khaki sofa faced the side wall, which housed a fireplace and a TV mounted above it. A dark leather recliner sat to the couch's left. To the right was an overstuffed chair in the same light brown as the couch. Gold accent tables sat next to both chairs, and a maple coffee table occupied the area in front of the sofa. Light oak floors ran throughout the main floor, interspersed with rugs.

To his left was the dining area. The maple table and white upholstered chairs seated six. A gold pendant light hung above it. On the taupe walls, she had a series of wooden shelves covered in plants.

Beyond the dining area, an island separated the space from the kitchen. The speckled granite counters sparkled in the overhead lighting, which also gave some shine to the eggshell gray cabinets. More plants sat on a shelf above the sink.

He wandered into the living room, glancing down the hallway. The stairs turned off to the left. Two doors went off to the right, and he assumed one went to a closet, because there was no vacuum sitting in the middle of the floor. At the end of the hall was a door that led outside.

Asher perched on the couch and took out his phone to send a quick text to Edie. *I'm here.*

Dots appeared on his screen, then, *Did she let you in?*

He smirked and responded. *She did. Not sure how long it'll last. She was cleaning and went to change. We haven't talked yet.*

Don't let her throw you out. She needs you. I know you feel the weirdness too.

She wasn't wrong. He wasn't sure he was as convinced about the danger as Edie, but he definitely wanted to investigate more.

I'll do my best. Try not to worry.

Sure. An eye roll emoji accompanied her reply.

His smile grew. He could almost hear her snort.

Clicking off of his messaging app, he opened his email, thumbing through the work messages that had arrived while he'd been traveling, answering a few. Just because he was a former CIA analyst didn't mean he was out of the intelligence game. It was just a different kind of intelligence now, and he was more choosy about what he did and who he worked with. Most of his contracts were for companies who wanted to beef up their security. Or for those who had a breach and wanted someone to track the perpetrator down. He liked those the most. Finding someone and waltzing in through their digital back door was extremely satisfying. And now, if he took too long or failed, there were no lives on the line. Just dollars.

The doorbell rang. Standing, Asher pocketed his phone and went to answer it. He hoped Esther had already paid for the pizza. He didn't have any cash on him. Not American money, anyway. Airport exchange rates sucked, and all the banks were closed by the time he landed in Portland.

Opening the door, Asher greeted the young man in a polo and hat with a national pizza chain's name emblazoned on them.

"Hi." The kid smiled and opened the insulated bag he held. He pulled out the pizza box and handed it over.

"Thanks. Did my friend already pay for it and leave you a tip?"

The kid nodded. "It's been taken care of, yes."

"Great. Have a good night."

"You too."

Asher closed the door and turned, heading for the kitchen. Esther appeared as he set the box on the island.

"Perfect timing." He glanced her way, taking in her appearance. She'd showered, turning her coppery hair a deep shade of auburn. It hung in damp waves around her shoulders. Instead of the oversize shirt, she now wore a white long-sleeved tee with her school district's logo on the front and the name down the sleeves. Gray leggings covered her legs, and she wore thick socks on her feet. She was still cute.

"I'm starving." She walked to a cabinet and took out two plates, passing him one.

Asher added a couple of slices of pizza to his plate.

"Do you want a soda or something?"

"Sure. Anything you have. I'll drink it all."

She opened the fridge and took out two cans of Coke, handing him one, then put two pizza slices on her plate.

"Do you want to eat at the table?" He tipped his head toward the dining room.

"We can sit in the living room. I hardly ever use that thing." She tipped a finger toward the table. "When my parents come over is about the only time it gets used. And not even all the time then." Ripping some paper towels off the roll, she passed him some.

Asher took them, then gathered his dinner and headed for the living room. He waited for her to choose a seat—the recliner—then sat on the couch. The scent of hot cheese, tomatoes, and Italian spices tickled his nose as he lifted a slice and took a bite. Idly, he wondered how long she'd wait before she asked him to explain his presence.

One slice later, he got his answer.

"Can you explain what's going on now, please?"

Asher washed his food down with a quick swig of soda. "So, after you talked to Edie Wednesday, she showed up at my house and asked me to do a background check on the Tylers. Said she was worried about you. I did a quick check and discovered that it's highly unlikely Rob Tyler is Leah's biological father."

The slice of pizza in her hand hovered near her mouth. She blinked at him with wide eyes. "What?" She lowered her food back to her plate. "You're sure?"

"Yes. He was in prison when she was conceived. Even if she was early, he was still in jail for months before and after."

"Holy crap. So who's her real father?"

"I don't know, yet. I also don't think Connie Tyler is who she says she is. I can't find a record of her prior to her marriage to Rob, except for Leah's birth certificate. The woman on the marriage certificate doesn't exist. Her birth certificate, social security number—all that checks out, but she has zero credit or work history prior to marrying him. It's possible she lived with family and didn't have to work and never used a credit card, but at her age, that's highly unlikely. They've also only been married for five years. Leah was four when they wed. Has the girl ever said anything to hint at having a different last name?"

"No. And she always calls Rob her dad. But I don't see

what this has to do with my safety. I mean, yeah, they live in a rough part of town and he's creepy, but I've been more weirded out by the hoodie man outside their house and mine than—"

Asher held up a hand. "The hoodie guy was at their house too?" That was the first he'd heard of that.

"Well, I'm not sure if it was the same guy. But there was a man in a hood on Wednesday when I left their place."

"Describe the men." He set his plate on the coffee table and took out his phone so he could take notes.

"Um, they were similar in height and build. Probably around five-ten or so. Average build. Wednesday, the man had on a gray hoodie and dark jeans. Last night, he was in jeans and a black hoodie. That's all I could see. Both times, his hands were in his hoodie pocket, and he either had his head down or it was in shadow. I can't tell you a skin color because of that."

Asher typed the man's description into his notepad app. "Do you think it was the same person?"

She shrugged. "Maybe? I'm really not sure. I wouldn't think so. I live a long way from the Tylers, and I didn't notice anyone following me."

"Were you looking?"

Her mouth flattened, and she looked away. "Not really, no."

He gave a quick nod. "So it could be the same man. But the question is, why would he follow you? And if it's not, why was there a man standing outside your house?"

She picked at her pizza crust. "Now that you say it out loud like that, it sounds even weirder. And I don't know who it could be. I don't talk to many men outside of work."

"It could be someone random that you met at a store. Some stalkers only need a smile from a woman to become fixated on them."

Her eyes grew round, and she blanched. A curse floated through Asher's head. He probably shouldn't have said that.

"Sorry. I'm not trying to scare you. I usually go over details with the guys and Edie. This is stuff they're used to hearing. Ford keeps me away from the people we protect for a reason." Truthfully, he was much more comfortable talking to people through a chat box or email than in person. He knew he could be charming, but he also tended to say what was on his mind. And he thought out loud a lot. It helped him see the bigger picture.

"It could be, too, that it was just some random person on the sidewalk last night," he continued. "Maybe he stopped to think or took a call, and you couldn't see the earbuds in his ears. This could all be one big coincidence, and nothing is going on."

She rolled her lips in, glancing away before nodding. "I hope that's what it is. I don't want to think that some lunatic is obsessed with me."

He didn't either. "There's one more possibility we need to consider." And this one actually scared him more than if she had a stalker. "It could be someone following you to get information about the Tylers. If Connie fled from an abusive relationship or from an unsafe situation, that person could be looking for her and their child."

"God, that kid has been through so much. She was normal and healthy until an infection destroyed her heart muscle. I know she misses being the way she was. To think she had to change her identity too—" Esther shook her head. "I don't know how she's as normal as she is. Especially with Rob Tyler as her dad—sorry, stepdad."

"Tell me more about him. I know he has some convictions for drugs. There were some burglary ones in his past too."

"What kind of drugs?"

"Meth."

She scrunched her nose. "I've never seen any evidence of drug use. But I've only been with Leah for a couple of months. Since school started. He's rude and creepy, but she's not afraid of him. Not really. She doesn't want to upset him, but it's more of a case of she doesn't want him to yell than that she's afraid he'll hit her or something. I've seen kids afraid of their parents beating them. She doesn't act that way."

"What about her mom?"

"I've never met her."

"Never?"

"No. She's always at work when I'm there. Except this week, she's been locked in her bedroom. Leah said she's sick."

Asher lifted an eyebrow. "And she's locking herself in her room?"

"I mean locked in a euphemistic sense. She's avoiding Leah to keep her from getting sick, so she's staying in the bedroom. Leah's immune system is still weak. Even a cold could cause a lot of problems for her."

"Gotcha. You're sure she's there, though?"

That made Esther frown. "Actually, no. I'm only going off of what I've been told."

"Is it possible Connie Tyler doesn't exist?"

"No," Esther was quick to respond. "Leah talks about her. I don't think a child could lie that convincingly about having a mother. It's too natural, and she mentions her too much."

"Okay. At least we're not dealing with a phantom. I'll keep digging. In the meantime—"

Esther lifted a hand. "Why did you come? And don't give me that crap about appeasing Edie. She's pushy, but she's not that scary."

Asher smirked and a shudder raked down his spine. "Honey, I'd rather tangle with a mountain lion than your sister."

Esther chuckled. "You just have to get to know her. She's a teddy bear."

"With you. You're her sister. But she doesn't take crap from any of us. And with the pregnancy hormones? She was a little manic last night."

"Last night?" Esther groaned. "She showed up at your house after our movie, didn't she? It wasn't a phone call. I assumed she called you and told you."

"No. No phone call. She and Jordan appeared around eleven. She's part of the reason I'm here. You didn't see her. She's truly stressing out about this situation, and it can't be good for her right now. So, I'm here to help alleviate some of that. But I'm also here because I can't discount what I've learned and all the things happening. A weird guy outside your house and a woman who isn't who she says she is? Something's not right."

"I don't need a protector. Edie might be the black belt, but I'm not helpless."

"I didn't say you were. But it's always better to have another set of eyes, Essy."

She huffed and picked up her pizza, taking a bite. While she chewed, she stared at a point over his shoulder. Asher could tell she was thinking about what he said. He let her. She'd come around to his way of thinking, eventually. Because at the end of the day, she didn't want to stress her sister out, either, and she was uneasy about the man in the hoodie. That was evident in how her posture had changed while they talked about him.

Asher made it almost through his second pizza slice before she spoke again.

"So, what's your plan? Do you become my shadow? Because that—" She broke off and shook her head. "I won't like that."

He had to tread carefully here. Leaving her unprotected

wasn't an option, but he wanted to give her space too. She was more easy-going than Edie, but she still had a stubborn streak. If he pushed too hard, she'd balk. "I'd like to stay here with you. Just so I'm close," he added when her eyebrows dipped and her mouth opened with the beginnings of a protest. "The nearest hotel is over a mile away. And while I sprang for the roomier SUV when I rented a car, I'd rather not sleep in it. It is October in the Pacific Northwest."

Those dark red eyebrows of hers dipped even lower. "Fine. You can have the guest room."

"And here's the part you might not like. I hacked my way into the Oregon education system and entered a substitute teaching license for myself. I also put myself on the district secretary's schedule for an interview with the superintendent tomorrow to become a sub for the district." He'd had a rather productive layover in Los Angeles.

Again, she opened her mouth to protest, but he held up a hand. "Being in the same building with you will be less conspicuous than me sitting outside in a car all day."

Her lips slammed shut. "You're bordering on a shadow, Asher."

"I know, but I need to be close by. I won't be in your class-room, but I'll be around if you need me. I'm also going to follow you to your tutoring job."

"Oh, uh-uh." She stood up, waving a finger at him. "That *is* shadowing."

Asher rose and moved around the coffee table to stand in front of her. "Essy, that part is non-negotiable. You saw the hoodie man outside their house. It's a rough neighborhood. Honestly, I don't know why the district sent a young woman there to tutor the girl in the first place."

"I volunteered." Fists clenched, she glared up at him. "I need the money so I can fly down to visit Edie more than once a year."

His jaw worked. "You should let me invest some of your savings. Then you won't have to take dangerous assignments."

"That would have been nice to know before, but what's done is done. I'm not leaving that kid in the lurch because I got a little freaked out."

"Then you'll just have to put up with me following you there. I'm not saying you can't go to the store or out to eat without me. But for the most part, I want to be around. Just until I get a handle on what's going on here."

"You—" She raised a finger, pointing it at his face. "Ugh! You're lucky I love my sister and that she's pregnant. If it weren't for that, I'd tell you to go home."

A grin slashed over his face. "I know."

"You're not endearing yourself to me by being a cocky bastard."

Surprise pulled a quick laugh from him. "You're more like Edie than I thought."

Esther rolled her eyes and spun away, flopping back into her chair. "Good. Maybe it'll help you remember I'm not a pushover. I might avoid conflict, but that doesn't mean I do it at the expense of my mental health."

A surge of pride filled him. He liked that she knew her own mind well enough to know her boundaries and wasn't afraid to stick up for herself. He'd seen her with Edie and knew she could give as good as she got, but the week she was in Costa Rica, she'd been fairly reserved with everyone else.

"I'll do my best to be unobtrusive. I just want to keep you safe, Essy."

She huffed, raising her pizza slice. "I'm sorry. I know you do. I just—I don't like this. Any of it." She ripped off a chunk of crust, and shoved it between her teeth, chewing angrily.

Asher moved closer and crouched in front of her. He touched her knee. "I know you don't. But keep in mind, my presence here will move things along faster than if I hadn't come. I'm not constrained behind a wall of monitors."

Esther swallowed her food, her gaze connecting with his. Warmth seeped into his fingers from her legging-covered skin as he stared into her bright blue eyes.

"I hope so. Because I don't want to live like this." A tremor started in her chin. "I don't like being afraid when I step outside my house."

Asher moved his hand up to cradle the side of her face. "I won't let anything happen to you, Esther. You have my word."

Just like that, Asher knew he wasn't leaving until he was a hundred percent certain she was safe. It had nothing to do with reducing Edie's stress level or figuring out the puzzle of who was hanging around, and everything to do with the woman staring back at him with watery blue eyes.

Eight

The shower on the other side of Esther's bedroom wall kicked on. She glanced over, then rolled her eyes. "Ignore it, Essy. Don't think about what he's doing." Spreading the pages of her book wider, she focused on the words.

She made it through a paragraph before her mind wandered. An image of Asher in swim trunks flashed through her mind. On her trip to Costa Rica, she'd spent some time at Edie's friend Max's house. He had a private beach and had a volleyball net set up, so they'd all gone down to play. Asher had walked down the stairs to the beach wearing a t-shirt and flip-flops. He'd ditched both before the action started. It was the first time she'd seen him without a shirt. She hadn't known a computer geek could look so good. He was all rippling muscle and hard planes, topped by a megawatt smile, great hair, and a sexy beard. It wasn't right that any man could look so good. Men like him were supposed to be reserved for Holly-wood, where they were unattainable to mere mortals like her.

Esther snorted. He wasn't attainable for her, either. If he ever did settle down, it would probably be with some exotic, dark-haired beauty he met in Costa Rica. A woman as worthy of a magazine cover as himself. Not a freckled redhead who burned in the shade.

Her phone rang, thankfully pulling her from the hole her thoughts had descended into. She snatched it off the night-stand and saw her sister's face on the screen. Swiping to answer, she lifted it to her ear.

"You have a lot of nerve sending him here," she said in lieu of greeting.

Edie chuckled. "I didn't send him. He went on his own."

Esther hummed. "Whatever. Your new brand of crazy sent him here. Now he's staying in my house and wants to follow me around at school."

"How's that going to work?"

"He hacked into the education system and gave himself substitute teacher credentials."

Edie laughed. "Of course he did. It's a good thing he's a good guy. I'd hate to think someone with nefarious intentions could do that."

"Stop enjoying this. He's actually here for a serious reason."

"You're right. I'm sorry." An apologetic tone entered her voice.

Esther sighed. "No, I'm sorry. My life is on a rollercoaster, and I don't like it. It's making me grouchy." So was the thought of a naked Asher in the hall bath.

"Well, he's there to stop the ride. Give him a chance, Essy."

Again, Esther hummed.

"I'm serious. He knows what he's doing. Anyway, I just called to check on you. Make sure you had an uneventful day." She paused, then chuckled. "Well, uneventful in the sense that Hoodie Man stayed away."

"As far as I know, he did. I kept all the blinds closed and never left the house."

"You need some cameras outside. Especially at your front door. You can't see who's there."

"Yeah. I think we'll probably do that tomorrow. Asher has a plan, but he didn't share it all. We discussed more of the big picture stuff. I'm just along for the ride at this point."

"I'm glad you're taking it seriously."

The memory of the terror she'd felt seeing that man outside her window resurfaced. "Yeah, well, I'm more than a little weirded out by everything. And I know I protested the idea, but I'm glad he's here." Knowing Asher was sleeping down the hall helped calm her. She knew that if something happened in the middle of the night, she didn't have to handle it on her own.

"Me too. I think I'll sleep better tonight knowing you have him there with you." Edie's voice softened, and then she let out a grunt. "These—feelings—are seriously inconvenient. I hope this goes away once this baby's born."

Esther smiled. "You'll probably always worry a little more now. But it won't be to the extreme. You could talk to your counselor there. She might be able to help you." Edie had been seeing a therapist since her return from Arizona to help her deal with all the things that had resurfaced during the events there. It had helped, and they still met at least once a week.

"I probably will, because I can't live like this for the next eight months. I don't think Jordan can, either."

"Your husband is a saint. He'll handle it in stride. He knew what he was getting into when he married you."

Edie barked a short laugh. "He did. And it's why I love him. He accepts me; faults and all." A loud yawn came over the line. "Oh. Sorry. I think I'm going to let you go. Fatigue is another unwelcome side effect of pregnancy. I can't get enough sleep."

"That too shall pass." Esther smiled.

"I know. But for now, I'm going to bed. I'll talk to you soon. Try not to give Asher too hard of a time, yeah?"

Esther glanced at the wall again. "I'll try not to."

"Good. Love you."

"Love you too. Bye."

"Bye."

Pulling the phone away from her ear, Esther hung up. The shower cut off. She picked up her book, trying to drown out the image in her brain of Asher climbing from the tub and wrapping a towel around his waist.

It didn't do a lot of good. She reread the same page several times while he finished in the bathroom, then wandered down the hall to his bedroom. It wasn't until she heard the guest room door shut that she was finally able to push the image of him wet and naked from her mind and concentrate on her book. Eventually, she fell asleep, only to be bombarded by dreams of Asher frolicking in the sand and swimming through the waves.

When her alarm went off the next morning, she smacked the off button, then glared at the clock with gritty eyes. She debated going back to sleep and skipping church, but she'd promised Jenny that she'd teach Sunday School today.

Groaning, she sat up and pushed the covers off, then got out of bed. Her little house didn't have a master suite, so she gathered clothes and poked her head into the hallway, making sure the coast was clear. Running into Asher before she'd showered and was fully awake was not the way she wanted to start her day.

His door was still closed, so she darted into the bathroom and locked the door. Turning on the shower, she let it warm for a moment, then stepped in. Hot spray blasted her chest. She tipped her head and let the water run over her hair and down her back as she turned away from it. Some of her grogginess washed away with the water.

After soaping her hair and shaving, she washed the rest of her body, then got out. The cooler air outside the shower pricked her skin, and she hurried into her clothes. Deciding not to dry her hair, she whipped it into a quick braid, then did her makeup. When she finished her morning routine, she left her pajamas in the hamper and exited the bathroom.

"Where are you going all gussied up?"

Esther froze on her way to the stairs at the deep voice behind her. She turned and about swallowed her tongue.

Asher stood in his doorway, shirtless. Dark hair dusted his sculpted pecs, then narrowed into a line that split his perfect abs. It disappeared beneath the waistband of a pair of blue and gray plaid pajama pants that hung so low on his hips she could see the vee of his obliques and the hard ridge of his hipbones.

She jerked her gaze up, but it didn't do her ability to speak much good. He had a serious case of bedhead that only made him sexier.

He arched an eyebrow at her. "Esther?"

"Huh?" His question finally registered. "Oh, um, church."

He yawned and swiped a hand over his face. "It is Sunday, isn't it? Give me a few minutes and I'll go with you."

"You don't have to. I'll be fine." It was church. If anywhere should be safe, it was there.

"It's not that. I wouldn't mind going just because. I usually attend an online service from my church back home. One here in the U.S., I mean. It'll be nice to go to a service in person."

"Oh." She wouldn't have pictured him as a church-going type. But then she didn't know him very well, either, and probably shouldn't be making those kinds of assumptions. "Well, I need to leave in about twenty minutes. I was headed down to drink some coffee and eat breakfast before I left."

He nodded. "I'll be down soon. Make me a cup?"

"Sure."

"Thanks." A hint of a smile crossed his sleepy face, then he stepped back and closed the door.

"Holy crap," Esther muttered under her breath. She needed to be more careful in the mornings. The sight of him fresh from sleep put all sorts of naughty ideas into her head.

Rolling her shoulders, she turned around and went downstairs.

Ten minutes later, while she sat at the island, sipping coffee and reading the morning news on her phone, Asher rounded the corner from the stairs.

Once again, her brain stuttered and her ability to form a coherent sentence fled. If possible, he looked even better in his light blue dress shirt, charcoal slacks, and maroon tie. The fabric hugged his muscular body but wasn't so tight that it looked like he was about to pop a seam. It was just snug enough to hint at the body beneath.

"Morning." He crossed to the coffeemaker and filled the mug she'd left on the counter for him. "Mmm... that smells good." He raised the cup and took a sip, then looked at her. "What do you have for breakfast? I haven't had a chance to go to the grocery, so I'm at your mercy this morning."

She stared at him, still unable to speak.

He frowned. "Esther, are you okay? You seem a little off."

"I'm fine." *Geez. Get it together, girl.* "Um, I had fruit and yogurt. There are eggs in the fridge. And bread for toast in the pantry. I have some protein bars in there too."

He nodded once and set his mug down. "That works. Thank you."

She hummed and looked at her phone. Staring at him wasn't helping her ability to think.

But she couldn't help it. Glancing up through her lashes, she watched as he walked into the pantry, then came back out a few moments later with the bread and the cooking spray.

"Which cabinet has plates and bowls?" He gestured to the cupboards.

Esther pointed.

"Thanks." He opened it and took out a bowl, then went to the fridge and grabbed two eggs and some sliced cheese.

Her pretext of reading forgotten, she watched him cook a quick egg sandwich using the microwave and the toaster. It took all of three minutes.

"I need to remember that egg trick. That looks good." She nodded to his plate as he sat down next to her.

"It is. You get creative when you're a broke college student who only has a hot plate and a microwave, and the cafeteria is closed because you spent too much time in the computer lab."

Esther chuckled. "Or in my case, the library. I kept a stash of protein shakes and yogurt in my dorm fridge for nights like that." She blushed. "And those frozen burritos."

Asher laughed. "Me too." He tucked his tie into his shirt, then lifted his sandwich and took a bite.

"Why did you bring a tie?"

He glanced down, chewing. Holding up a finger, he swallowed. "I wanted to be prepared for anything. I have a suit jacket upstairs too, but I didn't figure church warranted a full suit."

"It probably doesn't even warrant the tie. We're not terribly formal."

He lifted a shoulder. "I always wore one growing up, so I still do when I go."

"Where's home for you?"

"Michigan. I grew up near Kalamazoo."

"Do you still have family there?"

"My dad. We're not terribly close, but I go home at least once a year for a visit, and we email."

Esther wrinkled her nose. "I couldn't imagine only seeing

my dad once a year. My mom, either. It's hard enough with Edie being so far away."

"You grew up differently. My mom died when I was just a kid, and my dad worked two jobs to keep us afloat. I spent a lot of time with my grandparents and was close to them, but they're both gone now."

"I'm sorry. That must have been tough. What happened to your mom?"

"Aneurysm. I was three." He took another bite of his sandwich.

"Oh, wow. I can't imagine."

"I don't remember much about her. She smelled good, that I remember. And she had a pretty singing voice. But my grandparents—my dad's parents—were great. They stepped in right away, so I never felt neglected. Like any kid who's lost a parent, sometimes I wished I had a mom to go to school functions with, but my grandma would go, so I didn't completely miss out. And I turned out okay." He sent her a crooked smile.

"You did, yes. What about your maternal grandparents? Were they in the picture?"

He shook his head. "Mom moved to Michigan from out of state for college. The University of Michigan. She and Dad met there. Her family lives in Wisconsin. My grandparents on that side are still alive, but I've never had much to do with them. My grandmother hasn't been well for years and couldn't travel, so I didn't see them much. I have an uncle there, too, and a couple of cousins. What about you? Do you have extended family around?"

She nodded as he finished the rest of his sandwich. "I have a couple of aunts, and they live in the area with their families. We have a few cousins. All four of my grandparents are still alive too." Her eyes widened as she remembered who would be at church. "Oh, no." She covered her face.

"What?"

"My family will be at church. My parents and my mom's parents. Oh, this is bad. They'll have all kinds of questions about you." She removed her hands and looked at him. "I can't tell them about my troubles. My dad will go ballistic. You think Edie's bad? Nope. Dad will literally pitch a tent in my front yard."

"Just tell them I'm your boyfriend."

"We can't do that!" He was out of his ever-loving mind. "That'll lead to even worse questions. We can tell them you're here for work."

A single dark eyebrow rose. "Doing what, exactly? My business is online. I can literally work from anywhere with an internet connection. Why would I come here?"

Her hopeful expression crumbled. He had a point. "Okay. But my boyfriend? Really?"

"I don't know what else to tell you, Essy. We need to explain my presence somehow. And that makes the most sense. Even if I stay here today and you go to church alone, this town isn't that large. Someone's going to notice my car outside your house every night. It'll get back to them one way or another. Wouldn't you rather address the problem head on than let it blindside you?"

She huffed. "Actually, I'd rather not address it at all." She lifted her coffee cup and took a big gulp. It hadn't occurred to her what other issues Asher's presence in her life would cause. If they told everyone they were dating, it would explain why he was hanging around, but then she'd have to field all the questions about what went wrong when he left. "This would be easier if Mom and Dad hadn't met you."

"True. But honestly, you're making this into a bigger issue than it is." He tipped his head back, draining his coffee.

Was he for real? "You do know this is my life you're complicating, right? I have to live it when you leave."

"I know. But what I mean is, we can tell people I came up

to see if we can make something of how we feel, but I can't stay because of work obligations. We can fake a long-distance thing with everyone for a while, then tell them a few months from now that we decided to end it."

Esther frowned at her coffee mug. While that didn't sound that complicated, she still detested the idea of dealing with it all. But she didn't see another way. He was here, and as much as she hated to admit it, she felt better with him around.

"All right, fine." She pushed away from the island, standing, and shook a finger at him. "But you keep your hands to yourself."

One side of his mouth kicked up, and he touched two fingers to his temple. "Scout's honor."

Esther let out a soft snort and headed for the sink and away from the teasing glint in his eyes. "Why do I get the feeling you were never a Boy Scout?"

He chuckled. "I'll behave."

She certainly hoped so. It was a tenuous thread holding back the urge to wrap her arms around him so she could feel what that perfectly sculpted body of his felt like pressed up against hers.

NINE

Asher slipped a finger beneath his shirt collar and tugged, questioning why he'd decided to wear a tie. It had been years since he strangled himself with one. Even at all the weddings he'd been to recently, he hadn't worn one; the attire had been much less formal. But as he got dressed this morning, his grandmother's face had popped into his head, and he'd heard her reminding him as a boy to straighten his tie as they left the house for church. So, he'd put one on.

Truthfully, it wasn't the tie that had him feeling restricted. It was the need quietly pulsing through his veins for the woman who sat beside him. With her hair plaited and her makeup minimal, she looked demure and ladylike in her colorful maxi skirt and pale green blouse. She was the type of woman he'd always wanted. Not the flashy, overly made up, rail-thin models he tended to attract. He wanted a lady. Someone kind and polite, but passionate. One who didn't care if her hair wasn't always perfect or that her clothes weren't part of the latest trend. Just someone who was real. Esther fit that bill perfectly.

"Take the next left. The church is on the right." She pointed ahead, breaking into his thoughts.

He nodded and slowed. When they left the house, he'd asked to drive. Not only because he was more comfortable being in the driver's seat in case something happened, but because he'd parked in the driveway behind the single-car garage that housed her vehicle. To take hers, he would have to move his car, anyway. It just made sense to take his rental.

Turning the corner, he saw the church just down the street. The parking lot wasn't too crowded yet, but they were a bit early. He pulled in and parked.

Another car pulled in as he shut the SUV off, and Esther let out a little grumble.

"Are you ready for this?" She nodded toward the car. "That's my mom and dad."

He flashed her a quick grin and unbuckled. "Yep." Yanking on the door handle, he got out.

Rounding the hood, he held out a hand to Esther. She paused near the headlight and stared at it.

"Take my hand, Essy. You want them to think we're dating, right?"

She took a deep breath and laced her fingers with his.

"Smile." He tugged her closer. "They'll think I'm an ogre."

That made her chuckle softly. "They will not. You charmed the pants off them in Costa Rica."

"People's public personas can be much different than their private ones."

"True, but they know Edie wouldn't associate with someone who wasn't a good person." She grumbled again. "I hate giving them false hope that I found someone they like."

A voice in the back of Asher's mind called out that she might not be as deceptive as she thought. He could see himself with this woman. How they'd make it work, he didn't know. But it wasn't out of the realm of possibilities.

"Esther?" Her mother, Faye, walked closer, then stopped as she got a good look at Essy's companion. "What—? Asher, what are you doing here?" Her gaze dropped to their clasped hands, and her expression brightened. "All right, spill." She waved a hand at their linked fingers.

"Hi, Mrs. Campbell." Asher turned up the wattage on his smile and aimed it at Faye.

"Don't turn that charm on me. When did this happen?" She glanced at her husband. "Did you know about this?"

Conner shook his head. "No. Why would she tell me before she told you?"

"We haven't told anyone. Not even Edie knows," Esther said.

Asher made a mental note to text her and tell her to act surprised when her mother called to talk about this.

"We're just—" Esther paused and looked up. "Seeing where this goes."

Asher smiled, squeezing her hand, then turned to her parents. "The truth is, your daughter captivated me the moment I saw her. We've been chatting the last couple of months through email, then on the phone. I finally asked her if I could come visit and see if we can make something of this. Our situation isn't normal or uncomplicated, but you can't make something work that you never try to do in the first place."

"Very true," Conner said. He swept an arm out toward the church. "Let's go in, shall we?"

They made their way inside, where Asher helped Esther out of her jacket and hung it up on the coat rack along with his own.

"Faye!"

Asher glanced over as someone called Esther's mother's

name. Faye raised a hand and waved to the other woman, who beckoned her over.

"Go on, Mom. We can't join you in the sanctuary, anyway. I'm teaching Sunday School today. Asher's going to help."

"Oh." Faye's brows knit together. "All right. Maybe we can have lunch afterward?"

"Can we take a raincheck?" Asher asked. He didn't want to put anymore stress on Esther to keep up appearances than necessary. Besides, they had other things to accomplish today. "I planned an afternoon of activities for us."

Faye's expression brightened. He could see in her eyes that she liked the idea of him courting her daughter. "Of course. Perhaps one evening this week we can all have dinner."

Esther directed a smile at her, but Asher could see from the fine lines at the corners of her eyes that it was forced.

"Sure, Mom."

"Great." Faye smiled.

The woman across the room called Faye's name again.

"We'd better go before Liz has a stroke," Conner said.

Faye rolled her eyes, looking very much like her daughters in that moment. "It's not like it's gourmet fare we have to get ready. And she can handle the coffeepot on her own."

Conner took her hand and pulled her away. "I know, but she needs the affirmation that she's doing it right. And you're so good at making her feel accomplished."

"Oh, stop." She lightly tapped him on the chest, chuckling. Turning her head, she smiled at Esther and Asher. "Asher, we're glad you're here. Essy, I'll call you, and we'll set something up, all right?"

"That sounds good, Mom." Again, she smiled her tight smile.

Asher slid closer and untangled their fingers to lay them on her back at the base of her neck. When Faye and Conner turned away, he gave Esther a gentle squeeze. "You might want to work on that fake smile. Your parents were too excited to see it this time, but next time?"

She huffed. "Come on." Leaving him behind, she swiftly moved off.

In a couple of strides, he caught up to her. "It's not that terrible, you know."

"What's not?"

"Pretending to be dating."

She halted abruptly, turning to face him. "It's not that. It's —" She broke off, pushing him toward the wall as a middle-aged woman approached. Esther offered her a quick smile, waiting for her to pass.

Asher didn't think she was aware she'd left her hand on his chest after she nudged him back. He wasn't about to break it to her. He liked it there.

"It's not that I'm upset about the pretend dating thing or that I think it's hard. It's—" She paused, pulling the corner of her bottom lip in to chew on it as she thought.

"It's lying to your family, isn't it?" he said softly.

She released her lip and nodded. "Yeah."

"Well, we'll do what we can to limit our interaction with them. I'm not sure we can avoid dinner, but maybe I can fake a work emergency to get us out early."

"Maybe we'll figure out what's going on and you can go home before it even happens."

"Yeah, maybe." Although, part of him hoped that wasn't the case. Now that he was here, he didn't have much desire to leave.

Ten

The light tinkle of a little boy's laughter drew Esther's attention. She glanced up from helping Daphne with her Bible craft to see Bryant King giggling at Asher, who had a streak of glitter on his face. Asher's tongue poked out from between his teeth as he attempted to line up the holes and poke yarn through them. The booklet Esther had the kids make looked tiny in his big hands.

He aimed a bright smile at Bryant as the piece of blue yarn slid through the holes. Esther's heart stuttered as she took in the sight. He was so gentle with the kids. And hands on. When she explained the craft, he'd rolled up his sleeves and jumped right in to help. It really wasn't fair that a man so pretty was also so kind. She needed to resist him; there was no future for them—not that he'd even give her a second look—but he was making it damn hard.

Movement at the door brought Esther out of her thoughts. She looked over and saw Leila Kite come into the room and frowned. What was she doing here? She didn't have any children.

The woman glanced around the room, quickly zeroing in on Asher.

Ah. It suddenly made sense. One of the moms must have mentioned Esther's helper.

A predatory smile slid over Leila's face.

Esther looked at Daphne. "Excuse me a moment, sweetie." She stood, heading Leila off before she could get across the room. "Hi, Leila. What can I do for you? Did you come to help the kids with their Bible study craft? You're a little late if so. It's almost time to pack up."

Leila paused, her smile turning down as Esther stepped into her path. "Oh. Um, no. I came to welcome our new member." She tipped her head toward Asher.

"He's just visiting."

"I still believe we should make everyone feel welcome here."

"I agree. But he's busy helping Bryant. You wouldn't want to interrupt a child learning to love Jesus, would you?" Esther knew she was playing dirty, but she didn't care. Leila wasn't here to help. She was only here to make a play for Asher, and it was an interruption Esther's class didn't need. And while she also knew it was rather un-Christian of her, she didn't like Leila Kite. The woman came to church because her family expected her to, not because she truly believed. And she never missed an opportunity to flirt—with single or married men.

"I'm sure you can wave and maybe say hello as we leave later." Though Leila and her family would likely be long gone before Esther and Asher left. They still had to clean up the room after the kids rejoined their parents.

"But—"

Esther walked forward, extending an arm to turn Leila around. "You should go find your parents. They're probably getting coffee to go, I imagine. I need to help the kids finish their projects before their parents arrive. Thanks for stopping in. Next week, come earlier. I never turn away help when we're in the thick of crafting." Plastering a wide smile on her face, she ushered the woman out the door.

Leila tossed a glare over her shoulder but left without incident.

Esther puffed out her cheeks as she released a breath. Some women had no boundaries.

Turning around, she went back to help Daphne, but the girl had figured things out herself and was putting the finishing touches on the front of her booklet. Esther glanced around, looking for anyone else who needed help tying their pages together. This group was rather young and hadn't mastered that skill yet, so she helped a couple more, then clapped her hands to get their attention.

"Everyone, put your last stickers on and color your last spots. Your parents should be here any moment." Most of the parents visited in the lobby for a few minutes after the service before they collected their children.

While the kids added more stickers and colored in the last of their pictures, Esther started gathering the yarn and construction paper they didn't use.

"Thank you for saving me."

She glanced back at Asher, who'd come up behind her while she sorted the paper by color into the file organizers on the shelf. "Oh. You're welcome. Leila's an opportunist and only interested in you because you're pretty. Besides, I didn't want her disturbing my classroom."

That crooked smile that made his dimples pop made an appearance. The glitter decorating his cheek only enhanced his adorableness.

"You're a good teacher, Essy."

"Because I don't want interruptions?"

"No. Because you care about the kids. Sometimes, that

care is all the kid ever gets. The world needs more teachers like you."

Esther felt her cheeks heat. "Oh, well, thank you."

"You're welcome." He took a quick glance around the room. "What do you want me to do?"

"Make sure all the kids have everything they showed up with and that they all have their booklet. Then just start putting things away. Although you don't have to be quick. Leila will linger as long as her folks will allow, so the longer we take to clean up, the less likely we are to have a second encounter with her."

His crooked smile widened. "Be a snail. Got it."

Esther chuckled. He turned to step away, but she snagged his shirt sleeve. "You've got—" She lifted a hand and motioned to the spot on her face where he had glitter on his.

Frowning, he raised a hand and swiped at his cheek, then looked at his fingers. Gold glitter shined on them. He sighed. "Why am I not surprised?" Using his sleeve, he wiped at his face. "Did I get it all?"

There were a couple of sparkles left in his short beard, but nothing crazy. "Yes."

"Great, thank you."

"Of course."

Backing away, she returned to helping the children pack up. Fifteen minutes later, all the kids were gone and the room was back in order.

"Are you ready?" Asher asked.

"I think so." She took another quick look around, but everything appeared to be back where it belonged.

"Let's go, then. I'm ready for lunch." He waited for her to exit, then flipped off the lights

"Is that part of your 'planned activities' for us this afternoon?" She turned her head, a curious smirk sitting on her lips.

He gave a low chuckle. "Actually, yes. We can grab a bite somewhere, then we're going shopping."

"Shopping? For what?"

"A doorbell camera."

Esther's shoulders sagged at the reminder of why he was here. "Oh."

"Sorry. Didn't mean to rain on your mood."

"You're fine. I just forget, you know?" They headed down the hallway toward the lobby. "Not enough has happened to make it something that's always on my mind. I still think you and Edie are overreacting, but I can see the merit of a doorbell camera. Even if all this wasn't happening, I should probably still have one."

"You should. Or a peep hole. Cameras are easier to install and safer."

They reached the main lobby, where a few people still milled around talking. Thankfully, Esther didn't see Leila.

"Looks like your mom and dad left already," Asher said.

Esther breathed a sigh of relief. She didn't want to have to put up the façade with them again. "Yeah." She waved at a couple of people but didn't stop on her way to the coatrack. They quickly donned their jackets and left.

Outside, she let herself relax a bit. They could just be themselves now.

"So, what's a good place for lunch?" Asher pulled the car keys from his pocket and hit the button on the fob to unlock his vehicle as they approached.

"Depends on what you're in the mood for."

He opened her door and stepped back so she could slide in. "We're on the coast, so how about fresh seafood?"

Esther didn't even have to think about where to go. "I know the perfect spot."

Asher got in, and she directed him to the beach where a local man with a food truck parked.

"Now, this is my kind of place." Asher set the brake and shut off the engine. "Some of the best food I've ever had has been at a food truck."

"Me too. And Jimmy makes some of the best." Smiling, Esther climbed out.

"I see we aren't the only ones who had the same idea." He nodded to the line four people deep.

"Yeah. We're actually not that late. There will be a longer line in about ten minutes or so."

True to her word, the line that stretched behind them when they finally got their food was three times as long.

"This is a nice spot." Asher commented as they sat down at a picnic table.

"It is. The tables are fairly new. Some locals petitioned the city to put them in. Before, it was just the trails down to the beach." She gestured toward the sign markers. "There are plans in the works to add some bathrooms and a foot wash station. All because one man parked his food truck here."

Asher popped a crab-stuffed fried ravioli into his mouth and immediately his eyes bugged out. "And can make amazing seafood. Holy crap, that's good." He shoved in a second bite.

"Right? He makes all his own pasta and never uses frozen ingredients. It's incredible." She speared her plastic fork into her chili-lime crab-stuffed baked potato. Savoring the taste, she glanced up, letting the sun warm her face. It had been a while since she'd seen it.

"Do you ever get tired of the sun in Costa Rica?"

He paused, a piece of ravioli just inches from his mouth. "Why would I get tired of the sun?"

She shrugged. "I just wondered if it was like the rain and people could get tired of it. I, for one, am glad to see it today."

He tipped his head and shrugged. "I don't mind the sun. But I spend a lot of time in my lair." He dipped a ravioli in the sauce that had come with his meal and ate it, rolling his eyes once more in ecstasy.

Esther looked down as her cheeks heated. She could imagine other ways he'd make that face. Sending a quick glance at him through her lashes, she speared a bite of potato. "Your lair?"

"I dedicated a room in my house to my computers. It's dark and cold, like a cave." He rolled a hand. "My lair."

Esther laughed. "All I picture is you as an evil genius, controlling the world from your desk."

He tipped his chin down and looked up, a wicked grin covering his face. "You're not far off." He lifted his head, his smile turning sunny. "Except I'm not evil. Well, not unless I have to be. Some people deserve everything I do to them."

She had no doubt. After what her sister went through in the spring and the stories she'd heard about the human trafficking ring Asher and the others broke up recently, she was glad there were people like him in the world. Because there were others who were truly evil.

Clouds scuttled in while they ate, threatening to hide the sun by the time they finished their meal. After disposing of their trash, they hopped back into the car, and Esther directed Asher to an electronics store in Coos Bay.

Inside, he led her to a section devoted to home security.

Her eyes widened as she took in the array of equipment. "I think I'm glad you're here. I wouldn't know what to get."

"We just want a basic doorbell camera. One you can wirelessly connect to your phone and with some decent cloud storage." He studied the shelves, then pointed. "That one."

Esther held up her hands. "Whatever you say."

He glanced at her, devilish merriment in his eyes. "Is my wish your command?"

A choked laugh bubbled up her throat. "What?"

He let loose a low laugh. "I'm kidding. Though it might be fun."

Esther's cheeks heated again. Was he flirting with her?

"Hi. Can I help you folks with something?"

Esther turned to see a man around her age approaching.

"We'd like to get that doorbell camera." Asher pointed at the display.

"Certainly." The man took a set of keys from his pocket and unlocked the case. He removed a box. "There you go." He handed it to Asher.

"Thank you."

"Can I help you with anything else?"

"Actually, do you have any motion-sensitive lights?"

"We do. Battery-powered or hard-wired?"

"Hard-wired."

Lights? Esther frowned. What was he talking about? "Asher!" she hissed. "Why are we looking at lights?" She followed him as he trailed behind the sales associate.

"I got to thinking. There isn't much lighting on the outside of your house. Motion-sensitive lights would be a good deterrent."

"We agreed on the camera." She couldn't afford a pricey system. Not to mention installation costs. He'd said "hard-wired" lights. That meant an electrician at the very least.

"I know, but you need better lighting."

The sales associate stopped in front of a display. "This is what we have. If we don't have the quantity you need, I can order them in."

Esther smiled politely. "Thank you. Could you give us a minute?"

"Sure. Just wave at me when you're ready."

"Perfect, thanks." Esther's voice trailed off as the man wandered away. She turned to Asher, her smile falling off her face. "I can't afford a bunch of extra security measures. I can do the camera." She glanced at the lighting display and the prices. "Even buy the lights. But the cost to have an electrician come out and install them is something else."

"I can do that. We just need to stop at a hardware store so I can buy the supplies. It shouldn't cost too much. And, you might not like this, but I'm buying it whether you pay me back or not."

"Asher." Her voice dropped with a low growl.

"Don't 'Asher' me. This is about your safety. I can't go back without telling your sister—"

"Don't you bring her into this." She stuck a finger in his face. "I will not have you guilt me into all the things."

"Essy—"

"No. I'll get the camera. But the lights..." She glanced at them again. They really weren't that bad in price. She could easily afford two if he put them in.

"Scout's honor, a hundred bucks in materials," he said.

His choice of words pulled a smile from her. "We've already covered you weren't a Boy Scout."

"But I'm still telling the truth."

Esther sighed, rubbing the bridge of her nose. "Fine."

A bright smile split his handsome face. "Let's go, then, before you change your mind." He lifted an arm and waved at the sales associate.

Minutes later, they walked out with the camera and two lights—one for the front and back of the house. She had a feeling Asher had wanted one for each corner, but she'd told the sales guy two lights before he could say anything. Asher hadn't contradicted her.

When they pulled into her driveway after stopping to get the wire and tools he'd need, Esther was done with shopping. And with her heels. She didn't normally wear heels this high; she was tall without them. But with Asher by her side, his height had given her the confidence to wear them. She knew she should have it anyway, but as a bookish introvert with flaming red hair, she tended to minimize the amount of attention she drew to herself. She had plenty of self-confidence, but that didn't mean she liked to be the center of attention.

"I probably should have asked before we left the hardware store, but do you have a ladder that'll reach above your doors?" Asher put the car in park and looked at her.

"I do, actually. And the attic has a pull-down staircase in the upstairs hallway."

"Awesome." He opened his door and climbed out. "I'll probably need your help, if you don't mind?"

"That's fine. So long as you let me change first."

"You don't want to climb ladders and walk around in your yard in pointy heels and a skirt?"

Smiling, she fished out her house keys. "No."

"I don't want to wear a tie and do it, either." He flicked the maroon silk.

An image of what he could do with that tie besides wear it struck her. Heat suffused her cheeks, and she turned away, thankful they'd reached the front door and she had to concentrate on letting them in.

Pushing the door inward, she hurried inside. With a quick detour to leave her purse on the island, she headed for the stairs. Asher was ahead of her. Unfortunately—or fortunately, depending on how she looked at it—there was enough sunlight streaming through the windows to see the globes of his perfect butt move beneath the thin fabric of his trousers as he climbed the stairs. She could imagine how it would look, flexing with each step, sans the pants. She hoped he put on jeans, though she wasn't sure that would be much better. She'd seen his jeans. He liked the kind that clung to his hips and thighs.

Why couldn't he be one of those computer geeks who liked the baggy grunge style?

They reached the landing, and she turned into her bedroom, thankfully shutting the door on the sinful deliciousness that was Asher Horn.

Esther wandered into her closet and stripped out of her skirt and blouse, kicking her heels into a corner. She'd put them away later; when she did laundry. Grabbing a pair of jeans, she stepped into them, then took a long-sleeved shirt off a shelf and slipped it over her head. Back in her bedroom, she found a pair of socks and slid them onto her feet. She'd put on her gardening shoes, which she kept downstairs in the laundry-slash-mud room.

Dressed, she left her room. Asher emerged at the same time and they went down together, but she made sure to go first. She was sure she'd get her fill of staring at his denim-clad butt while he was on the ladder.

Her inner wild child rolled her eyes, saying no, she wouldn't. Esther bit back a snort, knowing she was right. She'd never get enough of staring at his rear. At any of him, really.

"Can you get out your drill, a tape measure, and a sharpie while I grab the boxes from the car?" He glanced back at her as he walked toward the front door.

"Sure." She detoured toward the garage. Stepping through the doorway, she turned on the lights, then opened the overhead door, figuring it would be easier for him to just come through that way. The electrical panel was on the back wall.

Asher walked into the garage with an armload of boxes and bags. "All right. Let's start by marking where we want to put everything. Then I'll get the lights up. We'll do the camera last. It's the easiest."

"Sounds good." She followed him out front.

"I'm thinking on the corner of the garage, there, for the light." He pointed. "It covers the walkway and the drive. I'm not sure it'll cover your front windows, though. It'll be close."

"Wherever is fine. I'm just here to hand you things."

He tossed her a smile. "Let's go around back."

They rounded the corner of the house and repeated the process of staring at the façade. Asher picked a point in between the back door and the door that led out of the garage. Once they had locations figured out, he opened the electrical panel.

Esther hung back, not having a clue what to do. "How do you know how to do this? I thought your forte was computers."

"It is, but there's an electrical component to computer science. I've rewired buildings so they have the infrastructure to run high-tech systems. Not often, but I know how to do it. A couple of lights are simple."

"If you say so."

Mouth twitching with a suppressed smile, he shut the panel door. "Come on. Where's your ladder?"

For the next hour, she followed him around with boxes and tools, passing things to him and even crawling up into the attic to help as he threaded wires down the walls.

"I'm glad it's not hotter." Esther fanned her face as they closed up the attic. It had been warm up there, and she was sweaty. And itchy from the insulation. They'd worn masks to keep from inhaling any they kicked up, but it stuck to her sweaty skin. She needed a shower. It would have to wait, though. They weren't done yet.

Out back, Asher set the ladder against the house and climbed up to attach the light, before they moved around front to do the same. Once both were up, he flipped the main breaker back on.

"Go wave your arms at the one out front. Once we know they work, I'll change the setting so they don't come on unless it's dark."

Esther left the garage. As she broke the plane of the garage door and rounded the corner, the light turned on. "Well, that was easy." She went back inside. Asher was coming in through the back door. "It works. Does the one out back?"

"Yep." He closed the electrical panel. "Let's get the doorbell camera up."

"Why don't you set up the Bluetooth and the cloud stuff? I can attach the bracket."

"Oh. Are you sure?" Asher tipped his head to the side.

"I can handle a doorbell."

"All right, then." He shrugged and walked over to the workbench along the wall and picked up the doorbell box, opening it. "Here you go." He handed her the mounting bracket and some screws. "You'll need the drill."

She nodded once, then picked up the tool.

"What email address do you want me to attach this to?"

She told him.

"Do you have a specific password in mind, or do you want me to make up something?"

"Just make up something." Tools and parts in hand, she left the garage.

Standing in front of her door, she studied the doorframe. She wasn't quite sure how high to put it. It needed to be high enough to catch people's faces, but not ridiculous. The fisheye lens would help with that.

Esther set her things down, then walked up to the door like she was going to knock. Closing her eyes, she raised her hand to where she thought the doorbell would be, then opened them. That was a good height.

With the sharpie from her back pocket, she marked the spot on the frame, then set about screwing the bracket into place. Once she had it mounted, she stepped back to admire her handiwork.

Not bad.

"Are you ready for this thing?"

Esther jumped slightly, not having heard him approach. She spun around, forgetting about the flowerpot behind her. At the last second, she saw it and tried to avoid walking into it, but failed. She kicked it and lost her balance.

"Oh!" Arms windmilling, she lurched to the side.

"Whoa, there." Asher's arms clamped around her and his hands splayed over her back, hauling her into his solid chest.

She grabbed hold of his biceps. "Thanks." She looked up. *Hello.*

Deep, dark brown eyes stared back at her from a face that was closer than it had ever been. Her gaze flicked to his full lips, then back to his eyes.

Color stained her cheeks, and the heat spread south, warming the rest of her.

"Are you all right?"

"Um, yeah." She pushed against him, needing some space before she let her inner wild child do what she wanted to do and kissed him. "I'm good." She turned to the bracket she'd installed. "Does that look okay?"

He walked toward it. "Looks fine." Raising the camera, he slid it onto the mount. It clicked into place. "Do you have your phone? You need to download and log in to the app."

Esther pulled her phone from her back pocket. He walked her through the process, and soon she could see what the camera saw.

"That's cool." She glanced up. "Thank you." And she meant it. Until now, when she actually saw it in action, she hadn't given much thought to how having the camera would make her feel. But it gave her a small sense of security to be able to know who was at her door before she opened it. If Asher hadn't come—hadn't hauled her to the store and picked it out—she probably never would have installed it.

"You're welcome." He winked, then turned and leaned over, moving the flowerpot she'd kicked back into place.

Esther picked up the drill and empty packaging.

"Esther?"

"Hmm?" She glanced at him. "What are you doing?" He was leaning down, looking at the ground on the other side of the porch, behind the shrubs.

"Did you step into the flowerbed while you worked?"

"No. Why?" She moved closer.

"Someone's been in here. There are footprints." He pointed.

"What?" She walked to the edge of the porch and looked down. Sure enough, man-size footprints compacted the dirt.

The blood drained from her face. She leaned against the house. "How old are they? Could it have been the guy in the hoodie?"

Asher squatted to get a better look. "If it was, he came back. These look fresh. It's rained since then. Heavily. They were probably made yesterday or this morning."

Which meant whoever it was, came up to the house with Asher in it.

Esther glanced down the street and hugged herself against a sudden chill. That scared her even more than the guy staring at her on the sidewalk. If the person wasn't afraid to get close with Asher around, what would they do if he wasn't?

Eleven

Raindrops pelted Asher's car windows as he waited in the parking lot outside Esther's school. After their discovery yesterday afternoon, he'd decided to play it safe and take her to work. The original plan had been for her to drive herself, and then he would meet her at the Tylers' after school and sit outside while she tutored Leah. Now, though, he was driving her. He would still wait outside, but he was her ride instead of just her shadow.

The scent of his stale coffee wrinkled his nose as he took a drink. It was hours old, but it still had its kick, which he needed. Last night, he'd tossed and turned, unable to get it out of his mind that someone had peeked in her windows with him in the house. He'd tried to convince himself that maybe the guy didn't know it was a man staying with Esther. Maybe he thought she had an old friend in town, or a cousin. And he was sure the guy knew she had company. Part of the reason Asher parked in her driveway and not on the street was because he wanted their mystery man to know Esther wasn't alone.

But that hadn't mattered.

He didn't understand how Dean and the others did this sort of thing. Asher had stress during their operations, but it was a different kind of stress. More, hurry up and get it done, and less, why won't the bad guy cooperate? He just hoped the new doorbell camera and security lights would net them a lead. Asher needed more to go on than a man in a hoodie.

An electronic bell cut through the air, signaling the end of the school day. The side door opened, and a stream of children filed out on their way to the waiting buses. Esther said she had car rider duty, which meant she had to stick around for a little while after the bell rang.

It didn't take long for the teachers to work through the line. Fifteen minutes after the bell rang, Esther exited the front doors of the school.

Asher pulled out of his parking spot and met her at the edge of the sidewalk. She slid into the passenger seat, setting a large tote bag between her feet.

"Hey." She reached for her seat belt.

He smiled at her and pulled away. "Hey. How was your day?"

"Long. I think I'm going to have a bunch of snotty kinder-gartners in a day or two. A couple of them were sneezing a lot. That's usually a precursor to a cold rampaging through my classroom." She sighed. "How was your day? Did your inter-view go well?"

"It did. I expressed my desire to get to work as soon as possible, so she said she'd have her secretary input my informa-tion into the sub system today. Hopefully, I'll get a call tomorrow and will be in the building with you."

"You're lucky our super is a woman. I bet you smiled and she agreed to anything you said."

Asher pressed his lips together, holding back a smirk, and glanced in his side mirror. "Maybe." He definitely wasn't above using his looks to get what he wanted when it was important. That wasn't to say he'd never used them for trivial things. He'd done some dumb stuff when he was younger. Now, though, he reserved the dimples for situations where it mattered.

Esther chuckled. "Just don't ruin it for future subs by doing a terrible job."

"I won't. I like kids. It helps that I'm a big one myself." He let his smile free and aimed it at her.

She rolled her eyes. "No argument there."

They reached the traffic light at the main road. He'd input the Tylers' address into his GPS earlier and it told him to turn now. Following its prompts, he was soon pulling up outside their house.

"This really is a rough neighborhood." He leaned forward, looking through the windshield at the houses lining the street. Most of them needed a coat of paint or new siding. Rusted chain link surrounded some of the yards, which in many cases, were more bare patches of dirt and weeds than grass. Ancient, dented and rusting vehicles sat in front of a couple of the homes. One of them had its wheels missing.

The Tylers' house was one of the nicer ones. Its dingy exterior definitely needed a refresh, but the paint wasn't peeling—much—and the yard and landscaping were tidy. Only the crumbling concrete stoop really screamed "decay." And while the older model sedan in the driveway looked like it had seen better days, it was clean and appeared to have decent tires. Someone in the house cared and was trying.

Esther pulled on the door handle and opened the door a crack, then reached for the handles on her tote. "Are you sure you want to sit out here for an hour? I'll be fine in the house. You can come back and get me."

"I'm sure. I'm going to people watch while you're inside." He wanted to take note of anyone who paid particular attention to the Tylers' house.

"All right. Well, I'll be back in an hour." She pushed the door open and stepped out.

"Call me if things get weird."

"Things are usually weird with Rob, but if they get weirder, you'll be the first to know." She closed the door.

A slight frown knit Asher's eyebrows together as she walked to the door. She knocked, and he heard the muffled bark of a small dog inside. A moment later, the door swung open. The man who answered did so with a scowl. His gaze flicked to Asher's car, then he said something to Esther. He couldn't see more than the side of her face, but it was enough to know she replied. Whatever she said must have been satisfactory, because Rob stepped back and let her in.

Asher's anxiety level ratcheted up as the door closed. He didn't like her being in there on her own. Not after what he'd discovered about the man and what she'd said about him. But he didn't have a choice. Being close by was the best he could do.

He lifted his coffee and took another drink, grimacing again at the taste. Why was he still drinking it? Opening his door, he dumped the contents onto the road. He was tempted to get out and walk around. See if any curtains fluttered or if anyone disappeared back into their houses. He didn't see anyone watching, but he could only see into the windows of a few homes on the street from this vantage point.

Glancing down the road, he decided to wait for a bit. People would let their guards down if he waited until she'd been inside for a while. He reached into the backseat and lifted the satchel he'd brought into his lap. Digging inside, he removed a tablet and flipped open the cover to take notes. Asher jotted down the license plate and vehicle description for every car close enough for him to read. Right now, he didn't intend to do anything with the information, but he'd have it if it became necessary.

Thirty-five minutes into his wait, a man walked around the corner down the block. He wore a dark tan hoodie, which was up over his head, obscuring his face.

Asher sat a little straighter.

The man walked toward him, head turned slightly to the side, his gaze on the Tylers' house. Asher lifted his phone, opening the camera app and snapped some pictures. Dean would yell at him for not having a proper camera, but it couldn't be helped. He'd do the best he could to enhance the images later. Not that it would do much; he couldn't see the guy's face.

Getting closer, the man's attention shifted. He looked away from the Tylers' and perused the street. Sunglasses covered his face. With the hood pulled low, all Asher could see was a chin. The man was white.

Twenty yards away, the man paused. He'd spotted Asher's car.

"Come closer, you bastard," Asher muttered. He wanted a better shot of his face.

But the guy didn't listen. He turned around and briskly walked away.

"Oh, uh-uh." Asher got out of the car and hurried after him. He didn't know what he'd say when he caught up, but he'd make up something.

"Excuse me. Sir?" Asher called.

The man glanced back, then began to jog.

Asher muttered a curse and picked up his pace. "Sir?"

The guy took off at a full sprint.

"Hey!"

His shoes slapped against the potmarked concrete sidewalk as he chased after him. The man rounded the corner, blocked from view by the houses. Asher ran faster, not wanting to lose him. He soon made it to the corner, but when he turned onto the next street, it was empty.

Slowing to a jog, he glanced between the houses and listened. A little dog barked across the street, but the animal was inside. Asher could see it through the front window. It stared at him and yipped.

Running all the way to the next intersection, he paused and glanced both ways. There was no one on the street. A glimpse inside the few vehicles parked along the road showed that they were empty. He muttered a curse and turned around. With his head on a swivel, hoping to catch a glimpse of the guy, he made it back to his car.

Angry that the man had gotten away, he got in and slammed the door. Whoever that was knew this neighborhood well. The question was, did the man live around here, or had he been watching the Tylers' home long enough to know the neighborhood?

"Dammit!" He smacked the steering wheel.

Either way, Asher wouldn't likely see the man around here again.

TWELVE

The ceiling fan whirred over Esther's head, tousling the fine hairs resting on her forehead. She rolled over for the hundredth time and huffed. Sleep was not coming easily tonight. Now that she was alone and had nothing to do but listen to her thoughts, she couldn't make them shut up. Who was the man Asher saw? Why was he watching the Tylers' house? Why would he run away? Was he the same man who'd stared at her through her window? She didn't know—had no way to find out. But her brain didn't care. It kept cycling through the questions, keeping her awake.

Esther rolled over and picked up her phone, opening the doorbell app. Her darkened street stared back.

"Ugh." She turned off the screen and set the phone down. "You need to stop, Essy. It'll alert you if someone's there. Go to sleep."

She flopped onto her back and put a pillow over her eyes.

But what if they're out of range and staring, *like last time?*

With a groan, she flung the pillow to the side and sat up, pushing the covers away. She wasn't sleeping anytime soon, so she might as well do something productive. Leah's birthday was at the end of the week. When Esther left today, she'd asked Rob if she could bring the girl a small birthday cake. Surprisingly, he'd agreed with little fuss. She could make the cake and freeze it, then it would be ready to frost Thursday evening.

Wandering downstairs, she rounded the corner, debating which flavor cake to make, and didn't see Asher in the living room until he spoke.

"What are you doing up?"

A shriek ripped from her chest, and she flattened herself against the wall. Heart thumping, she covered it with her hand. "Why are you sitting in the dark?"

"I'm working."

Of course he was. All normal people worked in the middle of the night and without the lights on. "You should be sleeping. Especially if you're going to spend all day with grade schoolers tomorrow."

"Which is exactly why I'm working. I have other projects that need my attention. Ones I can't work on while I'm in a classroom with kids."

A wrinkle formed between her eyebrows, and she pushed away from the wall. "Like what?"

"Just stuff. I do a lot of digital security analysis. Plus, I couldn't sleep, so..." He shrugged. "Why are you up?"

"My brain wouldn't shut off. I'm going to bake a cake." Pivoting on the ball of her foot, she headed for the kitchen.

"A cake?" Curiosity fueled a cute frown on his face. "What?"

She heard him get up and walk toward her. "Cake. You know, that stuff you eat for your birthday?"

"Whose birthday?" He stopped beside her.

"Leah's. She'll be ten on Friday." She went into the pantry and loaded her arms with flour, sugar, cocoa, baking powder, and baking soda.

"Here, let me take that."

"I've got it." She spun, deftly gliding around him.

"Nice move."

She tossed him a smile as she set her things down. "Thanks. I was a competitive dancer and a cheerleader in high school." A memory surfaced, and her smile turned sly. Edie would kill her, but she needed something to distract her from Asher's yumminess. "You want to know a secret?"

"What?"

"Edie was a cheerleader too."

His eyes widened. "No! You're kidding."

She shook her head. "Nope. All four years of high school. And I have photographic evidence to prove it. I get this cake in the oven and I'll show it to you."

Asher spun, staring at her cupboards. "Where are your cake pans?"

Esther laughed. "Slow down. I have to mix it up first."

"I can still get the pan out and get it ready for you. And turn the oven on."

He had a point. "Cabinet beside the stove," she said. "Get the two round ones."

While he got the pans out and greased them, Esther set to work measuring ingredients into the mixer she took from the island.

"What do you want the oven set to?"

"Three twenty-five," she answered.

She heard the beeps as he set the oven to preheat.

"So, what kind are you making?" He came closer to stand beside her.

"Chocolate. Leah loves M&M's, so I thought I'd make a chocolate cake and decorate it with the candy."

"That's cute. And her parents didn't object? Or didn't you ask?"

"I asked. Rob actually didn't have a problem with it. He seemed more surprised than anything. He just told me that she'd like that, then thanked me." That part had surprised her. She hadn't expected him to say yes, let alone thank her for doing it.

"Well, I'm glad he didn't give you any grief. He might not be Leah's biological father, but it sounds like he cares."

Esther agreed. The man was gruff and gave her the creeps, but he was kind to Leah. He put up with all the craziness of her life without much of a fuss. "He does, yes."

"So, what do you want me to do?"

"Hand me the pans you prepped."

He picked them up and set them next to her. She detached the mixing bowl from the stand and split the batter between the pans. After tapping them lightly on the counter to get the air bubbles out, she rounded the island and put them in the oven. With a few quick taps, she set the timer, then turned around and gave Asher a wide smile. "You ready to see Edie as a cheerleader?"

"Yes. Can I take pictures to use as blackmail if I ever need it?"

Laughing, Esther led him toward the stairs. "I'd love to say yes, but I value my life. And my relationship with her."

He chuckled, following her upstairs. "Yeah, she probably wouldn't speak to you for a while."

"She's still going to be ticked I showed you. But there are just some things that aren't meant to be hidden away. Edie as a cheerleader is one of them." Reaching the landing, she led him into her bedroom and went into her closet. All her old photos were in a box on a shelf. Standing on her toes, she reached for it. Her fingers grazed the edge. Why did she put it up so high?

"Here. I'll get it." Asher stepped up behind her.

Heat from his body radiated into her back as he reached over her head for the box. Esther didn't dare move. Any direction she went, she'd end up touching him. At this hour, her defenses were at a minimum. Self-preservation meant staying right where she was.

His hand closed around the box, and he brought it down, handing it to her as he stepped back.

She cast a quick look at him and took it. "Thanks." On swift feet, she high-tailed it out of the closet's confines and into the bedroom. Sitting down on the bed, she lifted the cardboard flap.

The mattress dipped as Asher sat next to her. She planted her feet so she wouldn't slide toward him and kept her eyes down. Perhaps looking through the pictures in her room wasn't the best idea. But they were already seated and she had the box open, so it would be a little strange for her to suddenly stand up and run away.

Doing her best to ignore the two-hundred pounds of yummy male magnetism next to her, Esther leafed through the packs of photos in the box until she found the ones from high school. It didn't take her long to locate the ones from her junior year—Edie's senior year. She flipped open the envelope and pulled out a set of pictures, quickly flipping through them.

"Is that homecoming? Don't tell me she was homecoming queen too?"

"Pfft, no. Sierra Wells took that honor." Esther rolled her eyes, then chuckled. "On the phone the other day, Edie said she wanted to bring Jordan home for a visit just so she could sit in the local coffeeshop and show him off to all the girls in high school who turned their noses up at her."

"Even though she was a cheerleader they did that? Didn't that automatically make her one of the 'cool' kids?" He air-quoted.

"To a degree, yes. But she didn't hang out with them—at least, not all of them—outside of cheer. Edie always had her nose stuck in a book or was doing something else on her own."

"What about you? Were you a party animal?"

"No. I went to more than Edie, but I still spent a lot of time with a few close friends and by myself." She glanced at him. "You?"

"Actually, no. I know I'm not shy and will be the first to dance when there's music, but I didn't have your typical high school experience."

"Oh? How so?"

"I graduated at sixteen. I probably could have skipped another grade, but my dad wouldn't let me. He didn't think I was mature enough for the older kids. Which I probably wasn't. My first year of college was rough. I remember feeling very, very young. But once I made a few friends who were nerds like me, it wasn't so bad. They kind of took me under their wing and kept me safe, so that was nice."

She fixed her gaze on him for several long moments. "You know, Edie said you were smart—a genius—and I've sort of seen that in action, but until now I never really thought about what that meant. Or just how smart you really are."

He lifted a shoulder, a red flush creeping up his neck. "It's not a big deal. I am who I am. I've always felt that way."

His words pulled a smile from her. "That's a great outlook to have. I wish more kids were like that. More accepting of themselves, you know?"

"Yeah. But it takes some mental toughness and a family to support it. I probably would have been more self-conscious about it if not for my dad and my grandparents. They helped me accept my intelligence by being vocal about loving me for me."

A sharp pang went through Esther's heart. He was right. Not every child had that.

Clearing her throat, she looked down at the pictures, quickly flipping through them to find the ones she wanted. "This one is from senior night." She handed him a picture of

Edie and their parents at the homecoming game. They smiled at the camera, Edie holding a single red rose and all decked out in her cheerleading uniform.

"Oh my goodness." Asher let out a soft laugh. "That's priceless."

She handed him another one. It was the same picture, but now she was in it too.

"You two looked alike even then. Almost like twins."

"We've been mistaken for twins. More than once." With the right makeup, they looked nearly identical. They'd fooled a couple teachers before as a prank.

Esther flipped through more photographs, finding several more images of Edie and herself in their cheerleading garb.

"Mom and Dad have video of our routines. And from tumbling classes when we were really young. I'm sure they're saving it to use to embarrass us with our children sometime down the line."

Asher gave a soft chuckle. "No doubt."

Esther opened another pack and shuffled through the pictures. These were from prom.

Asher let out a low whistle. "Wow."

"What?" She glanced at him.

He nodded to the pictures in her hands. "You looked great."

She pulled the photo from the envelope and held it up, smiling at the memories that assailed her. "That was a fun night. It was Edie's senior prom, my junior, so we both got to go. We danced until they shut it down, then went to the after-prom and danced some more. My feet hurt so much the next day—for several days, really—but I'd have done it all over again."

"Sounds like fun. I never went to prom."

"No?"

He shook his head. "I was too young. My birthday is in

mid-May, so I was only fifteen when we had our senior prom. What girl wants to go with a guy who can't even drive?"

"Then they were dumb. I bet you were cute even at fifteen." She blushed as she realized what her words implied.

His wolfish grin confirmed it. "You think I'm cute?"

Esther rolled her eyes. "Don't even act like you don't know. It's not attractive. I doubt there's a living, straight woman on the planet who wouldn't find you gorgeous."

"Maybe, but I'm not with any of them, am I? And I asked you."

The heat in her face climbed higher. What was he getting at? "Why does it matter?"

He put the pictures on the bed behind them and leaned closer. "Maybe because I find you cute too." His dark eyes captured her gaze and held it. "Not just cute. Beautiful." He lifted a hand to smooth a tendril of hair off her temple. "You're beautiful, Esther."

Ooooh, Lord. What on earth was he doing? "Asher..." Her forehead wrinkled as she frowned, confused.

His fingers trailed over her cheek to skim the edge of her bottom lip. "Would you stop me if I kissed you?"

Would she—what? Esther blinked several times, attempting to process what he said. Was he serious?

One side of his mouth lifted in a shy smile. "Sorry. Sometimes my filter doesn't work." He dropped his hand and started to lean back, but Esther grabbed a handful of his t-shirt.

"No." She shifted closer. "No, I wouldn't stop you."

The smile on his face slowly died, and an intensity darkened his eyes, turning them into midnight pools.

He brought his hand back up and wove it into her hair, bowing his head. Esther held his gaze until his face blurred, then closed her eyes. A breath later, his lips brushed hers. Just a touch. But it was enough to send a torrent of heat rushing through her. As it radiated down her spine, he pressed his lips to hers again, harder this time. The electric burn picked up speed, rushing down to her toes, only to fly back up to pool in her belly.

A soft whimper escaped her. She wrapped her arms around his shoulders and sidled closer. The hand in her hair held her head steady as he deepened the kiss. He slipped his other arm around her back, engulfing her in his embrace.

For long moments, he nipped, then soothed her mouth, tasting her. She returned the favor, learning he liked it when she sucked on his bottom lip as much as she liked it when he did it to her. And that his dark hair was as silky as it looked. The cool strands curled around her fingers.

Distantly, a chime broke through the spell they'd woven. Esther's eyelids fluttered as her mind registered that the sound wasn't going away.

In a blink, the source of the noise clicked. She sat back abruptly, staring at him with wide eyes. "My cake," she whispered.

"Cake?" His brows dipped, then smoothed out. "Right. The cake." His hands fell away.

During their kiss, the photo box had slid to the side. Esther righted it and set it on the bed. "I better go check on it."

He gave her a jerky nod and ran a hand through his hair. "Yeah." He cleared his throat. "Go ahead. I'll put the pictures away."

Esther pressed her swollen lips together and nodded once. Thoughts bounced around her brain, refusing to form into words. He'd addled her brain, and she needed a moment to gather herself. She knew it was a chicken move, but she did the only thing she could.

She fled.

Thirteen

"Okay, kids. Let's quiet down." Asher waited a moment for the group of kindergartners to look at him. They'd been working on an alphabet activity for the last twenty minutes, and he could tell that most of them were done. The noise level had increased dramatically. "Your teacher left a list of videos for us to watch on learning sight words. Do you want to watch from your seats or sit on the carpet?"

A chorus of "Carpet!" rang through the room, making him grin.

"Sounds good. Come have a seat."

The group converged on him, settling into spots on the eight-by-ten rug at the front of the room. Asher picked up the remote from the desk and aimed it at the projector to turn it on.

The screen stayed blank, and he frowned. "Is there another way your teacher turns the projector on?" he asked the kids.

"No," one said.

"She uses the remote," said another.

He tried again, but got the same result. Heaving a sigh, he

let his arm fall to his side, then walked to the projector hanging from the ceiling. Tipping his head back, he looked for a power button. Finding it, he flipped it on. The lights lit up, but nothing appeared on the screen. "Well, fudge."

Giggles echoed off the classroom's painted cinderblock walls.

"I'm going to run next door and ask Miss Campbell for help." He edged toward the door. "Stay seated. I'll be right back." Turning, he dashed out the door to Esther's classroom next door. He didn't know how he got so lucky to be right next to her on his first day, but he was glad fate was on their side.

He rapped his knuckles on her door, then poked his head in. Twenty-some sets of eyes swung his way, but he was only interested in one. He caught Esther's gaze at the front of the classroom, where she stood pointing at the screen and talking to her students. "Hey. Sorry to bother you. I need a hand." He offered her a quick smile.

"Of course." She looked at her class. "I'm going to let the video play. I want you to pay close attention and tell me which sight words you see when I come back." She lifted the remote in her hand and pushed a button. The video started up.

Asher frowned. What the heck did he do wrong that his wouldn't work?

She met him at the door. "What's up?"

"How did you do that?"

"Do what?"

"Make your projector work. I found the power button, but it won't do anything else." He led her away from her classroom and into his.

"Miss Campbell!"

"Hi, Miss Campbell!"

Several of the students waved, greeting her as they walked in. A wide smile wreathed Esther's face. Asher stared at her, momentarily forgetting where they were. That bright, guileless smile she bestowed on the kids transformed her entire face. There was no artifice when she dealt with the kids. No barriers thrown up against her emotions. She was completely open and one hundred percent herself.

"Hello." Esther waved back at his class. "Are you guys having fun with Mr. Horn?"

"Yep!" several of the kids said.

"He's goofy," one boy remarked.

"Yeah, he makes silly voices," a little girl said.

"Oh, really?" Esther shot him a side glance, amusement sparkling in her eyes.

Asher lifted a shoulder, a smile toying with his mouth. He wouldn't apologize for being himself. He didn't think she wanted him to, though, judging by the look on her pretty face.

"He made all the animals in the book have different voices," the same girl said. "We wanted him to read more, but he said we had to do our ABCs." She pouted.

"We'll read more later, Violet. We still have hours left in our day."

Her pout quickly reversed itself.

Asher looked at Esther. "Show me how to work this thing." He picked up the remote. "You'd think with all my fancy degrees and all the secure computer systems I've penetrated, I could best a video projector. Nope."

She grinned. "In your defense, these projectors aren't that user-friendly." She pointed to the remote in his hand. "Aim it at that cabinet and press input." Her hand swung toward the closet behind the teacher's desk.

Asher did as she said. "Okay, now what?"

"Press two, then enter."

He followed her instructions and the screen lit up. "All right, now we're cooking, kids." He grinned. "Thank you,

Miss Campbell." He offered her a little bow, making the kids laugh.

She chuckled. "You're welcome, good sir." Crossing one leg behind the other, she curtsied. Smiling, she straightened. "If you have any other problems, come knock again."

"I will." He walked her to the door. "Thanks for saving me, Essy."

At the door, she turned her head. The mirth in her eyes faded as they made eye contact. Asher felt the lightness from moments ago morph into the same driving need he'd felt last night when he'd kissed her. He wanted to do it again, but didn't dare with so many young eyes on them.

The same spark lit her eyes for a moment before she looked away. "You're welcome. I, uh, better get back to my class." She motioned to her classroom and stepped back.

"Thanks again."

She offered him a quick smile, then turned and hurried into her room.

He stared after her for a moment, wishing he could follow. Not because he didn't want to be in his classroom alone, but because he wanted to be with her. He'd found her interesting the first time they met, but as they spent more time together, he kept wanting to learn more. The kiss last night hadn't helped. He didn't think he was alone in that, either.

Asher shut the door, returning to his class. Eventually, they'd have to confront their growing feelings. What that meant for the future, he didn't know.

He clapped his hands together, getting the kids' attention. "All right. Who's ready to learn about sight words?"

Fourteen

"Esther!"

At the whispered exclamation from the doorway, Esther glanced up from her desk and the lesson plan she'd been working on, a peanut butter sandwich in her left hand. "Hey, Liv." She smiled at her colleague. Liv Spellman had started at the school the same year Esther did and also taught kindergarten. The two had become fast friends.

Liv hustled into the room, her rounded pregnant belly preceding her. Edie's face flashed through Esther's mind, and she was hit with another pang of jealousy. An image of Asher's smile and the remembered feel of his silky hair clutched in her fingers swiftly followed.

Whoa, girl. Slow down.

Even if the kiss meant something and a relationship bloomed between them, they were still a long way off from adorable, squishy, brown-eyed babies.

Not that she believed she and Asher would ever have a relationship or that their kiss meant anything. Sure, it had been pleasant—okay, more like earth-shattering and mind-blowing—but it was just a kiss. They were alone, and they'd been stuck together for days. And they'd shared a moment. That's *all* it was.

"Girlfriend, who's the hunk subbing for Tamara?" Liv stopped in front of Esther's desk and pointed a finger at her. "And don't pretend you don't know. I saw you two get out of the same car this morning."

Crap! Of course she did. "Um, he's an old friend of my sister's."

Liv arched an eyebrow. "That man is a friend of Edie's? How?"

"Military. They met through that. He wasn't military, but did some... other... stuff." She didn't want to divulge Asher's real backstory. Not all of it. It didn't make much sense for a genius hacker with his own version of a supercomputer for a brain to be subbing in a kindergarten classroom. "He decided he liked the area up here, so while he looks for a job, he's staying with me and subbing for the district to stay busy in between interviews." Esther resisted the urge to pat herself on the back. That was a pretty plausible backstory. Especially for something she came up with on the fly.

"Oh. He's staying with you, you say?" A wicked gleam entered Liv's eyes. "What's that like? Is he sleeping in your guest room or with you?"

"Liv!" Esther's face heated. "He's staying in the guest room."

Liv cackled. "I bet that won't last long."

"Why not? He's just a friend."

"Uh-huh. Sure." Liv winked, not even trying to fight the smile that blossomed on her face. "One who's put a pretty shade of pink on your face. You can't sit there and tell me you don't find him attractive."

"Of course I do. Have you looked at him? But that doesn't mean anything else can happen." Esther pressed her lips together as soon as the words left her mouth, realizing what she'd said. She sent up a silent prayer Liv wouldn't notice.

"Anything *else*?"

Esther bit back a groan.

Liv grabbed a chair from a nearby table and lowered herself onto it, holding her belly. "What happened?"

"Nothing."

"Not nothing. You're red now. Spill."

With a huff, Esther set her sandwich down and ran her hands over her face, then stared at her friend for a moment before she answered. "We shared a few... nice kisses last night. That's it. And that's all it can be."

Liv hummed. "Honey, if I were you, I'd jump all over that man. I don't know how your sister didn't, but you need to count your blessings."

"Yes, well, your pregnancy has made you extra horny, so you'd jump on any man who offered, I'd think."

Liv pressed a hand to her heart. Mouth rounded and brows dipped, she gave Esther a horrified look. "I would not. My Neal is enough for me."

Esther grinned. "Neal and your nightstand friend."

A quick laugh burst from Liv's chest. "This is true. It never runs out of stamina. Just batteries."

They shared a laugh.

"The books tell me my libido will calm down in the third trimester. I'm almost there, so we'll see. Neal can't wait. He told me the other day he never thought he'd ever think he could have too much sex."

Esther's face heated for another reason. She waved her hands. "TMI, Liv. TMI."

Laughing again, a quick knock on the open door had them both turning. Esther's chuckle died in her throat at the sight of Asher standing there. Her body heated and her brain whispered, "He'd never get tired of sex. Look at him. The man runs marathons."

She bit back another groan. If she survived his presence in her life, it would be a miracle.

"Hey, Essy. Sorry to interrupt. I can eat in my classroom if you'd rather chat with your friend." He held up the lunch sack he'd packed alongside her this morning.

"No, no." Liv pushed to her feet. "You're fine. We were just chatting. Girl stuff. I need to go grab my own lunch. The kids will be back from recess before we know it." Smiling, she waggled her fingers and walked out of the room.

Asher strode in, pulling up the chair Liv had just vacated. Esther bit back a laugh as he folded his long frame into the child-size seat. "I have other regular chairs." She nodded to the desk chair across the room by a long table.

"This is fine." He opened his lunch bag and took out the cold meat sandwich. "So, we've been noticed, huh?"

Esther frowned as she picked up her peanut butter. "Why would you say that?"

"She didn't ask who I was or how you know me."

"Oh. Right." She took a bite of her sandwich, wishing he'd drop it. She did not want to discuss Liv's opinion on their living situation.

"So, what did you tell her? About how you knew me?"

"Mostly the truth. I said you were Edie's friend from her military days." She held up a hand. "But I didn't disclose what it was you did back then. I also told her you decided you wanted to live up here and were staying with me and subbing while you looked for a job."

A crooked smile crossed his face. "Good. I was actually hoping something like this happened."

"You were? Why?"

"Because linking myself to you gives me better access to

the staff. I'm not the new guy. I'm Esther's friend. They'll be more accepting and more talkative if I need information."

"Information? On what?"

He lifted a shoulder. "Don't know. But if I need it, I can get it."

The hair around her forehead fluttered as she blew out a quick breath. "I think I'm glad I don't think like a spy."

"I wasn't a spy."

"No, but you were close enough. Normal people don't think like you. Or my sister."

He tipped his head. "I guess that's true. So, anyway, what did she say?" He sent her a devilish smile that melted her insides.

Covering her reaction, she narrowed her eyes at him. "That's between me and her." She flicked her fingers toward his lunch. "Eat your sandwich."

Asher barked a laugh. "I thought we were buds." He took a bite.

"That doesn't mean I spill the tea on my other *buds*."

Amusement danced in his dark gaze. "You and Edie have the same ferociousness. You just hide yours under a calm exterior."

She lifted a shoulder and tossed him a saucy smile. "It's the red hair." Chuckling, she polished off her sandwich, then reached into her lunch sack for the container of strawberries she brought. "How was your morning? Other than not being able to work the projector."

"I could simplify that whole system in less than an hour. It's ridiculous." He shook his head. "Other than that, things have gone well. The kids are great."

"It sounds like you met them at their level with the story voices. That helps. Learning should be fun at this age."

"At any age, it should be fun."

"True." She wouldn't argue with him about that. Some of

her favorite classes had teachers who made the material interesting. "So, what do you want for dinner tonight? We should probably stop for groceries on our way home." She stared at a point over his shoulder as she went through her mental list of what was left in her fridge, freezer, and cupboards.

"If we can find the ingredients, I could make a dish I learned in Morocco."

"Morocco?" Her gaze connected with his. "Man, I'm starting to think I should have followed in Edie's footsteps. She went there too. I've always wanted to go. The Marrakesh markets look like so much fun. She brought me some stuff from there, but it's not the same."

"Maybe one day you can go. You're still young."

Esther wrinkled her nose. "Maybe. It's just a matter of finding someone to go with me. Maybe I can convince Edie and Jordan to go. They can leave the baby with Mom and Dad. Mom will love it."

"See? You have a plan. So, does this mean you want that Moroccan dish for dinner?"

Fifteen

It was trash day.

Asher stared at the trash can at the curb outside the Tylers' house. The lid was still closed. Looking down the street, it appeared as though the garbage truck had yet to come.

He glanced at the Tylers' front door. Esther went inside twenty minutes ago. It was safe for him to wander a bit. Maybe take a peek inside that bin. But he didn't know whether anyone could see the trash can from inside the house. The last thing he needed was to have Rob Tyler rush out, demanding to know what he was doing.

But it was large enough he could hide behind it. Just reach in and pull a bag out and go through it while he crouched low.

Asher reached into the backseat and grabbed the small backpack he'd brought. From the front pocket, he took out a pair of black nitrile gloves and put them on, then opened his car door and got out.

Glancing up and down the road, he strolled toward the garbage can. Eyes still roving the street, he paused next to it. Once he was sure no one was watching that he could see, he flicked his wrist and opened the can's lid. A peek inside revealed a small bag of trash on top. It looked like maybe it came from a bathroom. He snagged it and quickly dropped into a crouch behind the trash can.

"Show me your secrets," he muttered, picking the knot out of the ties. With the bag open, he rummaged through the sea of tissues, empty toilet paper rolls, and discarded makeup wipes.

A flash of silver caught his eye, and he reached for it. Lifting it free, he turned it over, reading the label. It was an empty azithromycin packet. Esther had said Connie Tyler was sick last week.

He pocketed the used blister pack. There were a few people he knew who could run it for prints. It could tell them who Connie really was. Because if Connie Tyler was really Connie Tyler, he'd dismantle his lair and never stick his nose behind someone's firewall ever again.

The revving of an engine as a car turned the corner echoed through the damp air. Asher glanced over, then hurriedly retied the trash bag. Standing, he tossed it back into the bin as the car passed, then closed the lid. He'd really like to go through the other bags, but it was too risky to pull them out. What he'd found, though, was great. Hopefully, it would yield some answers.

Back in the car, he scrolled through his email contacts until he found one of the people he thought could help and shot off a quick message. Zach came back a minute later, agreeing to test the package for prints. When they stopped at the store for groceries, he'd get some mailing supplies and send the blister pack off first thing in the morning.

Asher spent the rest of the hour watching the traffic that passed by and keeping a lookout for the guy who ran away yesterday. The neighborhood stayed boringly quiet. While he kept watch, he googled specialty grocery stores, knowing he'd need some spices most places wouldn't carry. By the time Esther exited the house, he'd found one and was ready to leave.

"I'm starving. Let's go get food," she said as she slipped into the car.

Asher started the engine. "Yes, ma'am."

"So, did that guy come back?"

He shook his head as he pulled away from the curb. "No. But I did a quick search of the Tylers' trash. I found Connie's empty antibiotic package. I have a friend who's agreed to run it for prints."

Esther wrinkled her nose. "You wore gloves, right? Because that's gross."

Asher grinned. "Yes."

"Good."

"How was your session?"

"Oh, fine. Leah's excited about her birthday. She said her parents agreed to take her out to an actual restaurant for dinner."

"Isn't that dangerous for her?"

"I asked the same thing, but she said her doctor told them if they went when it wasn't too crowded and she wore a mask with high filtration when she wasn't eating that she should be all right. Her immune system is poor, but it's not non-existent. School's a bigger risk just because kids are little germ factories."

He let out a snort. "That's for sure. I had one kid today who I sent to wipe their nose I don't know how many times. It was like a faucet."

"Yep. Been there. I had a couple out today. That cold I thought was brewing finally hit."

"How are you not sick all the time? You must have an immune system made of titanium."

Esther chuckled. "I've been doing this for several years. You build up immunity. During student teaching and my first year as a full-fledged teacher, I caught most everything. Since then, I get maybe one or two illnesses every year, and they're never that bad. Some cold medicine and I'm fine."

"I hold out no hope I won't get something this week. You might have to dip into your medicine stash to save me." He flashed her a cheeky grin.

She sent him a sunny smile. "I'll dig it out and put it where you can find it."

Asher let out a low laugh. "Thank you."

A few minutes after they left the Tylers', he turned into the parking lot of the store he'd found in his search.

"I don't normally shop here." Esther got out of the car, staring up at the store's façade with a curious furrow to her forehead.

"I wanted to make sure I could get everything I needed."

"What are we having, anyway? You didn't say."

The store's door swished open, admitting them.

"Tangine. It can be made several ways, and with many different spices. I found a recipe I liked a lot years ago and make it routinely at home." Just the memory of the mix of spices and rich sauce had his stomach growling. "It gives me leftovers and then I don't have to cook as much."

"Well, I can't wait to try it." She grabbed a shopping cart, dropping her purse into the child seat, and followed Asher.

Winding their way through the aisles, they both added things to the cart as they went.

"How do we split this?" Esther asked when they reached the registers.

He grabbed several items and set them on the belt. "I'll pay. You can get the next load."

"You're sure?"

"Yes."

Together, they got everything unloaded. Asher paid for their groceries, and they left.

"What's that?" Esther pointed at the car. Under the windshield wiper, a piece of paper flapped in the breeze.

"Probably a flyer." Asher hit the button to open the back hatch, and they unloaded the groceries. Ready to go, he reached over the doorframe, snatching the paper from under the wiper and unfolded it. His forehead wrinkled with a frown as he read the single word written on the sheet.

Thief.

"What's it say?"

He turned it around so Esther could see. Her eyes bugged out when she read the single word.

"Do you think someone saw you take the blister pack from the trash?"

"I'm not sure. Seems like a strong response to going through someone's garbage." Asher looked up, eyeing the parking lot. A woman exited the store, pushing a cart to a black SUV, a baby in the basket. Across the aisle, an older woman unloaded her groceries into the trunk of a silver sedan. A man in athletic pants and a t-shirt jogged toward the doors. No one looked out of place.

But Asher could feel eyes on them. They pricked the back of his neck, making the fine hairs there stand on end. "Let's get out of here." Stuffing the note into his pocket, he opened the car and slid inside. Zach now had two things to run for prints.

Sixteen

Steam filled the bathroom as Esther got ready for work. She swiped at the mirror with a towel, then picked up her foundation. She'd opened the door after she dressed, but some of the humidity lingered. It didn't help that Asher had already made the room muggy when he took a shower before her.

Dabbing her face with a makeup sponge, she smoothed out the foundation, then applied highlights and bronzer. With a dab of blush, a few strokes of eyeshadow, and some mauve lipstick, she left the bathroom. All she needed were her shoes and her phone, and she could go caffeinate herself.

Her footfalls were silent on the thick cream carpet as she entered her bedroom. Wandering into her closet, she picked out a pair of brown boots to go with her outfit, then sat on her bed to put them on. The zippers slid up with a quiet rasp.

Reaching over, she snatched her phone from the nightstand. The screen lit up as she lifted it, showing she had a text.

Esther frowned. Who would text at this hour?

A quick glance revealed it was from Liz. Esther groaned as she read it. Her friend wanted to know if she was ready to do the two-step on skates tonight. They had a team-building exercise she'd forgotten all about.

For a moment, she contemplated not going. The team-building events weren't mandatory. Not everyone went. Especially the teachers who had kids in sports. But Esther enjoyed the evenings. They always went somewhere fun or interesting, and she'd learned a lot about her colleagues through these events. She knew not every school district had things to foster relationships with its staff, and she was grateful hers did.

Heaving a sigh, Esther pulled up the keyboard to text her back.

I completely forgot. There better be pizza at this thing. And cookies!

Dots appeared as Liv texted back.

There always is. What are you going to do about your buddy? He can come, you know. I'm bringing Neal. You know the administration encourages us to bring our significant others to these things.

Esther sighed and responded.

Asher is not my significant other. He's just a friend.

The dots appeared again.

Bring him anyway. He'll liven things up.

A laugh bubbled free. That was for sure. It didn't matter that he was gorgeous. Just the fact Esther brought someone would get everyone talking. His looks would only add fuel to the fire.

As much as she wished she could get around bringing him, she didn't think she could convince him to stay at home. She doubted he'd let her out of sight. Not after that note left on his car yesterday.

She texted Liv back.

I'll think about it.

Her response was quick.

Don't think. Do.

Esther chuckled under her breath. Liv had an agenda, and she was pretty sure it was driven by hormones.

The phone clicked as she turned the screen off. Getting up, she returned to her closet. Staring at the shelves, she grabbed a pair of black leggings, a plain pale-pink t-shirt, and some thicker socks, shoving them into a backpack. Her boots worked with the outfit, so she skipped the shoes.

Gear in hand, she headed downstairs.

Asher glanced up as she entered the kitchen, the smile of greeting on his face morphing to a slight frown as he saw her bag. "What's that for?"

"So, I forgot about a thing I have this evening. My school does a team-building exercise once a month, and it's tonight. You're welcome to come. But you'll want to pack some casual clothes. We'll have to change at the rink. It's right after I get done at Leah's."

"Oh. All right. Let me go up and grab some stuff. The coffee's ready." He pointed at the coffeemaker.

"Bless you." She needed the jolt.

"You're welcome."

She was already pouring as he left the room, a grin on his face.

Seventeen

Oh, man.

Asher stared at the sign of the building he'd just pulled up to. This wouldn't end well.

He clenched his teeth, working his jaw as he shut the car off. Maybe she wouldn't make him skate. Maybe he could get away with being a cheerleader.

She glanced at him with a bright smile as she yanked on her door handle. "Come on. They'll start the party without us."

He opened his own door, turning away so she couldn't see the reluctance on his face. "Wouldn't want that."

Crowd noise and the low rumble of skates on the hardwood arena deck filled Asher's ears as they entered the building. Esther paused, glancing around, then pointed.

"They're over there. Let's get our skates first, though." She turned left, heading for the rental counter.

The teenage girl working the counter smiled at them with a mouthful of braces. "Hi. You guys need skates?"

"Yes, please," Esther said. "Size eight. But inline skates." She glanced at Asher.

"Um, a thirteen. Regular ones." Yep. This really wouldn't end well. If she was getting inline skates, that meant she was good at it. He'd be lucky to stay upright no matter what skates he wore. They needed training wheels, like bikes.

The girl walked away and came back a moment later with their skates. Esther paid for the rentals before they joined her colleagues.

A pregnant woman squealed as they walked up. "You brought him! Good for you, girl."

Some of Asher's apprehension faded as a blush crept up Esther's neck. At least he wouldn't be the only one embarrassed during this outing. He smiled and waved at the woman. "Hello. You're one of the other kindergarten teachers, right?" He remembered seeing her yesterday. Today, he'd been in a second-grade classroom.

She nodded. "Liv Spellman. This is my husband, Neal." She gestured to a dark-haired man with glasses sitting next to her. He tipped his chin in the universal male hello.

Asher reciprocated. "Nice to meet you."

"Esther, introduce us to your friend," an older woman said.

"Oh, um, sure." She went around the seating area, naming individuals, then explaining who he was and why she'd brought him. He was glad to hear her give the same explanation she gave Liv yesterday. They needed to keep their stories straight.

Once introductions were made, Liv smacked a hand lightly on her table. "All right. You two go change. I talked the manager into turning on a line dance in about ten minutes. I don't plan to wait on you."

"Honey, are you sure you don't want to sit this one out tonight?" Her husband sent her a concerned look.

"I'll be fine. I've been skating since I was a kid. I promise not to do any jumps, but I'm steady enough on my feet I can roll around. I even asked my doctor about it; you know this. She said I'd be fine so long as I took it easy."

Neal rolled his eyes. "Easy is the keyword there, babe. I think your definition is different than hers."

Liv laughed. "Probably."

Asher's misgivings ratcheted up a little more. He was about to be shown up by a pregnant woman. Inwardly, he rolled his eyes. At least he'd give Esther an entertaining evening.

He touched her arm. "Come on. Let's go change."

They set their skates down and headed for the locker rooms on the other side of the arena.

"Are you okay?"

He glanced at her, then twisted, avoiding a collision with a group of teenage boys. "I'm fine."

"Really? Because you seem a little tense."

"Nope. A-okay."

"Yeah, sure you are. Don't lie to me, Asher. You don't have to tell me what's going on, but don't lie, all right?"

Asher stopped. Tipping his head back, he let out a long breath. "Sorry. You're right." He looked at her. "And you'll find out soon enough why I'm edgy, so I might as well tell you now." He paused, his jaw working once more. "I can't skate."

A frown narrowed her eyebrows for a quick moment before her expression smoothed out. "You can't skate? How is that even possible? I mean—" She raised a hand, palm up, and gestured to him. "You're not exactly unathletic."

"Running and swimming are wildly different to skating."

"True. But it's about balance. And you surf. I've seen you. I think you'll be fine. It might take you a few minutes to get the hang of it, but you'll be chasing me around the floor in no time."

"Chasing you?" That sounded like a challenge. "Oh,

honey, I won't be the one doing the chasing once I figure things out."

She tipped her head, a sly smile toying with her lips. "Want to make a friendly wager?"

He barked a laugh. There was more of Edie coming out. The two women were so different, but so much alike. "Sure."

"If I'm still skating circles around you by the end of the night, you have to dress up in an inflatable costume and be one of those surprise birthday-gram people for Leah's birthday. Balloons, birthday song and all."

"Deal." He'd do that even if he lost. "And if I win, you have to let me put up a full security system at your house."

She narrowed her eyes at him. "I don't have the money for that, Asher."

"Did I ask you to pay for it?"

Her blue eyes flashed fire as she balled her fists.

"Well?"

"Fine," she ground out through clenched teeth.

A smile spread over Asher's face. He held out a hand. "May the best skater win."

"Oh, she will." She shook his hand, her glare shifting to a cocky grin. "She will."

Eighteen

S he was going to lose.

Asher had started off wobbly, but he was picking things up fast. His first few trips around the arena, he'd held the railing and hugged the wall, his knuckles white as he tried to coordinate his feet. But his hesitance had been short-lived. A few minutes ago, he'd broken away from the edges and was rapidly figuring out the motion to stay upright and move at a quick clip.

"This isn't so bad. I don't know what I was afraid of."

Esther tossed him a quick smile. "Looking inept in front of a group of strangers?"

He chuckled. "Probably."

They rounded the short side, and he increased his pace, pulling away from her.

"You might want to slow down," she yelled. As quickly as he'd picked it up, he wasn't ready to make a quick turn, and they hadn't worked much on braking yet.

But he ignored her.

Esther quickened her pace, hoping to catch him before he reached the corner, but his long, powerful legs propelled him forward faster than she could close the gap. She could only watch and pray he didn't trip over his feet as he leaned into the curve.

For a moment, she thought he'd make it. He slid one foot in front of the other, rounding the bend. But then she realized he hadn't leaned far enough or moved his feet fast enough to make it. She straightened, letting herself glide as she watched the inevitable.

He let out a short cry of surprise as he drifted off course toward the wall. Luckily, they were padded. At the last second, he twisted, turning his body so he hit on his side and not his face. He bounced off the pads and landed on his butt on the floor.

She glided to a stop beside him. "You okay?"

He looked up, exasperation written all over his face, then broke out into laughter. Leaning forward, he draped his arms over his knees, red-faced as belly laughs rolled free.

An answering chuckle bubbled up from her throat until she was laughing right alongside him.

After a moment, he looked up. Still chuckling, he said, "Maybe I wasn't quite as ready to beat you as I thought."

Grinning, she shook her head. "No. Not quite."

"Give me a hand, would you?" He extended an arm.

Esther grasped his hand to steady him as he got to his feet. His right foot shot out, throwing him off balance again. Her smaller stature—and the fact that she was on skates—was no match for his heavier mass.

With a shriek, she went down, landing with her face buried in his lower abdomen, and her hand in the apex of his right thigh.

A sharp wolf-whistle came from behind them.

"You go, girl!"

Esther glanced up in time to see Liv skate past, a wide smile on her face.

Asher laughed.

"It's not funny." She pushed back, her hand brushing his crotch.

His laughter died, and his brown eyes turned molten. Esther paused, ensnared in his gaze.

"You guys need help?"

Esther blinked and looked back. A roller rink employee had skated up to them and now stared down at them with a concerned frown on his pimply face.

She cleared her throat and moved away from Asher, but didn't get up yet. "No, we're fine. Just lost our balance."

The teenager gave her a thumbs up and skated away.

Esther closed her eyes and took a breath, trying to corral her wayward hormones. They wanted to find out more about that bulge she'd inadvertently touched. Now wasn't the time or place for that. She wasn't sure there was one, but it sure as hell wasn't now.

Getting a foot under herself, she pushed to her feet, then spun around and offered Asher a hand. "Don't pull me down this time."

He took it, changing the way he situated his feet to give himself a better foundation. "I'll try not to."

She tipped her ankles inward, creating a wedge shape to help stabilize them, and held on as he hauled himself up.

Almost upright, his left foot rolled. Esther grabbed his shirt and pulled him close. He put a hand on her hip, steadying them both.

Her nose landed in the crook of his neck and shoulder. She couldn't help herself and took a deep breath. His spicy male scent filled her senses. Heat suffused her face and pricked her scalp. She bit her lip so she wouldn't bite the tendon millimeters from her mouth.

His low, strangled growl rumbled through her chest, not helping her situation.

"These things have a mind of their own."

"They sure do," she muttered. Her hormones were certainly screaming loudly in her head.

"I'm glad I didn't get rollerblades like you."

Esther blinked. Rollerblades? Some of the fog cleared from her mind. He'd been talking about the skates. Not that his hormones had a mind of their own.

More heat flooded her cheeks, but for a different reason this time. What was she thinking? Asher was just trying to learn to skate. He didn't need her sniffing him and wondering what it would be like to stroke the wicked devil in his pants.

She pushed back, breaking out of his hold. "Me too. I'm not sure we'd ever get you off the floor." Skating backwards, she beckoned him forward. "Come on. Get your sea legs under you again." She very much wanted to just skate away, but it wasn't an option. He'd just follow her. So, she figured it was best to distract them both.

"Teach me how to do that."

"What? Skate backwards?"

"Yes."

Smirking, Esther skated further away, executing a quick spin. "I'm not sure you're ready. You did just crash trying to go around a bend."

"Because I was going too fast. I can handle slow." Asher pushed off, coming after her.

The intensity in his dark eyes sent a delicious shiver down her spine.

"And I've already proven I'm a quick study." He put his hands together, his intense gaze morphing into a soulful puppy-dog look. "Teach me, oh masterful one. Please?"

Esther laughed. "Fine."

Smoothly spinning away again, she moved out to the middle of the rink, distancing them from the crush of skaters.

"It's all about shifting movement and pushing with your feet." Going slow, she showed him.

It took him a few tries, but soon, he glided backward, though awkwardly.

He sent her a bright smile. "I'm not the most graceful skater, but I'm moving." Reversing direction, he skated toward her.

Esther spun away, skating a ring around him backward as a devilish smile crossed her face. "No, you're definitely not."

"Hey, no fair." He reached out, trying to snag her arm, but she moved out of his reach.

Her grin widening, she crooked a finger. "Come get me. We still have a bet to settle."

Nineteen

Cool night air whispered over Asher's still overheated skin as he got out of the car at Esther's. He opened the rear door and retrieved his backpack, then walked around to her side, waiting while she gathered her things. "I had fun tonight. I didn't think I would when I saw where we were."

She backed out of the car, slinging her bag over her shoulder, and smiled up at him. "I'm glad. I love skating. Liv and I go a lot. You picked it up pretty quickly." Her smile broadened. "But you still lost our bet."

He had. Quite spectacularly. Cornering still made him uncomfortable, so around every bend he'd slowed. Esther hadn't. She'd whipped around them like a professional Indy car driver, red ponytail flowing behind her, waving the checkered flag on his defeat.

"The question now is which inflatable to buy for you to wear?" She laid a finger on the tip of her chin and looked away in thought.

The mischief in her eyes set off the firestorm of need that had been building in Asher's gut all evening. Her adorableness was officially off the charts, and he couldn't take it anymore.

Crowding her against the car, he brushed the flyaway hairs back from her face. "I'll wear whatever you want, wherever you want."

The smile on her face faded as their gazes locked. Asher slid his hand back, cradling the side of her head as he leaned closer. Giving her every chance to back away, he held her gaze, making sure she knew his intentions. She brought a hand up to clutch his wrist, but she didn't push him away. Asher closed the distance and kissed her.

This time, he was prepared for the onslaught of need that punched him in the gut.

Or so he thought.

It didn't surprise him, but it still stole his breath. The only thing his body wanted was her. Not air or anything else. *Just Esther.*

So, he gave it what it wanted and deepened the kiss, supercharging the flames already racing through him. Plunging into the depths of her mouth, he tasted her, learning every corner. She did the same. In moments, they were pressed together, their hands roaming and the passion flaring higher.

The ache in his pants became almost unbearable, and he pulled back, needing to know where she stood on where this was going. He knew where he wanted it to go, but he was a man; it's where his body always wanted to go.

Forehead pressed to hers, he sucked in a breath. "Essy, I want to take this inside. If you don't, that's fine, but we need to stop before I explode."

She sucked that bottom lip between her teeth and nibbled on it, pulling a strangled groan from him. He wanted to be the one to bite that lip. Of their own accord, his hands squeezed her butt, tipping her belly into his hips.

Her eyelids fluttered and her mouth parted. Asher clenched his teeth and forced himself not to pounce.

She slid her hands up his chest to tangle in his hair. "When you said you'd wear anything I wanted, did that include nothing?" A sexy smirk emerged as she spoke.

"Hell yes." Asher pounced.

With one tug, he had her body molded to his. Burrowing his fingers into her hair, he loosened her ponytail, pulling out the band that held it in place. The silky tresses cascaded over his hand. He gripped her hair, holding her steady as he deepened their kiss.

The wind gusted, blowing strands of the unbound tresses over their faces. Asher pulled back to stare at her. "We should take this inside. But first... are you sure?" He searched her now midnight blue gaze, looking for misgivings. All he saw was raw, unadulterated need. It matched what burned in his chest.

"I know it's crazy. It might not end well. But I don't care. Edie's always telling me I'm too cautious. I've never had anything—or anyone—give me a good enough reason not to be."

"And I do?"

"Yes. I want to pinch myself every time you look at me like I'm beautiful. I know I'm pretty, but I'm not a supermodel."

Asher growled. "Supermodels don't hold a candle to you. In a sea of them, I'd always find you." Her happy smile, bright blue eyes, and the smattering of freckles on her pretty face held his attention more than the most exotic face ever would. She was stunning.

Color bloomed on her cheeks. "In any case, I like how you make me feel. It's not just the beauty thing. You make me laugh. And you listen."

He held her gaze, digesting her words. "I don't want this to be a one-time thing, Esther. I know it will complicate things, but I think I want this to be more than a fling that only lasts for as long as I'm here." He hadn't given the two of them much serious thought, but now that it was staring him in the face, he couldn't imagine going back to his life without her being a part of it. Especially if they finished what they'd started. "If you're not all right with that, we need to go inside and go our separate ways for the night."

He could see the debate raging in her mind through her expressive eyes. A hint of fear and uncertainty appeared, but need and something else he couldn't put his finger on pushed it away. The apprehension stayed, but determination held it at bay.

"I'm up for that. Wherever it might lead us."

TWENTY

This was madness.

Esther buried her face in Asher's neck, inhaling his sweaty, masculine scent as he carried her up the stairs. They'd stumbled inside, where after they removed their jackets, he'd whisked her off her feet, cradling her to his chest. It had sent the last of her misgivings running. Whatever happened in the future, she refused to worry about it now. Edie was right. She needed to live a little.

How could she ever expect to find the happiness her sister had if she never put herself out there? Her introverted lifestyle didn't really lend itself to meeting men.

Here was one basically dropped into her lap.

And he liked her.

She needed to take advantage of that. Especially since he was stunningly handsome and just as kind.

He turned into her bedroom, flipping on the lights with his elbow before carrying her to the bed.

"You still sure?" His low voice rumbled through her as he glanced down, meeting her gaze.

She brought a hand up, threading her fingers into his hair.

"Yes." Stretching her neck, she kissed him, telling him with more than words just how ready she was.

He moved again, and a moment later, the mattress pressed against her backside. Asher lowered himself next to her, sliding a thigh between hers as he kept their mouths fused.

She gripped the hem of his t-shirt at the back of his waist, twisting the material in her hands. Her knuckles grazed warm skin near his spine. She wanted to feel more. Wanted to feel his hands on her bare skin. She wanted all of him. Everywhere.

Her body clenched at the thought. It had been a long time since she'd been with a man. Years. When her last relationship ended, she hadn't been interested in dating for quite a while. Once she was, no one intrigued her enough to want to get beyond a couple of dates. It had been over a year since she'd been out with anyone.

He shifted, bringing his pelvis into contact with her hip. Esther felt the growing ridge in his jeans and an answering heat pooled in her core. She might not have been on a real date with Asher, but it didn't matter. She knew what she needed to know.

But the contact brought up another issue. One she hadn't thought of until now. She pushed him back. "We need protection. I'm not on the pill." And she didn't keep that stuff in her house. Her love life sucked, so there was no need.

He rose up slightly and reached into his back pocket, producing his wallet. "I have one, so we need to make it count. And for the record, I don't sleep around. When I was a teenager, my grandpa and my dad drilled it into me to always carry one. I admit, I used it a couple of times when I was young. Now, though, it's just a habit to keep one on me."

"Well, I'm glad. Because I don't want to stop to go to the store." She took the wallet, tossed it on the bed, then dragged him back down for another searing kiss.

All talking ceased as their need took over. Esther tunneled

her hands beneath his shirt, bunching it up around his shoulders. He peeled it off, giving her an up-close look at what she'd so far only admired from a distance. Fingers trailing over his lean, well-defined muscles, she dedicated herself to learning every inch of his torso.

Deep into her exploration of the ridges and valleys of his abs, she barely noticed her leggings coming down until his fingers slid through the wet heat at her center. She broke away from his lips, moaning as he slicked the wetness over her eager lady bits and found the hidden knot of nerves. Her hips left the bed, chasing his touch.

"Take your top off. Let me see that beautiful body." He growled, nipping just below her ear.

Esther slid her arms from her sleeves and drew her shirt over her head, leaving her in her lacy pale blue bra.

The hand not teasing her core picked at the lace cup. "This too. Take it off."

She started to ask why he didn't do it himself when he speared her with two fingers. All the breath left her lungs on a keening cry.

She understood now. He was a little busy driving her insane.

Arching her back, she wiggled her arms underneath herself —no small feat, since he continued to stroke her inner walls— and unfastened the clasp. The fabric loosened.

Asher hooked a finger between the cups and pulled, freeing her arms as he tossed it over the side of the bed. He latched onto one breast, teasing the tip, even as he continued his mind-numbing assault below her waistline.

Esther writhed on the bed. Her body didn't know where to go or what to do. With every nip, stroke, and touch, he overwhelmed her senses.

Every thought in her head ceased, making way for the bright light of ecstasy that ripped through her brain and down her nerve endings. She cried out, clamping her knees together, holding his hand in place as she rode the wave.

Eventually, the waves died down, leaving her lounging languidly. Her body relaxed, letting him go. He moved away from her, getting up.

"Where are you going?"

"Nowhere." He unzipped his jeans and shoved the material down his legs.

Some of Esther's tranquil feeling faded as her body woke up again. He'd exposed thick, muscular thighs and the outline of something she couldn't wait to wrap her hand around.

Kicking out of his jeans, he hooked his thumbs in the top of his boxer-briefs. In one smooth, fluid movement, he whisked the material over his hips. It fell down his legs to pool on the floor and left her staring at the long sweep of his manhood.

Her body wept, anticipating what was coming. She crooked a finger at him and raised her knees. Fire blazed in his eyes as he put a knee on the bed and crawled between her thighs. Rolling his hips, he brushed through her wetness as he hovered above her.

"Condom." Esther slapped at the bed, looking for his wallet. He'd better find it fast. Before she threw caution completely to the wind.

One long arm reached past her head, snagging the billfold. He sat back on his haunches and flipped it open, removing the foil packet and tossing the wallet on the floor with their clothes. The wrapper crinkled as he tore it open. A moment later, he'd sheathed himself and was hovering over her again.

"Remember how I said we need to make this one count?"

She nodded, liking where his thoughts were going. She didn't want vanilla sex. Not if they only had one chance tonight.

"Roll onto your side."

Esther rolled. He brought her top leg up, letting her bottom leg slide under him as he shifted closer. His hand skimmed her calf as he lined himself up with her entrance and pushed forward. The angle was unlike any other, and it gave him access to her entire body, of which he took advantage. Esther clutched the sheets as his hands roamed over her torso, down to her core to tease her, and then back up, all while he slowly rolled his hips, teasing a different part of her body. She both loved it and hated it; she couldn't touch him.

Finally, she decided that wasn't acceptable and bent her top leg, pushing against him. He let her go, and she scooted away, quickly rolling up to her knees to come at him.

"I take it you didn't like that position?"

She grabbed handfuls of his hair. "It was fine, but I couldn't do this." She latched onto his mouth. He locked his arms around her waist and toppled them onto the bed, hauling her over his body to straddle his hips. Scooting up the headboard, he bent his knees, trapping her in the vee he created.

Reaching between them, she wrapped his silken length in her fist and squeezed. His deep groan vibrated her insides down to her soul.

Ready for more, she lifted and swirled him through her folds, then sank down. His fingers dug into her flesh as he gripped her hips. Their moans mingled, echoing through the room. Hands on his shoulders, she held on as they moved together, taking each other to the heavens.

When her climax hit, white spots burst in her vision. He swallowed her shout of pleasure with a soul-searing kiss. Esther grasped his face and held on as her body floated away, carried on a sea of ecstasy and an emotion she couldn't name. It wasn't love; maybe love-adjacent. His firm but gentle touch left her feeling cherished and appreciated.

Slowly, she floated down from the planets and the stars,

regaining some awareness of her surroundings. But mostly, her mind focused on the man in her arms and the embrace they shared. He continued to nip and suckle on her lips, drawing out the pleasure their union created. She didn't want to move, but knew they needed to shower and do all the things that needed done before they went to bed.

But for now, she was content to stay here and let the little moments feed the feelings growing deep within.

They'd started something tonight, and she wasn't ashamed to say she was greedy and wanted more.

Twenty-One

"Are you ready for this?" Esther looked at Asher, a wicked smile on her face as she reached into the backseat of his car for the item they'd bought yesterday evening. "Because I am."

With a huff and a sigh, he took it as she held it up. "I was set up. How was I supposed to know you were practically a professional?"

Laughing, she gathered the handles of the tote between her feet into one hand and opened the car door. "You could have asked." Her smile softened as she put one foot on the pavement. "But we both know you would wear that even if you won the bet. Just because it would make Leah smile."

It should surprise him that she had him pegged already, but it didn't. He'd been more open with her than any other woman he'd ever dated. At least this early on, anyway.

But she'd struck a chord in his heart, and she'd come into his life at the right moment in time. He was primed and ready for something permanent, so he hadn't held back like he had in the past.

"Give me about five minutes, then come knock. Don't forget the cake."

He'd need at least that long to get dressed and inflate the suit. "Sounds good, and I won't."

She got out and walked up the path to the house. Asher waited until she was inside before he climbed out and opened the package containing the inflatable unicorn suit they'd picked out. Esther had wanted an M&M to go with the cake she made, but it hadn't been one of their choices at the party store.

Shaking out the nylon suit, he broke open the package of batteries from the small bag on the rear driver's side seat and put them in the pack that powered the small fan. After tucking the battery pack into the pocket inside the suit, he shoved his feet through the leg holes. He hoped it wouldn't ride too far up his calves. The height for this thing topped out at six-foot-two. He was six-three.

The shiny fabric rustled as he drew it up over his shoulders. He felt it inch up his legs, the elastic pulling his pant legs up with it. Cool air whispered over his shins. It was definitely too short. At least the inseam wasn't riding up his butt.

After turning on the fan, he zipped himself in and closed the car door. While he was still relatively deflated, he rounded the car and opened the rear passenger door, picking up the cake box and bouquet of candy flowers for Leah. He'd asked Esther why they couldn't buy real ones, and she said it was a bacteria risk.

Figuring it had been five minutes, and now fully inflated, he walked up the sidewalk to the house, hoping he didn't trip. The plastic set into the neck wasn't the clearest stuff in the world, so he couldn't see the best. Suit swishing with every step and the unicorn's wings flapping behind him, he reached the front door without incident, though. He knew he looked ridiculous, but he didn't care. If it made Leah smile, he'd wear the suit every day and wave at her through the window while Esther helped her with her lessons.

He tucked the candy flowers under one arm and knocked on the metal screen door. It rattled in its frame. The dog barked, the sound growing closer as it neared the door. A moment later, he heard a man's gruff voice, then the inner door swung open and a scowling man Asher presumed was Rob appeared. He held a snarling black and brown Chiweenie in his arms. The man tried to maintain his stern expression, but Asher could see the smile in his eyes.

"Hi. I'm with Esther." Asher offered the man a smile, but wasn't sure he could see it with the unicorn's head dipping with the slightest movement. Maybe he wasn't as inflated as he thought.

"She mentioned you. Come in." Rob pushed the screen open and stepped back.

Asher maneuvered through the door, careful to stay out of reach of the dog's pointy teeth, and swished his way through the living room behind Rob.

"They're set up in the kitchen." Nearly there, Rob paused and looked back. "Thank you for doing this. Leah—she hasn't had much joy the last few years."

"You're welcome." Asher studied the man through the filmy plastic obscuring his vision. Whatever Rob's reasons for allowing his name to be on Leah's birth certificate, something told him they weren't all selfish. It seemed he truly cared for the girl.

Crossing the threshold into the kitchen, Esther and Leah looked up from the table. Esther slapped a hand over her mouth, mirth dancing in her eyes. But it was the sunny smile on Leah's face that held his attention.

She giggled softly. Moments later, that giggle turned into many giggles, then belly-clenching laughter when Esther snort-laughed. Asher glanced at Rob and saw a genuine smile on his face.

Setting the box down on the table, Asher decided to ham it up. He spun in a poor imitation of a pirouette. Pulling the candy flowers from under his arm, he swept into a low bow and held them out. The girl cackled and took the bouquet.

He hopped into a standing position and—still hamming it up—stood like a flamingo. He knew it wasn't logical, but it didn't matter. Unicorns weren't real, so he could do whatever his little heart desired.

"Happy birthday, Leah," Esther said.

"This is awesome." The girl wrapped her arms around Esther's neck. "Thank you, Miss Campbell."

"You're welcome, sweetie. But thank your dad. He okayed all of this."

Leah turned to Rob, bestowing a cheerful smile on him. "Thanks, Dad. This is a great day. I can't wait to go out to eat tonight too."

"You're welcome, pumpkin." He came closer and ruffled her hair, smiling at her. "As soon as your mom gets home, we'll go. She's looking forward to it too. Especially after being cooped up last week and over the weekend because she was sick."

"Let's tell Asher the Unicorn thank you for the delivery, then we'll dig into your cake. I'm betting your dad won't mind if you spoil you dinner just a little." She cast a quick look at Rob.

"Nope. It's your special day, pumpkin. A small piece will be fine."

Leah pulled the box closer and opened the lid. "M&M's! Oh, yum!" She looked at Asher. "Thank you, Mr. Unicorn."

Taking his cue to leave, Asher jumped, lifting his arms above his head as he performed a quick scissor movement with his feet. With a flourish, he executed a pretty darn good split jump through the kitchen doorway for a grand exit. Laughter, and the dog's wild barking, followed him through the living room as he swished toward the front door.

Grinning ear to ear, he exited the house, swishing all the way back to the car. He wasn't upset he'd lost his bet with Esther. Seeing Leah's smile and hearing her laugh had been worth every sweaty second.

And he was definitely sweaty. The suit didn't breathe well. Even with the fan, moisture dripped down the sides of his face. His dance moves hadn't helped.

He opened the liftgate and reached for the zipper, ready for the cool outside air.

Pain blasted through the back of his head as something slammed into him. He toppled forward into the car, and the world went black.

Twenty-Two

Esther smiled and waved at Rob and Leah as she left the house forty-five minutes later. Leah had breezed through the work Esther brought, and she figured since it was the girl's birthday, there was no harm in ending a little early.

The door creaked as she exited. Still smiling, she glanced toward the curb. Her smile faded as she realized Asher's car wasn't there.

"Where the heck did he go?"

With a sigh, she dug her phone out of her bag and called him. It rang five times, then rolled to voicemail. She tried again and got the same result.

Hanging up, she propped a hand on her hip and stared at the street. She didn't know whether to be angry or concerned. Why would he leave her here alone? He'd been adamant about following her here and sticking around while she was inside.

Maybe he'd decided to run a quick errand. She was early, after all.

Blowing out a soft breath, she stepped off the porch and wandered over to the corner of the house by the driveway, leaning against the dingy siding. She'd wait until it was officially time for her to be finished with her tutoring session. If he wasn't back by then, she'd call again. She wasn't sure what she'd do if he didn't answer. Maybe call her dad for a ride?

Esther crossed her arms and ankles, settling in to wait.

Ten minutes later, he hadn't returned. She waited five more, and when he still didn't appear, she called him again.

Once more, the call rolled to voicemail.

She let out a huff as she ended the call. Where could he be? And why wasn't he answering?

Not wanting to lurk outside the Tylers' house any longer, she decided to call her dad. If Asher showed up before he arrived, great. If not, she'd text him and tell him she got a ride home. She was sure he had a good reason for leaving.

Dialing her dad's number, she waited a few rings for him to pick up.

"Hey, sweetie. What's up?"

"Can you come get me? Asher was my ride, but he's disappeared."

"Disappeared? Where did he go?"

"I don't know. He was gone when I came outside, and he's not answering his phone."

"That's odd. He's not that type of person."

"I know. Look, can you just head over here? We can talk more on the ride home. I'm not that comfortable standing out here alone."

"Where are you?"

"My home tutor student's house." She gave him the address.

"Okay, I'm on my way. Ten minutes."

"Thanks, Dad."

"Of course." He hung up.

Esther dropped her phone back into her purse and settled in to wait.

Her gaze tracked from one end of the street to the other,

looking for the man in the hoodie. She hadn't seen him since the day he stood outside her house. Asher said he hadn't been back since he chased the guy off. But that didn't mean he wasn't lurking somewhere. There were plenty of places for him to hide.

Behind cars. Behind trees and shrubs. Even in the shadows of the houses.

And she couldn't see around any of it. She didn't plan to go look, either. At least here, she had the house to her back so no one could sneak up on her. But that didn't stop her heart from beating a little too quickly or keep awareness from pricking her skin.

Eleven nerve-wracking minutes later, her dad rolled up in his black truck. Esther shot off a quick text to Asher, telling him she was headed home, then scurried away from the house and down the drive, climbing into the passenger seat.

"Hi, sweetie. I was hoping he'd be here when I pulled up."

"Me too. I don't know where he is." She snapped her seatbelt into place.

Conner pulled away from the curb. "He didn't say anything about leaving?"

"No. He came inside and helped me celebrate Leah's birthday for a few minutes, then went back out to sit in the car. He's never left me here alone."

Her dad's eyebrows pulled together. "Wait. What? Why wouldn't he leave you here alone?" His gaze sharpened. "Is something going on?"

Esther sighed, knowing she either needed to think of some quick lie or just spill the beans.

A lie would just trip her up later, so she went with the simple truth. "So, Asher and I weren't really dating when he came up. We are now," she was quick to add. "But when he first arrived, it was to put Edie's mind at ease."

"Edie?" He paused, frowning, then quickly continued. "What does she have to do with this?"

"There have been a few—strange things happening to me lately. Nothing crazy. Just odd. Like Rob Tyler making me uncomfortable. He hasn't done or said anything. He's just—creepy." Esther shrugged the uncomfortable feeling away. "Anyway, I've seen a man in a hoodie lurking around. Both at the Tylers' and at my house. Edie was worried, so Asher volunteered to come up and check things out. That's why he was my ride. He takes me to the Tylers', then just sits in the car and keeps an eye on things until I'm done. Today shouldn't have been any different."

"Maybe you should call Edie. See if something happened there that needed his attention. He's their computer man, right?"

"Yes." She unlocked her phone and went into her contacts. "I guess I could try." She found her sister's name and tapped it, then put the call on speaker. Edie picked up after a couple of rings.

"Hey."

"Hey. Have you heard from Asher?"

A beat of silence passed. "Asher? No. Why?"

"Because he left me high and dry outside the Tylers' house."

"What? He didn't say *anything*? Not a text or a voicemail?"

"Nope."

"That's weird."

"Right? I called Dad. We're on our way back to my house."

"Hi, Edie," Conner said.

"Hi, Dad. Um, let me call Ford. See if he knows anything or can reach him. I doubt it, though. He and the others are out on a boat on a fishing trip. But I'll ask. Hang tight. I'll call you back."

Before Esther could respond, Edie hung up.

Pressing her lips together, her jaw working, Esther set the phone down and leaned back against the seat. This was so weird. If Ford or one of the others didn't call him away on something urgent, she couldn't fathom what would make him leave without telling her.

Unless he didn't go willingly.

The thought hit her like a bolt of lightning. Her breath seized in her lungs, trapping the air as they refused to work.

No.

Was Hoodie Man more of a threat than they'd realized? But why would he go after Asher? He'd been watching her. It would make more sense for him to take her.

Except he couldn't get to her because Asher was always around.

A ball formed in her stomach. Maybe the guy took Asher with the intent to kill him, so he could get to her.

She shoved that thought away and slammed a heavy door on it.

No.

She couldn't think like that.

He was fine.

He had to be.

Esther stared out the window the rest of the way to her house, her mind busy with all the reasons why he could have left. Some of the thoughts were utterly absurd, Like, he'd gotten his pants caught in the costume's zipper and ripped them and had to go home to change. She tried not to think about the more ominous reasons why he hadn't returned.

Her phone rang as her dad turned onto her street. She fumbled with it, her heart in her throat, praying it was Asher.

It wasn't.

Her sister's smiling face graced the screen.

Quickly, Esther answered, hoping Edie had good news. "Hello?"

"Ford said he didn't call him. Neither did any of the guys. He asked if they should head back. I told him I wasn't sure. What do you think? Do they need to come in?"

Conner turned into the driveway—the empty driveway— and put the truck in park.

"Maybe. We just pulled up to the house. His car isn't here."

"If you can't get a hold of him or he doesn't show up in the next couple of hours, you need to call the police. He can be impulsive, and he can also get stuck in his head when he's work- ing. It's possible he got a lead on the case there. But it's odd he wouldn't at least text you or arrange a ride to get you home."

"Maybe he did text, and I didn't get it. Service around here can be spotty." She'd missed calls and texts from her parents in the last month because of a lack of coverage. Sometimes it was the weather, other times it was just crummy cell coverage.

"True. All right, give him a couple of hours. If he's still MIA, call the cops and report him missing. Then call me. I'll get the guys to come back, and they can do what they do best. Was he in his car?"

"Yes."

"The car rental agency might be able to help you out. They put trackers in their vehicles. The cops can get a warrant to access the data."

"Okay." She made a mental note to mention that if she had to call the police.

"I wouldn't worry too much yet. I know that sounds crazy from the woman who's been worrying about everything lately, but there are many reasons he could be out of contact. Keep me posted, though, all right?"

"I will. Thanks, Edie."

"You're welcome. Talk to you soon."

"Yep. Love you."

"Love you too. Bye."

"Bye." Esther hung up.

"What did she say?" Conner asked.

"That he might be working and not paying attention to anything else, and to give him some time."

Conner's head bobbed. "Sounds like a good plan. Do you want me to stay?"

Esther inhaled a breath, then let it out, glancing at her front door. "No. I'll be fine. If I need you, I'll call."

"You're sure?"

"Yes. Thanks for picking me up." She gathered the handles of her tote and opened the door.

"Okay. Let me know later how everything turns out. Your mother and I can come over and lend some moral support if you need to call the police."

"I will. Thanks, Dad." She slid out of the truck seat.

"You're welcome." Conner lifted a hand in farewell.

Esther gave him a strained smile and shut the door, then headed up the path and inside.

Silence echoed in her ears as she shut the front door behind her. She hadn't realized how much of a difference his presence made before. It was amazing how quickly she'd grown accustomed to the noise a second person brought to a house. Without Asher, her house felt like a tomb.

Locking the door, she moved into the kitchen and set her tote on the counter. She cast a quick glance around, unsure what to do.

Do what you always do, her inner voice prompted.

Right. Of course. It was just like any other day after work. She needed to change clothes, then figure out dinner. She'd make something elaborate tonight. It would help take her mind off Asher.

Heading upstairs, she quickly shed her school clothes and donned a pair of lavender leggings and a light sage green cropped sweater. In just her socks, she went back downstairs to the kitchen and opened the fridge, eyeing its contents. She had a bunch of Roma tomatoes to use, so she decided to make her own pasta sauce. And her own pasta. That would eat up a good hour.

Pushing up her sleeves, Esther got to work. After taking all the vegetables she needed for the sauce from the fridge and washing them, she set them on the island, then grabbed an onion from the bowl on the counter. She dug out her cutting board and a bowl, then removed a knife from the block, the blade making a metallic *shink* sound as she withdrew it from the wood. It wavered in her hand, and she clutched it until her knuckles turned white, trying to still the tremor. Playing with sharp objects when she was upset probably wasn't the best idea, but she needed to do something to calm her racing mind.

With the first cut through the green pepper, her loud thoughts dimmed the slightest bit. By the time she got through the tomatoes, she felt less scattered and more in control. Whatever the reason Asher had disappeared, she'd handle it in stride. There really wasn't another option.

But when she got to the onion, tears welled in her eyes.

Esther sniffed and swiped her face on her sleeve.

It's the onion. That's all.

She was scared to admit anything else. Didn't want to acknowledge the loud voice in the back of her mind screaming at her that he hadn't left willingly. That he wouldn't do that to her. Not without communicating his plans.

Just because she would handle that scenario with grace, too, didn't mean she wasn't also terrified of what it meant.

Twenty-Three

A headache pulsed through Asher's skull and into his eyes. He struggled to focus as he came awake. The low hum drumming through his ears didn't help. Where was he?

He rolled—or attempted to—but didn't get far. His hands were bound behind his back. The fabric of the unicorn costume bunched around him, twisted, further restricting his movement.

So did the seat back in front of his face. He was in the back of his rented SUV.

And the car was moving.

But who was driving?

Lifting his hips, he tried to free up some of the fabric so he could sit up, but it refused to budge.

Asher growled and tried to muscle his arms apart. The costume swished, and he kicked the tailgate as he strained against his bonds, but he stayed stubbornly bound up.

The vehicle made a sharp right turn; hard enough to tip him to the side, and he rolled into the wheel well, smashing his face on the plastic.

"Watch it, asshole!" He didn't care if the guy knew he was

awake. He probably already did with all the thrashing he'd been up to.

The world outside dimmed, and the car slowed. Asher struggled to right himself, so he could see where they were. The costume fabric had loosened some, but it was slick, and in the tight space without the use of his arms, he kept sliding against it.

A moment later, the car stopped and the engine cut. The interior light came on as the driver got out.

Instead of getting up, Asher wiggled onto his back. He'd kick this jackass in the face the moment he opened the hatch.

A shadow passed the window, then a few seconds later, the tailgate lifted. Asher lashed out, but connected only with air.

Light blinded him from a flashlight, and the man's low chuckle sounded from several feet away. "Did you really think I was that stupid?"

"I don't know. You kidnapped me in broad daylight. That's pretty dumb." He squinted, turning his face away from the brightness. The guy had one of those megawatt flashlights —the kind that were as bright as the sun. With the headache he already had, the light made it a million times worse. But maybe that was the man's plan. Disorient him so he couldn't think well enough to plan an escape.

"In that neighborhood, even if someone saw something, they won't tell. There, the cops are the enemy. Who are you?"

Asher froze, confused. "What? Why did you abduct me if you don't know who I am?"

"Because you were in my way. Who are you? Who hired you?"

"No one hired me. I was there with a friend."

"Esther, yes."

"How do you know her name?"

"I know a lot of things. But not who you are. Again, what's your name?"

Asher hesitated, but decided for now, to play the man's game. "Asher."

"Asher what?"

"What does it matter what my last name is?"

"Because I like to know who I'm dealing with. Don't make me hurt you."

Asher didn't need to see past the bright light to hear the hammer being pulled back on a handgun.

"What's your name?"

"Asher Horn."

"See? That wasn't so difficult. How do you know Esther?"

"I told you; we're friends."

"Funny. I've never seen you around before this past week."

Asher's focus sharpened. Just how long had this man been watching Esther? "I don't know what to tell you, man. We've been friends for a while." He decided to feed the man the lies they'd constructed to tell others. "I live out of town for now. I'm here looking for a job and staying with her while I job search and house hunt. Now, how about you tell me who you are?"

"No. But thank you for that information."

Asher heard rustling. The light bobbed. Then, in one quick movement, the man leaned into the car and plunged a needle deep into Asher's thigh.

"What the hell, man?" He tried to move away, but with his hands behind his back and the limited confines of the car, he could do little more than twist.

It wasn't enough. He watched the man inject something, then back out of the car.

"Enjoy your nap."

The guy stepped back and shut the hatch. A moment later, the horn honked once and the locks engaged.

Muttering a curse, Asher kicked at the window. His vision

swam and what should have been a powerful kick barely thudded on the glass.

No. This shouldn't happen so fast. Intramuscular injections took time to be absorbed.

Unless the guy got lucky and hit a blood vessel.

Or he was a pro and knew how to make one stick count.

That thought didn't fill him with comfort.

Seconds passed, and the car interior swam wildly in front of Asher's eyes. Blackness edged the corners of his vision. He fought against it, weakly kicking at the window again.

But it was no use.

The blackness took hold, and he sank onto the cargo area floor.

Twenty-Four

The living room curtain flopped back into place as Esther let go of it. She turned, glancing at the wall clock. Over two hours had passed since Asher took off. She couldn't wait any longer. It was time to contact the police.

Traipsing into the kitchen, she picked up her purse and car keys. She figured she'd get better results if she showed up at the police station rather than calling to make a report. Perhaps if she was adamant enough that something was wrong, they'd let her speak to a detective.

After stuffing her feet into a pair of canvas shoes, she exited the house through the garage and climbed into her car. Moments later, she was headed down the road.

Nerves twisted her stomach in knots and threatened to expel the meager amount of pasta she'd forced down earlier. She had a terrible feeling Asher hadn't taken off in hot pursuit of a lead.

Just minutes after she left her house, she turned into a parking space outside of the local police station. Heron Ridge wasn't large, and their police department reflected that. But they were large enough to have several patrol officers and a detective on staff. Hopefully, they could help her. If not, well, she'd call Edie and the cavalry. One way or another, she'd find Asher.

Warm air hit her as she stepped inside the building's vestibule. A man at the desk sat up straighter as she entered.

"Good evening. How may I help you, miss?" His voice came through the speaker embedded in the glass, giving it a tinny, electronic sound.

"Hi. I need to file a missing person's report."

"Okay. Adult or child?" The man slid a notepad closer and picked up a pen.

"Adult."

"How long has this person been missing?"

"Just a couple of hours."

His expression shuttered, and he laid the pen down. "Ma'am—"

Esther held up a hand, cutting him off. "I know what you're going to say. He hasn't been gone long enough. But if you'd let me explain, you might think differently."

The officer eyed her for a long moment. Esther held his gaze, her back ramrod straight. She wasn't leaving until someone heard her out.

"Okay. Explain."

She didn't hesitate. "My name is Esther Campbell. I'm a teacher at Heron Ridge Elementary. As part of my duties, I'm a homeschool tutor for a child who can't attend regular classes due to a medical condition. It's not in the best part of town, and I haven't felt safe there lately. I told my sister about it. She's a former military officer, and she knows people. She told one of her friends, and last week, he showed up at my door, offering to help. Part of that help is he's been driving me there and waiting for me. Today, we did what we always do, but when I left my student's house, he was gone. Car and all. He didn't text or call. Never mentioned he planned to leave before I got out of the car. I don't know where he went. I ended up calling my dad to come get me because I didn't have a way home. You have to understand. Asher isn't some flighty man who couldn't be bothered to wait around. He's a former CIA analyst with a genius-level intellect. If he left, he'd tell me."

Again, the officer stared at her, this time with a disbelieving smirk on his face. "You had me up until the CIA part. Go home and take your meds, lady."

"Excuse me?" Esther narrowed her eyes at him. "Listen, I am not a nut job. My sister is Edie Campbell. Do you know who that is?" In their small town, military heroes were well known. Especially ones who'd been wounded in action.

The man sat back. "I do."

"And wouldn't it make sense that she knows someone like that?"

"I suppose it would."

"Great. Can I talk to the detective on duty?"

The officer sighed. "Ma'am—"

Again, Esther held up a hand. "Please? I'm worried. This isn't like him."

Chewing on the corner of his mouth, the officer stared at his phone, then sighed. "Fine. But I can't promise you he'll do anything yet."

Relief flooded her veins. "That's fine. At least I'll have the ball rolling."

The man picked up the phone and dialed an extension. A moment later, he spoke. "Hey, I've got a woman up here wanting to file a missing person's report. I think you need to hear her out."

A beat of silence passed, then he nodded. "Thanks." He hung up and looked at Esther. "You can come back." He reached for the wall, then the door to her left buzzed.

"Thank you."

Esther walked over and pulled on the handle to let herself in. She paused at his desk on the other side.

"Fill this out." He pushed a clipboard toward her.

She wrote her name and other information on the paper, then handed it back. He gave her a visitor's badge, then stood up.

"Follow me." Rounding the desk, he led her through a metal detector, then down the short corridor to an office, where he rapped his knuckles on the semi-closed door.

"Enter," came a muffled male voice from inside.

The officer pushed the wooden door inward before he stepped back and motioned for her to precede him. Esther moved forward, getting her first glimpse of the mid-fortyish detective with salt and pepper hair behind the metal desk.

He rose, revealing a tall, lanky body that said he ran a lot, and offered her a tired, but polite smile. "Come in, ma'am, and have a seat. I'm Detective J.D. Stroud."

Esther tried to return his smile, but knew she failed. It had probably looked more like a grimace. She sat down, folding her hands in her lap. "Esther Campbell."

The door returned to its semi-closed state as the officer left.

"Officer Weyland said you want to file a missing person's report?"

"I do. And I want to ask that you hear me out before telling me it's too soon. Also, I promise you, I'm not crazy."

He arched an eyebrow. "You know, most people who are crazy say they aren't."

Esther let out a soft huff. "Please?"

His mouth flattened. "Fine."

"Thank you." Not waiting for him to change his mind, she launched into a thorough but condensed version of why she thought Asher had been abducted and hadn't just left. Starting with her sister and how Edie knew Asher, she moved on to why he'd come to Oregon and what had happened since he'd been here. She also touched on the mystery surrounding the Tylers. By the time she'd laid everything out, Detective Stroud's skeptical expression had changed to one of concerned curiosity.

"So, he just disappeared on you this evening? Car and all?"

"Yes. Edie told me to mention he was in a rental car. That you might be able to use that."

"It's possible. Do you know where he rented the car?"

"Portland Airport." She named the company whose sticker she'd seen in the corner of the windshield.

The detective wrote it down. "Give me a description of your friend."

"Um, he's tall. Maybe six-two or three. Dark hair. Brown eyes."

"Age?"

"Thirty-three."

"What about weight and build?"

"He's fit. He runs marathons. I'm not sure about weight. Maybe one-eighty? One-ninety?"

"Okay, what about his clothing? What was he wearing?"

Esther chuckled softly, remembering how he looked when she last saw him. She waved a hand. "Sorry. To help me celebrate my student's birthday, Asher put on an inflatable unicorn costume. Leah loved it. The last time I saw him, he was wearing that. Underneath, he had on khaki-colored jeans and a dark purple dress shirt."

Detective Stroud wrote that down, then nodded. "All right. I'll get a flyer made up. Make some calls and go visit—"

The door swung inward, startling them both. Esther turned around to see Officer Weyland.

"I'm sorry to interrupt. Detective, we just got a call about a shooting and a child abduction at Little Nicky's Pizzeria."

Esther's blood ran cold. That was the restaurant Leah mentioned they were going to for dinner.

"Officers are on scene, and K-9 is en route," Weyland continued.

"Witnesses?" Detective Stroud pushed back from his desk.

"Just an elderly couple on their way out of the building. Report from the scene says the shooting victim is critical. Medical just got there."

"Okay. Tell the units on scene I'll be there soon."

Officer Weyland nodded once, then ducked out of the room.

"Miss Campbell, I'm sorry, but I need to go. I promise—"

Esther stood. "I think the cases are connected."

Stroud paused and frowned. "I'm sorry?"

"Asher and the incident at Little Nicky's. My student—Leah—she said her family was going to Little Nicky's for dinner for her birthday."

His gaze sharpened. "You're sure?"

"Yes. She was so excited about it, I could hardly keep her on task. She hasn't been to a restaurant in years, Detective. Years. I heard all about their plans. More than once."

He stared at her for a beat. "Okay. On the off-chance you're right, I want you close by to answer questions." He rounded the desk and ushered her toward the door. "You're coming along."

TWENTY-FIVE

Esther's heart lurched into her throat as Detective Stroud turned the corner near Little Nicky's. An ambulance turned out of the lot, the siren coming on as it hit the road. Stroud pulled to the side to let it pass. Esther's gaze followed it, wondering who was inside. Whoever it was must be truly critical. The paramedics hadn't been on scene long.

The car bumped over potholes as Stroud took his foot off the brake and rolled forward again. Red and blue strobe lights pulsed through the night, giving the scene an eerie vibe that did nothing to settle her heart back where it belonged.

Stroud pulled up behind a county cruiser and cut the engine. "You stay with me. Hopefully, you're wrong, and I can have a uniform take you back to the station to get your car."

"I'm not wrong." Though she prayed she was. Unbuckling, she followed him out of the vehicle.

They ducked under the crime scene tape. Esther stayed glued to Stroud's side, not wanting to get in anyone's way or contaminate the scene. He led her to a uniformed officer near the front of the building. The man was hunched over, speaking to someone she couldn't see.

"Meigs."

The man glanced over his shoulder, then straightened. Esther let out a gasp as she caught sight of the person hidden behind him. While she'd never seen the woman in person, she'd seen pictures. Connie Tyler, with her white-blonde hair and high cheekbones, was striking, and recognizable even with her tear-stained, puffy face.

Stroud glanced at Esther. "What?"

"I told you I wasn't wrong. That's Connie Tyler. My student's mother."

He let out a soft curse. With a quick tip of his head, he motioned the officer to the side.

Meigs stepped away.

"Mrs. Tyler?" Stroud's voice, though firm, held a note of compassion.

Connie looked up from her seat on the bench in front of the restaurant.

"I'm Detective Stroud. Do you know this woman?" He pointed at Esther.

A slight frown marred Connie's face. "Should I?"

"She says she knows you."

"I'm Esther Campbell." She hadn't mentioned to Detective Stroud that she'd never met Leah's mother.

Connie's frown turned curious. "Leah's teacher?"

It was Stroud's turn to frown. "Wait. You know the name but not the face?"

"We've never met. I'm always at work when she's there. Rob—" Her voice caught, and she paused to swallow before continuing. "Rob is the one who deals with Leah's schoolwork."

Esther glanced around, suddenly realizing Rob was nowhere in sight. A pit formed in her belly. The call had been for an abduction *and* a shooting.

Connie stood up and folded her arms, hugging herself. "I don't understand. Why are you here?"

Stroud spoke before Esther could. "Mrs. Tyler, can you tell me what happened?" He took a small notebook and a pen from his pocket, flipping to a blank page.

Sniffing, Connie swiped at her face. "Um, we—we were leaving. Walking to the car. Right over there." She extended an arm, pointing past them to her right. "Leah was so happy. She'd had a great day." A soft smile lit her face, and she glanced at Esther. "I heard all about what you and your friend did for her. Thank you."

Esther cleared her throat to rid it of the lump that had suddenly formed. "You're welcome."

Connie's expression sobered, then went distant as she recalled what happened. "We were maybe ten feet or so from the car when a man popped out from a couple vehicles down, pointing a gun." She closed her eyes, and a tear trickled out. "He came up so fast. Grabbed Leah from between us. I remember screaming. Then Rob charged at the guy, yelling for him to put Leah down. He—he—" She broke off with a sob. More tears tracked down her face. She drew in a shaky breath that ended on a soft hiccup. Opening her eyes, she looked at Stroud. "The man shot Rob. Practically point blank. Then he was gone. He just—tucked Leah under one arm and took off that way." She gestured toward the parking lot entrance.

"He wasn't parked in the lot?"

Connie shook her head. "I ran after him, but he was too fast for me. By the time I reached the sidewalk, he was gone. I don't know where he parked, but it wasn't in the lot."

"Okay. Did you recognize him?"

"No."

Esther narrowed her eyes. There'd been an ever-so-slight hesitation to that single word. She was no psychologist or investigator, but she was a kindergarten teacher. She'd honed her lie-detection skills on five- and six-year-olds. There was something about Leah's abductor that triggered something in Connie's memory. "Are you sure?" she asked the other woman.

Connie turned silvery blue eyes on her. She held Esther's gaze for a moment. A hardness glinted in their depths and made Esther frown. She had no proof, but she'd bet Connie Tyler was hiding something.

"I'm sure." She turned to the detective. "He had a hood pulled low and wore black gloves.

Hoodie Man.

Who was that guy? What did he want with Leah? And Asher?

"What else can you tell me about him? Height, weight, race, age?"

"I didn't see his face, but he was probably about six feet tall. Thin, but not skinny. I'm not sure about race. White, I think. There was some skin showing above his glove when he put his arm around Leah."

"Okay. Did he say anything?"

"No. He just grabbed Leah, then shot Rob and took off running."

"Mrs. Tyler, is there anyone who would want to hurt your family?"

"No."

Again, there was that slight hesitation on the beginning of the word. Almost like a stutter, but so slight, it was barely there.

"You're sure?" the detective asked. "You didn't even really think about it."

"Why would I need to? I live a boring life. I work and go to the grocery. Rob takes Leah to most of her doctor's appointments, of which there are many. Other than that, we're home all the time. We don't socialize. We don't have time. There isn't anyone who'd have a beef with us." Connie shifted her arms, tightening her hug around herself.

Stroud pressed his lips together. Esther wanted to ask questions, but didn't dare.

Moisture trickled down Connie's face again. She sank onto the bench. "What am I going to do? I just want my baby back."

Esther spared Stroud a quick glance as she moved forward and sank down beside Connie. "She's a strong kid. She'll be okay until the police find her."

Connie nodded, raising a hand to wipe at her face as she sniffed. "I know you're right. Thank you. I still don't understand why you're here, though. Is the detective your dad or something?"

"No. My friend—the one who helped me surprise Leah for her birthday?" She paused, waiting for Connie to acknowledge she knew who Esther meant.

"The man in the unicorn suit?"

"That's him. He's disappeared too."

Connie's eyes widened. Then, just as suddenly, she reared back and stood up, aiming a glare at Esther. "Your friend did this?"

"What?" Esther's eyes rounded, and she rose to face the angry mother. "No. Asher would never. I think their disappearances are related somehow, but he didn't take her. I was at the police station, filing a missing person's report on him, when the call came in about Leah."

"Mrs. Tyler, do you know Asher Horn?" Stroud asked.

"No. I've never heard the name before."

Esther noted there was no hesitation in her voice this time.

"Why do you think they're connected?" Connie demanded of Esther.

It was Esther's turn to hesitate. For one, she didn't want to talk out of turn. She doubted Stroud brought her along so she could inject her speculation into his case. And two, she didn't want to upset Connie if she happened to be wrong. Ultimately, she decided to go with a basic truth. "Someone's been lurking around outside your house. I thought they were following me, because I've seen them at my place too. Asher was with me, not just to help surprise Leah, but to make me feel safer. He's been my shadow for the last week."

Connie's brows dipped. "Why would someone kidnap your friend and my daughter?"

"I don't know. But their disappearances have to be connected. It's too coincidental."

"All we have at this point is conjecture." Stroud closed his notebook and tucked it into his pocket, along with his pen. "I'll look at all angles for both disappearances."

"I don't care what you do. Just find my daughter. She—she could die"—her voice broke—"if she doesn't take her meds."

"What are the meds for?" Stroud asked.

"Anti-organ rejection. She had a heart transplant in late August. If she goes too long without them, her body will reject her heart. It can be irreversible."

"How much can she miss—"

"None," Connie said, not letting him finish. "At this stage, missing any doses could cause rejection fairly quickly." Tears gathered in her eyes again. "Unless you can find her in the next hour or so, she's going to miss a dose. She takes them every twelve hours. At eight a.m. and eight p.m."

An ache speared Esther in the chest. Connie was right. They were on a ticking clock.

TWENTY-SIX

A drumline danced in Asher's head again, pounding out a tattoo as he woke. He shifted, and a deep groan that felt pulled from the pits of hell rolled from his chest. His mouth worked, trying to bring some moisture into its parched depths. He felt like he'd sucked on cotton balls.

His hands were no longer bound, so he worked one elbow under his chest and pushed, sitting up. The muscles in his shoulders and back protested, and he grimaced but made it upright. Pressing the heel of his hand to his temple, he shifted off his hip and onto his butt before leaning against the chilly wall at his back.

He blinked, trying to bring the room into focus. His eyes were as dry as his mouth, and his head felt floaty yet from the sedative.

Gradually, a bit of moisture returned, and he could make out his surroundings. Dank, dirt walls enclosed him; a small window set near the ceiling was the room's sole source of light. Outside, a streetlight cast a glow inside. He couldn't see much beyond his immediate vicinity, which consisted of a filthy, lumpy mattress on the ground. As far as he could tell, he was in a basement or a cellar.

His captor had uncuffed him, but had left him dressed in the deflated unicorn costume. The fabric still bunched around his torso. It also trapped heat. A chill skated up the back of Asher's neck as the clamminess of his clothing underneath the nylon costume registered. He knew where all the water in his body went; into the sweat now dampening his clothes.

Grimacing as he moved, he lifted his hips, yanking on the fabric to untwist it. Weak from dehydration and the effects of whatever sedative his captor gave him, his hands slid off, and he smacked himself in the face.

"Fuck!" He covered his cheek, attempting to soothe the sting.

A whimper sounded from the corner. Asher froze, then lowered his hand and squinted into the dim light. "Hello? Is someone there?"

Springs creaked, and another whimper echoed softly through the room. The high pitch sent his heart racing. That sounded like a kid.

Asher renewed his efforts to get out of the unicorn suit.

It took another minute of fighting with the slick fabric before his uncoordinated muscles managed to shove it over his feet. Once he was free, he climbed to his knees, not trusting his balance enough to get to his feet yet, and crawled across the room toward the sound.

The whimper grew and turned to a soft cry. Asher paused just feet away. It was definitely a child.

"Hey, honey." He kept his voice soft and soothing. "It's okay. I won't hurt you. I'm stuck down here too." He squinted, trying to see through the shadows. The kid was up on a cot, backed into a corner where there was little light. "How about you come out so I can see you?"

The soft cries continued, and the kid didn't move.

"It's all right. I want to help and get us both out of here." When he still got no response, he decided to try a different tactic. He'd make friends the way he always did; he'd use his words. "My name's Asher. What's yours?"

He didn't get the response he'd been hoping for, but the cries stopped, and he heard a soft intake of breath, like a gasp. Taking it as a win, he shifted, sitting down. The child moved, extending one leg into the light. A pink sneaker encased the kid's foot below purple leggings.

"How long have you been down here? I've been asleep. You're not hurt, are you?"

He waited a beat, another question on the tip of his tongue if the kid didn't answer. But she did.

"No," came the whisper. "Are you Asher the Unicorn?"

All the breath left Asher's lungs. Her voice was stronger on the question, but he didn't need to hear it to recognize her. "Leah?" He scooted closer and rose to his knees.

"Yeah." Her reply wobbled. "I want my mommy, Mr. Asher."

"Oh, honey. I bet you do. Can I sit with you?"

She sat up, leaning into what light streamed in through the window, and nodded. Wet streaks coated her cheeks and her blonde locks hung around her round face in disheveled hanks. She looked scared, but not hurt, for which he was thankful. An injury with her medical condition could create some serious problems.

Asher braced his hands on the bed and pushed up on unsteady arms, then sank down onto the creaky cot beside her. Immediately, she leaned into him. He wrapped an arm around her and gathered her to his side, holding her close. "It's okay, Leah. You're safe with me. We're gonna get out of here."

"Where's Miss Campbell?"

"I don't know. Whoever took us hit me over the head

outside of your house and knocked me out. How long have you been here?"

He felt one small shoulder flex in a shrug. "I don't know. Awhile. You were already sleeping over there when he brought me down."

"I'm sorry I wasn't awake."

"It's okay. I'm just glad I'm not alone. I don't like dark places." Her voice descended into a whisper again as she finished.

He squeezed her shoulders gently. "Did you recognize the man who took you?"

Asher felt her head roll against his side.

"No. He just grabbed me after dinner. And he—he shot my dad, I think." Her words wobbled, and she sniffed.

He wouldn't doubt that. The guy had seemed willing to use the weapon he'd brandished. He glanced down at Leah, wondering again if she was hurt. She hadn't said one way or another. "How are you feeling? He didn't hurt you, did he? And I know you take a lot of medications. Are you doing all right without them?"

She pulled back to look up at him. "I'm fine. And he gave me my meds."

A frown marred Asher's forehead. "What? He gave you your medicine?"

Leah nodded. "I think he took them from my house. My parents mark some of the bottles with the date when we open them. When we got here, he sat me down in the kitchen and gave me the ones I take at night. I saw the writing on the bottles."

Asher's frown intensified. What did this guy want with Leah? How did Esther play into things? Was she involved because she was around? The man said he'd been watching her specifically, though. It didn't make any sense why he'd take Leah if it was Esther he wanted.

"How do we get out of here, Mr. Asher?"

That was a great question. One he didn't have an answer to. Yet. "I'm not sure, sweetie. But we'll figure it out. And I'm sure people are looking for us." If Esther hadn't called Edie yet, she would soon. There wasn't a force on earth that could stop his friends from finding him.

Their captor was about to find out who Asher really was.

Twenty-Seven

Keeping one eye on Detective Stroud, Esther stepped away from the organized chaos happening around her so she could call her sister. She'd wanted to go with Connie Tyler to the hospital, but Stroud said he couldn't spare another car to take her anywhere yet. She didn't know why she couldn't ride in the same one that whisked Connie away.

She squinted at the detective. She had a feeling he didn't entirely trust her and wanted to keep her close. But that meant, for the moment, she was stuck.

Esther leaned against the corner of the building and tapped Edie's name in her contacts. It rang once before her sister answered.

"He's not back, is he?"

"No." Esther sighed. "And there's more. I went to the police station to file the missing person's report. When I was talking to the detective, a call came in. For a shooting and a child abduction. Leah's been kidnapped and Rob Tyler was shot. They're not sure he's going to make it."

"Are you serious? What the hell? Okay. I'm calling the

guys in. Give me a rundown on what you know, so I can brief them."

"It's not much. Connie Tyler said a man came up and grabbed Leah as they were walking to their car after dinner. Rob tried to intervene, and the guy shot him. She said he was wearing a hood and took off running out of the parking lot with Leah under his arm."

"Did she follow him?"

"Yeah, but she couldn't catch up. She said by the time she reached the sidewalk, he was out of sight."

"Are there side streets close? Where was this?"

"Little Nicky's."

"Oh. Yeah, that neighborhood is a maze."

"Yep."

"Did you get a description other than a guy in a hood?"

"No. I don't think she was being completely truthful."

A short pause came over the line. "Why would she lie? I mean, her daughter's in danger and her husband got shot."

"I know. But there was just something about the way she hesitated—just a fraction of a second—that said she wasn't being completely honest. I think she knows more than she's letting on and doesn't want to tell the police."

"It could be she's scared about revealing her past. Maybe she'll tell us. We don't have any authority to do anything, though."

"Maybe. I'd like to try to talk to her alone, but I can't get out of here to get up to the hospital and try."

"Hold off for now. As soon as we hang up, I'm radioing Ford and telling him to come in. I'm sure Brooke will give us the use of her jet. Ezra can fly everyone up as soon as they get back. I need twenty-four hours, Essy."

"Asher and Leah might not have that long, Edie." Her voice grew thick as she thought about the danger the two of them were in. Asher could already be dead.

"I bet they do. I'm not sure why the guy took Asher, but I'm betting Connie Tyler's past has come back to haunt her and that's why he took Leah. This guy has a plan, and it's not to kill her."

Esther rubbed her temple, a headache beginning to pound behind her eyes. "But where does that leave Asher? I can't just sit here and do nothing. Give me something to do. What do you guys need?" She needed a distraction. It would drive her crazy to sit around and wait on Edie and her friends to arrive.

"See if you can get a list of witnesses. The guys will want to talk to them when we get there. And maybe see if you can find out which businesses nearby have outdoor security cameras. It'll save us time if we already have that information."

"How are you going to access it, though? Asher's the one who gets into everything electronic."

"The old-fashioned way. Ask nicely. Don't worry, Esther. We know what we're doing and can adapt."

"I know. I do... It's just..." She broke off and growled, beyond frustrated.

"I get it, Essy." Edie's voice was softer now. "There's nothing like not knowing if someone you care about is okay. But you have to trust me. Trust us. Just like I had to trust my team when Jordan was missing."

"Yeah." Esther blew out a breath. "Okay. I'll go see what I can find out. Let me know when you'll all be here, okay?"

"I will. Keep me posted if things change."

"Yep."

They said goodbye and hung up. Esther shoved her phone into her bag and glanced around the parking lot. It was still organized chaos. Crime scene techs were near the Tylers' car, going over the ground with a fine-toothed comb and taking dozens of pictures. An officer stood sentry at the entrance, blocking the drive. Others stood with groups of potential witnesses, while Stroud and the police chief conducted interviews. They had people in two groups; those who needed to be interviewed, and those who had been.

She wandered closer to those with whom Stroud and the chief had already spoken. Lingering at the fringe, she listened.

After several minutes, the consensus seemed to be that no one had seen much of anything except for an older couple several people gestured toward. Esther turned toward the restaurant, studying the pair sitting on a bench alone.

A jolt of recognition made her eyes widen. She knew them. They went to her church.

Emboldened by familiarity, she walked over, stopping a few feet away. "Mr. and Mrs. Tinsdale."

The couple looked up, and the wife smiled. "Esther. Hello, dear."

"Hi." She lifted a hand and waved, returning her smile. "May I sit with you?"

"Of course." Sue Tinsdale nudged her husband in the side, motioning for him to scoot.

"Thank you." Esther perched on the bench next to her.

"Such a terrible thing, isn't it? Did you see what happened?" Sue asked.

"No. Did you?"

"We sure did. That man came out from behind a truck and just plucked that little girl right off the pavement. Her poor dad tried to stop him."

"It was a terrible sight," Herb Tinsdale said, shaking his head.

"Did you see the guy? His face, I mean."

"No. He had that infernal hood over his head." Sue crossed her arms and shook her head.

"But he was in the restaurant earlier." Herb leaned forward to look at Esther.

"He was not," Sue said. "That young man sitting alone was not the same guy."

"He didn't have the sweatshirt on, but he had on the same pants."

"They were jeans, Herbert. Many people in the restaurant had on jeans."

"Don't tell me what I saw, Susanna. It looked like the same man to me."

Esther waved her hands to break up the argument. "Did you tell the police this?"

"I wanted to, but she told me I was mistaken." Herb aimed a gnarled finger at his wife.

"And you still are," Sue shot back.

Herb pressed his lips together and sent her a quick look before continuing. "I didn't mention it because, well, she's right. I don't always see what I think I do. My mind likes to make connections that aren't there, and I didn't want to get a young man in trouble if he didn't do anything wrong."

Esther looked out at the two groups of witnesses. "Do you see the man anywhere now?"

The couple followed her gaze. Herb adjusted his glasses.

"I don't," Sue said.

"No. He's gone. But he left before we did. I saw him get up and walk out."

"How long before you left was that?"

"Ten minutes or so, I guess."

That was plenty of time for him to retrieve a hoodie and hide before the Tylers came outside.

"Miss Campbell."

Esther looked up. Detective Stroud walked toward them, a scowl on his face. She plastered a bright smile on hers. "Detective."

"What are you doing?"

Pulling on every school play she'd ever acted in—all of which were in elementary school—Esther faked a frown. "What do you mean?"

"I don't need you interfering with my witnesses."

"Oh." She glanced at the elderly couple. "I wasn't. The Tinsdales go to my church. I came over to say hello. We did, however, discuss what happened tonight. Herb has something you need to hear."

Stroud's gaze sharpened, and he focused on the older man. "Oh? Did you remember something new?"

Herb shifted, casting a quick glance at his wife, who sighed and shook her head.

"Mr. Tinsdale?" Stroud said when the man hesitated.

"Go on, Herb. It might be nothing, but it might be important too," Esther said.

The old man huffed. "Fine. There was a young man in the restaurant. He kept staring at the Tylers' table, and I swear he had on the same pants as the man who attacked them."

"The same pants?"

"They were jeans," Sue said, rolling her eyes.

"But they were the same kind of jeans," Herb retorted. "Anyway, from my seat, it looked like he was watching them. I don't know if he was. He wasn't there long. Maybe twenty minutes. He arrived after they did, ordered an appetizer and a drink, then left about ten minutes before us."

Stroud pulled out his notebook and pen. "Describe this man. Other than his clothing."

Herb scratched at his temple and scrunched his nose. "He was a white guy. Six feet tall, maybe a little less. Fit, from what I could tell. He had on a black jacket over an olive-green t-shirt. There was something on the front, but I couldn't see what it was."

"That's a really great description, Mr. Tinsdale," Stroud said, sounding genuinely impressed.

Herb smiled. "Thank you. I did quality control for years. I notice details."

Sue snorted. "When you want to." She looked up at

Stroud. "He gets these fanciful ideas sometimes. Makes those connections between unrelated things. I've said for years he needs to write a book, but—"

Stroud held up a hand. "You're right. That could be the case this time. But I have a missing child to find. No details are too small to look into." He gave her a polite smile, then turned to Herb. "What about age and hair color for this man? Did you notice either of those things?"

Herb's head bobbed. "Yeah. His hair was a real light brown. And he was probably early thirties."

"Mid," Sue said. "Mid-thirties."

Stroud made notes. "Okay. I'll have the manager check their security tapes for the man, then I'd like you to confirm it's the right person before we proceed. Give me a few minutes." He shifted his weight, ready to head off, but paused and caught Esther's gaze. "Thank you, Miss Campbell."

Esther offered him a tight smile and nodded once. "Just find them, Detective."

Twenty-Eight

A frown wrinkled Esther's forehead, and she huffed a soft sigh as a chime penetrated her dreamless sleep. Blinking slowly, she stared at the wall across from her couch, disoriented for a moment before her brain registered the noise. It was her phone, which she'd left on the coffee table after she'd come downstairs, unable to sleep. She didn't remember nodding off.

Esther sat up and reached for the phone. Her sister's face was displayed on the screen. She answered the call. "Hello?"

"So, we have a bit of a problem. Well, not a problem. Not exactly. More a change in plans."

Leaning forward, elbows on her knees, Esther scrubbed a hand over her face. "What?"

"The guys are back, but they're all getting sick."

"Sick? What?" She groaned. That was just... great.

"Yeah. It started with Max. A bit of a cough, fatigue. Now he's spiked a fever. Sam has one, too, and the rest of them are starting to get that throat tickle that says it's coming. Margot and Annabeth think it's the flu."

Esther groaned. "How did they get the flu?"

"Probably from Margot's girls. With the clinic build in full swing, she's had them with a sitter. They aren't the only kids there, and they were sick last week. Max thought he'd avoided it, but apparently not."

"Great. So what are we going to do?"

"I have a plan. Ezra's not sick. He didn't go on the fishing trip. Amy's pregnant again, and her morning sickness is ten times worse than mine. Margot's not sick, either, so she's going to keep an eye on her and everyone else while he flies the rest of us up there to you."

"The rest—" Esther paused, frowning. "Who are you talking about?"

"The girls. Me, Audra, Brooke, and Annabeth."

Esther groaned. "I know you've done some bodyguard stuff, but this is different."

"And it's nothing we can't handle. Audra's a former spy. Brooke has resources coming out her ears. Annabeth can be our go between with Dean and his investigative prowess while he's laid up. We've got this. Now, I need to go pack. We'll be there in less than twelve hours. Probably like nine. It's close to eight hours in the air and we're leaving very soon."

"Um." Esther ran a hand over her face and through her hair, her still sleepy brain trying to process everything. "Okay."

"Everything is going to be fine, Essy. We'll find them. Oh, one more thing. Audra said she's going to call someone to help us with the tech side of things, so that person might call you while we're in the air."

"Oh. All right. Do you have a name or anything?"

"No. Just answer your phone, no matter what."

A yawn stole over Esther's face. "I will."

"Good. I'll see you soon."

"Yep. Thanks, Edie." An ache bloomed in her chest. She didn't know what she'd do without her sister.

"You're welcome."

They bid each other farewell and hung up.

Esther set the phone down and leaned on her elbows, covering her face. She liked Edie's confidence, but she also knew that the guys worked as a well-oiled team. Audra and Brooke might have great resources, but the issue was lining up those resources in a timely fashion, so the investigation didn't stall.

She huffed and dropped her hands. There was no use worrying about it. She couldn't control any of it or magically make the guys feel better. The circumstances were what they were, and they needed to use them the best they could.

Pushing to her feet, she went into the kitchen to make some coffee. Sleep wasn't an option, and she couldn't sit around and do nothing. But she wasn't sure what to do, exactly.

What Asher said about how Rob Tyler couldn't be Leah's father rumbled around in her brain. Maybe she could dig into Connie's past. And Leah's. There were probably news articles about the girl. She remembered hearing about fundraisers for her—had contributed to some. She'd start there. It might end up being a dead end, but she couldn't just sit idle.

While the coffeepot gurgled, she ran upstairs to grab her laptop. Computer and steaming mug of coffee in hand, she parked herself on the couch again and opened her web browser.

And stared.

She didn't know what to type. Information gathering wasn't her thing. Not like this. She surfed the web for art projects and gourmet coffee. Not dirt on a past someone didn't want found.

Esther sucked in a breath and held it for a moment. What would Asher do? Where would he start?

She let the air out of her lungs and tapped the keyboard with her nails. Social media?

It could work. If Connie had a presence there.

Only one way to find out.

Esther logged into one of her social media accounts and typed Connie's name into the search bar. A list populated, but none of the profile pictures looked like Connie Tyler. She tried Leah's name, hoping there was a page dedicated to supporting her transplant journey.

An icon with a ribbon around a heart caught her eye. "Bingo."

She clicked on it. Leah's smiling face stared back at her. Esther cruised through the list of people following the page; most were teachers or other people in their community. There were some she didn't recognize.

She set the laptop down and got up to retrieve paper and a pen. She'd go through them and write down the ones that might warrant further investigation.

Once she finished with that platform, she logged into another and did the same thing. On the third and fourth ones, she didn't find any info on Connie or Leah. But she'd gathered a small list from the others. It probably wouldn't pan out to anything, but she felt productive.

With the social media platforms scoured, Esther paused, tapping at the keyboard again. She wasn't sure what to do next.

The AI button in the corner of the page caught her eye, and an idea struck her. Couldn't those things search by picture?

She clamped her teeth down on her bottom lip. Maybe she could find a family photo.

Pulling up a search engine, she typed Leah's name and their town into the search bar. A local news article popped up, and she clicked on it.

"Yes!" she hissed, seeing the image that appeared. Saving it to her computer, she cropped it so only Connie's face appeared, then went back to the search engine and used the AI image search tool. It was a long shot, but she could get lucky.

Her phone chimed.

"Oh!" She jumped, startled by the sudden noise, jostling the computer. At least she hadn't been taking a drink.

Esther leaned forward and picked up the phone, her heart hammering in her chest. An international number appeared. "Whoa. Who did you call, Audra?" She slid her thumb over the screen and answered it. "Hello?"

"Hi. Is this Esther Campbell?" The lilting, female British voice sounded pleasant and kind.

"Yes."

"Brilliant. My name is Jo Richardson. Audra asked me to call you. Fill me in. I got the basics from her, but she said you have all the particulars."

"I guess so. What do you want to know?"

"Start from the beginning. It'll help me build a picture of what's going on and where I need to focus my search."

Esther gave a weary sigh. She was getting tired of recanting this story. But she did it, anyway, starting with what she first told Edie and going all the way through what she heard from the Tinsdales at the pizzeria tonight.

"I was just about to look through the results of the image search I did on a picture I found of the Tylers from a news article," she finished.

"Send that to me. I'll get better results than those pathetic excuses for AI searching." She gave Esther her email address.

Esther chuckled. "I think I like you," she said as she opened her email.

Jo laughed. "While I don't aim to please anyone but myself, I'm glad."

That was a good philosophy to have. It was impossible to please everyone. The only person whose opinion should matter was one's own. Esther felt that if she couldn't live with herself, it was hard to expect others to do the same.

Attaching the full image to an email, Esther clicked send. "There, sent."

"Cheers, thanks. All right, let's see what we've got." A short pause came over the line. "Nice looking family. Poor kid. How's she doing? Health-wise, I mean. I know she's in a spot of bother right now."

"She's been doing well. Her doctors are happy with her progress."

"That's good to hear. My sister had a kidney transplant when she was seventeen. Lupus. It's rough. Okay... let's see."

Esther scrolled through the images on her computer while she waited for Jo. It was a lot of pictures of blonde women. But none of them matched.

"Hmm..."

The note of curiosity in Jo's voice piqued Esther's attention. "What?"

"I'm sending you a picture. Look at it and tell me if you think it looks like Connie Tyler."

"Okay." Esther clicked into her inbox. A moment later, a message arrived. She opened it and clicked on the attachment.

"Did you get it?"

"Yes." Esther tipped her head, staring at the young woman on the screen. And she was young. Late teens. But she looked like Connie. "It looks a lot like her, yes. Who is she, and where did you find that?"

"It's from a social media post on a school web page. She was in a group. There aren't any names. It just says 'French Club.'"

"What school?"

"Pierpoint High School in Pennsylvania."

Esther typed it into her browser and found the web page. "I wonder..." She opened a new tab and let her voice trail off.

"What?"

"So, I have a subscription to a website that contains an online archive of yearbooks. I'm on the reunion committee for my class. Anyway, I'm wondering if her yearbook is on there." She logged into the website.

Jo let out a soft snort. "Love, you missed your calling. That's good thinking."

"Thanks." Esther typed the name of the high school into the search bar. "Is there a year on that post?"

"Yes." Jo read it off.

"Perfect, thank you." Esther added it. Her heart thudded as the screen went blank while the search started. When it refreshed, a list for the school appeared. She let out a soft squeal. "We're in business. Okay. Going back fifteen to twenty years..." She scrolled, then clicked on a year. "We're lucky. This isn't a large school." It would still take her a little time to look through all the grades, though.

"What's the name of this website and what's your login information? I can use my software to find a match."

"Oh. That would be faster, yeah. Okay." She gave Jo the information. Through the phone, she heard a flurry of typing.

"We just need to give it a minute to work. The news article picture is a good one, so hopefully—wait."

Esther sat up at the note of interest in Jo's voice. "What? Did you find something?"

"I think so. I'll send you this. It looks like her name is Lindy Nieman." More typing ensued, then, "Hmm... That's interesting."

"What is?" Jo was killing her with all the vague lead-ins.

"Her parents were murdered almost eleven years ago. She disappeared, and the police assumed that whoever killed them killed her too."

A deep frown pulled Esther's eyebrows down. "Whoa. They didn't suspect her of doing it?"

"No, it doesn't look like it. Hang on. I'm reading news articles on it."

Esther huffed. She could do that.

Annoyed at being out of the loop, she typed "Nieman murders Pennsylvania" into her web browser and clicked on the first article that came up.

"This says they found blood from a third person at the scene. Lindy's. Enough of it for the cops to think she'd been gravely injured."

"Hence the theory she was killed too." Esther skimmed her article. It didn't mention the blood, but it talked about how the mail carrier found the bodies the next day. Apparently, the front door had been left a jar and there was blood smeared on the doorjamb.

"So, maybe she witnessed the murders, was wounded herself, and then ran?" Jo surmised. "This article says they dredged the lake behind her parents' property for her body, but didn't find it. Doesn't mean it's not there, though. If she was disoriented from blood loss, she could have stumbled right into it."

"Maybe." But Esther couldn't help but think about how Rob Tyler wasn't Leah's biological father. Who was? Did that person have something to do with Lindy's parents' deaths? News articles weren't going to tell her any of that. Detective Stroud wouldn't like it, but she needed to talk to Connie.

"I'll keep digging into this girl. See what else I can turn up," Jo said. "Is there anything else you want me to look into?"

"Um, not now, no."

"Okay. If you need me, call me at this number or send me a quick email. I might not answer the phone if I'm busy with something, but I will let you know right away that I got your message."

"All right. Thank you, Jo. I appreciate it."

"Of course. Asher's my friend too. I want to find him as much as anyone."

Esther highly doubted that. What she felt for Asher went far beyond friendship. So, unless Jo and Asher had a similar relationship in the past, Jo's concern didn't hold a candle to Esther's. Her heart was bruised and bleeding. Every moment without him was another chunk of it being lopped off.

Clearing her throat, Esther tried to make herself sound not so depressed. "He's lucky to have so many friends who care. I'll let you know—or Audra will—if we need anything else."

"Sounds good. Please keep me updated on things?"

"Of course."

"Cheers, thanks. Bye."

"Bye." Esther hung up. Taking a moment to process the conversation, she stared blankly at her computer screen. A smiling Lindy Nieman stared back at her. Dressed in a yellow cap and gown, she was sandwiched between her parents. They looked like a quintessential happy family. Esther couldn't help but wonder what went wrong. How did the parents end up murdered? Why did Lindy run?

She sat back, bringing the computer with her and balancing it on her thighs. Jo wouldn't be the only one doing some digging.

Twenty-Nine

"You look like hell."

Esther rolled her eyes and stepped back to admit her sister and her friends into the house. "Thanks, Edie. It's good to see you too. Love you."

"You know what I mean." Edie answered Esther's snarkiness with an eye roll of her own, then hugged her tight. "Did you sleep at all?" she asked as she let go.

"After I talked to you? No. I did a little before that, but only a couple of hours." She glanced past her sister at Audra. "Your contact called. We made some headway."

"Brilliant. Let us dump our stuff and we'll go over things and come up with a plan, yeah?"

Esther nodded. "Edie can stay in my room with me; two of you can take Asher's room, and one of you can sleep down here."

"I'll take the sofa," Audra said.

"That works." Edie headed for the stairs. "Essy, did you change bedsheets yet?"

"No."

"Okay. I'll grab a set from the linen closet for the spare

room. Brooke, Annabeth, if you want to come with me, I'll show you where you'll be sleeping."

While they went upstairs, Esther turned to Audra. "You can stow your bag in the corner over there, if you want. Or we can put it in the laundry room."

"Wherever. I'm not picky."

"That corner is fine." Esther pointed to a spot by the front window. "The laundry room is kind of tight."

"Sounds good." Audra walked over and deposited her bag. "So, what did you and Jo discover?"

"Connie Tyler's real identity."

Audra's eyes widened. "Seriously? It was that easy?"

"With facial recognition and AI, yes."

"That makes me worry about the future of undercover work. I'm glad I'm out of that game."

Esther plopped back down on the couch, sinking into the cushions. "How is normal life treating you?" Audra had retired from her job with Britain's Secret Intelligence Service just a few months ago.

Following Esther's lead, Audra sat in the recliner. "It's been an adjustment. I'm not used to having so much free time. Though Brooke's been keeping me busy."

"That's right. Edie mentioned Brooke asked you to head up security for the new resort."

"All I can say is, I'm glad I have Sam and the others to help me implement the security system. Once the place is up and running, I can see myself in charge of day-to-day operations. But the actual system? That's not my forte. She hired an outside consultant too."

"She's aiming for next year, right?"

"Yeah. June. The building's exterior is done. So are the private cabins. It's all interior work now and hiring staff."

Esther couldn't wait to see it. Knowing Brooke, it would be elegant and luxurious, but affordable. The woman was as rich as Midas, but she was down-to-earth. She wanted the resort to be for everyone.

Clatter on the stairs drew her attention. Edie, Brooke, and Annabeth rounded the corner from the short hallway.

"All settled?" Esther asked.

"Yes," Edie replied. "Fill us in. What did you find out?"

Esther stood, picking up her laptop from the coffee table before walking over to the island. She opened it. "So, I found a family photo of the Tylers from a news article. Jo ran an image search on it and found a match to Connie Tyler from a social media picture at high school in Pennsylvania that's a good fifteen years old. There were no names with the picture, but because I'm one of those planning types and am on every committee under the sun, including my class reunion committee, I have a subscription to a yearbook website. Jo searched it and we found her. Connie's real name is Lindy Nieman. Her parents were murdered just shy of eleven years ago. The police thought she'd been killed, too, but dumped elsewhere. Her body was never found."

Brooke scoffed. "Because she's been living under an assumed name. Are we sure she didn't murder them?"

"I mean, it's possible." Esther lifted a shoulder. "She probably would have just found out she was pregnant. Maybe they didn't want her to keep the baby? I don't know why, though. She was an adult at the time. Just out of college. I don't think she killed them, though. The police found a significant amount of her blood at the scene. I think she was wounded, maybe left for dead. Or she was wounded, taken, and then escaped."

"I think we should talk to her," Annabeth said. "Go straight to the source and get answers."

Brooke chuckled. "Dean's rubbing off on you."

"Well, it worked when we looked into my sister's death." Annabeth shrugged.

"I agree with you," Audra said. "Having her daughter missing, and the fact that we already know who she is, will probably make her more willing to talk."

"Then let's go." Esther closed the laptop. Stroud would just have to deal with her interfering. If she shared this info with him and he tried to take over, Connie might clam up. Especially if she'd been involved in her parents' deaths. Esther didn't care about that. She just wanted to find Asher and Leah.

The group filed out the door and into the SUV Edie rented at the airport. Esther gave her sister directions to Leah's house.

As they turned down the Tylers' street minutes later, Audra let out a soft groan. "Crap. I was afraid of that." She peered through the window, gaze fixed on the police car parked in the driveway.

"How do we get past them?" Brooke asked. "We can't just waltz up there and knock. I mean, we can, but I doubt we'll get inside. And even if we do, the cops will want to listen in. Do we want that?"

"No," Esther said. "She might not talk if the police are involved."

"Essy, do you think you could talk your way in?" Edie asked as she drove past the house. "She knows you."

"Maybe. But you and Audra might ask better questions."

"You did pretty well on digging up dirt on your own," Brooke said.

"Only because I had Jo's help. It was talking to her that got me thinking."

"Okay, so we need to lure her away or sneak in." Audra frowned, a thoughtful wrinkle to her forehead.

"Or you do what you do best." Edie grinned.

Esther groaned. "What are you thinking?"

Edie lifted a shoulder. "Audra, you spent a lot of time pretending to be someone else."

"And?"

"So, what if Esther goes in? Just to offer sympathy. But once she's past the cop, she convinces Connie to play along with what's about to happen."

"What do you want to do?" Annabeth asked.

"We pretend we're Connie's co-workers, and we heard about Leah. We've come to offer support. Audra can lie us past the cop."

"That sounds good." Audra leaned forward. "Circle the block and park. You should go in with Esther, though. The police officer might recognize you. It'll make more sense for you to be with your sister. He or she will know you're not Connie's co-worker if they recognize you."

"Good point." Edie stopped at the stop sign and made a right-hand turn. "Everyone in agreement?"

A chorus of "Yes" echoed through the car.

"Awesome."

They circled the block, and parked down the street, out of view of the Tylers' front windows. She and Esther got out and walked down the sidewalk.

"You good to do this?" Edie asked. "I know you don't like lying."

"In this case, I'll make an exception. We have to find them." Her voice broke, and she blinked furiously to keep the tears at bay. She'd cry later.

Edie stopped her with a hand on her arm. Esther looked at her, still battling back tears.

"Oh!" Edie's eyes widened. "You fell for him, didn't you? I hoped this would happen." A wide smile wreathed her face.

"I know you did. But now is not the time to discuss it. None of it will matter if we don't find him." Esther marched away, hanging onto her emotions by a thread.

She so missed Asher's smile and his quick wit. It still boggled her mind how hard and fast she'd fallen for him. But it shouldn't surprise her. The man was brilliant and funny, but most importantly, kind. He had a heart of gold and wouldn't hesitate to do anything he could to help someone. He just checked all the boxes for what she wanted in a partner. The last couple of days without him, all she'd been able to do was think about their time together. Her mind had analyzed all the little details and every flicker of a feeling that had passed through her heart since he'd arrived. It hadn't been terribly hard to recognize she'd fallen in love with him.

Heart aching, she walked up the Tylers' front steps and knocked on the door, Edie close behind. Buster barked from deep inside the house. The officer who answered was one Esther recognized. She'd gone to school with Landon Garner.

"Esther? What are you doing here?" His gaze traveled past her, taking in Edie standing at the bottom of the steps, and his frown deepened.

"Hi, Landon. I heard about Leah and her dad. She's my student. I came to talk to Mrs. Tyler."

"I'm not supposed to let anyone in."

"Why not? Is Mrs. Tyler a suspect?"

"No. Detective Stroud didn't say why. Probably so we don't upset her."

"How about you ask her if she'll talk to me?"

"I can pass along a message."

"Officer Garner? Who's at the door?"

Esther leaned around Landon at the sound of Connie's voice. "It's me, Mrs. Tyler. Esther Campbell. Leah's teacher."

"Let her in," Connie said, walking closer, holding Buster. The dog's bark turned to a whine, and he wiggled in her arms as he saw who'd come to visit.

"Ma'am—"

"I'm not a prisoner, Officer Garner. And this is my house. Either let her in, or I'm going out."

Landon sighed and stepped back.

Esther didn't hesitate. She hurried in and quickly took charge, fretting over Connie like the best church grandma in existence.

"How are you holding up? I can only imagine how you're feeling." She wrapped an arm around Connie's shoulders and steered her toward the kitchen, giving Buster a quick scratch. The dog licked her hand. "We should have some tea and chat."

She glanced back, spearing Landon with a look as he attempted to follow Edie. "Would you mind giving us some privacy? I'm sure we'd all like to unload some stress without a stranger listening in—no offense."

His mouth flattened, but he nodded. "I'll be in the living room if you need me, Mrs. Tyler."

Esther didn't give Connie a chance to respond. She ushered her through the kitchen door to the small table.

"Rob never mentioned you were so pushy."

"I'm not normally. We need to talk."

Walls went up in Connie's eyes, and her shoulders went back.

"Have a seat." Esther gestured to the table.

Edie crossed to the cabinets and started opening them. "Where do you keep your tea? Or would you rather have coffee?"

Esther knew what her sister was doing; she was giving legitimacy to Esther's spiel for Landon's benefit. Edie could also see the living room from where she stood. He wouldn't be able to eavesdrop if he couldn't get close enough without being seen. She just hoped he didn't call Stroud.

"I've had enough coffee to keep me awake for the rest of my life," Connie said. "Tea is in the skinny cupboard by the fridge. Mugs are to the left of that. What's going on?"

Esther and Edie shared a look, then Esther decided to just rip the bandaid off. "We know who you are."

The walls in Connie's eyes slipped, letting panic shine through loud and clear.

Esther held up a hand. "We won't tell anyone. In a minute, some of our friends are going to knock on your door, pretending to be concerned co-workers. You're going to convince Landon to let them in, then we're going to have a frank discussion about who took your daughter and our friend Asher." She motioned between herself and Edie. "We know you had your reasons for running all those years ago, but you need to come clean. It might be the only way we find them."

Connie's panic turned to despair. "It wasn't supposed to be like this," she whispered.

"We're going to fix it," Esther promised. She nodded to Edie, silently telling her to text Audra.

"No." Connie shook her head. "No one can."

"Honey, you don't know me and my friends." Edie looked up after sending the text. "You lucked out getting Esther as Leah's teacher. She knows people. Including me."

Connie stayed silent, the set to her shoulders and the thinly veiled panic in her eyes saying she didn't believe them. Esther couldn't do anything about that right now. She'd need convincing, and the only way to do it was to just get on with things.

Edie filled the teakettle with water and set it on the stove to heat. It had barely warmed when there was another knock on the door.

Buster barked and squirmed in Connie's arms.

"He's getting up," Edie said, watching Landon.

Murmurs reached them a few seconds later.

"Connie? Sweetie, it's Audra from work. We're all just worried sick about you and your family."

Esther bit back a smile at Audra's Americanized voice. She nudged Connie and tipped her head toward the door.

The other woman stared at her for a moment, a flash of defiance in her eyes, but soon stood. "This better be worth it." She put Buster outside in the backyard, then exited the kitchen.

"Poor Landon," Esther murmured, getting up to stand in the doorway with Edie.

"I almost feel sorry for him. But he shouldn't have been put in this position," Edie said.

Esther agreed. Stroud was being rather protective. Maybe he'd noticed Connie's hesitation when answering his questions last night too.

Landon glared at the group of women as they traipsed inside. He gave the door a toss behind Annabeth, and it shut with a little more force than necessary. Esther stepped back as Connie led the others into the kitchen.

"Hello," Esther said, holding out a hand. "I'm Esther, Leah's teacher. This is my sister, Edie." They needed to make this look legit. Landon would question things if they seemed to know each other right off the bat.

"I'm Audra. These are my friends, Brooke and Annabeth."

"We were about to have some tea. Would you like to join us?" Edie asked.

"That would be lovely," Audra said.

With pleasantries exchanged, they moved deeper into the kitchen.

"Tell me what's going on," Connie said, keeping her voice low as they settled around the table. Edie stayed near the stove and Annabeth leaned against the wall while the others sat.

"Esther, you start," Audra said, dropping the accent.

Connie's eyes widened at the transformation. "Who are you people?"

"We'll get to that," Esther said. "But I'm going to start at the beginning, okay?"

The woman nodded.

"When I took this job, it was for the extra money. I didn't give a thought to where it was or anything like that. But—and I don't mean any offense—you don't live in the greatest neighborhood. Being here sometimes gave me the heebie-jeebies, and I told Edie that. My sister is a former Army officer. She lives in Costa Rica now, which is why I wanted the extra cash; so I could go see her more. Anyway, she's one of several former military and government agent-type people who live in the same area down there. Remember how I said last night I was concerned about someone lurking outside your house and mine?"

Connie nodded.

"Asher is a friend of Edie's from Costa Rica. When I mentioned to her what was going on, she got concerned and talked to him about it. He's a former intelligence analyst. The man can find information buried beneath layers and layers of red tape and hogwash." Esther lowered her voice. "He discovered some discrepancies in Leah's birth certificate and your identity. It was enough to make him come up here as a favor to her."

Connie shot out of her chair, her eyes flashing with panicked rage. "I knew it was his fault! You two brought this upon us!"

Esther stood and patted the air. "Please keep your voice down, Mrs. Tyler."

"Everything okay in here?" Landon appeared in the doorway.

Balling her fists, Esther kept her back to him and silently implored Connie to assure him they were fine.

The woman stared at her for a long moment, then glanced at Landon. "We're fine. I'm just upset about Leah."

"Maybe you all should go. Give her some space."

"No, they're fine," Connie said. "I'm fine. You can go back to the living room."

He rested a hand on the butt of his holster and tapped his fingers as he studied her. "All right. If you're sure?"

"I am." She seemed to shrink in on herself as she crossed her arms, clutching her sleeves.

With a quick nod and another long look at the group, he walked away.

Esther looked at Edie, waiting for her to signal they were safe to continue their discussion. After a moment, Edie nodded once.

"Let's sit back down." Esther motioned Connie to sit in her chair.

Her expression still wary and angry, Connie lowered herself to the seat.

"Asher and I didn't do anything to trigger someone coming after you. Whoever it is, was already here. I think we got in their way, which is why Asher was taken."

"You said you know who I am," Connie whispered.

"Yeah. Last night, one of Audra's contacts and I dug into your family. We found some old photographs and tracked you down with your high school yearbook. We know your real name is Lindy Nieman."

All the color bled from Connie's face. She grasped the edge of the table, her knuckles turning white with her grip. She closed her eyes for a moment and a tear trickled out. "I haven't heard that name or even thought of myself as that woman in so long."

"What happened?" Annabeth asked softly. "Why did you run away and change your identity?"

"Because Leah's father is a sick son of a bitch. I didn't discover that until it was too late. I was already pregnant." She sat back, wiping at her face with her sleeve, then crossed her arms. "Bradley and I met in college. We were both engineering majors. But he—he was on another level. Like MacGyver, almost. He was always making something out of nothing. I found him fascinating. And handsome. We'd been dating for several months and things seemed fine. He was a little possessive, but nothing terrible. It wasn't until we got close to graduation that his demeanor changed. He started coming up with excuses why we couldn't go visit my parents or making plans for us when he knew I had plans with friends. If I pushed back, he'd guilt me into canceling what I wanted to do and into doing whatever he wanted."

"What did your friends and family say?" Brooke asked.

"They told me he was being controlling, but didn't push the issue too much. At least, my friends didn't. My parents were more vocal about it. Especially after I found out I was pregnant. That's why I was at their house."

"Did Bradley know about the baby?" Audra asked.

"No. I knew something about our relationship wasn't right, even if I didn't want to admit it to myself." She glanced down at her hands in her lap, picking at a catch on her fingernail for a moment before she looked up again and answered. "When I suspected I was pregnant, I took the test in a bathroom at school and left it in the trash there. A couple of days later, he had to work late. I didn't have a car. He'd convinced me we could save up for a house faster if we only had one car payment, so I sold mine. I typically didn't go anywhere I couldn't walk or ride a bike to when he was working, but that day, I called my parents and asked if they would pay for a taxi to drive me the two hours to their house. They said yes without hesitation. I packed up my stuff and left." Shifting, Connie wrapped an arm around her waist and raised the other, her fingers covering her mouth.

The teakettle whistled. Edie shut it off, then busied herself making several cups while Connie continued.

"When I got there, I told them what was going on and that I was scared. As much as I didn't want to be pregnant or to have any sort of connection to Bradley moving forward, I couldn't bring myself to have an abortion. I wanted Leah from the moment I found out about her." Her face crumpled, but she quickly drew in a breath and swiped at the moisture on her face again. "Mom and Dad told me they'd do whatever they could to support me and the baby. I went to bed that night still scared, but at least I had some hope."

"He figured out where you went, didn't he?" Edie's voice was quiet.

Again, Connie nodded. "Yeah. He showed up about twelve-thirty that night. Made a racket, banging on the door. Dad answered it to tell him to go away. I hung back, but I could see him. There was a wildness about Bradley I'd never seen before. He was completely unhinged. When he refused to leave, Dad said he'd call the police, then tried to shut the door. Bradley kicked it open. Dad—" she broke off with a choked sob. "Dad fell back, landed on the floor. Mom rushed over to help him up, and I ran forward to try to make Bradley back off. He shoved me, and I hit my head on the corner of the foyer table on the way down. It tore up a big flap of my scalp and made me black out. Just for a minute." She indicated the side of her head.

Edie handed her a cup of tea. Connie wrapped her fingers around it, but didn't drink.

"When I came to, he had a small statue—a cast of my parents' hands—in one hand and was using it to hit my mom. My dad was already lying in a pool of blood."

Brooke gasped, and she and Annabeth both covered the lower half of their faces. Esther's stomach turned.

"I knew I had to get out, or I was next. While he was"— she swallowed hard—"distracted, I picked up my mom's keys and purse and slipped out the open front door. I just drove. No idea where to go. Bleeding."

"Why didn't you go to the police?" Brooke asked.

"Because I was terrified I wouldn't win. That they'd believe *him*. And then—if I wasn't arrested for their murders —that I'd end up right back in the same place. Under Bradley's thumb. Except then it would be our child, too, who he could control. I—I just couldn't."

"How did you become Connie Tyler?" Audra asked. "Changing your identity isn't something most people know how to do. Especially young women who come from good families. They never have a reason to know people who know how to do that."

"Short answer? I got lucky. After I fled, I drove for a couple of hours with a sweater I found in the backseat pressed to the side of my head. Once I finally felt like I'd put enough distance between myself and... and..." She flip-flopped a hand. "Anyway, I stopped at a rest area and used the first aid kit in my mom's car to clean myself up enough to not scare people, then I put on a jacket my mom left in her car, went inside, and cleaned up some more. I needed gas and caffeine, so I got back on the road and stopped not long after at an all-night gas station. The clerk there was some older, curmudgeonly type of man. He took one look at me and knew something was wrong." She rolled her lips in, pressing them together for a moment before continuing.

"Drake Camden and his wife, Carlie, saved my life that day. And Leah's. Somehow, he convinced me to come into the back to their breakroom. While I sipped on water and snacked on some crackers, he called his wife, who was a retired nurse. She showed up and got enough out of me to know I wasn't in a good place. I know it was dumb to trust strangers, but something kept whispering that I could trust them. Carlie took me back to her house, stitched me up, got me into some clean clothes, and let me sleep."

Connie twirled the tea mug in her hands, staring at it without seeing it. "When I woke up the next morning, I thought for sure they'd demand answers, but they didn't. They told me I was welcome to stay as long as I needed. It only took me a couple of days to decide I wanted to tell them the truth. I needed help to stay away from Bradley, and they deserved to know who I was after being so kind."

"So they know who you are?" Audra asked. "The old you and the new you?"

"Yes."

"Are they still living?" Edie asked.

"Yes. As far as I know." Connie moistened her lips and tapped her nails on her cup. "After I told them what happened and how I didn't want to go back, Drake called in some favors. He'd run with a rough crowd for a while when he was younger and still knew people. One of his buddies was really good at forgery, and he created a new identity for me. I've used it ever since, and it's always held up, even on our taxes and when I married Rob."

"Was he a friend of Drake's too?" Brooke asked.

"Sort of. He's the son of a friend. Rob needed some stability in his life after he got out of prison, and I needed someone who'd not only be willing to defend me and my child, but could help provide for her. I was terrified to use my degree, since Bradley's in the same field, so I've never worked anywhere that needed beyond a high school education. But that meant we were living near the poverty level. I could barely make ends meet. There were no extras in our lives, and I didn't take any unnecessary time off work. That worked fine until Leah got sick." She ran her thumb along the edge of her cup.

"Five years ago, she contracted a simple bacterial infection, but it somehow made it to her heart. I couldn't afford to take time off work, but she had to have treatment or she'd die. I was desperate, so I called Drake and Carlie. That's when Drake mentioned Rob."

"So you just married a man you didn't know?" Brooke gave her a curious frown.

"I did it for Leah. I met with Rob once before I agreed and laid out everything. That it would be in name only, and that he'd help take care of Leah. He was in a bad place and needed a fresh start. I knew it was a gamble, but I didn't see any other way. I know he's not the friendliest man, but there was something in his eyes when we met. He was as desperate as I was. So, we agreed to let Drake's friend put his name on Leah's birth certificate. I introduced him to Leah as her father, then we got married."

"She doesn't know Rob's not her biological father?" Annabeth asked.

"No. I never talked about her dad, and she never asked. She was only four at the time, so she wasn't asking too many questions yet. Honestly, if this hadn't happened, I would have never told her. Rob's been good to us. He completely turned his life around and became the husband and father we needed. I'm truly grateful for all he's done." Her face crumpled and a cascade of tears ran down her face.

Esther covered one of Connie's hands. "I'm sorry. How's he doing? We never asked."

"It's touch and go. He's sedated in the ICU. I wish I could be there, but the police want me at home in case the kidnapper contacts me." She snorted. "But if it really is Bradley, he won't. I'll never see Leah again."

"That won't happen," Edie said. "Not with us involved. You didn't see his face last night?"

Connie shook her head. "No. He had a hood up and a baseball cap underneath, and he never spoke. The build was right, though. And there's one other thing."

"What?" A curious frown dipped Esther's eyebrows.

"Leah's medications are gone."

Esther's eyes rounded. She glanced at Edie and their friends.

"You're sure?" Audra asked.

Connie nodded. "When I got home, I noticed Buster didn't come running. He was outside, and we didn't put him out there before we left. It put me on alert, so I went through the house quick. That's when I noticed her meds were gone. Some of her clothes are missing too."

"Did you tell the police this?"

"No." Connie hung her head. "I didn't want them to ask too many questions or start digging too deep into my past. But I think that's inevitable now."

Most likely, Esther agreed. "Okay, so where do we go from here?" She turned to Audra and Edie. "We're assuming Bradley is behind this, yes? Especially with the fact the medications are missing?"

The two women shared a look. Esther frowned, sensing they had something to say she wouldn't like.

"Yes," Audra said. "But we also don't want to discount other possibilities."

"Such as?" Esther raised an eyebrow, unsure what other possibilities there could be.

"That this is about you," Audra said.

Esther's other eyebrow joined the first one, and they both arched higher. "What? Why would it be about me? Why would Leah be involved?"

"I was mulling this over on the plane ride here," Audra glanced at Edie, whom Esther didn't think looked surprised by the turn in the conversation. "It's possible someone is obsessed with you. It could be Bradley, or it could be someone else entirely. Asher was in the way, so the guy took him out. As for Leah, Edie and I think he could be trying to create a family for you. Or using her as a lure, so you're a more willing participant."

"No." Esther sat back and stared at Audra, then her sister. "No. Because if that's true, Asher's probably already dead, and I can't accept that." The ache in her chest that had been present since Asher disappeared grew two sizes, opening a yawning hole in her heart. He couldn't be dead. She refused to believe it.

"None of us want him to be dead," Edie said. "But we need to consider the possibility."

"You can consider it all you want. I refuse." Esther pushed back from the table and stood. She needed to get out of the house and get some space before she exploded. Without another word, she spun on her heel and left.

THIRTY

Asher shifted, trying to get comfortable propped up against the wall on Leah's cot. The girl had been sleeping a lot, which worried him a bit. He didn't know if that was normal for her. Their captor had left her meds at the top of the stairs with their food this morning, but Asher was worried she was getting sick. The dampness wasn't ideal for her already suppressed immune system. It would just bring it down more. Not to mention their environment exposed her to a host of bacteria she wasn't used to.

He glanced at the window set high into the wall, attempting to gauge the time. His smart watch was missing, along with his phone. Their kidnapper was savvy enough to know someone could track Asher through both devices. It also kept him guessing about the time of day. Once it got dark, he planned to camp out near the top of the steps and ambush the guy when he brought them dinner and Leah's evening medicine. He wished he had a weapon, but there was nothing down here except their beds and the toilet paper in the small bathroom tucked under the stairs.

Leah moaned softly in her sleep and snuggled deeper into

his side. Asher brushed the hair away from her face. She was cool to the touch, which encouraged him. Maybe it was just her brain's way of coping with the situation.

It would be nice if his did the same, but he'd had the opposite reaction. He barely slept last night. He couldn't help but wonder who had taken them and why. How it was tied to Esther. Asher could understand his abduction with her involved, but not Leah's. It made more sense that this was about Leah. But why was Esther involved? Why was he? Because they were in the way? But how would the guy know that? Asher hadn't been involved until recently, and the guy had been around long before that.

A long breath left his chest. He'd been thinking in circles all night. It wasn't getting him anywhere, and he had a headache from it. The only saving grace was he knew Esther would have called Edie by now. That meant Ford and everyone else were involved. Asher was confident they would find them.

Leah moaned again, a little louder. Asher picked her up and put her on his lap, tucking her into his chest and rocking her slowly.

Once more, he said a prayer the girl wasn't getting sick. He tacked on another that his friends found him before anything bad happened.

THIRTY-ONE

Esther retreated to her bedroom when they returned to her house. Audra was going to call Jo and have her look into Connie's ex, Bradley. Until they had more information, there wasn't anything they could do. And Esther needed some time alone. Her sister and friends had followed her outside not long after she'd walked out. She'd sat in the passenger seat on the way back and stared out the window, giving single-word answers as she grappled with her feelings. She didn't want to deal with them. It hurt to think about what Asher could be going through. And despite her refusal to consider he might be dead, the thought had crossed her mind. It was like a spear to the gut. Her insides twisted up, and she couldn't breathe.

Throwing herself onto the bed, she stared at the ceiling. A cloud of scent enveloped her. Asher's scent. She should have asked Edie to change her sheets too. Her interlude with Asher might have only lasted a few days, but they'd spent every night together in her bed. She was thankful the rest of the house didn't hold his scent. The memories were bad enough.

The tears she'd been holding back finally burst free. A guttural sob slipped past her lips. She turned and buried her face in her pillow. Asher's scent hit her again, stronger, and the torrent of emotions and tears hit harder.

For several minutes, she sobbed into the material. When the bed dipped and a hand touched her shoulder, she turned and saw her sister through watery eyes.

Edie crawled up next to her and wrapped Esther in her arms. "Shh. He's fine. It takes a lot to kill one of the Wagner Brigade. Asher might not be former military, but he's not defenseless. I mean, he's been living with us all these years and gets roped into our sparring sessions regularly."

Esther continued to cry on Edie's shoulder, listening to her soft, soothing voice. She hadn't lost hope that he was alive, but the fear was there. It felt good to get it out.

Slowly, her tears stopped and her sobs turned to hiccups and sniffles.

"Feel better?" Edie asked.

"Yeah." Esther sat up and wiped her face with her sleeve. "Sorry."

"Don't be. You care about him. You're allowed to be upset."

Esther bobbed her head. "Still. It just hit me. And once the tears started, I couldn't stop them. I guess they needed to run their course. How are you not a blubbering mess? I'm not the hormonal one." Edie was remarkably calm. Considering the worrywart she'd been lately, it seemed strange.

"I'm in my element. Delving into issues like this, finding solutions—it's what I do. That it's Asher involved just drives me more. I'm definitely worried, but the doer side of me is keeping the worrier side in check." She gave Esther's shoulders a quick squeeze. "Come on. We're going to do a Zoom call with Dean. See if he's up to some research."

Taking another swipe at her face, Esther scooted toward the edge of the bed. "Can you give me a couple minutes? I want to splash some cold water on my face."

Edie offered her a soft smile. "Sure. We'll be down in the living room when you're ready."

"Thank you."

"Of course." Edie reached over and enveloped her in a tight hug. "I love you, Essy. We'll find him. Leah too."

Esther hugged her back, but remained silent. She didn't trust herself to speak without descending into a blubbery mess again.

Edie left, and Esther walked down the hall to the bathroom. She had to keep her gaze on the mirror and not look at the vanity. Asher's toothbrush, deodorant, and razor decorated the countertop.

Teeth clenched, she wet a washcloth and pressed it to her face, letting the coolness sink in and soothe her red, puffy eyes. Once she felt semi-presentable, she hung the cloth on the towel bar to dry and went downstairs.

Annabeth handed her a cup of tea as she sat down. "It's herbal," she said. "I thought you might like it to calm your thoughts."

"Thank you." Esther took it with a soft smile.

"Okay, are we ready?" Audra sat down and picked up the television remote. When no one objected, she switched on the TV, then connected her computer to the larger screen. The Zoom window popped up, Dean's name in the middle of it as the call connected. A moment later, Margot's face appeared.

"Margot?" Annabeth frowned at the TV. "Where's Dean?"

"Puking in the bathroom. You all *owe me*. Big time. I am on my own with two wild two-year-olds and five grown men who are in the midst of the flu. Plus, the clinic build hasn't stopped just because everyone's sick. Please tell me you're making headway there and can come home soon?"

"Sort of," Annabeth said. "We need Dean to do some

research, but it sounds like it might be better if we try on our own."

"Are you at Max's house?" Brooke leaned closer, peering at the screen.

"Yes. It was easier to have everyone together, so I could keep an eye on them, and his house is the biggest. The girls have already had it, so it doesn't matter if they're exposed."

"What about you?" Edie asked.

"I'm a doctor. My immune system is as hardy as they come. What does 'sort of' mean, Beth?"

"We have some leads," Audra said. "But don't worry about—"

"Hey, ladies." Ford wandered into the room, looking like he'd gone five rounds with a championship fighter and sounding like he'd spent the night before screaming at a concert.

Brooke gasped when she caught sight of her husband. Esther saw her eyes widen.

"Oh, honey. You look terrible."

"I don't feel any better. Fill me in. What have you all found out?"

"I'd like to know too." Max walked in, looking and sounding much like Ford.

"Should we wait for the others?" Edie asked, arching an eyebrow.

"No." Ford waved a hand, then broke off to cough. "Sam and Jordan are sleeping. Dean's still in the bathroom. Talk before we pass out."

Margot aimed a glare at the men, focusing the majority of it on Max as he sat down next to her. "You should be in bed."

"I'm fine. I need to hear what they have to say."

"Right, let's dig in, shall we?" Audra said.

Esther was thankful the former spy didn't want to waste time. She was starting to feel like Edie, now that she'd had a good cry. The determination to find Asher and Leah was pushing away her urge to curl up and sob again.

"We're good," Max said. "Go."

"So, Esther uncovered Connie's true identity with the help of a former colleague of mine," Audra began. "Her name is Lindy Nieman. Her parents were murdered almost eleven years ago by her former boyfriend—Leah's father. All of this is verified. We just returned from talking to Connie. We have two theories. The first is that it's him, and Asher was just in the way. The second is that it's someone stalking Esther and Leah was taken as an incentive for Esther to cooperate."

"I don't like that one," Max said, then coughed. "It leans more toward Asher being dead."

"Not just that," Ford said. "It's a stretch to think someone would kidnap a child to get to Esther. My money's on the dad."

"Which is where we're focusing for now," Edie said. "We wanted Dean to run some background on him. But, Audra, maybe we can get your friend to do that instead?"

Audra nodded. "I think that's a good idea. Dean could probably do it from bed, but I don't want him to miss something because his brain's foggy."

"Probably a good idea." Ford coughed again. "Any other leads? Car? A description the police can release to the public? Witnesses?"

"Connie said she never saw the man's face or heard him speak, which is why she can't be sure if it was Bradley," Esther said. "I talked to the elderly couple who witnessed the abduction. Herb and Sue Tinsdale. They described a man they saw inside who Herb says was watching the Tylers. Sue's not so sure, but it was enough to get the detective on the case to pull camera footage."

"You need to get that footage," Ford said.

"And do what with it, babe?" Brooke asked. "Asher's the

one who would be able to work his magic on it, but he's not here."

"Give it to that friend of Audra's. I have a feeling this person is a lot like Asher in what they do."

"She is," Audra confirmed.

"Then use her as much as you can. If money's an issue, I'll come up with some funds somewhere."

"It won't be," Audra said. "The only problem will be time. She's busy."

He nodded. "Do the police know about the dad?"

"No," Edie said. "Connie's reluctant to come forward with the information because of what happened to her parents. She's terrified of this guy. Can't say as I blame her. You didn't hear her story. He's—something."

"We did ask her if we could share the information with the police," Annabeth said.

"You did?" Esther gave her a sharp look.

Annabeth nodded. "It was after you left. Right before we joined you outside. Audra asked if she minded if we spoke to the police. She said she'd rather we didn't, but she knew it was all going to come out, anyway, and she wanted Bradley to pay for what he'd done. She said she was ready to come forward and face whatever consequences there were for her, so she agreed. Really, she just wants her daughter back safe and sound. We can do a lot, but we can't do everything. Like put Bradley in jail if he's behind this. She also told us to tell you she's sorry Asher got involved in her family drama. She doesn't think it's likely this is about you any more than Ford does."

The lump in Esther's throat returned, choking off her words. She nodded and pressed her lips together.

"What's Bradley's last name?" Ford asked.

"Lennox."

Esther repeated that in her mind. Connie must have told them that after she left too. She'd never heard it before.

"We'll do some digging here as we're able, but don't count"—he broke off, coughing—"on"—he coughed again—"us." The last word barely made it through. Waving a hand, he got up and left the room.

"He sounds awful," Brooke said.

"They all do," Margot said. "The girls weren't this sick."

"Man-flu is a thing," Annabeth said.

"I know. I just never expected to experience it large-scale."

"We're not that bad," Max said.

She sent him a look, arching an eyebrow. "Says the man who texted me to come hand him the television remote from his dresser."

"I was comfortable all snuggled up. I finally wasn't cold."

Margot rolled her eyes, but a smile toyed with her mouth. She turned to the camera. "I'm hanging up now. When Dean told me you wanted to call, I set the girls up with some paints. I need to go check on them."

Max's eyes widened. "You gave them paint unsupervised? In my house?"

"Relax. They're on the tile in the back living room inside their play yard."

"On the—" He broke off with a hoarse groan. "Margot, that's Saltillo tile. Even washable paint will stick like glue." He stood up, grumbling. "I'm gonna be on my knees scrubbing —" He paused, swaying slightly.

Margot shot to her feet and grabbed his arm to steady him. "Slow down, killer. I put a tarp down and a sheet over that. Your tile should be unscathed."

"You could have led with that," he said, running his free hand over his face.

She chuckled. "And miss watching you panic? Never." She glanced at the camera again. "We'll talk to you guys later. Yell if you need us."

"Will do," Edie said.

Margot leaned down and clicked the mouse, and the screen went blank.

"We are definitely going to pay for leaving her there with all of them," Annabeth muttered.

Edie's mouth tipped up. "Probably."

"I, for one, am glad we're not there, though." Audra shook her head. "I think we should stay here until they're all better. That does not look fun." She leaned forward and picked up her phone, sending a text. "I'm messaging Jo. To see if she's free for a quick call."

The message no sooner went through than she had a reply. "Yep. Okay." Setting the phone down, Audra picked up the laptop.

"So, what's the current bet on when Max and Margot get married?" Edie asked.

Annabeth rolled her eyes. "Never, if you ask her. He's 'just a friend,'" she air-quoted, pitching her voice up.

Brooke snorted. "He says the same thing."

"Right? It's so wrong." Annabeth shook her head. "I've never seen two people who belong together more. He's so good with the twins. And he's been just what Margot needed to get over Tad's abrupt departure from their lives."

Esther didn't know much about Margot's past. Only what Edie had told her and what she'd gleaned from her week in Costa Rica. If she didn't know better, she'd think they were a couple. That those kids were his. One day, it would hit them. The love. She knew that from experience. She hadn't wanted a relationship with Asher, but her feelings didn't care. They wanted him, and nothing would stand in their way.

"What have you got?"

Jo's voice broke through Esther's thoughts.

"A name," Audra said. "Bradley Lennox. He's Lindy Nieman's ex-boyfriend. She said they met in college. He's possibly working as an engineer. She said they were both engineering majors, and that he was really gifted. See what you can find out about him. An address would be amazing. Also, do you think you can hack a security system and get some footage of a guy the witnesses to Leah's abduction fingered?"

"Oy. You don't ask much."

A smile tilted Audra's mouth. "I know you can do it. And if it's not Bradley Lennox, then we need to find out who it is. It could be no one important. Just a diner with a staring problem. But you'll work faster than the police."

"Stroke my ego, why don't you? Fine. I'll let you know when I have something." The computer made a *boop* sound.

Audra closed the lid and set it on the table. "Well, I guess now we wait."

Esther's jaw clenched. Jo's fingers couldn't work fast enough.

Thirty-Two

A low groan went through the ceiling above Asher's head. He peered up through the darkness, listening. Their captor was on the move.

"Is it time, Asher?"

"Maybe." Asher sat up, nudging Leah back. "You stay here and keep quiet; just like we talked about, okay?" He'd clued Leah in on his plan earlier, not wanting her to be surprised if things turned chaotic.

Getting up, he kept an ear tuned to the ceiling as he made his way to the stairs. Tiptoeing to the top, he crouched down against the wall. Judging by the light level outside and how long it had been dark, he'd guess it was about time for dinner and Leah's meds.

Minutes ticked by. Blood pulsed in Asher's ears and his calves burned from holding his crouch. But he didn't dare move. He could miss his window of opportunity. He'd have one chance at this. If he failed, he'd end up cuffed again. Or worse.

The small sliver of light coming in under the door flickered. Asher heard the slide of metal at the top of the door and the bottom. He listened intently but didn't hear the jingle of keys. Was the door only bolted and not locked? That could be a good or a bad thing.

The knob rattled. His muscles tensed.

In a blink, the door flew open. Before Asher could react, their captor stuck a long pole through and jabbed it at him. The end made contact with Asher's upper arm. He heard the snap of electricity at the same time all of his muscles seized.

Unable to control his body, Asher tumbled down the stairs, slamming into the steps with a harsh thud. His head struck the railing as he reached the bottom, amplifying the ache already there. He landed on the dirt floor in a heap, unable to breathe for a long moment.

Through the ringing in his ears, he heard the man descend the steps. He stopped on the last tread and stared down. In his hand, he held a taser attached to a pole.

Jesus. No wonder it hurt. Asher knew he needed to move, but his muscles still refused to cooperate. Every movement he made was uncoordinated and slow. At least he could breathe again.

"Do you think I'm an idiot?" The man jabbed Asher's abdomen with the modified taser.

The groan Asher let out quickly cut off as his lungs seized.

"I've got this whole room wired with surveillance. If I didn't need you to keep an eye on the girl and to keep her calm, I'd have killed you when I took you. This is your one and only warning, Mr. Horn. Do it again, and Miss Tyler will be on her own."

He jabbed Asher again.

A buzz whined in Asher's ears, and the already dim basement grew darker. The man's heavy tread up the stairs barely registered.

But the soft hands on his face and a light swaying just feet away did. He blinked, hoping to clear his vision. Stars danced above his head, bringing light to the sound in his ears.

"Asher? Asher, are you okay?"

Leah's voice came through a long tunnel, reaching him on the last of the echo. He tried to reply, but all that came out was a strangled moan. Her face danced in front of his eyes, lit by a halo coming off the lantern they'd found under her cot.

Mustering up every ounce of strength he could find, he rolled to his side. It wasn't up, but it was one step closer to being that way.

The movement helped clear his head a little. Some of the stars receded, and the buzzing decreased in volume. He tried talking again. "Lee—" His hand brushed her arm. It was all he could get out.

"It's okay. I'm right here. Are you okay? Are you hurt anywhere?"

He wanted to laugh and tell her everything hurt, but he couldn't. He was in too much pain.

With a grunt, he shifted, getting an arm beneath himself so he could push up. Muscles quivering, and with a false start, he finally made it to a sitting position. After taking a moment to regain a modicum of strength, he tried his vocal cords again.

"I'm—I'm okay." He swallowed. "Sore." And he would be for a while. Being shocked was no joke. He'd been tased as part of his CIA training. It had left his muscles achy for a couple of days. This time, it would likely be far worse.

Wincing, he scooted back until he hit the wall. He was still too shaky to sit up unsupported for long.

"Can I do anything?"

Asher rolled his head side-to-side against the wall. "No. I'm okay. I just... need a few minutes."

Holding the lantern out in front of her, Leah crawled over the dirt floor to sit beside him. Her warm weight settled into his side. Even though his arm still felt like a load of bricks, he lifted it to tuck her in more securely. They both needed the connection at the moment.

"I'm sorry, Leah." He wished he'd done a more thorough search of their prison. Maybe he'd have found the cameras. Now, he couldn't take the chance and search for them. He didn't doubt that their captor would keep his word, and Asher couldn't leave Leah alone. His only hope now was if the guy decided they needed to move.

"Did he—" Asher broke off with a wince as he shifted. "Did he leave food and your medicine?"

"I'm not sure." Leah lifted her head.

"Could you go look? I still can't move much." He had feeling in his limbs, but the muscles quivered and tingled to the point they felt like limp noodles.

Leah got up and ascended the stairs, the light bobbing as she moved. Several moments later, she came back down with the lantern hooked over her arm by the handle and a metal tray tucked against her chest.

"This looks disgusting."

A smile cracked Asher's mouth. She sounded like a typical kid. "Eat it anyway. You need the calories. Your body is still healing."

In the lantern's glow, he saw her mouth pull to one side as she grimaced. "This is like that crap from that book, *Oliver Twist*. I mean, I know it's oatmeal, but it looks like gruel." She set the tray down between them.

Asher took one of the bowls and picked up the spoon. A glop of oatmeal plopped back into his bowl. She wasn't wrong. He glanced at the tray. "At least he gave us fresh fruit."

"Yeah, but it's melon and grapes. I don't like melon."

"You'll have to tell him that when he comes back."

"Why would he listen?"

"Because he wants you alive, and from what he's said, happy." Asher mulled over the man's words. He'd been clear his focus was Leah. That Asher was only alive to keep her comfortable. But why?

Asher had a feeling it might have to do with Leah's parentage. Was the man holding them hostage her father? If so, what did that mean for Connie? And what did he want with Esther?

THIRTY-THREE

Wake up.

Esther's dream abruptly ended at the simple command that floated through her mind. She blinked at the ceiling, confused.

Rolling over, she glanced at the clock. The digital display glowed a bluish white and read two thirty-two.

Why was she awake?

Flopping onto her back again, she closed her eyes. Maybe she could get back into her dream. It had been a good one. She'd been strolling with Asher on the beach.

But an uneasiness kept her mind from shutting down. Something had awakened her.

Heaving a sigh, she pushed back the covers. She'd go downstairs, make sure all the doors and windows were locked —they were because she and Edie both checked before going to bed—then come back up and try to sleep again.

"What is wrong with you?" Edie mumbled from the other side of the bed.

"My brain woke me up for some reason and won't let me go back to sleep until I check all the doors and windows."

Edie groaned. "Hang on. I'll go with you."

"No. You stay here. I probably just heard Audra downstairs and with all the craziness happening, my sleeping brain decided it was foreign and needed to be checked out. I'll be back in a few minutes."

"You're sure?"

"Yes. Go back to sleep." Before Edie could say anything else or follow her, Esther left the room.

She tiptoed down the stairs, not wanting to wake Audra on the couch if she wasn't already awake.

Creeping around the corner of the hall, she headed for the back door.

"You heard it too?"

Esther yelped. Her hand landed on her chest, and she spun around to see Audra standing behind her. "Dear God in Heaven! Geez, Audra."

"Sorry. I didn't mean to scare you. What did you hear?"

"I don't know." Esther frowned. She'd really thought her mind was making up things. "I was dreaming and my brain just told me to wake up. What about you? I take it I wasn't imagining things?"

"No. The motion light in the backyard came on, and I heard scraping at the back of the house. By the time I got over here and looked out, there was nothing."

A quiet clink came from the garage. Both women spun toward the sound.

"What was that?" Esther breathed.

"Stay here." Audra held up a hand as she crept forward. She paused at the knife block and pulled a knife from the wood. "Talk about déjà vu..."

"What?" Esther whispered.

"Never mind. Stay put."

Esther didn't listen. She shuffled forward, staying close to Audra's back. They only made it a few steps when they heard the door leading to the yard from the garage slam shut.

"Dammit!" Audra ran forward.

This time, Esther didn't follow. She whirled and ran for the back door. Pressing her face to the glass, she peered outside and saw the backside of a man fleeing the illuminated circle of the security light and into the darkness. "He's running!" she yelled, hoping Audra heard.

A moment later, Audra burst through the garage door and into the yard, chasing after him.

Footsteps sounded overhead. A few moments later, they were on the stairs.

"What's going on?" Edie burst into the kitchen.

"Someone was in the garage." She wished now she'd listened to Asher and let him put up cameras and perhaps install a security system. Luckily, the man hadn't made it into the house.

Edie hurried forward and nudged Esther to the side, throwing the door open.

"Edie, no." Esther grabbed her arm. She knew what her sister wanted to do. "You can't go after them."

"The hell I can't!"

"You're pregnant. You can't go running into the unknown. Jordan will kill us both if you put yourself in danger like that."

"He doesn't have to know." Edie twisted her arm free.

"Edie!"

Edie huffed. With a quick glare at Esther, she turned her fierce look onto the yard and the darkness beyond. "Fine."

"What is going on down here?" Brooke rounded the corner, Annabeth on her heels.

Esther quickly explained what happened.

Annabeth shook her head. "We need to call the police. I think we touched a nerve with our digging."

"That or the guy just wants Esther—"

A sharp crack rent the night.

"That was—" Brooke started.

"A gunshot." Edie nodded. She stepped out the door. "You can't stop me this time, Essy. Audra could need help."

"I'm calling the police." Brooke already had her phone in her hand.

Edie took off, barefoot, through the grass.

"Edie!" Esther took several running steps after her sister, then growled in frustration. "Dammit!" She ran a hand through her hair and turned around. Brooke had her phone to her ear, talking to the emergency dispatcher.

Letting out a soft groan, Esther let her hand fall back to her side. There was no keeping secrets now. Detective Stroud would skin them all when he learned everything they'd kept from him.

Within minutes of Brooke's call, sirens pealed through the neighborhood. Soon, flashing lights illuminated her yard and the houses around hers. Esther watched from the window as several police officers exited their cars and ran around the side of her house. A man she recognized walked toward her front door. It was Detective Stroud.

She let out a soft huff and went to answer. Might as well get the inquisition over with.

When she opened the door, he was on her front stoop, hand poised to knock. With a quick frown, he lowered it.

"Since when are detectives some of the first ones to arrive on shots fired calls? Don't they usually wait until the heat dies down to investigate?" Esther was genuinely curious.

"I recognized your address when the call came in over the scanner."

She blinked at him, surprised. "You know my address? Better yet, you were awake?"

He lifted one shoulder. "I couldn't sleep. And I know your

address because it was on the report you filed about your friend. Can we stop the small talk and you let me in?"

"Right. Sorry." She stepped back. Once he was inside, she closed the door.

"What happened?" He glanced toward the hall as Brooke and Annabeth moved away from the back door and came toward them. "And who are they?"

"Friends. So—" She sucked in a breath, then let it out slowly. This was not a conversation she wanted to have. "You were right to suspect I might stick my nose into your investigation."

He narrowed his eyes at her, then crossed his arms. "What did you do?"

"Called my sister."

"The one who sent your friend who disappeared? The former CIA guy?"

"Yes."

He sighed, his frown deepening as he stared past her at Brooke and Annabeth. "Which one of you is the sister?"

"Neither of them," Esther said. "She and Audra ran after the shooter."

His arms dropped and his eyes rounded. "They what?" Exasperation colored his tone. "Was dispatch aware of this? Do my officers know?" He reached for his radio.

"I told the dispatcher they went after the guy." Brooke stepped closer.

"Someone broke into the garage," Esther said. "It woke me and Audra up. When we went to investigate, he ran out. Edie, Brooke, and Annabeth came down, hearing all the commotion. We all heard the gunshot, and that's when Edie went after them."

"Were either of them armed?"

"Audra had a kitchen knife."

"You know there's a saying about not bringing a knife to a gunfight, right?"

Brooke scoffed. "That doesn't apply to Audra."

"Let me guess." Stroud's tone was dry. "She's CIA too."

"British intelligence, actually," Brooke replied.

His short chuckle dripped disbelief. He swiped a hand over his face. "So, what are you two, then? FBI? DEA? Some other alphabet soup agency?"

"No. I'm an executive for Appalachia Resorts," Brooke replied.

"I'm a doctor," Annabeth said.

"We're losing the point." Esther waved a hand. "I called Edie, looking for help to find Asher and Leah. I know it's your job, but she and her friends—not just these"—she gestured to Brooke and Annabeth—"have resources well beyond yours. When we talked earlier, I wasn't entirely truthful with you. Actually, I wouldn't say that. I just failed to mention some things."

"Such as?"

"What Asher found when he was looking into the man I saw lurking around the Tylers' house."

"He knows who it is?"

"No. We do now, but he doesn't. We uncovered some things about Connie Tyler's past that could have bearing. She doesn't want it getting out, but she agreed that it might be necessary."

"What might be necessary? Miss Campbell, you need to tell me what you know. Right now."

"I'm trying to." She glared at him. "Connie Tyler's real name is Lindy Nieman. Her parents were murdered almost eleven years ago. It's possible the man who murdered them is the same man who took Asher and Leah."

"And who would that be?"

"Leah's biological father, Bradley Lennox."

Stroud muttered a soft curse, closing his eyes for a moment. "When did you find all this out?"

"We've known something was off about Connie for over a week. That's part of the reason Asher came here. But we've only known Bradley's name since yesterday. A friend of Audra's did some digging."

"Is Bradley the man you saw tonight?"

"I don't know. I didn't see his face. Even if I did, I don't know what he looks like. We haven't been able to find a picture. We have someone on it, though."

"Your friend's friend?"

"Yes."

"Tell them to stop searching. I'll handle it."

"No offense, Detective," Brooke said, breaking into the conversation. "But you don't want her to stop. We'll find answers quicker than you will. You can do the physical part, but leave the information to us."

Stroud's expression hardened. "Ms.—" he paused, waiting for Brooke to fill in her last name.

"It's missus. Mrs. Wagner."

"Mrs. Wagner—"

Brooke cut him off. "You have no clue who you're dealing with. The woman chasing the intruder took down the Brogan crime family in Las Vegas. My husband, and hers"—she pointed at Annabeth—"took down a murderer. So did Edie and her husband. We're not amateurs."

He pinched the bridge of his nose, muttering under his breath.

"We're wasting time arguing about this, Detective," Esther said. "Do you want to find Leah and Asher or not?"

"Of course I do," he shot back, pinning her with a steely-eyed glare.

"Then let's work together."

Finally, he nodded. "Fine. I knew you were up to something, for the record. The officer at the Tylers' house reported that you'd stopped by. Along with friends of Connie's from work. I'm guessing it was the rest of you lot?" He glanced at Brooke and Annabeth.

"It was." Esther's head bobbed once. "We needed to confirm what we found out, and we wanted her side of the story."

Stroud ran a hand over his hair. "I guess I need to have another conversation with Mrs. Tyler."

"Be gentle with her," Esther said. "She was just trying to protect her daughter. Bradley Lennox is not a good man."

Understanding lit his gaze. "I will be. Now, can I talk to this friend of your friend's? I have questions."

Esther shared a look with Brooke and Annabeth, unsure what to say. Her instinct was to say no. Jo couldn't get officially involved. And it wasn't her call, anyway. She turned to Stroud. "I doubt it. But we'll talk to Audra when she returns."

"Sounds good." He wandered over to the dining table and pulled out a chair.

"What are you doing?" Wrinkles creased Esther's forehead.

He took his notebook and pen from his pocket and laid them on the table, along with his radio. "Waiting."

THIRTY-FOUR

Esther smothered a yawn behind her hand. The adrenaline had worn off an hour ago, and she was fully aware it was the middle of the night. Audra and Edie needed to hurry up and get back so Stroud could talk to them. An officer had radioed a few minutes ago that they were on their way back. They'd lost whoever they were chasing.

She glanced at Stroud and caught him looking at his watch. At least she wasn't the only one feeling the hour.

Another yawn stole over her face, more intense than the last one. "Goodness." She stood. "Detective, would you like some coffee? Because I need some."

"If you're already making it, sure."

She nodded once, then looked at her friends. "Brooke? Annabeth?"

They both responded in the affirmative, looking as weary as Esther felt. She peeked at the clock on the stove as she entered the kitchen. It was nearly four a.m. At least it was Sunday. She didn't have to worry about work. Just church. Her parents would freak out when they found out what happened—and they would find out. It was a small town. But she'd worry about that later. There was no use borrowing trouble.

As Esther busied herself adding water and grounds to her coffee machine, the front door opened. Audra and Edie entered, along with two uniformed police officers; one a local policeman and the other a county sheriff's deputy.

"Welcome back," Esther said. "I'm making coffee."

"I don't need it," Audra said. "That run woke me up."

"Same," Edie said. "I just wish we'd caught the guy."

"We would have if someone hadn't stopped us." Audra tipped her head toward the county sheriff who held the knife she'd left the house with. "I was right on his heels when this guy came screaming around the corner in his car and cut me off."

The deputy shot an annoyed glance at her, then walked toward Esther. "She said this belongs here. Where do you want me to put it?"

"In the sink."

"Yes, ma'am."

"Would you like some coffee?" She gestured to the gurgling machine.

"Oh, um, no ma'am. Thank you." He put the knife down with a clink of metal-on-metal.

She turned to the other police officer and raised an eyebrow. He shook his head.

"You're Audra?" Stroud rose from his spot at the table and came closer, eyes pinned on the dark-haired woman.

Her brow wrinkled. "Yes. And you are?"

"Detective J.D. Stroud. I need to talk to your friend. The one feeding you all your information."

She blinked at him once, her face serene. "No, you don't."

His lips flattened, then he turned to the officer and deputy. "Give me a quick account of what happened. Obviously, you found them." He motioned to Audra and Edie.

The deputy nodded. "Two streets over, yes. I never saw the man they were after. She said he crossed the street just before I came around the corner."

"And I'd have had him if you hadn't." Audra crossed her arms and cocked out a hip, raising a haughty eyebrow at the man.

"Ma'am, you had a knife. I couldn't let you keep going."

Audra scoffed. "You wouldn't have even if I didn't."

"Not on a shots fired call, no. I'm just glad we already knew you two were chasing him."

Brooke aimed a grin at Audra. "You want your badge back, don't you?"

"Like you wouldn't believe," she said through clenched teeth, her eyes flashing with anger.

"Anyway," Stroud said, rolling his hand.

The deputy turned his attention to Stroud. "Anyway, after I detained them, your guy showed up." He gestured to the officer. "They gave him a quick description, and he went after the man, but he slipped our net. I don't think we could get enough units into the area quickly enough to prevent him from leaving."

Stroud clicked his tongue and ran a hand through his hair. "Okay. Do you have anything else to report?"

"No," the deputy said. "Patrol is still combing the area, and a crime scene unit is processing the place where he shot at them."

"Bloody bastard is lucky I didn't catch up." Audra scowled. "He didn't miss by much."

"Which is why you—"

Audra held up a hand, cutting off the deputy. "I can assure you I've seen more action and been in more dangerous pursuits than you'll ever experience. So, please, don't patronize me."

The deputy's annoyed stare came back, but he stayed silent.

Esther saw Stroud's mouth twitch in amusement.

"Okay, thank you. You two may go." Stroud tipped his head toward the door.

With a final glare, the deputy traipsed outside, following the local officer.

When the door closed, Stroud turned to Audra again. "Your friends filled me in on who you are. We've agreed to work together to find Leah and Mr. Horn. I need to talk to your colleague."

"Again, no, you don't. We can relay anything you want to ask."

"That may be so, but it's much more efficient if I do it myself."

Edie raised a hand, gaze fixed on Audra. "How about we just call her now and put her on speaker? Then you don't have to give out her information, but he still gets to ask his questions."

Audra stared at her for a beat, then nodded. "With the understanding that she's helping in an unofficial capacity. Her name can't appear in your records."

Stroud folded his notebook closed and stuffed it in his pocket.

"Good. Give me a moment. I just need to grab my phone." She left the kitchen, heading into the living room.

Finished making coffee, Esther wandered over to her sister's side. "You okay?"

"I'm fine." A small frown formed between Edie's eyebrows. "Why wouldn't I be?"

"Oh, I don't know... middle of the night run, adrenaline, baby..."

"I'm fine. Tired, but fine. And don't you dare tell Jordan

the guy shot at us. He's already not happy that we all flew up here on our own."

Esther held up her hands. "No worries there. That's a conversation you can have by yourself."

Footfalls on the hardwood heralded Audra's reappearance. She walked into the room with her cell in her hand and looked at Stroud. "Remember, you never spoke to her."

He mimed zipping his lips.

She tapped the screen and a ringing filled the room.

"Aud, I told you I'd call if I had something. I'm at work." Jo's whispered voice came over the line.

"There have been some developments. You're on speaker with all of us, plus a local detective."

"What? What happened? Wait. Hang on. I need to find somewhere private."

Rustling sounded, then the murmur of voices. Eventually, things quieted and Jo spoke again.

"Okay. I'm away from Dumbo ears. Fill me in."

"Someone tried to break into Esther's house just a little while ago. Edie and I chased him, but he got away thanks to some local intervention." Audra shot a dark look at the detective.

Esther rolled her lips in. Those poor cops would probably never gain her forgiveness. She couldn't blame her, either. She wished they hadn't stopped her too.

Jo let out a soft grunt. "Isn't that a rub? Okay. What do you need from me?"

"Have you had any luck getting info on Lennox?"

"I found a picture. And I'm running a background check, but not much is coming up. Like your girl, Lindy, he disappeared after her parents died. It'll take some time to run facial rec against the old license photo I found. I haven't been able to"—she paused for half a second—"do that other thing we talked about."

Esther shot a quick look at Stroud to see if he caught her hesitation. His eyes narrowed slightly, but he didn't comment. She was glad. All the digging they'd done was one thing. None of it was illegal. Hacking the pizzeria's security system definitely was.

"Did he have any criminal history?" Stroud asked.

"No. And I'm betting his new identity doesn't, either."

"I agree," Esther said. "From the way Connie described him, he's highly intelligent. I think he only lost control back then because she wouldn't bow to his wishes. Since then, I'm betting he's buttoned up his emotions. He'll be a model citizen."

"What else have you checked?" Stroud reached for his notebook, then grimaced and dropped his hand.

"The standard social media sites. There aren't any profiles with that name. Not even old ones."

Esther hadn't expected her to find any. But it did make her think of something. "What about engineering societies?"

"That's a good idea," Edie said.

"Engineering?" Jo said.

"Connie said they both majored in engineering," Esther said. "She works in a field loosely related to that. With his intelligence and the behavioral traits he shows, he probably wouldn't want to give up his career. If he could fake a new identity, I don't think it would be out of the realm of possibility that his new persona included new credentials as well."

"I'll run a check. We might need a name first, though. I'm not sure how many of those organizations have pictures of their members."

"It's still worth a shot. If we can locate him in one of those, it might give us a place of employment," Audra said.

"Do you have information on the parents' deaths?" Stroud said. "I'd like to contact the department that handled the case and review their files."

"I'll send everything I have to Audra. Including the image I found of Lennox. I was planning to package all this up on my lunch break, but since you're all awake, I'll do it now."

"Thank you," Audra said. "We appreciate it."

"Do you have any more leads?" Jo asked.

"No. Wait." Audra's spine straightened. "Can you set up a flag for pharmacy break-ins within, say, fifty miles of here? Leah's medicines are missing, but I'm not sure how long they'll last. He might need to get more."

"Leah's medication is gone? What?" Stroud frowned. "Mrs. Tyler didn't mention that."

Audra held up a finger, making him scowl. Esther didn't think he found her attitude so amusing now that she directed it at him.

"Yep," Jo said. "Can you get me a list of her drugs?"

"Probably."

"Brilliant. Send it over, and I'll add it to the algorithm."

"Sounds good. Thanks."

"No worries. I'll speak to you soon." There was a soft click, then silence.

"When did you plan to tell me her meds were gone?" Stroud demanded. "And why didn't Mrs. Tyler mention it?"

"Because she didn't want you digging too deep into her background," Edie said. "But that cat's out of the bag and you now know what we do."

Audra's phone pinged. "She sent the photograph."

Stroud moved toward her. "Let me see that."

She turned the device around.

From her position, Esther caught a glimpse of a handsome blond man.

"Hell." Stroud glowered at the screen. "Add ten years and make the hair a little darker and you've got the guy from the restaurant."

"You're sure?" Brooke walked over to take a look.

"One hundred percent."

"Should we put that on the news?" Esther asked. "He doesn't know we know his identity. What if he decides it's not worth it and kills one or both of them?"

Stroud's expression turned thoughtful. "I could put out the still from the restaurant surveillance. Call him a person of interest. It might give him a sense that we don't know as much as we do, but still get the public looking for him. Because like it or not, we need a lead on his whereabouts. We won't find Leah and your friend without that."

"I agree," Audra said. "Just be careful about your wording. We don't want to spook him. I don't think he'll harm Leah. But Asher's a different story."

Esther's heart clenched. The urge to run and hide from the conversation hit her again, but she planted her feet. Wallowing in her fear wasn't productive. They—she—needed to stay proactive. "What can we do? And don't say stay out of your way."

"Actually, you all have been helpful. Just keep me looped in to anything you discover. And please don't go off on your own if you get a lead?" His voice and eyes pleaded with them to agree.

Esther just stared at him, unwilling to promise anything. She knew she would do whatever was necessary to bring Asher and Leah home safe. Her sister and their friends would too.

Edie caught her eye, understanding in her gaze. She offered Stroud a smile. "I can promise you we'll be careful. That's as good as it gets."

THIRTY-FIVE

It took everything Esther had to get through the school day on Monday. She'd contemplated staying home, but decided she needed the distraction. There was nothing she could do sitting around her house. But she'd been absent-minded all day and not the kind of teacher she wanted to be for her students. Tomorrow, she'd stay home.

Which was why she was still holed up in her classroom, twenty minutes after the end of the school day, prepping plans for the sub. She'd talked to her principal during lunch and got the okay to take the next couple of days off. If things went beyond that, she could take more, but it put pressure on the substitute pool. And she might go stir-crazy sitting at home without anything to do.

"Hey, girl."

Esther glanced up to see Liv in the doorway. She gave her friend a tired smile. "Hey."

"I heard about what happened. I'm sorry I couldn't get over here before now. It was one crisis after another today." She wandered into the room and perched on a desk nearby. "And why the hell are you here?"

"Because I thought it would be better than sitting at home twiddling my thumbs."

"Was it?"

Esther lifted a shoulder. "Maybe. I don't know. I'm taking the next couple of days off, though. I wasn't with it enough to teach well today. I'm just finishing up some lesson plans for the sub, then heading home."

"Good. Do the police have any leads?"

"Some. But things are at a standstill until something pans out or something else happens."

"I don't want to think what that something might be." Liv shuddered.

Esther didn't want to contemplate it, either.

"Do you need anything?"

"No. My sister came up." She didn't mention Edie's friends. It would just bring questions Esther didn't want to answer. "And I have my folks. I'm okay."

"You're not, but I get that you're trying to keep a brave face." Liv heaved herself up, putting a hand on her swollen belly. "I'll get out of your hair so you can finish your prep. If you need anything—"

"I will call." Esther smiled. "Thank you."

"Of course." Liv waddled toward the door, pausing for a moment to glance back. "I hope everything works out okay. I like Asher. And Leah must be terrified."

The emotions Esther had closed off knocked at the door. She pressed her mouth into a flat line and nodded. "Thanks."

Liv gave her a soft smile, then left.

Esther blew out a breath, then sucked in another one through her nose, holding it for a second. She was tired of feeling like a train wreck. Another cryfest alone in her room was probably in order. This time, though, she'd probably do it in the shower. As much as she loved her sister, she didn't want to share her emotions—just get them out.

Shaking off the melancholy, Esther dove back into her lesson prep.

As she neared the end—finally—her phone dinged. She paused to look at it. It was a text from Edie.

Are you almost done? You said you'd text and to give you half an hour, but it's been forty minutes.

Esther tapped the screen and replied. *Almost. You can head over. I should be done by the time you get here. Or shortly after.*

Dots appeared on the screen, then, *Sounds good.*

Incentivized now, knowing Edie was on her way, Esther banged out the last bit of her plans and hit print. Pushing away from the desk, she left her classroom and went down the hall to get the papers from the workroom printer. With them in hand, she went back to leave a copy on her desk and get her things.

Double-checking she had everything and that her room was in order, she flipped off the lights and headed for the front doors, stopping in the office to leave a copy of her lesson plan in the principal's mailbox, just in case something happened to the one on her desk.

"Hi, Esther." The office manager, Nan, smiled when Esther walked in.

"You're still here?" Esther held out her lesson plan.

"Only for a few more minutes. I had some things to catch up on. Is this your plan for the sub?"

"Yes."

"Perfect. I'll make sure Becky gets it."

"Thanks, Nan."

"Yep. Oh! I almost forgot." Nan shuffled through the pile of papers on her desk. "I was going to stick this in your mailbox, then got busy." She held up a white envelope. "A courier dropped this off for you earlier."

With a frown marring her face, Esther took the letter. "Did they say what it was or who it was from?" She turned it over in her hands and saw a logo for an educational store in Coos Bay in the corner.

"Just that it was a promotional thing from that store."

Esther sighed. "Now I'm getting junk mail at school too? That's just great." Chuckling, she waved it as she backed toward the door. "Thanks, Nan."

"Not a problem. I hope you have a good evening despite —" She stopped and flopped a hand back and forth.

"Yeah. Me too." Smile fading, she pushed a shoulder into the door and waved again as she left. Outside, there was no sign of Edie yet, so Esther sat on the bench near the entrance and opened the envelope. She did like the store and shopped there regularly for supplies. Maybe it was a coupon she could use on her next visit.

Except it wasn't.

Esther's blood ran cold, making her hands tremble as she read the typed lines on the single sheet of paper she'd unfolded.

If you want to see your friend alive, bring me Lindy. 2247 Sorrell Lane. Come alone. If I see anyone other than you two, he's dead. I'm watching.

If there'd been any doubt in her mind that Bradley Lennox was involved, it had been erased with the use of Connie's real name.

Her head lifted, and her gaze darted from one corner of the parking lot to the next. She stared at the shadows, wondering if someone was hiding.

If he was, she couldn't leave with Edie. He'd know.

But how was she supposed to leave the school without a vehicle of her own?

Esther's eyes tracked the sidewalk that eventually led out to the street. She'd have to walk. Get far enough away her sister wouldn't see her when she drove in, then call an Uber.

She set off down the path, away from the school, nearly

running in her haste to get out of sight before Edie arrived. She also wanted to see if someone truly was following her. The beginnings of a plan had formed in her mind.

Grateful she'd worn boots today and not regular heels, or even flats, she broke into a jog once she was out of sight of the school. Edie would come down the main road, so Esther's plan was to duck into the adjacent neighborhood. There was a gas station on the other side where she could have an Uber pick her up.

All along the way to the intersection, Esther glanced back every few yards, but saw no one. If Lennox was there, he had mad tracking skills. She never caught a glimpse of anyone.

At the stop sign, she turned, dashing into the sea of ranch-style homes. Still keeping watch, she dug her phone from her bag and pulled up her rarely used Uber app. Hopefully, it wouldn't take too long for someone to reach her.

She picked the type of car she wanted and typed in her pickup location. After a few more clicks, her ride was confirmed and on the way. She had twelve minutes.

Esther didn't hesitate. With another look over her shoulder, she called Edie.

Her sister picked up on the second ring. "Where are you? I just pulled in and don't see you."

"I got a note. A courier dropped it at the school, and the office manager gave it to me on my way out. I'm supposed to get *Lindy* and take her to the address listed on the letter."

A short pause came over the line. "Wait, what? The letter said Lindy? Not Connie."

"Yep."

"And he left you an address? What is it? Wait, hang on. I need something to write with."

Esther heard some rustling, then a soft clatter.

"Shit. Stupid console... Sorry. I hit the bottom of my bag on the armrest and dropped it. I'm ready now."

"Twenty-two forty-seven Sorrell Lane."

Edie repeated it back as she wrote it down. "Okay. Did he give a timeframe?"

"No. The note says he's watching, but I haven't seen anyone. I don't see how he could be sure I'd get the letter today. What if Nan had just put it in my mailbox? Even if I hadn't taken the next two days off, it would be tomorrow before I'd see it if she did that."

"Good point. It could be he's just prepared for you to show up whenever."

"Do you think that's where he's holding them?"

"No. I think he's got cameras on site, so he can see when you arrive, but they're not there. I bet they're nearby, though. This is good. This gives us a solid area to look. Where are you? I'll come get—"

"No! No, you can't. I need to do what he says. You call the others. Come up with a plan. But I'm taking an Uber to the Tylers' house, collecting Connie, then going to that address."

"Esther..."

"I know you don't like the idea, but we need to make it look like we're following his instructions. I doubt he'll harm Leah, but Asher could be in real danger."

"What about the officer Stroud left at her house? He's probably still there. You have to get past him."

"Let me worry about him. But don't tell Stroud. Not until you hear from me that I've got her and we're away from the house."

Edie's sigh turned into a growl. "I really don't like this."

"I'm not asking for permission. And we're wasting time. Go back to my house and talk to the others. I have to go." Esther stabbed the button to end the call before Edie could respond. It probably left her fuming, but she didn't care. Edie needed to trust her. Esther had faith in her sister and their friends. Edie needed to lay off the control freak side of her personality.

Hustling through the neighborhood, Esther made it to the gas station with two minutes to spare. So she didn't look like a weirdo, loitering outside, she went in and grabbed a drink—which she needed after her jaunt—and watched out the windows for her ride. A quick glance at the app showed "Amanda" was two blocks away.

Time to go.

Esther went to the register and paid for her drink, then went outside. The white sedan with Amanda behind the wheel pulled in a few moments later. Lifting a hand, Esther flagged her down.

The driver's window rolled down. "Hi. Are you Esther?"

"Yes." She showed the young woman her phone with the reservation.

"Great. Hop in."

"Thanks." Esther got in the back and buckled up.

"Where to?"

She gave the woman the Tylers' address. Amanda arched an eyebrow, recognizing the neighborhood, but said nothing. Within fifteen minutes, they were pulling up out front of the house.

"There you go. Do you need me to wait?"

"No, but thank you." Esther opened her door, ready to step out.

"All right. Have a nice evening."

"Yep, you too. Thanks." Climbing out, Esther closed the door and walked up the driveway, leaving the woman a tip on the app as she went. She stowed her phone and knocked on the door.

Landon answered once again.

His face fell, and he crossed his arms when he saw her. "Back again?"

"Yep." Esther stepped forward, aiming to walk past him, but he wouldn't budge. She huffed and gave him a bored stare. "I don't have time for this, Landon. Let me in."

He held her gaze for another moment before shaking his head and stepping to the side. "Don't get me in trouble again."

A pang of misgiving went through Esther's chest. She didn't want to cause him problems, but there were far bigger things at stake than a reprimand from the police chief. So, she lied. "I won't."

"Esther?"

Connie looked up from her seat on the couch.

"Hey. Can we talk?" Esther tipped her head toward the kitchen.

Landon let out a soft groan. "Yep, I'm getting in trouble again."

Esther ignored him and headed for the kitchen, knowing Connie would follow. Her gaze flitted over the window. Buster was outside, nose in the air, watching a butterfly. If she wasn't so stressed, she'd smile.

Connie joined her as she sat down at the table.

"What's going on?" Her eyes widened, and she lowered her voice. "Did something happen?"

Esther nodded. She reached into her bag and withdrew the note she'd received. "I got this at school today." She slid it over the tabletop. "Don't react when you read it. We don't want to set off Officer Garner's radar."

A fine tremor went through Connie's fingers as she unfolded the note. Her quick intake of breath was her only reaction. After she read it, she folded it up and pushed it back. "What do we do?"

"We're going to sneak out of here. I don't think he's actually watching. I ditched my sister just to be safe and didn't see anyone following me. I think when we go there, we'll be watched, but right now—and when I got the note—

he didn't have eyes on me. Edie's on it. She and the others will come up with a plan. But you and I are going to show up alone."

"Okay." Connie clutched the edge of the table. "How do we sneak out, though? This house is small. My car is in the driveway, but he could run out and block the drive before we can leave."

Esther bit her lip, thinking. They needed to incapacitate him in some way without harming him. "Do you trust me?"

"Yes."

"Then follow my lead, okay?"

"All right."

Getting up, Esther went out to the living room with Connie right behind her. Landon sat in a chair, staring at the kitchen.

"Landon, we have a favor to ask."

He lifted an eyebrow, his eyes clearly skeptical. "What's that?"

"Connie said she has some pictures of Leah—from when she was little—in a box at the top of her closet upstairs, but she can't reach it." She glanced at Connie. "I guess Rob put some things away and that was one of them. She wants to show me the pictures. Could you get it down for us?"

His expression cleared, and he stood. "Sure. It's in the master bedroom closet, you said?"

"Yes," Connie replied. Her gaze darted to Esther, then back. "I'll show you."

Esther followed behind, praying Connie had a walk-in closet. That would be the best way to trap him. Otherwise, they'd probably have to shove him down, then close him in the bedroom. She wasn't sure how, though. The door locked from the inside.

Upstairs, Connie led Landon into her bedroom. Esther hung back, scanning the hall and the rooms they passed for something to keep the door closed. But nothing caught her eye.

While Connie led him over to the closet—which was not a walk-in—Esther's gaze roved over the room. Panic started to set in, quickening her heart rate and making her palms sweat as still nothing snagged her attention.

Think, Esther! What could she do? Wedge the door?

No. It swung the wrong way.

She could tie it shut. *If* she could find something long enough to reach across the hall to the other door. But she didn't see anything in here that fit the bill.

Her gaze landed on a charcoal-colored tree holding necklaces and bracelets that looked like it was made of iron. Esther bit her lip, casting a quick glance at Landon before sidling closer to where the piece rested on the dresser. If it really was metal, maybe she could break the doorknob off on this side.

"It's up there." Connie pointed to the stash of things on the shelf. Luckily for them, her closet wasn't that well organized. Landon would have to wade in to get to the stuff at the back.

Landon stretched, moving a stack of sweaters to the side. A hat fell off and into his face. He frowned. "Are you sure it's up here?"

"Yes. It's just buried. They're old baby pictures. Not something I look at all the time, you know?"

"Right." He shuffled forward a step. The clothes hangers tipped as he pressed against them.

It was now or never.

Taking one long step to the side, Esther picked up the tree. *Yes!* It was solid.

Adjusting her grip, she quickly sidled closer to Connie.

The woman's eyes flicked to hers, rounding as she saw what Esther held.

Knowing they wouldn't get a better chance. Esther set the

statue on the bed and silently moved in behind Landon. With all the force she could muster, she put both hands on his back and shoved.

Landon pitched forward with a shout of surprise. He grabbed at the clothes, but they slipped off their hangers, falling to the floor with him.

"Run, Connie!" Esther turned and ran, snagging the tree as she went. She pushed Connie through the doorway, then raised the statue high before bringing it down on the bedroom-side doorknob. The force jittered up her arm, making her fingers tingle. The knob bent but didn't break. She hit it again, bending it further.

Scrabbling came from the closet, along with several colorful male curses. Esther smashed the doorknob one more time, and it snapped off.

"Oh, thank goodness," she breathed. Hooking a hand around the door, she yanked it shut as she fled into the hallway.

"Will that hold him?" Connie hovered a few feet away, her blue eyes round as saucers.

"I think so, but we still shouldn't stick around to find out."

A thud hit the door. "Esther!" Landon bellowed from the other side. "Let me out of here!" He let out a frustrated growl. "Why do you do this to me? I thought we were friends."

"Sorry! It's important." Touching Connie's arm, Esther backed away. "Let's go." Together, they turned and ran for the stairs. Banging from inside the bedroom followed them down.

"Where are your keys?" Esther asked as they reached the first floor.

"In my purse." Connie ran around her to the table along the wall by the stairs and grabbed her bag. "Let's go." She headed for the front door and flung it open.

Esther caught it, right on her heels. Together, they ran

down the front steps to the car in the driveway. "Do you know where Sorrell Lane is?"

"Yes." She shoved the key in the lock on the driver's side and yanked the door open. "Get in."

The lock on the passenger side popped up when she pressed a button. Esther opened the door and fell into the seat. She buckled up as Connie backed down the driveway and onto the road. "Follow the traffic laws. We don't want to get pulled over."

The car slowed a bit, and Connie nodded. At a more normal pace, she maneuvered the car out of town. Sorrell Lane was a country road. Within minutes, they were surrounded by fields, trees, and old farmhouses.

They passed 1516 Sorrell Lane, and Esther leaned forward. "Slow down. We're close."

Half a mile later, she saw the mailbox. "There."

Connie slowed and turned onto the gravel drive. A once white two-story house sat fifty yards away. Overgrown bushes hid the front porch, and it looked like one of them might have grown through the window.

"I know you said they probably wouldn't be here, but this seems like the perfect place to hide when you don't want to be found, doesn't it?" Connie brought the car to a halt in front of the garage, leaving enough room for her to turn around.

"Yeah. But I still think they're elsewhere."

"So, what do we do now?"

Esther stared out over the property, hoping her sister and their friends were on their way. She didn't know what Lennox wanted with them, and she didn't want to leave this property without someone following behind. "We wait."

Thirty-Six

I *need a ball.*

Asher shifted, his restless energy seeking a way out. It didn't matter that his muscles were on fire from the taser or that the drumline was back in his head. His brain worked just fine and it wanted desperately to come up with an escape plan.

At home, he ran. Sometimes he bounced a tennis ball off the wall in his lair while he puzzled out smaller problems.

This was a big problem, but running wasn't an option.

He squeezed his eyes shut and tried to force his mind onto other things.

Esther's face popped into his head. An ache formed in his chest. He missed her so damn much. She'd invaded his dreams a lot over the last few days. He'd run the gamut of emotions; from joy at seeing her bright smile and the laugh lines that formed at the corners of her beautiful blue eyes, to a passion so intense he ached with it. He missed her laugh. Missed seeing her roll her eyes at him when he said something ridiculous. He even missed her soft snore when she was deep asleep.

He missed *her*. Full stop.

After the third or fourth dream, where he'd awakened happy, only to have his heart ripped out of his chest when he realized he was still in this dank hole in the ground, the true reason hit him like an axe to the skull.

He loved her.

That thought had rattled around in his head for several minutes, continuing to flummox him, until it finally settled. The warmth from the feeling banished everything else, and he'd clung to it since. He *would* get out of here so he could tell her how he felt. Dying without her knowing wasn't an option.

He also hoped he'd get to do more than tell her. He wanted what his friends had. The happy marriages; the babies on the way. It didn't take much to envision that life with Esther. Asher would be damned if he'd let some psycho take that away from him.

A high-pitched beeping permeated the floorboards over his head. He glanced up, wincing as his sore muscles protested the movement.

"What's that noise?" Leah sat up next to him.

"I'm not sure." It was one they hadn't heard before.

A moment later, heavy footsteps sounded overhead. Something had their captor's attention.

The footsteps paused for several seconds, then started again, faster. He was running.

Asher pushed to his feet when a door banged closed.

"Did he leave?" Leah asked.

"I think so." Asher walked up the steps to listen at the door. They'd heard him come and go before, but never so quickly.

He went back down the stairs. "Something's happening."

Angling his head as he thought, he weighed their options. They could play it safe. He could sit back down, and they could wait. Or he could risk the taser—or worse—again and attempt to make something that would get them out of here or defend them when he came back.

His gaze connected with Leah's. She'd complained of a scratchy throat this morning.

They were out of time. He needed to get Leah out of here.

"Okay, sweetie, here's what we're going to do. I think I can make something to aid in our escape."

"With what? There's nothing here."

"There's enough. Can you get my unicorn suit? I want you to rip out the fan and the wires."

She got up while he crossed to his mattress on the floor. Getting to the springs wouldn't be easy without a knife. Neither would removing them. But he couldn't let it stop him. It was time to leave.

Asher heard the rip of fabric and glanced back. Leah had the costume's fan in her hand and was hurriedly yanking the wires free from the suit. It gave him an idea. "Bring me the fan when you're done."

She gave the wires one last yank and pulled the entire unit free. Climbing off the bed, she walked over to him. "What are you going to do with it?"

"Right now, I'm going to use the plastic like a knife." Palming the fan, he slammed it down. His knuckles scraped the floor, but the fan stayed stubbornly intact, so he did it again. This time, it cracked. Pulling on the pieces, he separated a chunk, giving him a nice point he could use to dig into the heavy mattress fabric.

"What do you plan to do once you dig into the mattress?"

"Use the springs. I noticed when he unlocked the door the other day it's bolted. I don't think it's locked. I might be able to twist the springs into a long wire we can slip under the door to open the bolts." It was a long shot, but it was better than sitting around waiting. "I can twist more together to make a shiv."

"What's a shiv?"

"Basically a knife, but it's more for stabbing than cutting."

"Oh. What happens if he has a gun this time?"

Asher's movements faltered for a fraction of a second. He didn't want to think about that. "Let's not borrow trouble.

THIRTY-SEVEN

What was taking so long? Esther glanced at her phone. Edie hadn't texted her with any updates. It had been forty-five minutes since she left the school and ten since she and Connie arrived at the farmhouse.

"What happens when he gets here?" Connie asked. "I know you said your sister is working on a plan, but he's going to want us to go with him. If she's not here..."

"I know. I was just thinking the same thing. And he won't let us take our phones."

"Do you think he'll search us? Like, thoroughly, I mean?"

Esther cocked her head. "How thoroughly?"

"I'm wearing a sports bra. What if I tuck it under the back? We can tell him I left mine at the house when we ran from the cop guarding the place. Will your sister think to track mine?"

"She might. It might take a little longer for her to think of it, but it's worth a shot." Esther glanced around. "Get in the car and do it. Act like you need to sit down, so if he's watching on a camera, he doesn't get too suspicious. I don't know what kind of surveillance he has here. Some, obviously, or he wouldn't know we're here."

"Okay." Connie paced away, kicked at some tufts of grass, then marched back to the car. "Is this good?"

Esther smothered a smile. "It's great.

Connie threw the passenger side door open and flopped onto the seat. She left her legs hanging out, then as surreptitiously as she could, she took her phone from her purse on the floorboard and tucked it under her shirt.

"Are you good?"

"I think so." Connie hopped up and stormed away again. "Just don't let him touch my back. If he ever shows up."

Esther scanned the road again. She really thought he'd be here by now.

Two minutes later, the sound of a car coming down the road filled the air. They'd heard a couple others, so she wasn't too hopeful, but the sound grew louder and a dark-colored SUV came into view. It slowed as it neared the driveway.

"Is that him?" Connie came closer.

"Maybe. It's not Edie." Not unless she'd rented a different car. And quickly.

The car turned, and Esther could see a single male occupant in the front. It bumped over the gravel drive and came to a stop twenty feet behind Connie's car.

The man left the engine running and got out.

An audible gasp came from Connie.

A sickly-sweet smile spread over his face. He shut the door and walked closer. "Hello, Lindy."

"You son of a bitch, where's my daughter?"

"You mean our daughter?"

The blood drained from Connie's face, but her scowl stayed firmly in place. "No. You don't get any rights to her. You gave those up when you murdered my parents and left me for dead."

"The courts won't see it that way."

Connie scoffed. "How ever they see it won't matter, because you'll be behind bars for their murders."

"Hardly. You were the one there. It's your prints and blood they found at the scene. Not mine. You were angry at them. They found out you were pregnant and refused to support you. That made you angry. I mean, why else would you run and change your entire life?"

Esther laid a hand on Connie's arm before the woman could respond. Arguing with him wasn't getting them anywhere, and it didn't matter, anyway. "Where are Leah and Asher? What do you want with us?"

"Ah. So pragmatic. It's part of what makes you perfect."

A frown drew her brows down. "Perfect for what?"

"Get in. I'll explain at home."

Esther shared a look with Connie. She didn't like his choice of words. It was like he meant their home. Not just his, but a place where they'd all live. What was his plan?

The affable expression on his face hardened at their hesitation. "I said, get in the car." He produced a handgun from his waistband. "I won't ask again. Leave your phones with your vehicle."

Dammit, Edie. Where are you? Esther's gaze darted around once before settling on Connie.

"Now!" Lennox yelled.

Esther jumped and closed her eyes for a moment, hoping to slow her racing heart. They were out of time to stall. "Fine." She looked at him. "We're coming." Slowly, she took her phone from her bag and tossed it in through the open door of the car.

"You, too, Lindy." Lennox gestured toward the car with the barrel of the gun.

"I left it at home. We had to leave in a hurry to get away from the cop at my house."

Lennox's jaw worked. "The cops know?"

"No," Esther was quick to say. "You told me to bring her. I had to get her out of the house, and the only way was to trick him and lock him up, but we knew the door wouldn't hold him for long, so we ran. All she grabbed were her purse and keys. Her phone was in the kitchen."

He studied them for a brief moment. "Lift your shirt, Lindy."

She raised the hem, showing her pockets.

"Turn around."

Connie spun in a circle, holding her shirt up. Esther held her breath.

"Okay. Get in."

Knowing they really didn't have any other options, Esther headed for his car. Connie did the same.

As Connie approached, Lennox stepped into her path. Anger glittered in his light brown eyes. He grabbed her chin, pulling her close.

"Hey!" Esther reversed direction.

Lennox raised his gun and pointed it at her. "Stay there." His gaze stayed on Connie. "I looked for you. Spent months scouring the news and social media for any clue about you. I hoped you weren't dead. I knew I'd been a little... rough with you. But I didn't want you dead." He shook her. "Then I saw that picture of you and your little family. And I knew why you'd stayed hidden. You wanted to keep my daughter from me. I wanted you dead then." He squeezed harder, and Connie let out a soft whimper. She winced and grabbed his wrist, but he wouldn't let go.

"But after I watched you, waiting for the perfect time to strike, I realized it would hurt you more to take your precious child and to make you watch me raise her." He turned to Esther. "That's where you come in." He let Connie go with a hard push. She stumbled back, nearly falling. "Get in the car. There are handcuffs on the back seat. Use them."

Esther eyed him with tears swimming in her vision. What he wanted—it would be a fate worse than death for Connie.

"Get in!"

With a quick look at Connie, who now looked more defeated than angry, Esther got in the back seat.

Metal clinked softly as she picked up a set of handcuffs.

Oh, I don't want to do this.

But she had little choice if she wanted to save Asher and Leah. So, she wrapped the cold steel around her left wrist. With each click, her confidence that they would all make it out alive diminished a little more.

Thirty-Eight

"Okay, you hold that there..." Asher poked his tongue out as he wrapped the last strip of fabric around the bundle of springs he'd wound together. Pulling the material tight, he tied the final knot. "There." It wasn't perfect, but it would do some damage.

If he could get close enough. The taser pole had a longer reach. He'd just have to be quick and stay out of range as best he could.

"Let's go work on those bolts." Asher stood up, tucking the shiv into the back of his pants. He'd fashioned a hook earlier, but wanted to get both things done before he tried the hook tool.

At the top of the stairs, he slid the hook under the door. He'd bent the end, hoping it would give him a better angle of attack. All he needed was to get the bottom bolt out. He had enough mass and strength to bust through the top lock. He couldn't do both. He'd tried before he started the shiv.

The twisted springs scraped the door, sometimes knocking into the bolt, but he couldn't get the angle right to catch the latch. With a frustrated growl, he sat up. "I wish I knew what it looked like on the other side." It would be useful to know the lock's orientation. If he needed to push to open the latch rather than pull, he doubted he'd be able to open it.

Pulling the hook in, he added another bend higher up the twisted springs. The hook wasn't flush enough with the door. Hopefully, he still had enough leverage like this to pull on the latch if he managed to hook it.

A distant voice reached his ears. It was a man, shouting.

"Fuck!" he muttered under his breath. They were out of time. "Back downstairs, Leah. Go!" He ushered the girl down, then shoved the hook under her mattress, out of sight. He left the shiv in the back of his pants. His shirt covered it.

"The costume!" She pointed to the tattered fabric they'd left lying on the floor.

Asher picked it up and rolled it into a ball, stuffing it in a corner by his bed. He couldn't do anything about how it looked, but he could hide it as best he could. He also dragged the thin cotton blanket up over the ruined mattress. His hope was their captor wouldn't look at the camera footage, assuming that since everything looked the same, they'd behaved while he was out.

With another quick look around the room, Asher backed toward Leah's cot. Everything looked as it had when the man left.

The voice grew louder. But there was something new. A softer, higher-pitched voice. Then another joined in, rising over the other two. This one he recognized.

"Goddammit," he whispered. What the hell was she doing here? If she'd let herself get captured to rescue them, they would have words later. Lots of words. She was a teacher; not a cop or a bodyguard or any other profession that lent itself to rescuing people.

The bolts holding the basement door in place clacked and scraped. A moment later, a shaft of light came down the stairs.

"You two." Their captor's voice carried down the steps. "Get up here. And don't try anything."

Leah looked at Asher with round eyes. "I don't want to go up there."

"I know, but we need to. This is our chance. Stay close and do what I tell you, okay?"

She caught her lip between her teeth and nodded.

He helped her off the bed, then took her hand, leading her toward the steps. Their captor stood at the top, a pistol clutched in his right hand.

Cautiously, Asher mounted the stairs. Two from the top, he paused. "You want to back up so we can come out?"

The man took a step to the side. "Move." He flicked the gun.

Asher moved Leah to his other side, putting himself between her and the man as they cleared the doorway.

"Mom!" Leah broke free from Asher's grip and dashed across the kitchen to the platinum blonde standing hand-cuffed next to Esther.

"Leah!" The woman looped her arms over Leah's head. A sob ripped from her chest as she clutched her daughter.

Asher only watched them for a moment before turning his gaze to Esther. She looked no worse for wear. In fact, a low anger simmered in her bright blue eyes.

"That's enough," the man said. "Leah, come away from her."

Leah shook her head and tucked it into Connie's chest. She held Connie tighter around the waist.

"I said, come here."

Again, Leah shook her head.

"You will listen to me! I am your father."

Leah froze. Asher's eyes widened. *What?* He'd considered

the possibility, but not hard. Suddenly, many things made sense.

Slowly, Leah lifted her head to look at her mom.

"I'm sorry, baby," Connie said, her voice cracking. "It's true."

"No. No, my daddy's name is Rob."

Connie's hand fisted in Leah's shirt, and she closed her eyes. A tear leaked free. "It's complicated, sweetie. But Bradley's right. He's your dad." She aimed a glare at him. "As much as I wish he wasn't."

The hammer cocked on the gun as Bradley drew it back. He pointed it at Asher. "Get her away from Lindy."

A ball formed in Asher's chest, pushing on his heart. He did not want to rip that girl away from her mother.

"You're of little use to me now, Mr. Horn. I won't hesitate to kill you if you don't cooperate."

Asher sent him a deadly glare. Two steps. That's all it would take to put him within swinging range of Bradley's face. But he couldn't risk the man accidentally firing his gun. There were too many people in the confined space.

He turned to Leah and held out an arm. "Leah, honey, come stand with me. Just for a bit." He looked at Connie, silently pleading with her to urge Leah to let go.

Choking back a sob, Connie lifted her arms and shifted. "Sweetie. Go with Asher."

"No!"

"Please, honey. We need to do what Bradley says." She framed Leah's face and bent close, whispering something to her. Asher couldn't make out what she said.

Whatever it was, it worked. Leah eventually nodded and backed away. Asher held out a hand, and she took it, latching onto his side with her other arm.

"What are we doing?" Esther asked. "You have all of us here. What do you want?"

A cold smile slid over Bradley's face. His eyes turned as hard and flinty as stone. He shifted the weapon away from Asher, keeping it raised, but now pointed at the wall. "It's simple, really." He shrugged one shoulder, his nonchalance in direct contrast to the anger running through his expression. "I want the family I was denied."

THIRTY-NINE

Esther swallowed—or attempted to. Her mouth was drier than the Mojave. What did that mean? The family he was denied. And how did she and Asher play into that?

"I understand why you didn't want me to be a father to our child, Lindy. With me around, you couldn't slack off and be a terrible mother like you have been. I wouldn't have let us live in that filthy, crime-ridden, cesspool of a neighborhood. Or let our daughter catch a deadly disease if I'd been in the picture. She'd have had the finest things and gone to the best schools. Although, I have to say, I'm impressed with the quality of some of the teachers at Heron Ridge." He gestured to Esther. "Obviously. And I have no doubt she'll be a better mother for Leah than you ever were."

A *what*?

No. No, no.

His plan was suddenly extremely clear. He wanted her to replace Connie in the family unit. "I'm sorry, no." Esther backed up a step and waved her hands.

His gaze flicked to her, but he ignored her and continued to address Connie. "And you're going to watch it all from a cage I built, just for you. For the rest of your life, you get to watch us raise Leah. I guarantee she'll prosper more than she ever would with you."

"You're mad!" Connie shook her head. "How will she prosper when you'll never let her leave the property? Because you won't be able to, you know. She knows too much. Knows who you are and what you've done."

"She'll do just fine, because she'll know if she says anything, you and Miss Campbell will die."

Connie looked at the girl, a fierceness in her eyes. There was also a wildness there. Esther knew the woman would do anything to protect her child.

"Honey, I don't care what happens to me," Connie said. "You sing your brand-new heart out to anyone who'll listen. He can kill me a thousand times over. I just want you to live." Her voice broke.

"But do you speak for everyone?" Lennox asked.

"Yes." Esther didn't hesitate. She caught Asher's eyes, telegraphing an apology. She knew he wasn't happy she was here. She'd seen it when he looked at her after he came up the stairs. He was glad to see her, but he hated that she'd put herself in danger to save him.

The set to his jaw told her he understood, even if he didn't like it.

Lennox's eyes narrowed. "I'm sure you'll both rethink that once you see what death is really like."

All the action in the room moved in slow motion for Esther over the next few seconds. She saw the glint of evil intent enter Lennox's eyes a fraction of a second before he extended his arm to bring the gun around. As his gaze traveled toward Asher, her feet moved of their own volition.

"No!" The word ripped from her soul.

She didn't think.

As the gun came up, she dove.

The noise and the punch to her side came at the same time. All the breath left her lungs; long before she hit the floor.

"Esther!"

Asher's voice rose over Leah's scream and Connie's shout of dismay. Hands touched her, but she didn't know whose. They felt too small to be Asher's.

Blinking slowly, she raised her head. Scuffling broke through the numbness settling over her. Connie's face swam in her vision.

"Esther! Esther, look at me."

She blinked again but couldn't hold her eyes open. Her head lolled to the side. The hands that touched her shoulders and arm a moment ago now framed her face.

"Esther, stay awake."

She wanted to, but the numbness encroached further.

And it had a friend.

The cold. Ice invaded her veins.

"Asher!"

Esther managed another slow blink and saw Connie look behind her.

"Asher, let him go. I need your help!"

Let who go? Wait. Lennox? Is that who she meant? Why would Asher let him go? He'd just shoot someone else. She tried to get her elbow beneath her to sit up and protest, but she could do little more than twitch her arm.

Another hand landed on Esther, this time on the top of her head. It was much smaller than the first.

"It's okay, Miss Campbell. Mommy and Mr. Asher will take care of you."

Leah's whispered words floated down the tunnel Esther drifted in. Her eyelids fluttered closed.

She was so cold.

And sleepy...

The tunnel grew darker; the light fading as she slipped deeper into it.

"Esther!"

Asher's voice echoed through her head.

Her brow wrinkled. Why did he sound so far away?

She didn't know, but she couldn't force her eyes open to find out why. Didn't want to.

Sleep crooked a finger, welcoming her into its arms and promising warmth. With a sigh, she embraced it, banishing the cold. It pulled her down until the darkness took over and her mind went blank.

FORTY

"You son of a bitch! Come here!" Asher grabbed at Bradley's clothing, scrambling to get a hold on the man after he'd kicked out of Asher's grip. At least he wasn't armed anymore. When Esther went down, he'd run at the man, knocking the gun free from his hand. It had skittered under the table, out of reach of anyone. Asher wanted to use the shiv still tucked into his belt, but didn't dare take one hand to reach for it. He was having enough trouble getting a grip on Bradley.

"Asher, please! She needs help!"

The plea in Connie's voice finally registered. He glanced back, his muscles freezing as he saw the growing pool of blood surrounding Esther.

His momentary lapse was all Bradley needed. A booted foot landed on Asher's cheek. He fell back with a grunt, momentarily stunned.

Bradley's gaze caught his. For a second, his eyes flicked toward the gun. It was past Asher, beneath the table. The debate in his gaze brought some awareness back to Asher's brain. He shifted, ready to stop him.

But Bradley didn't do what he expected. Instead, he turned and ran. A moment later, Asher heard the front door open, then slam shut.

"Asher!"

The panic in Connie's voice banished every thought he had about going after him.

He got to his feet and hurried to her side. Esther was unconscious.

"We need to find a phone and call for help."

Connie's eyes widened, and she reached behind her back, shoving her hand beneath her shirt. "I forgot! She told me to hide it so we could be tracked." When she brought her hand out, she held a cellphone. With a few taps, she called for help.

Asher glanced around, looking for something to staunch the flow of blood from Esther's abdomen. "Leah, see if you can find a towel."

The girl got up, moving away. Asher put his hands over the hole in Esther's shirt and pushed. She groaned but didn't open her eyes.

He felt moisture gather in his as blood welled between his fingers. *God, this was not happening.* "Hang in there, Essy," he whispered. "You can't die on me."

"I found some!" Leah thrust some kitchen towels in front of him.

Asher took them and pressed them to Esther's belly. "How long until the ambulance gets here, Connie?" She was losing so much blood. If they didn't get her help soon—he didn't want to think about it.

Connie held up a finger, giving the dispatcher directions to their location. He was glad Bradley hadn't blindfolded her and Esther on the way here.

"Ten minutes," Connie said, finally.

A grimace crossed Asher's face. That was too long. But

they didn't have a choice. He'd just have to do everything he could to keep her from bleeding out until then.

Connie hung up with the dispatcher. "What do you want me to do?"

"Do you know if she called our friends to help find me and Leah?"

"Yes."

"Is one of them Edie? Or Ford?"

"Edie. I met her."

"Okay, call her. Get her here so we can get the team on finding Bradley." He rattled off Edie's phone number from memory. "Put the call on speaker."

Connie dialed.

"Hello?" Edie's voice came over the line, cautious.

"Edie, it's Asher."

"Holy shit, you're alive!"

Despite the seriousness of their situation, he couldn't stop the chuckle that slipped out at the incredulity in her tone. "I am. But we have a few problems. Esther's been shot and Bradley got away."

A short pause came over the line.

"Tell me you're joking. Or that I heard you wrong."

"No. She—" He stopped, having to swallow around the sudden lump in his throat. "She dove in front of me. Bradley was going to kill me, and she dove in front of the bullet." He swallowed again, blinking back tears. "She's alive, but uncon-scious. The bullet hit something vital because she's bleeding heavily. Connie already called for help. She said you're in town, and I know you're going to want to come here, but I need you to track down that asshole."

"Asher—" The word came out choked.

He heard her take a shaky breath. "I know, Edie. I know. I'm doing everything I can." Again, he swallowed around the lump in his throat. "I love her too."

Another choked sob came over the line, then a harsh intake of air. "Where are you? So I know where to start looking for Lennox."

Asher felt the grip he had on his emotions slipping, but he managed to repeat the address Connie had given the dispatcher.

"He was in a black SUV," Connie said. "At least, that's what he brought us here in."

"Do you know what make?"

"Chevy."

"Okay. We'll do what we can. Asher, you keep me updated on my sister."

"I will, Edie."

The line clicked as she hung up without saying goodbye.

He closed his eyes for a moment, gathering himself. Talking to Edie, putting into words what Esther had done, had shattered the door on his feelings. One more swift kick and everything would be free.

He couldn't lose it, though. There was too much on the line.

So, he shored up the door and focused on Esther. The towels he'd pressed against her abdomen were soaked. Leah had brought extras, so he added more to the stack and continued to press down.

Turning his head to ask Connie to look for a first aid kit, he caught sight of Leah and the words stuck in his throat. The girl stood next to her mother, arm wrapped around her shoulders, while Connie clutched the girl to her side. Leah's gaze was fixed on the blood seeping through the towels and coating his hands. Her lower lip trembled and silent tears tracked down her face.

Asher glanced away, his jaw working as he struggled to hold on to the precarious grip he had on his emotions.

Don't lose it, man. Esther needs you, and Leah doesn't need to see you fall apart.

He bit his tongue, using the pain to maintain his composure. Once he was sure he wouldn't crack if he talked, he looked at Connie. "Can you see if there's a first aid kit anywhere?" Maybe they'd get lucky and there would be one with some QuikClot in it.

Connie got up.

"If nothing else, bring back more towels." The ones he'd added to the stack were turning red.

She nodded and ushered Leah out of the kitchen.

Asher glanced down. Blood smeared his hands and stained the knees of his pants. *God, there was so much blood.* He said a quick prayer she'd last until they could get her to a hospital. He didn't know what he'd do if she didn't make it.

FORTY-ONE

Asher stared at his hands, the scene from the farmhouse running on a loop through his mind. Dried blood occupied the creases of his nails and under the short tips. A streak he'd missed when washing them decorated the side of his right index finger. He rubbed at the spot, causing some of it to flake away. He should probably make another visit to the men's room and wash it off, but he didn't want to leave the waiting room. It had been several hours since the trauma team at the hospital here in Eugene had taken Esther back for surgery. Any moment now, those doors could part and someone in green scrubs would walk through, asking for Essy's family. He wanted to be available when that happened, so he didn't have to wait for them to come back.

Even though they couldn't really tell him much because he wasn't related. The details would have to wait for Edie to return from chasing down Bradley, but he'd at least know if Esther was alive.

He glanced at the clock, willing someone to come out and tell him that. There was no certainty they would. The sickly gray pallor she'd had to her skin wouldn't leave his head. When the paramedics arrived, the most senior member of the team had taken one look at her injury and radioed for a helicopter. The thought was the bullet had hit her liver.

Asher hoped that was all it hit.

Commotion near the door drew his attention. He looked up to see a man walk in, flashing a badge at the volunteer at the desk. The elderly woman gestured in Asher's direction. The cop turned, and Asher sat up straighter.

"Asher Horn?"

As the man approached, Asher stood. "Yes. You are?"

"Detective J.D. Stroud. I've been working your kidnapping case, and now Miss Campbell's shooting. How is she?"

"I don't know. She's still in surgery."

The detective's head bobbed a couple of times. "Okay. Can we chat while we wait?"

"Of course."

"Good, good. Let's use one of their consultation rooms." Stroud gestured to the bank of doors lining one wall.

"Sure. Just let me tell the receptionist where I'll be."

"She knows. I already asked if we could use a room."

"Oh." Asher's brow wrinkled as his addled brain tried to shift gears. He'd been locked in his thoughts too long. "All right."

Following Stroud across the waiting area, they settled into one of the consultation rooms.

"Now, I know you're probably eager for me to dive into what happened today, but I want to start at the beginning. Walk me through the last few days." Stroud flipped open a pocket notebook and clicked his pen.

Asher took a deep breath, forcing his mind to think back to Friday. "I helped Esther surprise Leah for her birthday. She wanted to do something extra fun and exciting for the girl, so she made her a cake and we bought an inflatable unicorn costume. Everything was fine when we got there. I put on the suit, went in, did some silly dancing, then left Esther to finish the day's lesson. I was at the car, taking off the costume, when someone—Lennox—bashed me over the back of the head. When I woke up, I was handcuffed in the back of my SUV, and we were in a building big enough for him to drive inside. But it wasn't a garage."

"You're sure?"

Asher nodded. "I couldn't see the walls. And the ceiling was high. It was too dark to see much of it, but it looked like metal rafters."

"Okay, so industrial?"

"Most likely. He opened the back tailgate long enough to drug me while we were there. The next thing I remember, I came to in the basement."

"Was Leah there already when you woke up?"

"Yes."

"And you don't remember how you got into the basement?"

"No." Asher frowned. "And I didn't have any weird bruises, so he either carried me or had me strapped to something to bring me down. Probably the latter. He seemed fit, but I'm not small, and he wasn't that big. I never asked Leah about it. She might know. Not that it's important." He waved a hand. "Anyway, I tried to ambush him on Saturday, but he had infrared cameras placed around the room that we didn't know about, and he ambushed me instead." His hand went to his stomach. It still hurt. "He rigged a taser to a pole and shocked me with it. Several times. After that, I didn't try anything. Not until we heard him leave in a hurry earlier."

"Why? What made you think you needed to do something then?"

"It was just the suddenness of it. It was quiet upstairs, then suddenly an alarm of some kind sounded and he was running out the door. I knew something was up, so I decided to risk getting caught. I dug into my mattress to get to the springs and I made a hook so I could try to unbolt the door. I made a shiv too." He reached behind his waist and pulled out the homemade weapon, giving it to the detective. "You should probably take that. I forgot I had it until now." The only thing on his mind since the farmhouse was Esther. First on keeping her alive, then praying that the surgeons could fix her.

Stroud took the shiv and looked at it, turning it over in his hands. "I found the hook. Twisting the springs together was genius. This is too. How much time did you have?"

"Before he came back with Esther and Connie?"

The detective nodded.

"Thirty, forty minutes, maybe."

Stroud stilled and blinked several times. "That's... that's impressive."

Asher shrugged one shoulder. "I was determined."

"I guess so." Stroud laid the shiv on the table beside his chair. "Do you remember hearing or seeing anything of note while in captivity? Other voices? Phone calls? Lights? Sounds outside?"

Asher stared at a point over Stroud's shoulder, thinking. "No. That house is pretty isolated, so there wasn't anything outside. Inside, he never talked on the phone, and he never had any visitors. We could hear him moving around. The pipes would clang when the water heater kicked on, so we always knew when he was taking a shower or doing dishes."

"He lived there with you?"

"Yes. From what I could tell. He rarely left."

"And alone?"

"Yes."

"Okay. Explain what happened today."

"Leah and I were attempting to unlock the bottom bolt on the basement door. I knew if I could get it open, I could bust through the top bolt. But Lennox returned before I could. Turns out it didn't matter. He called us up. Leah saw her mom and ran to her. That upset him. He revealed who he was to Leah, then demanded she come away from Connie. The girl didn't want to, rightly so, and Connie couldn't get her to step away, so Lennox demanded I take her."

"Did you?"

"Not by force. Connie and I managed to convince her to stand with me."

"Why didn't he want her with her mother?"

"Connie never told him about Leah. He accused her of being a bad mother and said he was going to make her watch while he and Esther raised Leah."

Stroud's eyebrows shot up. "Connie didn't mention that part when I talked to her. She did, however, say he tried to shoot you, and Esther jumped in front of you. Is that right?"

Asher flinched, seeing the moment in his mind. "Yes." He ran a hand through his hair, gripping the strands for a moment before he let go. "After Connie asked how he planned to keep Leah from contacting the authorities when she was out in the world, he said she'd stay silent to protect her mother and Esther. Both women told her not to worry about them. It was at that point Lennox decided they needed a demonstration. I was expendable, so he tried to shoot me." He paused, tears welling in his eyes again. He dashed them away with the back of his hand. "I still don't know what Esther was thinking."

"You want my honest opinion?" Stroud's voice was softer.

"Sure."

"She wasn't. I think she was protecting you; someone she loves. If she makes it through this, you better never let her go. You won't find a woman who loves you more."

A crinkle formed on Asher's forehead. Was that why she did what she did? Stroud's reasoning made sense, but the man also didn't know Esther. It was in her nature to protect people. To help them. Even if it hurt her.

Leah was case-in-point. Essy never would have continued to go to that neighborhood and put herself in danger if it weren't for the girl. Not that Asher blamed Leah. He didn't. He didn't blame anyone except Lennox.

"So, what happened after Esther was shot? Connie said you and Lennox grappled."

Asher jerked as he snapped out of his thoughts. "We did. I knocked the gun out of his hand when I tackled him, and it slid under the table. With the chairs in the way, we couldn't get to it."

"How come he got away? Not to be rude, but I met your friends and got some backstory. Aren't you some sort of former super-spy?"

"No. I worked in intelligence, mostly behind a screen. I'm not defenseless, but I'm not the warrior some of my friends are. And I didn't have the best hold on him when we went down. I grabbed his legs. It took all I had to hang on. When Connie's pleas for me to help finally registered, I looked back and saw Esther and all the blood." He stopped for a moment, looking at the dried blood on his hands again. Balling them into fists, he turned a bleak expression on Stroud. "It was a shock, seeing her like that. Enough so that I forgot what was happening for a moment. Lennox took advantage of my lapse and kicked me in the face." Asher pointed to the slight swelling on his cheek. "I was still between him and the gun, and the kick didn't faze me for long. After seeing Esther, I was ready to kill him. Apparently, he saw that on my face, and he ran rather than fight me to get to the gun."

"Why didn't you go after him?"

"Because Esther needed me."

A soft knock on the door interrupted their conversation. Stroud got up and answered it.

"I'm sorry to interrupt, Detective. The patient's sister is here and wants to speak with Mr. Horn."

Asher stood. "Edie's here?" He'd told her he'd call when he had news, so why was she here? Eugene wasn't a short drive from Coos Bay. Had she found something?

Stroud glanced at Asher, a frown marring his face. "You sound surprised. Why wouldn't she come to the hospital?" He crossed his arms and narrowed his eyes. "Esther told me about her sister's and her friends' backgrounds and what they do now. What are they up to?"

"Wait, you know about the work my friends and I do?"

"Yes. Those ladies are quite effective in digging up information."

Asher wasn't surprised at that. His friends—

His thoughts cut off mid-stream. A fierce frown pulled his eyebrows down.

Ladies? What?

"I'm sorry, who are you talking about?"

Stroud's brows dipped. "Esther's sister and her friends. There were four of them."

"You said ladies. The people with Edie are all women? There were no men?"

"No."

"Did one have a British accent?"

"Yes. And she called a friend that had one as well. I don't know who it was. No one would tell me her name."

Jo.

He'd bet his lair it was Jo. But where were Ford, Dean, Sam, and Max? And Jordan? He moved toward the door. "I need to talk to Edie."

"So do I, I think." Stroud pulled the door open wider and stepped out. Asher followed.

Edie stood a few feet away, flanked by Audra, Brooke, and Annabeth. They all looked stressed and worried.

"You look terrible," Edie said as she walked up to him and gave him a hug. "I'm so glad you're all right."

He hugged her back. "Thanks, Edie. Me too." He pulled away to look at her. "Why are you here? I told you I'd call with updates."

"We need you."

"What? Why? What happened?"

"After you called, we headed your way, hoping to intercept Lennox. It was a long shot, I know, and it didn't pan out. Anyway, the next step was to look for cameras, and we found some. But"—she hesitated slightly, her gaze darting to Stroud—"Audra's friend is having trouble gaining access. No one can hack a camera like you. We need a license plate to go any further."

"Hold on a second." Stroud held up a hand. "Hack? No. I can get warrants for—"

Edie slashed a hand through the air. "There's no time for that. The longer we wait, the more likely he changes cars and gets away. I'm not about to lose this asshole while waiting on some bureaucratic bullshit."

Stroud stared at her. Asher could see him weighing the pros and cons of her plan, but he didn't care what the detective decided. "You have your laptop?" he asked Edie.

Annabeth opened the tote she carried and produced it.

"We need to do this the right way." Stroud scowled.

Asher took the computer. "This is the right way. For us. You can stop me, but I guarantee Lennox will be long gone by the time your warrants come through." He didn't wait for the detective to respond; just spun on his heel and went back to the consultation room.

"Here's a list." Brooke handed him a piece of paper as he sat down. The whole group had crowded into the small room. "It's all the cameras within a mile of the farmhouse we could find. I wish it was a bigger list."

Asher looked at it, and his heart sank. There were only two businesses listed. "I'll see what I can do. Have you checked for doorbell cameras?"

"Not yet," Audra said. "When my friend had trouble accessing those feeds, we broke off to come talk to you."

"Okay. Go back and see what you can find. For those, we'll need permission and access from the people who live there. I can't get into those without knowing considerably more about the homeowners."

"How do you not need that from the businesses?" Stroud propped his hands on his hips, watching as Asher logged into Edie's laptop.

"Because internet companies are typically limited in any given area, and business internet even more so. Most businesses use whatever the locality's major supplier is. I don't have to backdoor my way into the individual businesses, just the internet supplier. From there, I can access the businesses routers and the devices connected to it. Residential doorbell cameras run on Bluetooth, typically to an app and a cloud server. Not only are there more internet options, but there are multiple brands of cameras. They're harder to access without the right information." He pulled up a browser and logged onto his server. From there, he found the main business internet supplier for the area and set about locating the back door into their system. "You guys go. See if you can get some footage. Just in case this is a bust."

Stroud sighed; the sound told Asher he was accepting defeat.

"You guys are going to sound like crazy people, knocking on doors like that. I'll send some officers with you. Maybe you won't get them slammed in your face, then."

"That would be great. Thank you, Detective," Brooke said.

"I'm staying here," Edie said.

Asher pushed out the chair next to him. "Have a seat. You can keep me company while I search, then help me go through video."

"I'll look into that building you said you woke up in." Stroud scooped Asher's shiv off the table, then headed for the door.

A thought occurred to Asher. "My car. Did you check with the rental company about the GPS?"

"It was deactivated shortly after the vehicle left the Tylers.'"

Asher wrinkled his nose. "Damn. Okay. I'd start with the area around where the data stopped. I don't think I was out too long after he hit me over the head. I woke up before we got there, and we didn't drive that far before he pulled into that building. It's possible he disconnected it there after he drugged me. That would take some time, and he wouldn't want to be too exposed. Not with me in the back."

Stroud nodded. "I'll check." Turning, he looked at the volunteer who'd stayed close after knocking. "I know this room isn't meant for this sort of thing, but they need to stay here."

She held up her hands. "It's fine. We have others. You do what you need to do, Detective."

"Thank you." With a nod, he slipped past her. "Ladies, follow me, please."

"Call us if you find something," Audra said. "We'll do the same."

Asher kept his eyes on the screen, typing away, but saw Edie nod out of the corner of his eye.

"We will," she said.

Silence descended as everyone left. Edie shifted in her seat, pulling her legs up to sit cross-legged on the chair.

"You okay?" He gave her a quick glance.

"Not really. But I'll be fine. Just keep me busy."

He understood how she felt. He was far from all right himself. If it weren't for the work that needed to be done to catch Lennox, he'd probably be close to screaming and throwing things.

"Do your parents know about what happened?"

Silence met his question. He glanced over again to see her wringing her hands together, staring at them.

"You didn't tell them? Edie…"

"I know, okay? I know I need to, but I—" She stopped and looked away. "I wanted to wait until she was out of surgery so I could tell them more. So maybe they could see her. Right now, they'd just come up and have to twiddle their thumbs like me."

"Okay, I want you to think about something for a minute, all right?" Asher raised a finger, focusing an intense gaze on Edie.

"What?"

"Think about that baby you're carrying." He tipped his finger toward her middle. "If it were that child in the operating room, and you were the parent sitting at home oblivious, would you want to stay oblivious or would you want to know? Even if you couldn't do anything. Would you want to know?"

Her jaw worked, and she stared at him for several long moments. "Dammit," she finally whispered. "Fine. I'll go call them."

"Good. And if you haven't eaten, find some food. A drink too. You need to take care of yourself."

Grumbling, she got up. "I'm not an invalid. Just pregnant. I'm fine."

"Just humor me, please?" He pinched the bridge of his nose. He loved Edie. Truly, he did. But she could try the patience of a saint some days. "I know you think you're superwoman, but I also know you will push yourself to the brink of exhaustion. And that line is closer now than you're used to."

Some of the indignation left her expression as the rationality of his words sank in. "All right. Do you want anything?"

He dropped his hand. "Coffee. And I wouldn't be opposed to a snack."

"Okay. I'll be back soon. If the doctors come out..."

"I will call you immediately. Wait. No. I don't have a phone. I'll have the receptionist call you." He made a mental note to get a burner cell as soon as possible. After he got into these surveillance systems, he'd take a walk and see if he could find a store that sold pre-paid phones.

"That works." She hesitated at the door. "I do not want to make this phone call. It's not Esther whom they should be worried about getting shot. It should be me."

"Life's not fair, Edie." If it were, Lennox would be dead, and Esther would be in his arms.

"No. No, it's not." She walked out.

FORTY-TWO

Not for the first time, Asher glanced at the industrial clock on the wall.

It was after eleven.

It didn't feel that late. But he'd filled himself full of caffeine while he worked. Between that and the anxiety from waiting for word on Esther's condition, he was wide awake. He supposed it wasn't all bad that there wasn't any news. If they were still working, it meant she was still alive.

Clenching his teeth, he turned back to his computer, watching the last of the footage from the list of businesses Brooke gave him.

As with the other, he found nothing of note.

Getting up, he paced around the room for several minutes. It was a decent size, with a few groupings of chairs and a couple of tables that several people could sit around. He knew he was likely driving Edie and her parents up the wall with his pacing—not to mention the other people in the waiting room—but he couldn't sit still. Breaking into the surveillance cameras had kept him focused, but now, without the distraction, he was already going a little stir-crazy. He couldn't imagine it would be much longer. Essy had been in surgery over five hours now.

"Hello?"

Asher reversed direction at the sound of Edie's voice. She held her phone to her ear. He walked closer, and she glanced at him.

"Uh-huh. Okay." She paused, listening. "I'll let him know," she said, before pausing once more. "No. No news yet."

When she paused yet again, Asher forced his feet to stay planted to the same spot so he didn't yank the phone from her hand and ask what the person on the other end knew.

Finally, she hung up. "That was Audra. They struck out near the place where you and Leah were held, but she had a thought to check near the abandoned farmhouse where he instructed Esther and Connie to go. Half a mile from there, they hit paydirt. She said the footage is grainy, but she's sending it to you to see if you can clean it up and get a plate."

Asher walked around her to the laptop he'd left on the table near their seats. He sat down and logged in, downloading the video.

Edie and Esther's dad, Conner, glanced over his shoulder as the footage played. "She wasn't kidding. How are you going to get anything from that?"

"Magic." Asher minimized the video and opened a program to clean it up. He pulled the footage into it and began messing with the different zoom levels and filters. "This might take me some time."

He tuned the room out, letting the task take hold of his mind. This is what he did best. Focus.

The team all thought he was just great at hacking. But it wasn't that. Yes, he could break into anything, but it wasn't just because he saw the path to get in. It was his ability to zero in and focus. That focus is what let him follow the dots. It was why he decried the moniker "hacker." If he applied his focus to other things—like cleaning up video footage—he could accomplish similar amazing things. He just happened to like computer tech, so that's where most of his focus went.

Twenty minutes into his task, Edie poked him in the side. When he let out a grunt and didn't look up, she poked him again. "Asher!" she said in a stage whisper.

Frowning, he glanced at her. "What?"

She pointed.

He followed her finger and saw a man in green scrubs standing at the reception desk. It was the same man he'd spoken to briefly before the O.R. staff wheeled Esther away for surgery.

Asher shut the laptop and stood as the man made his way toward them. Edie and her parents rose to face the doctor as well.

"Mr. Horn." The doctor nodded, then glanced at the people with Asher. "Are you Esther's family?"

"We're her parents," Conner said. "And this is her sister." He gestured to Edie.

"Let's all go into a room and talk." The doctor motioned to the row of doors along the wall.

Asher spun on his heel and headed for an unoccupied one. The doctor shut the door behind them.

"How is she?" Faye asked. "Is she going to make it?"

"First, let me introduce myself. I'm Dr. Kerns. I'm the trauma surgeon assigned to Esther. I'll start by saying she's alive. She has stayed that way through the entire operation. We had a moment where her heart rate went a little crazy during surgery, but she never arrested."

Asher said a silent prayer of thanks. That was a good sign.

"The bullet entered here." Dr. Kerns pointed to a spot on his upper right abdomen just below the ribcage. "It went through the lower right lobe of her liver and nicked her right kidney before lodging next to a posterior rib. She's incredibly lucky. It missed the large vein that runs through the middle of the abdomen, the inferior vena cava, by inches. If the trajectory had been the other way and the bullet went left through her body instead of right, we'd be having a much different conversation. We removed the section of damaged liver and repaired her kidney. She's not out of the woods; she lost a lot of blood and this is a major trauma, but I'm optimistic."

"Can we see her?" Edie asked.

"Soon. She's in recovery right now. Once she's moved up to the ICU, someone will be down to get you. Do you have any questions for me?"

They all shook their heads. Asher knew they probably would later, but for now, it was enough to know she'd survived.

"All right." Dr. Kerns rose. "If you think of something or have concerns, please let a nurse know and they'll get a hold of me."

"We will, thank you." Asher stood and shook the man's hand.

"You're welcome." With a polite smile, the doctor left.

Asher scrubbed his hands over his face. Weariness pressed down on his shoulders as the adrenaline he'd been running on ebbed with the knowledge that Esther would likely survive. His emotions were all over the place. He wanted to both cry and laugh.

Edie, though, had picked one. Tears streamed down her face as she sobbed into her mother's shoulder. Faye cried right along with her.

Conner caught Asher's gaze, moisture gathering in his eyes too. But an anger simmered underneath. For a moment, Asher worried it was directed at him. He wouldn't be surprised. Esther wouldn't be in the state she was if he hadn't let himself get clubbed over the head.

But Conner's words allayed his fears.

"You find that son of a bitch who did this to my baby. I don't care what you have to do. Make him pay."

The riot of emotion swirling in Asher's mind calmed as determination took hold. It would be his pleasure.

FORTY-THREE

A silence, cloaked in a heaviness like a summer rain on a humid night, enveloped Asher as the door to Esther's ICU cubicle snicked shut behind him. The hum of the machines on her IV pole and the hiss of oxygen coming through the mask on her face were the only sounds penetrating the stillness.

He stared at her, taking in her altered appearance. It had been a couple of hours since her surgery, but she was still pale, though no longer gray. Deep circles sat under her eyes, casting shadows on her pretty face. Her crowning glory, her beautiful coppery hair, had a dullness to it. As though it, too, knew her body's resources were needed elsewhere and had sent all of its reserves to heal her organs and replace the blood she lost.

Of their own volition, his feet carried him across the room to her bedside. He touched her fingers with one of his, expecting them to be cold to match the icy tone of her skin. But they weren't. Warmth seeped into his fingertip.

Asher perched a hip on the edge of her bed and picked up her hand. He brought it up and kissed the backs of her fingers. "Oh, Essy. I'm so relieved you're alive." Moisture gathered in his eyes, and he glanced away briefly, blinking to keep the tears at bay. "You shouldn't be here." His voice broke. "Shouldn't be in this bed, hooked up to all these machines." He sniffed. "Why did you have to jump in front of me? You have to know I'd rather take the bullet than have you hurt."

He skimmed her knuckles with his thumb. "God, baby." A lone tear trickled down his face, and he dashed it away. "This is such a mess. Lennox got away. Not scot-free. Audra and the others tracked down some doorbell camera footage of his car. I got a partial plate from it. I wish I could get more, but the camera was just too far from the road. Your detective friend, Stroud, has it now. I could have run it myself, but I needed a break." He squeezed her fingers. "Needed to see you."

Another tear fell, then another. Asher couldn't stop them now.

They just kept flowing. He slid off the bed and into the chair beside it, then pressed his forehead to the mattress next to her arm. The warmth of her skin anchored him and kept him from completely spinning out of control. She was alive, and the connection reminded him of that.

It took several minutes for his tears to ebb, but eventually, his mind broke through the sorrow over what happened and that earlier determination reared its head again.

He squeezed Esther's hand. "I doubt you can hear me, but just in case, I'm going to get him, Essy. I won't let him get away with anything he's done. So when you wake up, if I'm not here, just know I'm out keeping my word."

Asher rose to hover over her and press a kiss to her forehead. "I love you, Esther. I need you to get better so I can say that to you while you're awake." He kissed her forehead again, then squeezed her fingers and stepped back. "Get better, Essy. I'll be back."

Spinning on his heel, he marched out of the room, knowing what he had to do.

FORTY-FOUR

The chilly October breeze ruffled Asher's hair as he left the hospital. The streetlights cast shadows over the parked cars beyond the portico where he stood. He'd hired an Uber using Edie's laptop to take him to a store and was waiting for the driver to arrive. It was late—after one a.m.— but he needed a phone.

"What are you doing?"

He glanced back at the voice, frowning as he glimpsed the owner. "Go back inside, Edie."

She ignored him and walked closer, huddling into an over-sized fleece jacket. "It's chilly out here. Why are we outside?"

"I'm waiting on a ride. I don't know what you're doing."

She snorted. "Really? I would think it was obvious."

"Well, it's not." He had his suspicions, but he'd rather not think she believed he was about to go cuckoo. Or on a murderous rampage to put Lennox six feet under. She might join him on the latter, though.

"I'm just making sure you're all right. You went into Esther's room, sat in there for about fifteen minutes, and when you came back out, your eyes were red-rimmed, but you looked more determined than ever to find Lennox."

"I am. Not just for what he did to Esther. The man needs to be stopped."

"I know that."

"Then go back inside and let me do what I do."

"You sit behind a computer screen and find information. You don't go out in the field, Ash. That's more my thing."

"Yeah, well, you can't right now."

She crossed her arms and shifted, annoyance pinching her features. "I don't regret getting pregnant, but it sure is an inconvenience."

That brought a slight smirk to Asher's face. "In any case, I'm not doing fieldwork right now." Not yet. "I need a phone."

"Why didn't you ask me or one of the others to take you? Why hire a car?"

"I didn't want to take you away from your family. And the others all went back to Esther's to get some rest." He lifted a shoulder. "Uber seemed the easiest and most considerate way to get what I need."

She rolled her eyes and huffed, letting her arms fall back to her sides. "That's dumb. Cancel it. I'll take you."

"I can't."

She frowned. "Why not?"

"I used your laptop to book it, and it's still upstairs with your parents."

The stare she laid on him made him feel a bit like a bug under a microscope. His brows drew together, and he stared back. "What?"

"For a smart man, you sure can be stupid." She took her phone from her pocket and shook it at him.

"Why are you waving that at me?"

"Because you can log into your Uber from this." The look

of incredulity on her face morphed into concern. "Are you all right? I mean, you can have a brain disconnect from time to time, but this is a little much."

"I'm fine." He plucked the phone from her fingers and logged into his Uber account. "Maybe I need a little sleep."

"And food. Have you eaten?"

He paused, fingers hovering over the screen as he tried to remember the last time he'd had a meal. This morning. The gruel Lennox brought. "I had breakfast. And that snack you brought me earlier." The boost of energy and brain power from the small bag of trail mix she'd brought him had long since worn off.

Edie sighed. "You need Esther in your life. Just to keep you alive."

He grunted softly, not agreeing with or denying what she said. Some days, it was probably true. He'd made it to the ripe age of thirty-three without her, though.

"Come on." Edie tugged on his shirtsleeve.

Asher nodded, focused on the phone screen. "Yep. Hang on." He hit cancel, then confirmed it, before logging out. "All right. Ride's canceled. I'm at your mercy."

A wicked grin graced her face. "Careful, Asher. I know Esther conned you into wearing that unicorn suit, but I'm the sister with the truly devious mind. And pregnancy has made me cranky."

"So, we're stopping for ice cream, then?"

She tipped her head back and laughed. Asher chuckled, the lightness of the moment easing some of the tension in his body. There had been few light moments lately.

"Fine. Twist my arm." Edie grinned. "But you're buying."

That comment made him pause. He closed his eyes and groaned.

"What?" She stopped beside him.

"I forgot I don't have my wallet. It was in my car. Now I'm

glad you found me. I'd have gotten all the way to the store and had no way to buy the damn phone."

Edie paused for a beat. "Yeah, we're doing food first. Recharge those super brain cells of yours."

He followed her down the sidewalk and into the parking lot, where they got into Esther's car. Edie pulled out of the parking space and pointed them toward Coos Bay. At this hour, nothing was open in Heron Ridge.

Asher closed his eyes, shutting off his brain for the drive. Edie must have sensed he needed some time to himself, because she didn't try to make conversation until she pulled into the drive-thru for an all-night burger joint. He gave her his order, then tucked into his food when she passed it to him a few minutes later. In several bites, he'd devoured half of his sandwich.

By the time she'd parked and eaten a few bites of her soft-serve ice cream, he'd finished his burger and fries. With the food on board, he felt more awake and more in control of his thoughts and emotions.

"Thank you for dinner." He wadded up his trash and stuffed it into the bag. "I haven't had a decent meal in days."

She frowned. "I'm sorry. I should have made sure you'd eaten something more than the trail mix earlier."

"You're not my keeper, Edie. I don't need one."

"I know, but I am your friend. And you made sure I ate. I should've had the grace to do the same. I'm sorry."

"Don't be. You were worried about Essy and had a myriad of other things on your mind. I'm fed now and I'm fine."

She studied him for a long moment, then nodded. "All right. Let's find you a phone, then, shall we?"

"Finish your ice cream first." He pointed to the cup in her hand. "So we can banish the crankiness."

She rolled her eyes. "Fine." Dutifully, she popped a spoonful into her mouth.

Twelve minutes later, Edie had finished her ice cream, and they'd found a twenty-four-hour department store and purchased a pre-paid phone. He bought a pair of pants, too, to replace his blood-stained ones.

"Where to now?" Edie asked as they got back in the car.

"The hospital. I want another crack at that license plate."

She cranked the engine. "Didn't you already get a partial and send it to Stroud?"

"Yeah, but I want to look it up myself. He's taking too long."

Edie rolled her eyes as she pulled out of the parking spot. "It's only been a few hours, Asher."

"Exactly. Too long." He rolled his neck. "I wish I had my computers. They're faster than your laptop. No offense." He tore open the phone package so he could set up the device.

She held up a hand. "None taken. It works for what I do with it. You brought yours with you, though, right? We could drive back to Heron Ridge. You could work from Esther's house."

He grimaced, not liking the idea of being so far away. "Maybe. For now, I'll make do. Most of my programs are cloud-based, so I can access them anywhere. It's just the speed your laptop lacks." He powered on the phone and waited for it to go through its start-up process. "If we do go back to Heron Ridge, we should check out that address where my rental stopped pinging too. See what's there." Stroud had let that little tidbit slip earlier. Asher didn't think he'd realized it, either, and he wasn't about to inform the detective of what he could do with the information.

"We need to sleep first, Asher. It's late."

He glanced at the dashboard clock and blinked in surprise at the hour. His adrenaline was back, feeding his focus. Or maybe it was the food. Something had kicked him back into action.

"How about you drive back to Esther's and let me have the car? You can catch a ride with the others in the morning, can't you?"

She gave him a quick side glance. "That's not the point. You need to rest."

"I've been resting. For three days, I sat in a dank basement with nothing to do but sit around. I don't want to do that anymore."

"But you also got shocked, right? Repeatedly. And hit over the head hard enough you were knocked out. That's probably playing a big part in your absentmindedness."

"I'm fine. The food helped. If you won't lend me the car, I'll call another Uber." He knew it was a bit underhanded to point out how he could find a workaround, but he didn't care. Having Esther's car would make things easier for him.

Edie let out a soft growl. "You need to catch the flu too."

His brows dipped. "Excuse me?"

She turned a quick glare on him. "I've been enjoying the relative drama-free investigation with the ladies. You and the rest of the team can be a teensy bit melodramatic." She held up two fingers just millimeters apart.

"Melodramatic or not, we get the job done. So, can I have the car?"

Her hands clenched and unclenched on the steering wheel as she drove. "Fine," she finally huffed. "But I'm coming back to the hospital with you. I'm not leaving Mom and Dad there alone all night."

"You're sure? Those chairs aren't that comfortable to sleep in."

"I'm sure. The nurse said there's a lounge for ICU families that has recliners. I'll find that and sleep there. I just wish—" She stopped and didn't continue.

Asher looked up from programming the phone. "What?"

She glanced at him, then out the windshield, then back at

him. "Sleep isn't the only reason I don't want you going off alone. I won't stop you, but I just wish you'd wait until morning and take me or Audra with you."

"Edie—"

"Please? It's a safety thing. I doubt you'll run into Lennox, but he isn't the only criminal lurking at night."

His jaw worked. Asher's first instinct was to say no and do whatever he felt necessary. But he also understood her point. And he was not a field operative. "Okay. How about a compromise? I'll just drive around. I'll never get out of the car."

She snorted. "I know you, Mr. Impulsive. You'll see something that sets off your radar and want a closer look. Next thing you know, you'll be wandering into some abandoned building full of druggies and crazy people. Especially after being on the road for two hours just getting back to Heron Ridge. The drive will give your mind time to get antsy."

"It won't be that bad, Edie."

"The hell it won't."

Asher sighed and scrubbed a hand over his face. "Look, I *promise* I won't get out of the car. If I see something that I think warrants closer inspection, I'll take a picture, then either come back in the morning or call for help. Okay?"

She eyed him for a moment before turning back to the road. "If you die, I will bring you back to life and kill you again, understand?"

He smiled at her in the darkness. "Completely."

FORTY-FIVE

"Come on, you son of a bitch. Work," Asher grumbled at the laptop screen. When he'd run the partial of Lennox's plate, he'd gotten entirely too many hits, so he went back to the surveillance image and tried once more to sharpen it. He'd hit on a combo of filters that had enhanced it enough he could read another number, but the last two were still blurry. One was a two or a seven. The last was a three or an E. Or maybe an eight. He knew he could run all the possibilities, but the more digits he had, the fewer the number of results he had to sift through.

He had one more thing to try, then he'd run all the partial combos and see what came up. But hopefully, he wouldn't have to.

Tongue poking the corner of his mouth, he made a few more adjustments.

"Ha! Yes!"

His cheeks colored. He hadn't meant to be so loud. His gaze darted up. Several people in the atrium eyed him. He was glad he'd moved downstairs rather than staying in the ICU lounge. "Sorry." He waved a hand, then turned back to his computer. His tweaks had worked. He had the last two digits. A seven and a three.

With the new information, he restored the window for the license plate search he'd done earlier, and ran the full plate. Right away, a hit came back for a black Chevy Equinox.

"Whoa." Asher blinked and read the screen again. The car was registered to a woman. Vanessa Burnwell. Not what he was expecting.

"Okay, Miss Vanessa Burnwell. Who are you?" He ran her name using the information from her license plate registration and found a DMV record. She was on the young side. Late twenties. Using her photograph, he ran a search of social media, then minimized the window, letting it run in the background. With her name and birthdate, he ran a background check.

"Well, that's not surprising." He sighed as he scrolled through the information that popped up. She had a record for drug abuse.

Scrolling further, he realized she was currently in prison, five months into a three-year term. "So, how did Lennox get your car?" Did she sell it to him before she went in? Or give it to him? That would imply they had a relationship of some sort. He needed to talk to this woman. If they were friends or lovers, she could know where he might go.

He picked up his phone and dialed the number for Stroud that Edie gave him before he left her upstairs with her parents. The line rang five times, then rolled to voicemail. Asher held back a sigh and left a message.

"Hey, it's Asher Horn. I got the full plate for the vehicle Lennox drove. It's registered to a woman named Vanessa Burnwell. She's currently incarcerated in Idaho for drugs. I'm working on locating her social media accounts. Call me when you get this." He left his new number, then hung up.

The time on the phone registered as he set the device

down. No wonder Stroud hadn't answered. It was nearly three a.m. He should probably get some sleep, but he was still too keyed up. Getting a lead hadn't helped.

He tapped the keyboard, thinking. He could head back to Heron Ridge and check out the area where his rental's GPS stopped transmitting. He hadn't done that yet. Despite his eagerness to do so, he'd decided working on the license plate would be more productive. But now, he had to wait for his program to finish its search. That could be a couple of hours, or it could take multiple days. He was hoping it was only hours. He'd fed it plenty of information.

Asher closed the laptop and got up, tucking it under his arm. Pocketing his phone, he left the atrium and ventured out into the chilly October air.

A shiver went down his spine. He should stop at Esther's for clothes when he got back to town, before gallivanting all over the area. He'd changed his pants, but a coat would be nice.

He needed a shower too. There was an all-night truck stop not too far away. He'd seen it when he and Edie went out. He could run in there and clean up; get a hoodie and some fancy touristy boxers to tide him over. Then he wouldn't have to worry about disturbing the others.

Mind made up, he headed for Esther's car and got in.

Forty minutes later, he was clean, he'd had another snack and more coffee, and was on his way to his rental car's last known location.

The drive from Eugene to the coast ticked by at a snail's pace. Asher resisted the urge to set his cruise control, knowing the need to watch his speed would help keep him awake. Halfway through, he felt himself nodding off, anyway.

Shifting in his seat, he slapped his cheek and rolled his neck. "C'mon, Ash. You're almost there," he muttered to himself. Rolling the windows down, he let the cold air blast him in the face, then reached for the radio.

Rock music. He needed rock music.

Spinning the dial, he finally found what he wanted and cranked the volume up.

It did the trick. By the time he rolled into Heron Ridge, he was chilly and his ears were ringing, but he was wide awake.

"All right, where is this warehouse?" Glancing at the GPS, he turned into the industrial district, then switched the radio off. He hit the button to roll up his windows, his promise to Edie echoing in his mind.

Nothing jumped out at him. Graffiti decorated many of the buildings. Weeds poked through the cracked sidewalks and vacant lots of the places that weren't in use. In a couple of alleys, he saw homeless encampments. But nowhere did he see his car. He honestly hadn't expected to; though there was a part of him that had hoped it really would be that easy. More than likely, Lennox tucked it up in that building he'd pulled into, then transferred Asher to another car and left the rental behind. It could be broken down into parts by now, for all Asher knew.

Turning around, he drove back through the maze of warehouses and factories, this time at a slower pace. It all still looked the same. He could come back in the daylight, but he had a sinking suspicion it would take a tip from a member of the public before they found his car.

Leaving the industrial district behind, Asher checked the time. Stroud would be awake soon and would hopefully listen to his message. He debated taking a quick nap, but the fatigue he'd felt on the drive had disappeared.

Instead, he decided to go camp outside Stroud's house. He didn't trust the detective to keep him in the loop. And even if he did, Asher didn't like waiting on other people to do things. Stroud might not check his messages until he got to work. He might have other things to do before he could look into Vanessa. Asher refused to sit around all morning, waiting for Stroud to get back to him.

Pulling into an empty parking lot, he opened his laptop, noting that the search for Vanessa Burnwell's social media was still running. Hopefully, it would come up with something soon.

With a quick click, he opened a browser window and looked up Stroud's address. Memorizing it, he put the laptop away and drove out of the parking lot. It wasn't long before he was pulling up outside Stroud's house.

The windows of the two-story modern farmhouse were still dark. Asher glanced at the dashboard clock. It was just after six. Hopefully, the man was an early riser.

While he waited, he checked on the social media search, even though he knew it likely hadn't changed in the last few minutes.

A quick glance at the screen told him he was right. He shut the computer with a harsh sigh, then tossed it onto the passenger seat. Settling in to wait, he unbuckled his seatbelt and got comfortable.

The Strouds lived on a quiet street in a decent neighborhood. All the homes were on the newer side and well-kept, with weed-free grass, tall vinyl fences, and pristine concrete driveways.

Asher wrinkled his nose. He knew a lot of people liked the newer, clean and tidy look, but he much preferred his ramshackle beach house or even Esther's older two-story. They had character and didn't feel so cold.

Minutes ticked by. Lights went on in a house a few doors down, but the Strouds' stayed annoyingly dark.

He shifted in his seat as his mind wandered. An image of Esther's pale face crept into his mind, past the defenses he'd erected to help him stay focused. Swiftly on its heels was the memory of the bloom of deep red blood that formed on her clothing in Lennox's kitchen.

Asher's jaw worked, and he tried to force his mind onto other topics. Like what he was going to say to Stroud when he knocked.

But it didn't work. Half a minute later, the images were back. This was part of the reason he hadn't wanted to wait around and why he hadn't wanted to sleep. He knew the moment things quieted, his mind would spin through the last few days, and particularly the last twelve hours.

He closed his eyes and let his head fall back against the seat. "I don't want to do this right now," he whispered. But he knew it was now, or later, when he actually wanted to sleep.

So, he stopped fighting it and let the barrage of memories and feelings come.

They started with the pain in his skull when Lennox knocked him out, then the outrage and the tiny bit of fear he felt when he woke up handcuffed in the back of his car. Then the healthier dose of fear that accompanied the anger when he woke again in the basement of that house to find Leah there with him.

His abs clenched as he remembered the pain of being tased.

Fists clenched, he ground his teeth together. He was angrier at his own dumb ass for putting himself in that position than he was at Lennox. He should have searched the basement better, paid more attention. But he'd been so angry that he'd been taken and then so thrown off by Leah's presence he hadn't done his due diligence. And it had nearly cost him dearly.

Inhaling a breath through his nose, he opened his eyes and glanced at Strouds' house. Nothing had changed. He let out a low growl of frustration and sank his head into the headrest again.

This time, his brain went to the shooting. It replayed in his mind like an old VHS tape; playing, then pausing, then swiftly rewinding, only to play again. Over and over, he relived it.

Relived the fear that sucker punched him when Lennox pointed the gun at him. The terror that doused him like the iciest water when he turned around and saw Esther in a pool of blood. Even now, a hollow pit formed in his stomach and a jitteriness worked its way through his muscles.

That was a sight he never wanted to see again. Nor did he ever want to feel her fading beneath his hands or have her life literally seeping between his fingers.

Several tears tracked down his face, and he swiped at them.

He'd had his cry at her bedside earlier. Now was the time to find the man responsible. She was alive, and he couldn't do anything to help her heal. But he could catch the man who tried to kill her.

He opened his eyes again and looked across the street.

Wake up, dammit!

He glared at the Strouds' home and willed the lights to come on downstairs.

Annoyed, he plucked his phone from the center console, debating calling Ford. But he didn't really have a reason to. There was nothing Ford could do. Even if he wasn't sick and could get on a plane, they were in a holding pattern until they had more information.

Soft light glowed through the sheer curtains on the Strouds' front windows.

Finally.

Asher grabbed Edie's laptop and got out of the car. He jogged across the street and knocked on the door, forgoing the bell in case the Strouds had children still asleep.

The porch light came on a moment before the door swung inward to reveal a scowling Detective Stroud, who was still clad in his bathrobe.

"Horn, it's barely six a.m. What the hell are you doing here?"

"Did you read my text?"

"What? No. I haven't even had coffee yet. Or a shower. Go away. I'll call you when I get to the station."

He started to close the door, but Asher stuck his foot in the doorway. "I got a hit on Lennox's license plate."

Stroud's angry frown turned curious for a moment before he shook his head and glared at Asher. "I'll be in the office at seven-thirty."

Asher put a hand on the door this time. "If your wife stepped in front of a bullet for you, wouldn't you stop at nothing to bring her shooter to justice?"

Stroud narrowed his eyes, staring at him for several seconds. "Dammit. You play dirty." He stepped back and opened the door. "Keep your voice down. My wife and kids are still sleeping."

Stepping inside, Asher closed the door softly, then followed Stroud into the kitchen.

"You want coffee?" Stroud glanced at him as he stopped in front of the single-serve machine. "Or have you had enough that it's replaced the blood in your veins?"

"There's still a little red left, so hit me."

Stroud grabbed two mugs and put one under the spout, then added a pod and pressed start. Turning, he crossed his arms and rested against the counter. "What did you find? And how? Our techs weren't getting anywhere when I left last night."

"I wasn't, either, until I played with the image again. I managed to clean it up enough to get the last few digits. The car is registered to a woman from Idaho named Vanessa Burnwell. She's currently serving three years there on a drug charge."

Stroud pinched the bridge of his nose. "Do I want to know how you found all of this?"

Asher lifted a shoulder. "Most of it's public record. Or stuff that can be accessed with a private investigator's license."

"You don't have a private investigator's license."

Not contradicting him, Asher just stared. He didn't, but he didn't care.

Stroud huffed a short sigh. "So, what's her relationship to Lennox?"

"I'm not sure." He set the laptop down and opened it, showing him what he'd found. "I'm also running a facial rec program, trying to find her social media accounts. Maybe they'll tell us something. If nothing pops up, we'll have to talk to her."

"We?"

"You. Me. You and me. I don't particularly care, so long as it happens today."

"Look, I get that you're all gung-ho to take action, but police work is a process."

"A slow one. And I don't have to follow your rules."

His chin coming up, Stroud leveled a stern look on Asher. "So far, I've tolerated your antics because they've proven useful and mostly harmless. But don't push me, Horn. I won't tolerate you running around like we're in the wild and lawless old west."

Asher blamed the next words that came out of his mouth on stress and a lack of sleep. Because they certainly weren't ones that would win him any friends. "Respectfully, Detective, there's very little you can do to stop me. You have no idea who I am or what I'm capable of. With a few strokes of my keyboard, I can send your entire life into disarray. With a few more, I can give myself a new identity. One that would wipe Asher Horn off the planet. So, let's move past the bloviating and onto what truly matters, yeah?"

Blooms of color popped on Stroud's cheeks. Asher could see the anger seething just below the surface in his gaze, but he was beyond worrying about what the man thought. His only goal was bringing Lennox down.

"You know, I might be a small-town detective, but I'm far from dumb or unconnected. You'd be surprised at who I know and what I'm capable of."

"Honestly? I don't care. I want Lennox. Preferably in a hole in the ground, but I'll settle for seeing him in a cage."

The stern look on Stroud's face didn't waver. "I didn't think to check you for weapons. Should I?"

"I haven't been home yet."

At Stroud's rough intake of breath, Asher held up a hand. "But it wouldn't matter, because I'm not normally armed." He didn't bother to tell him that Edie and Audra might be, though. "I'm an analyst, not a field operative. Look, I'm not asking to lead the charge when we find Lennox. I'm just asking for you to feed me information so we can do it faster."

"Right, but if we don't do it legally, he'll walk."

"So, hire me as a technical consultant. I'll work dirt cheap on this case, and your department can utilize my proprietary software."

Stroud crossed his arms, the stern look morphing back to a curious one. "What sort of proprietary software?"

"It's basically just a bunch of algorithms that let me search legitimate databases faster." Sensing he had him on the hook, he pushed forward. "So, are you calling the prison, or am I?"

FORTY-SIX

The world came back into focus for Esther with a rush. The dull noise filling her ears became a roar of sound as her eyelids fluttered. Fuzzy ceiling tiles swam in front of her eyes.

Where am I? Her bedroom ceiling didn't look like this. What was that whirring noise? And the hissing?

The feel of her own breath on her face drew her attention to the stiff plastic strapped to her face. What—

An oxygen mask.

Everything rushed back.

The evilness in Lennox's eyes as he aimed his pistol at Asher.

Her instinctual urge to protect him.

She hadn't thought, just jumped.

Her hand went to her belly, feeling the thick bandages under the blankets. A heavy ache throbbed through her torso. What damage had it done? Would she ever be the same?

The door swung open, admitting sound and a shaft of light from the hallway. Through bleary eyes, she saw a nurse enter.

"Hi," the woman whispered. She stopped next to Esther's bed, smiling at her with tired brown eyes. "I'm Shawna. It's good to see you awake."

"How—how bad?" Her voice came out not much louder than a crackly whisper.

"Hang on. Let me get you a drink, then we can talk." She still didn't raise her voice.

Before Esther could ask why she was whispering, the nurse disappeared from view. A few moments later, the head of her bed raised, sitting her up a little more, and a set of hands holding a straw appeared in front of her face.

"Pull that mask down and take a sip."

Feebly, Esther raised a trembling hand to bat at the mask. Her arms weighed a hundred pounds each. Somehow, she got one to her face and lowered the clear plastic. Shawna slipped the straw between her lips, and Esther took a long draw of the cool liquid.

"Not too much. We don't want to upset your stomach." Shawna withdrew the straw and set the cup on the rolling table beside the bed.

"Why are you whispering?"

Shawna glanced over her shoulder and nodded at something behind her. "Because that's the first he's slept since you got here." She shifted so Esther could see.

Asher laid on the sofa under the window, a pillow tucked beneath his head and a thin hospital blanket over his long body.

"He passed out a couple hours ago. We've been tiptoeing around as we did our checks so we didn't wake him. Though I think it might take several minutes of your IV blaring before he'd wake up."

"How long was I out?"

Shawna glanced at her watch. "About twenty hours."

"Twenty—" Esther's head sank back into her pillow and she closed her eyes. "How bad is it?"

"You're a lucky lady. You lost a bit of your liver—which should grow back or get compensated for, because that's what livers do—and you have a hole in your right kidney, which Dr. Kerns sewed up for you. Things could have been much, much worse."

"And the surgery took that long?"

"Oh. No. You were under for several hours, but once Dr. Kerns was sure you were out of the anesthesia, he kept you mildly sedated until rounds this morning. You lost a lot of blood, and he wanted your body to rest. Things are looking good, though." Shawna glanced at the monitor above the head of the bed. "Your vitals have been stable since they brought you up here. And you're awake now. How do you feel?"

"Like I'm deep underwater. My limbs are really heavy, and there's just pressure—everywhere."

"I wouldn't expect anything else. But that should get better fairly quickly as the sedation wears off. How's your pain level?"

Esther rested a hand on her abdomen. "Um, it's okay for now."

"Good. Dr. Kerns put in an order for a pain pump for you. Now that you're awake, I'll get that set up." She pulled a pad of paper from her scrub pocket, then pressed a button on the monitor. The blood pressure cuff around Esther's upper arm inflated.

"Okay." Esther's eyelids fluttered. Her energy levels were laughably low. "Is there a timeline for how long I'll be here?"

"Several days, at least. It all depends on how quickly you recover and whether you have any complications."

Esther willed her body to cooperate. She did not want to stay a moment longer than necessary.

The cuff released its air, and Shawna wrote down the

results before tucking her paper and pen back into her scrubs. She offered Esther a sunny smile. "I'll be back soon with your pain pump. Do you want me to lay you down some more?"

"No. I'm fine like this." It felt better to sit up, actually. Things weren't as stretched out as they were lying down. "Thank you."

"Sure thing."

Once Shawna walked out of the room, Esther took a few moments to digest their conversation and to let her mind clear a little more. She'd essentially lost an entire day. What happened in that timeframe? Did the police catch Lennox? Was Leah okay? Asher appeared fine, so at least her mad dive to save him worked.

She scrubbed at her eyes above her oxygen mask, trying to rub away some of the grittiness. Sleep still pulled at the edges of her mind, but she wasn't ready to let it take hold again yet.

The movement made her slide down the mattress a little, increasing the ache in her back. Shifting, she only made it an inch before agony zinged through her side and her ribs. A grunt of pain escaped her, and she clutched at the sheets, waiting for the wave to pass.

Maybe she should hold off on moving until Shawna hooked up her pain pump. The backache wasn't that bad, all things considered.

"Essy?"

Asher's deep, sleep-roughened voice penetrated the pain waves. She looked over to see him sit up. A moment later, he stood and crossed to her side.

"Hey." He skimmed her hair back from her forehead. His touch did more to banish the pain than any amount of willpower. "Welcome back. Do you need me to get the nurse?"

"No," she managed to push out. The pain was receding. "I'm all right. I wanted to sit up."

"Do you want me to help?"

She rolled her head. "I'll wait until I have more pain meds on board. Shawna was just in here. She said she'll be back soon with a pain pump."

His head bobbed a moment before he yawned. "Oh, sorry."

Esther squinted up at him. "How much sleep have you had in the last few days?"

He waved a hand. "I'm fine. I slept at the farmhouse. It was fitful, but I'm sure I got plenty with all my naps. There wasn't much else to do."

"And since then?" She noticed even through her foggy brain he'd left that part off.

Asher lifted a shoulder. "A couple hours. But stop worrying about me. How are you?"

"Tired. Sore. But I'm fine."

He snorted. "No, you're not." He wrapped one of her hands in his. "Why did you do that, Esther?" One hand went to her face. His fingers skimmed her cheek as he brushed at her hair again. "I can't lose you."

A lump formed in her throat, choking off her words. She forced her dry mouth to swallow, but it only allowed a whisper to emerge. "I can't lose you, either."

The door cracked open with a soft knock.

Esther glanced over and saw Detective Stroud poke his head into the room.

"Can I come in?"

She pressed her lips together, wishing he'd waited just a little longer. What felt like a precious moment with Asher had slipped through her fingers with his arrival.

"What's up?" Asher straightened, but didn't let go of her hand.

Stroud came inside. "I got a hold of the prison housing Vanessa Burnwell." He turned to Esther. "And I was hoping you'd be awake." He offered her a kind smile that crinkled the corners of his eyes. "Welcome back to the land of the living. How are you doing?"

"I'm all right. Who's Vanessa Burnwell?" She frowned, not recognizing the name.

"I'll get to that. How much do you know about what's happened since yesterday?"

"Nothing. I just woke up a few minutes ago."

His face pulled. "Okay. Let me give you a quick rundown."

Esther's eyes widened as he went through all that had occurred. What stuck out, though, was that Lennox got away. She'd nearly died, and he was still roaming around out there. She understood why Asher let him go and was grateful he'd stayed to help her, but it stuck in her craw that the man had slithered away. Why couldn't he have tripped on his way out the door and smashed his head into something hard?

"So, this Vanessa woman is the key?" she asked.

"Possibly." Stroud tipped his head briefly in acknowledgment. "We won't know until we talk to her." He turned his attention to Asher. "Her attorney agreed to a video interview this afternoon. I'm not sure how much we'll get from her. He won't let her implicate herself in any wrongdoing. But nonetheless, I'm here to extend an invitation for you to sit in and *watch* the conversation. You'll be in the room, but you can't ask questions."

Esther looked at Asher. She could see he didn't like the idea of being sidelined, but there was little he could do.

He nodded once. "Fine. What time?"

"We should head out in the next few minutes."

"Okay. I'll find you." Asher's gaze flicked to the door.

Stroud backed toward it. "Five minutes. I'm leaving then, with or without you."

"I'll be there."

The detective tipped his chin, then turned and left.

Asher squeezed her hand. "I'm sorry. I don't want to leave you yet."

"It's fine, Asher. I'll just sleep, anyway. You'd just sit there and stare at me being unconscious."

A smile flirted with his mouth. "I'd probably sleep too."

She chuckled, then winced. "Ouch."

"Sorry. I'll do my best not to be funny for a while." He brought her hand up and placed a gentle kiss on her knuckles.

"It's fine." She gave him a soft smile. "Laughing isn't comfortable, but I enjoy your wit."

He ran a thumb over her cheekbone, staring down at her with a tenderness in his eyes that warmed her insides. "I'm quite happy you're still here to do that."

Esther lifted her free hand, grazing his forearm with her fingers. "Me too."

He tugged her oxygen mask lower and leaned down to brush his lips over hers. "I need to go. We'll talk more later?"

She nodded. "I'll be here."

FORTY-SEVEN

Asher walked out of Esther's room, reluctant to leave. He knew there was nothing he could do to help her heal, but it didn't change the fact that he wanted to just sit there in her presence and be thankful he could.

Stroud pushed away from the wall and tucked his phone into his pocket when he saw Asher emerge. "Ready?"

"Yep. Let's go." Tucking Edie's laptop under his arm, he followed Stroud down the hall toward the elevators. As they approached the ICU lounge, he saw Edie through the glass doors. She was camped in a recliner, reading a book, but glanced up in time to see him. Asher gave a quick tip of his head. Without question, she got up and met them as they passed.

Stroud sighed as Asher paused. "I invited you, Horn. This is not social hour."

"Invited him where?" Edie frowned.

"He finagled an interview with the woman who owns the car Lennox was driving." He'd told her about his discoveries this morning before he went to see Esther and subsequently passed out on the couch in her room.

"Let me tell Mom and Dad where I'm going."

"Now, hang—"

Asher waved a hand, cutting Stroud off. He glanced at Edie. "Go ahead."

She spun away, retreating through the glass doors. Asher turned to Stroud. "Trust me, it's easier to give in. She'd probably follow us, then make a ruckus at the station until you either arrested her or let her come back, anyway."

Stroud huffed and glared, but stayed silent. A moment later, Edie returned, and they traipsed toward the elevators.

"How's Esther?" Edie asked as they stepped into the lift. "Still sleeping?"

"No. She woke up not long before he arrived." Asher hooked a thumb toward Stroud. "She's groggy, but coherent. The nurse was going to hook her up to a pain pump now that she's awake to keep her comfortable. I imagine they'll try to get her up and at least into a chair later today."

"Did you get some rest? I poked my head in an hour or so ago and saw you passed out."

"I slept a little. I'm fine."

She hummed.

Stroud snorted. "Can you make him stay here tonight? Maybe take away his car keys so he doesn't show up at my house before the sun comes up?"

"He had info, and I'd have done the same thing." Edie gave the detective a pointed look.

"You all are nuts," he muttered.

"We prefer efficient," she said.

The elevator doors slid open, and they stepped into the lobby. Stroud led them out of the building to his cruiser. "You guys have a way to get back up here? I'm not sure I'll be able to bring you back."

"My rental is with Audra in Heron Ridge. She can bring us," Edie said.

"Sounds good." Stroud unlocked the vehicle. "Get in."

Asher let Edie sit in front, while he crammed his long legs into the back seat.

"Are you sure you don't want to sit up here?" Edie twisted in her seat as Stroud started the engine. "It's not a short trip."

"Positive. I'm going to check on my search." As of the time he went to sleep, he didn't have any hits on Vanessa's social media.

"How do you have an internet connection?" Stroud glanced in the rearview mirror.

"Hotspot."

"Oh. Right. Sorry. It's been a long day."

Asher knew the feeling.

Opening the laptop, he pulled up the search screen. It was done, and there were results. "Bingo."

"You got something?" Edie turned.

"Yep. Now we just have to hope the pages aren't set to private." That would take time, and he doubted Stroud would appreciate him breaching the platforms' firewalls to get to Vanessa's accounts.

The first account he clicked through had very little on it that was public. He scrolled through a few tags, looking at pictures of her with friends, but didn't see anyone who jumped out at him. The second account was much the same way. But the third one was a treasure trove. It looked like she'd tried to be an influencer, so much of her content was public.

A series of photographs from last year caught his attention. "Hello." He zoomed in. "Got you."

"What?" Stroud glanced back.

"Lennox is in some of her pictures. I don't think he knows it. She was taking selfies with some other women. He's behind them."

"He talking to anyone?"

Asher tipped his head, zooming in. "Yeah. There's someone there, but I can't tell who."

"You did all this legally, right? So I can use it?"

"Yes. Nothing I accessed was behind a firewall. And the search program I used is one I wrote. It's just basic facial recognition."

"Basic facial—" Stroud broke off, shaking his head.

Edie uttered a soft laugh. "I know, right? Sometimes, his genius boggles my mind too."

Asher rolled his eyes and kept scrolling. He didn't see it as anything all that extraordinary. Anyone could do what he did. He just followed a series of logical steps.

Engrossed in his task, the rest of the drive went by in a blur. He found several more inadvertent pictures of Lennox in different locations. Her acquaintance with him wasn't a one-time deal. She couldn't claim he was just "there."

Stroud pulled up behind the police station, then let them inside through the rear door. "Let's print off a few pictures from her social media quick."

He led them down a corridor, then turned into the bullpen and stopped at a desk. "Email me some."

Asher blinked, nonplussed. "It's faster to print them myself. Do you want to give me the password, or just let me crack it?"

Stroud released a short, incredulous chuckle. "You would, too."

"Yep. So what's the password?"

The detective recited it, and in minutes, they had a color copy of the clearest picture of Lennox from Vanessa's social media and were headed down a long hallway.

Stroud turned into a conference room with a television screen and a camera mounted to the wall. "So, my plan is to have you two in here, but you're observers, understand? I'll introduce you as consultants on the case, but you let me do the talking."

"What if we have questions?" Edie asked. "There could be things we think of that you don't."

"Run it past me first."

She stared at him for several seconds. "You're a bit of a control freak, aren't you?"

The detective let a beat pass, then turned away, ignoring her.

Asher nudged Edie. "Play nice. I don't want to get kicked out," he said, keeping his voice low. He was already on thin ice with Stroud after his stunt this morning. Actually, he was amazed the man had included him on the call. He figured the most he would get was a briefing after the fact.

She held up her hands, splaying her fingers, exasperation written on her face. "Fine."

They took their seats as Stroud got things up and running. A few minutes later, the screen came to life and a man and a woman appeared seated around a small table.

"Good afternoon," Stroud began. "I'm Detective J.D. Stroud. This is Asher Horn and Edie Campbell. They're consultants on my case. Thank you for meeting with us on such short notice."

"You're welcome," the man said. "I'm Ian Jackson. My client, Vanessa." He gestured to the woman in the orange jumpsuit next to him. "What can we do for you?"

"Miss Burnwell, can you tell me what you did with your vehicle when you were incarcerated?"

Her brow wrinkled, confused. "My car? What do you mean?"

"Did you leave it parked at your house? Did you sell it? Loan it to someone?"

"Oh. A friend said he'd take care of it for me. He sold it."

"You're sure he sold it?"

She nodded. "I got the money and paid off the loan. There was a little extra too."

"What was this friend's name?"

The attorney held up a hand. "Why the interest in her car? When you called, you said you needed her help with a kidnapping case."

"The car is involved in the kidnapping." Stroud got up and walked closer to the camera, holding up the still from her social media account. "Miss Burnwell, do you recognize this man?"

Asher watched recognition dawn in her eyes.

She shifted in her chair, suddenly a little wary. "That's Barry."

"How well do you know Barry?" Stroud lowered the picture, but stayed standing.

She lifted a shoulder and looked away.

"Is he the friend who sold your car?"

"No. That was Tyson."

"Did Tyson tell you who he sold the car to?"

"No. I just got a message that he'd sold it, and the money was in my account."

"I can confirm this," the attorney said. "I facilitated the loan payoff."

"Does Tyson have a last name?"

"Oliver."

"How about Barry? Does he have a last name?"

"Lennon."

Asher arched an eyebrow. Barry Lennon? It was just enough to be different.

"Did Tyson do something? Something bad?" Vanessa asked.

Stroud tipped his head. "Why would you think that? Was he prone to doing things he shouldn't?"

Again, she looked away. Asher so badly wanted to ask if he was the one who supplied her with drugs.

"Miss Burnwell?" Stroud prompted.

Her eyes darted to her attorney, then to the camera, then away. She shrugged.

"Do you have contact information for Tyson or Barry?" Asher couldn't stop himself. He didn't want to give her time to rethink things by running his question past Stroud first.

Vanessa nodded.

Stroud glared at Asher, then turned back to the screen. "Would you share that with us?"

"What's in it for my client?" the attorney asked.

"Knowledge that she might have helped bring a murderer to justice."

Jackson's eyebrows shot up. "Murder? You said kidnapping."

"This time, yes. But my suspect is also wanted for questioning in connection to a double homicide a decade ago."

The attorney leaned over and whispered something in Vanessa's ear. She nodded and he sat up.

"She would be willing to give that up for a written statement from you at her first parole hearing that she was cooperative and helpful."

"That sounds reasonable. So long as the information she provides is correct and doesn't send me on a wild goose chase. I'll be writing a different kind of letter, if that's the case."

"It's good info, I promise," Vanessa said.

"Then you have a deal, Miss Burnwell."

Forty-Eight

"Are you sure I can't run it with my software?" Asher frowned at Stroud as he and Edie crowded together in front of the detective's desk.

Stroud shot them a quick glare, then turned back to his computer. "Yes. Normal methods will work just fine for this." He logged into his computer, then pulled up a database, adding Tyson Oliver's name and phone number.

"Well?" Asher leaned forward.

"It's processing."

Edie tugged on Asher's sleeve. "Relax. My laptop isn't any faster."

With a short huff, Asher sat back. A moment later, Stroud picked up a pen.

Several seconds went by as he wrote.

Impatience got the best of Asher. He sat forward again, trying to read the man's handwriting upside down. "Stroud, I swear..."

The detective gave him a quick glance. "I found where he works and his address. He's got a couple of priors as well."

"For what?" Edie asked.

"Drug possession, like Vanessa."

"Did he do time?" she asked.

"No. It was marijuana, and the amounts were well below what they'd put him in jail for. He paid some fines." Stroud put his pen down and picked up the phone. He paused with the receiver near his face and arched an eyebrow at Asher. "Do you think you can keep your mouth shut this time if I put it on speaker?"

"No guarantees. But I'll do my best."

The detective's jaw worked, but he dialed, then hit the speaker button. The line rang five times, then rolled to voicemail. Stroud hung up and tried again. When it rolled to voicemail a second time, he did the same thing. On the third try, a man answered.

"Hello?"

"Is this Tyson Oliver?"

"Who's asking?"

"First, let me start off by saying you're not in trouble. Second, my name is J.D. Stroud. I'm a detective with the Heron Ridge Police Department in Oregon." He paused. "You still there?"

"Yeah. What do you want? I've never been to Oregon."

"You sold a car at the beginning of this year for a friend. Vanessa Burnwell?"

"What about it?"

"Who did you sell it to?"

"That was on the up and up. He gave me a cashier's check, and I gave him the title. Vanessa signed it in front of a notary her lawyer brought to the jail."

"Who bought the car?"

"Some guy I worked with. His name's Barry."

Asher, Stroud, and Edie shared a look. And the wording Tyson used caught Asher's attention. He grabbed the pad of sticky notes and a pen and wrote out his thought before shoving it toward Stroud.

The detective read it and nodded. "What do you mean, 'worked?'" he asked Tyson, voicing Asher's question.

"I haven't seen him in a while. The boss said he quit a few months back."

"So, you haven't seen him at all since he quit? Not even at a party?"

"No. I mean, he used to come to things we invited him to, but after he quit, it was like he just disappeared."

Asher scribbled another note, asking Stroud to text the man a picture of Lennox.

Stroud nodded. "Mr. Oliver, is the number I called you on for a cellphone?"

"Yes."

"I'm going to text you a picture. I'd like it if you could confirm if it's your friend, Barry."

"All right."

The detective picked up his cell and snapped a picture of Lennox from what they'd pulled from Vanessa's social media. He attached it to a message and hit send.

"Okay, I sent it."

"Hang on." Rustling came over the line, then a few moments later, "Yeah, that's him."

"He's the man you sold the car to?"

"Yes."

"Tell me more about him. What did he do for the company you both worked for? Do you know where he lives?"

"It was just basic construction, man. And I don't know where he lives. What does this have to do with Vanessa's car? Wait, did something happen to Barry?"

"He's fine, as far as I know. Do you have contact information for your friend?"

"I did, but the number doesn't work anymore. I told you, he disappeared."

"Okay. If you hear from him, would you call me? I need to speak to him."

"Um, sure?"

"Great, thank you." Stroud hung up before Tyson could ask more questions.

"Well, at least we know how he got Miss Burnwell's car and why it's still registered to her. He never bothered to go get new registration for it."

"Probably on purpose," Edie said.

"Agreed. But the question now is, where did he go?" Stroud tapped his pen on his notepad.

"I think he's still around here." Asher propped his ankle atop his knee, wiggling his foot as he thought.

Stroud frowned. "What makes you say that?"

"It sounds like he planned this. He bought a car no one would think to check on the registration for, he quit his job with little notice, and he changed all of his contact information and completely disappeared from his old life. His plan was to make a new life with Leah and Esther. I don't think he has a backup."

"That doesn't help us figure out where he is, though." Stroud sighed.

"No. But I don't think we need to. I think he'll show up again." Asher looked at Edie. "We just need to be ready."

FORTY-NINE

"Just go slow. We're in no rush to get inside."

Esther ground her teeth together to keep from snapping at Asher. She wasn't really angry with him. He was trying to be helpful. But she was so tired of everyone treating her like a child. And not even an older child. She'd returned to the infancy stage. All week, no one would let her do anything for herself.

Coming home was no exception. She'd given him a death glare when he asked if she wanted him to carry her into the house. He'd backed down, but had wrapped her hand around his arm before she could tell him she could walk by herself.

They reached the stairs going up to the porch. Esther raised a foot.

"Easy."

"Asher." She paused, foot on the step, and turned her head to shoot a glare at him. "Shut up."

Wisely, he stopped talking.

Esther navigated the steps, then pulled away from him to get through the front door. On her own, she headed for the couch. Sweat had already popped out on her brow. Just because she could do things on her own didn't mean she didn't tire quickly.

"Are you sure this is where you want to be? Wouldn't you be more comfortable upstairs in bed?"

The death glare came back out. "I'm fine. I've been in a bed for nearly a week. I don't want to sit upstairs by myself. The couch is fine."

Audra walked in from the kitchen, then, and flapped her hands at Asher. "Give her some space. Can't you see she's done with you lot hovering like a thick fog?" Her gaze took in Edie as well. "She has a voice. I'm sure if she needs something, she'll use it and ask. Right?" Her eyes flicked to Esther.

"Yes." Thank goodness someone in this house had some sense of reason.

Asher sat down next to her and took her hand. "Sorry, babe. I know I'm verging on smothering you."

Esther sighed and squeezed his hand. "I'm sorry too. I'm not trying to be a bitch. I just don't want to be treated like a little kid. I know my limits, and like Audra said, if I need help, I'll ask."

"Deal." Asher leaned over and kissed her cheek. "Do you need anything now?"

"A drink would be nice."

He hopped up. "Cold or hot?"

"Hot. Coffee, please."

"On it."

When he left, Audra took his place. Edie sat down across from her.

"Where are Annabeth and Brooke?"

"Grocery shopping," Audra said. "They should be back soon. How are you really holding up? And don't give me the answer that would please Asher."

Esther wrinkled her nose. Audra was too perceptive. "I'm sore and tired. And annoyed that I can't do the things I'm used to doing. Like showering. Having everyone hovering and constantly asking me if I'm okay and what I need is *exhausting*." She glanced at her sister only to see a sheepish look cross Edie's face. Esther lifted a hand briefly. "I appreciate everyone wanting to take care of me, but I'm sorry. It's tiring."

"You're right, it is. And of all people, I should know that. I do know that. I also know that telling you the hovering comes from a good place doesn't make it any better. From here on out, I promise to do my best not to ask a million times a day if you're all right or if you need something."

Esther gave Edie a tired but genuine smile. "Thank you. Can you run interference with Asher too? He's the worst one of you all."

Edie chuckled. "That's because he loves you and hasn't figured out how to handle that yet. With all that's happened, he hasn't had time to process. Asher is a man who definitely has to process stuff and file everything in all the right corners of his mind. Give him some time. He'll get there."

Esther stared, her mind caught on one word: love. Asher loved her? That would be wonderful, because she loved him too.

They really needed to talk. But this past week hadn't lent itself to a lot of alone time. If it wasn't one of her family or a friend coming and going from her room, it was a nurse or a patient care assistant. There was never a good time to start a conversation.

But she was home now. They could lock themselves in her bedroom and keep the world away. Tonight, that's what they'd do. Even if she had to play the sympathy card to get him to stay—because she had a feeling he'd balk at sleeping with her. He'd been treating her like spun glass, and would probably think he'd squish her or something if they shared a bed. She didn't care. She wanted to feel him next to her while she slept. She'd missed him. Missed the connection sharing a bed brought.

She wouldn't accept any excuses tonight.

Mind made up, she changed the subject. "So, do you have any new leads on Lennox's whereabouts?"

Audra's nose wrinkled in disgust. "No. He's a bloody ghost. Don't let your guard down. The working theory is he's a narcissistic knob and will come back and try again."

"Wonderful." Esther's shoulders fell. "Well, at least I'm homebound for the foreseeable future, so guarding me will be simple."

"True."

"Are Leah, Connie, and Rob safe?"

"Yes. Stroud got the Marshals involved, since Connie's parents were murdered in another state. They're in protective custody."

"Good." She'd heard Rob had been released from the hospital, and she'd gotten a homemade card from Leah. She hoped the police could track down Lennox soon so the family could go back to a normal life.

"How are they handling Leah's doctor's visits?"

Audra's forehead wrinkled. "I'm not sure. Probably through telehealth visits. Stroud mentioned something about a medic being part of their detail—and not just for Leah. Rob needs extra attention right now as well."

Esther blew out a long sigh. "I really hope this ends soon. That family has been through enough."

"I agree. Which is why Edie and I—and Asher took your hospitalization as an opportunity to wire your house from top to bottom with surveillance and security."

A deep frown formed on Esther's face. "What? Is that—"

"Don't even start." Audra cut her off. "It can come down after we catch Lennox. I'm sure Ford can repurpose the equipment somewhere else. It might not be a bad idea for us to have a security system we can use when needed."

Esther's mouth pursed, but she didn't argue. "Fine." She wasn't happy about having her home turned into a fishbowl, but she understood the need. It wouldn't be permanent; they'd eventually catch Lennox. Right?

FIFTY

The ache shooting through Esther's belly and hips threatened to take her out. While she was glad she was no longer basically bed-bound at the hospital, she'd done entirely too much moving around for her first day of freedom and was now ecstatic it was time for bed. She wanted nothing more than to stretch out and not move for the next eight to ten hours.

Wearing her softest, loosest pjs, she left the bathroom and made her way down the hall to her bedroom, using the wall for support. She rounded the corner and paused, eyeing the ten feet of open space between her and the bed. It was maybe five steps without support, but it felt like miles. Her body was utterly done.

Heavy footsteps on the stairs made her look over her shoulder. Asher appeared at the top of the steps.

"Hey." He hovered near the stairs, a hesitant look on his face. He'd been keeping his distance all afternoon and evening. Ever since her outburst. She wasn't sure if she'd offended him or if it was his way of respecting her wishes. Either way, it bugged her. She just wanted things to go back to the way they were.

"Hey. Help me to bed?"

Without a word, he walked forward, then put an arm around her waist, holding lightly onto her hip while he gripped her opposite hand. Esther leaned into him, letting him propel them across the room. With a wince, she sank onto the mattress and brought her feet up.

"Do you need anything else before you go to sleep?"

"Yes. You."

A slight widening to his eyes was the only emotion that crossed his face. "Esther..."

She rolled her eyes and let out a little chuckle. "Not like that. I can barely walk. I just want you here with me." She patted the sheets beside her.

"Oh. Are you sure? I wouldn't—"

"Asher, get your sexy, nerdy ass in this bed."

Fire roared to life in his eyes, turning the light brown depths the color of rich caramel. "For the record, I'm not tired yet." He reached for the collar of his shirt.

"Good. I'm not either."

He froze, then dropped his hand. "Essy, this isn't—"

"Don't finish that sentence. I know what you're going to say. All I want to do is talk and snuggle, Asher. That's it."

He blew out a breath, holding her gaze for a moment. "What about Edie? Wasn't she sleeping in here with you while I was missing?"

"Mom and Dad brought over a twin-size air mattress. Audra set it up in the guest room and moved in there with Brooke and Annabeth. Edie took the couch. Are there any other questions you'd like me to answer?"

A teasing glint entered his eyes, and those beautiful lips tilted up ever so slightly in a smirk. "No." In one swift movement, he whisked his shirt over his head. A second later, he unfastened his jeans and let them drop to the floor.

Esther bit her lip. Just because she wasn't physically capable of what her mind and body wanted, didn't mean she couldn't appreciate the sight before her. She'd meant it when she called him a sexy nerd. His big, beautiful brain was wrapped in a big, beautiful package.

He crawled into bed next to her and drew the covers up. Esther shifted, settling into the crook of his arm with a wince.

"Are you all right? Do you need me to move?"

"No. I'm just achy. I'm ready to stay in one place for a while."

He hummed. She could hear the lecture in that one sound. He was as aware as she was that she'd done too much today.

But she didn't want to talk about that. She wasn't even sure how to bring up what she wanted to talk about.

So, she drew circles on his chest with her fingernail and waited for him to speak. She'd figure it out.

Somehow.

Except he didn't talk. He stayed silent and drew his own circles on her shoulder as they laid there.

Head tucked, Esther rolled her eyes. The man was never without words. Why was he silent now?

Finally, she couldn't take it anymore. She pushed up on one arm and looked at him. "Are you all right?"

His eyebrows dipped. "Yeah. Why wouldn't I be?"

"You're quiet. You're never quiet."

His expression shuttered. "I'm fine."

Esther shook a finger in his face. "No. You're shutting me out. Why? Something's bugging you. Why won't you talk to me?" It was her turn to frown as her anxiety kicked in. "It's because of earlier, isn't it? Asking you not to hover doesn't mean I don't want you to talk to me."

"It's not that." He stopped and inhaled a breath, then pushed up so he was sitting.

Esther scooched up next to him and waited for him to continue.

He scrubbed his hands over his face and groaned. "I don't even know where to start."

Her ire with him fled as she saw the depth of uncertainty in his expression. He looked like a lost little boy. "Have you talked to anyone since that day?" She knew he hadn't talked to her. For most of her hospital stay, he'd been absent during the day. At night, he'd slip in after the nurses turned the lights down and curl up on the couch to sleep. While she'd appreciated his presence while she slept, she missed talking to him.

"Not really, no. Things have been a bit hectic."

"You can't keep all that bottled up, Asher."

"Who says I did?"

The look he sent her told her he'd had time by himself where he'd let loose. For that, she was happy. But that didn't mean he'd dealt with it.

"And?" She lifted one eyebrow.

"And what? I had a good cry. You're alive. All is well."

"That's such bull crap." She lightly smacked his chest. "You cannot boil all you went through down to that just because 'you had a good cry'." She made air quotes.

"What do you want me to say, Esther? That I feel like an idiot because I let myself get knocked over the head and kidnapped while in a ridiculous costume? Or that I feel like an even bigger idiot because I didn't do a good enough job canvassing the little prison Lennox put Leah and me in and I almost paid the price for that? How about how, if you look past both of those things, there's the fact that my ineptitude nearly got the woman I love murdered? If I'd been more vigilant, more like Ford and the others, I'd have kept my head on a swivel and—"

Esther laid a finger over his lips, silencing the flow of words. She swallowed around the ball of emotion clogging her throat. Had he really said he loved her?

She rolled her lips in, pressing them together for a moment before she eeked some words past the lump that refused to go away. "That's a good start," she whispered. Taking a shaky breath, she continued. "And you know what? I don't blame you for anything that happened. Neither does Leah nor Connie nor anyone else. I'm grateful you're not like your friends or my sister. They might have seen the attack coming and either ended up dead, or inadvertently left Leah all alone in that hole Lennox put you in."

The pain in his eyes briefly abated until he looked her over. His hand skimmed the soft fabric of her shirt near her abdomen. "Yeah, but—"

"No buts, Asher. I put myself in front of you. You didn't do this to me. And do you know why I put myself in front of you?" She only paused for the briefest of moments. "Because I love you too."

His hand fisted in her shirt.

"I don't want to—can't—live without you." She raised a hand to touch his face. Soft beard hair tickled her fingertips. "So, please don't blame yourself for anything that happened. Lennox is the only one at fault for any of this."

For several long moments, he stayed silent and just stared at her neck and the hair draped over her shoulder. When he finally looked at her, her breath caught at the emotion shining in his eyes. He looked like she'd given him the greatest present ever.

"You love me?"

She huffed a laugh. "Yes, you silly man. Why else would I launch myself—"

He cut her words off with a fierce kiss.

Esther let out a soft grunt of surprise, then blocked every

thought out of her head and just savored the feel of his mouth on hers. It had been far, far too long.

Asher's thumbs skimmed her cheekbones as he framed her face in his hands. All too soon for her liking, he pulled back.

"So, what do we do about this?" He rested his forehead on hers. His warm breath puffed on her face. "We've never really talked about it. Things were too new before Lennox turned our lives upside down."

"I told you where I stand. I don't want to do life without you. The rest is little details."

Asher barked a short laugh. "Little details, sure. Like where we'll live, and if this will be a long-distance thing for now."

"I don't want to do that." She bit her lip and glanced away, the reality of their living situation hitting home. "Maybe the details aren't so small." She waved a hand. "But they still don't matter. We'll figure it out."

His mouth ticked upward with a happy smile. "Yeah, we will. Because I don't intend to ever let you go."

Esther answered his smile with one of her own and fluttered her fingers over the planes of his face and into his thick, dark hair. She'd so missed being in his arms. "I'm glad. You know, Edie joked about setting us up. I blew her off, telling her we weren't suited. I've never been so happy to be wrong."

He chuckled. "I told her the same thing. Let's not tell her how wise she is. No need inflating her ego."

With a joyful laugh, Esther rested her forehead against his. "Deal."

Fifty-One

The buzz of the phone in his pocket drew Asher's attention away from Esther, who sat with her sister and mother, looking through the box of baby things Faye had brought over. While he was over the moon happy with Esther, he was not ready for a baby or any of the things that went with it, so he'd left them to their own devices while he got some work done.

Lifting his hip, he took his phone from his pocket. Stroud's name appeared. Asher's heart sped up, and he swiped to answer. "Hello?"

"Horn, I need you to come down to the station. The tip line's been inundated with reports of Lennox's vehicle. I need another set of eyes—good ones—to help me go through this stuff."

Asher closed his laptop and stood. "I'm on my way. Do you want me to bring Edie and Audra?"

"No. I need your computer expertise more than anything. They'll be bored."

Asher bit back a snort. He doubted it. The two women would find something to stick their noses into. But he didn't want to drive another wedge into his relationship with the detective, so he didn't argue. He'd just pried the last one loose. "All right, I'll see you soon."

"Thanks." Stroud hung up.

"Who was that?" Edie asked. "I heard my name."

"Stroud. The tip line got some hits on Lennox's car. He wants my help analyzing footage. I asked if I should bring you guys, but he said just me for now."

Her brows dipped, but she nodded. "Keep us posted."

"You know I will." He walked over to where they were seated and dropped a quick kiss on Esther's lips. "Don't get any ideas while I'm gone." He gestured between her and the box. "I love you, but we're not ready for that yet."

"Oh, I think we'll be ready sooner than you think." She flashed him a sweet smile.

Asher sighed, knowing he'd better wrap his head around a major life change sooner rather than later. Surprisingly, the thought didn't bother him as much as he thought it would, though. He wasn't ready to be a dad, but it wouldn't take much convincing. Not if Esther was the mom. She'd be great at it.

One thing at a time, though. They needed to figure out where they would live first.

After they caught Lennox.

Tapping her nose, he returned her smile. "I'll be back as soon as I can. The others should be too." Audra, Annabeth, and Brooke had run out to get Halloween candy for trick-or-treat tonight as well as supplies to make the tomato soup and grilled cheese on homemade bread Edie was craving. Rather than interrupt Edie and Esther's time with their mom, the three women had offered to give them some space and go get the ingredients.

"Git." Edie shooed him away. "The sooner you leave, the sooner you can come back."

He chuckled and held up his hands. "I'm going, I'm going." Walking away, he tucked his laptop under his arm, then grabbed his keys off the counter and let himself out the front door, arming the alarm system as he left.

The drive to the police station was uneventful. He pulled into a visitor's spot and went inside. The officer working the desk recognized him and buzzed him back. After signing in, Asher headed down the hall to Stroud's office.

He knocked on the detective's partially open door and stuck his head in. Stroud looked up. Asher tipped his head. "Damn. You look terrible. When was the last time you slept?"

"Well? Before you came to town. Get in here and sit your ass down." He motioned him inside.

As Asher walked in, Stroud turned a laptop around. "Can you enhance that? We need to know who's driving."

Sitting down, he set his computer on the other guest chair and pulled Stroud's closer. A few quick clicks on the photo enhancement menus and he shook his head. "I need to put it into my software. Yours is crap."

"So, log in and do your thing." Stroud waved his hands.

"Uh-uh. I'm not logging into a government computer with my creds and my software. You can send that picture to me."

Stroud eyed him from behind the desk. "What if I don't?"

Asher arched an eyebrow. They both knew that he could leave and back door his way into the police station's systems and get the picture with little effort. "You really want to play this game again?"

Fine lines appeared around Stroud's mouth as he pursed his lips and glared. He snagged the computer, spinning it around. Angrily, he pounded the keys. After a half a minute passed, he gave the device a small shove and sat back. "There. Check your email."

"Thank you." Asher picked up his computer and did just

that. In moments, he had the file downloaded and plugged into his photo enhancement software. "This might take me a few minutes." He spared Stroud a quick glance.

"I'll go get us some coffee." The detective pushed away from his desk and left Asher alone.

Tongue poked between his teeth, Asher clicked on menus and filters, doing his best to zoom in and not lose image quality. The camera this picture came from wasn't the best. It looked like the car was in motion, too, which didn't help.

Slowly, he zoomed in, cleaning it up with each magnification.

"You get anywhere?" Stroud walked in, carrying two cups of coffee. He held one out to Asher.

"Thanks." Asher took the cup and set it on the desk, too absorbed in his task to take a break. "I'm close."

Stroud stood behind him, looking over his shoulder. "That's definitely better than what our techs got it to. I still can't tell who it is, though."

"I'm not done yet," Asher muttered. He zoomed once more; close enough that this time they should be able to see a face.

The detective leaned down as Asher sharpened the image. "Hell."

"Yeah." A grimace crossed Asher's face. It wasn't Lennox. "You're sure that's his car?"

"One hundred percent. The techs didn't have any problem enhancing the view of the license plate. It's a match."

"So, who's driving, then?"

"I don't know." Stroud rounded the desk to sit down. "We'll have to run facial recognition and see if we can get a match. God only knows how long that'll take."

With a grunt, Asher opened his program that did that and started the process. His would be faster than any the detective could run. "Do we know where the car went? How many cameras caught it?"

"It was tracked coming out of Coos Bay. We lost it when he turned off on a country road."

"What about where it came from?"

Stroud paused, his coffee cup freezing inches from his mouth. He frowned. "I don't know. That's a good question." He set the cup down and pulled the keyboard for his desktop closer. "So, that image is from a camera on the highway, but the license plate popped closer to the center of the city." He glanced at the keyboard and pecked at the keys.

Asher got up and came around the desk, watching as Stroud moved through the camera footage on a split screen. "There." He pointed to a square.

"I see it." The detective clicked on it, bringing it full screen. "I know where that is. Let's check the next one."

It took them ten minutes, but they tracked the car to a residential neighborhood and caught it pulling onto a boulevard near a shopping center. The area it came from didn't have any street cameras.

"You know, there's a fairly decent-sized park there. And it's flanked by houses that all face it. I guarantee some of them have doorbell cameras. We might get lucky and catch Lennox handing the vehicle over to someone. Maybe even see him drive off in a different ride."

"Or we'll just see that guy driving." Asher pointed at the screen. It was possible, too, that it would be a wild goose chase, and they'd get absolutely nothing.

Stroud glanced back at Asher. "We won't know unless we look. You have time to go on a little mission?"

"Yes." Asher stepped back so Stroud could get up.

"Great. Text your buddies and tell them you'll be late for dinner."

FIFTY-TWO

"Oh my goodness! Edie, look at this one." Esther held up the tiny dress she'd unearthed from the box of things their mom brought over. The satin and chiffon lavender dress with tiny white flowers felt miniscule in Esther's hands.

"That was your first Easter dress, Edie," Faye said, a soft smile crossing her face. "You were only a few weeks old. All that fabric about swallowed you whole," she said with a chuckle.

Edie's nose wrinkled. "Yeah. It's... it's a lot."

Faye chuckled again. "Don't look so thrilled. I'm not asking you to put your baby in it. At the time, that was the height of fashion for baby girls."

"I'm sorry, Mom. I don't mean to sound..." She broke off and waved her head side-to-side.

"I know. And I get it."

Esther looked at the dress again. "Well, I, for one, think it's beautiful. I might snag it if I ever have a little girl."

A knowing look entered Faye's eyes. "Poor Asher. I think he better get ready quick."

Edie laughed. "He says he's not ready, but he'll do anything you want, Essy."

Esther held up a hand. "He's got some time. I want kids, but I'd rather walk down the aisle first. Maybe your second child and my first can be the same age."

A bright smile blossomed on Edie's face. "I'd like—"

Her words died as the overhead light went off and the hum of the furnace stopped.

"Did the power go out?" Faye frowned, staring at the light.

Esther caught Edie's eye. Her sister's expression had turned fierce.

"Stay here." Edie got up.

"Edith, you can't—"

"Mom, please. Stay put." Edie waved a hand.

Faye huffed and got up. "No. You're pregnant. I'm not letting you run into danger without backup."

"It's probably nothing." Esther slowly got to her feet, wincing as her incisions pulled.

"Seriously?" Edie sighed. "Sit down, Esther."

"I'm going to check the breaker box."

"I'll do it. You stay put. Mom, make her sit." Edie hurried away.

Esther crossed her arms and glared at her sister's retreating back. Edie knew she couldn't walk that fast.

"She's right, honey. You should sit."

"I'm fine. Why don't you go after her?"

The tinkle of glass breaking turned Esther's muscles to stone.

"What was that?" Faye turned toward the sound, which had come from the back door at the end of the hall.

"Mom, call 9-1-1." Esther reached for her phone to call Asher.

Shadows shifted and the air pressure of the room changed.

Someone had opened the door.

Esther pushed to her feet and grabbed her mother's hand.

"Esther, what are you doing?" Faye looked up from her phone.

"Come on," Esther hissed. "And keep quiet." Moving much faster than was wise for her healing body, she dragged her mom toward the kitchen.

"I still haven't called for help," Faye whispered.

"Me, either." Esther ducked behind the island, then peered over the top. She couldn't see the hallway from here, but there was nowhere to hide where whoever broke in couldn't see them. "Let's get to Edie."

Footsteps tracked across the wooden floor from the hall. Esther eyed the open space between herself and the door. If she could run, it wouldn't be a problem, but whoever was in the house was too close. Based on the footsteps, he or she was near the dining table.

Her mind whirled as she tried to come up with a plan. Asher had been gone almost thirty minutes. Audra, Brooke, and Annabeth should be back any time.

"Esther…" a male voice called to her in a sing-song tone.

Chills went up her spine.

"Esther, I know you're here."

"Mom, send a text to 9-1-1." Esther's voice was barely audible. "Tell them there's been a break-in and give them my address, then turn off your ringer."

Faye nodded.

Esther opened her texting app and sent a quick message to Asher. She silenced her phone and opened the cabinet door just enough to shove the device inside. She took her mother's when she was finished with her message and did the same.

"What now?" Faye mouthed.

Esther held a finger to her lips. She eyed the door again and prayed Edie wouldn't come through.

"Come, now, Esther. Don't make me search for you. I

know you're here. I watched your lady friends leave a while ago. Your boyfriend too. It's a shame you took that bullet for him. I am sorry for that. I didn't mean to hurt you. I should have killed him outside Lindy's house instead of taking him hostage. Would have saved all of us some trouble."

The door to the garage opened. "Well, it's not the breakers."

Faye darted out from their hiding place and grabbed Edie's arm, yanking her down. Just in time too. A bullet plowed into the wall near the door.

"Jesus! What the hell?" Edie pushed her hair out of her face as she maneuvered into a crouch.

No sooner were the words out of her mouth than Lennox appeared in front of them. In the dim light, Esther could see the glow of his white teeth as he laid a merciless smile on them.

"Well, hello, ladies."

FIFTY-THREE

Absently, Asher flipped his phone over as it buzzed in his hand. He and Stroud had just left the station and were on their way to Coos Bay.

The alert that appeared on the screen turned his blood to ice water. He muttered a curse.

"What?" Stroud asked.

"The alarm at Esther's is off. The power went out."

Stroud reached for his radio. "I'll ask them to check if it's her street or just her house."

Asher logged into the doorbell camera while Stroud talked to dispatch, hoping it was still transmitting. If the power was out, the Wi-Fi probably was as well. It would back up to the chip in the camera, but wouldn't sync to the cloud until the power was restored.

The live feed was down, as he'd feared, so he accessed the stored footage. He rewound it to the time he left, then hit play, speeding up the recording until he saw a vehicle drive past. After doing that several times, one caught his eye. It was a burgundy SUV. A nice one. It approached the house and slowed a little. Asher saw the glow of brake lights before it sped up and drove away.

A couple of minutes later, it returned, moving even more slowly.

He muttered another curse. "I think we might have a problem."

Pinching the screen, he tried to zoom in, but the car was too far away.

A message from Esther popped up on his screen.

Someone broke in. Called the police.

"What the hell does that mean, Essy?" Was she safe? Was the person still there? Was anyone hurt? Asher looked at Stroud. "Turn us around. Someone broke into Esther's. She said she called the police."

Stroud pulled a U-turn and hit his siren. "She say anything else?"

"No." He clutched the phone, staring at Esther's words.

As they rocketed down the road, Stroud called dispatch again to ask about the call Esther made to the department. Asher's jaw clenched as the dispatcher relayed that the call actually came in as a text and that they were unable to establish contact with them. Units were on their way.

"Could Lennox get in?" Stroud asked.

"Yes. But I'm not sure how far he'd get. Edie was there. Audra wasn't, though." He slammed his hand onto the dash. "Dammit, I should have brought them all with me to come see you."

Stroud's lips thinned. He stayed silent, but Asher noticed the car went a little faster.

FIFTY-FOUR

"Get up." Lennox motioned with the gun in his hand for them to rise.

Esther glared at him as Edie and her mother helped her to her feet.

He tipped his head, eyeing them. "All the Campbell women in one place. Esther, I see where you get your beauty."

"Oh, stop trying to be charming," Edie said. "We know you're not."

"You're right"—the smile disappeared from his face—"I'm not." He raised his gun.

It was like déjà vu for Esther. Except this time, she was saving her sister. Shoving Edie, she stepped forward. "Stop trying to shoot people I love."

He lowered the gun barrel toward the floor. "I'm beginning to question if you're the right mother for my daughter. What kind of person steps in front of a gun on purpose? Twice?"

Before Esther could react, he darted a hand out and grabbed hold of her arm, yanking her forward.

Fire ripped through her abdomen at the abrupt movement. She winced, but held back the cry of pain. Little more than a soft grunt escaped.

"But you're still better than that bitch, Lindy." He pulled Esther against him, putting his face next to her ear. "I bet you'll make smart babies too. So long as they don't get your penchant for chivalry."

Esther's stomach revolted as he nuzzled her neck.

Edie took a step forward. Lennox's gun lifted, aiming at her chest.

"Uh-uh-uh, big sister. You better watch your step. Little sister can't step in to save you this time."

Fury fairly shot from Edie's eyes, like bolts of lightning. She balled her fists at her side, and her chest heaved as she glared at him.

Lennox stepped back. "Let's go." He tipped his head toward the dining room.

Edie and Faye edged around him. Esther caught her sister's gaze as she moved past. The look in her eyes said she would pounce at the first opportunity.

Saying a silent prayer her ambush would work out in their favor, Esther let him propel her forward. Edie and their mother walked ahead. She saw Edie glance down the hall, then stumble. Faye caught her, holding her for a second before letting go.

"That's far enough."

They'd reached the living room.

"What are you going to do to us?" Edie asked.

"My plan was to sneak in, take Esther, and leave everyone alive."

"You still can," Esther said. "I'll go with you. Just leave them alone." She didn't really want to go with him. It was more of a ploy to stall him than anything else. Help shouldn't be far away. Even if he took her up on her offer, they likely wouldn't get far. There were multiple cameras Asher could access to get vehicle information. He'd find her before they ever left the area.

"Esther!" Faye's back straightened. "That's a horrible idea."

"It's fine, Mom," Esther said through clenched teeth.

"Esther Jean, it is not fine." Faye took a couple of steps forward, the mama bear coming out. She shook a finger in Lennox's face. "Listen here, you pathetic waste of space."

Esther chanced a glance at Lennox. Shock had made his mouth go a little slack. She bit back a smile.

"If you think I'm going to let you walk out of here with my baby, you're dumber than a box of stubby crayons. Even if you kill me and Edie, where do you think you're gonna go that Asher and his friends won't find you? Do you know what they can do? Do you know how they found you the first time?"

His shock morphed into curiosity. Esther widened her eyes, trying to tell her mother to stop talking. They didn't need to give away all the Wagner Brigade's secrets.

But Faye was too wound up to notice. She took a step closer. Lennox shifted, turning slightly as he put some space between them.

"Stay back." He aimed the gun in her direction, but Esther noticed he kept the tip pointed down.

She sent a quick look back. Was he second-guessing things?

"Go ahead. Shoot me." Faye tapped her chest, then held her arms wide. "See how well she cooperates after you kill her mother. Do it. Do it!" She lunged forward, making him spin.

The abrupt movement was too much for Esther's healing muscles this time, and she cried out in pain, sagging into his hold.

"Now!" Edie yelled.

What happened next was a blur. Faye dove to the side, while Edie dove forward like a linebacker. The muffled clink of pottery breaking registered a moment before pebbles, dirt, and shards of the terracotta planter holding Esther's little succulent rained over her head.

Lennox let out a grunt, his knees buckling, but he didn't go down.

Hands appeared around his wrist on his gun hand. Before Esther could see who they belonged to, another set of hands grabbed her upper arm and tugged. She fell away from Lennox. When she looked up, it was to see Edie.

"You go with Annabeth." Edie spun her away. Esther stumbled, shards of pain spearing her battered body at the sudden shift.

"I've got you." Annabeth grabbed onto her biceps, then readjusted her hold. Looping Esther's arm over her shoulders, she slid an arm around her waist and pulled her away from the skirmish.

Where did she come from? Esther didn't have time to ask. Chaos had erupted around her.

From behind them, Brooke came running, carrying a filet knife from the kitchen.

"Edie!"

Intercepting Brooke, Edie took the knife, then whirled, her red braid flying out behind her as she took two running steps toward Lennox and launched herself onto his back. The shift in his center of gravity yanked his arm up and out of Audra's grip.

Edie locked her legs around his waist and put the knife to his throat. "Drop it!"

He froze, but didn't drop the gun.

"I will happily stick this knife through your spine after all you've done, but kindly don't make me stain my sister's floor. She quite likes this rug."

When he still hesitated, she pressed the tip into his flesh. A bead of blood dribbled down his neck.

He let out a grunt and grimaced. "Oh, you're a fucking crazy bitch." He opened his hand and let the gun drop.

Audra scooped it up. Edie unwound herself from his torso, but stayed close.

"Get down," Audra told him.

Lennox dropped to his knees.

"On your stomach." Audra flicked the barrel of the gun to the floor.

"We need something to tie him up," Edie said.

"Already on it." Brooke walked forward, pulling the scarf from around her neck. She knelt down, putting a knee into Lennox's back.

He groaned and wiggled. "Damn. Move, lady. You've got bony knees."

"Oh, shut up, or I'll gag you too." Brooke wove the cloth around his wrists, then folded the ends over and around several times. "There. My husband taught me that knot. Get out of that, you bastard." She stood up and dusted off her hands. Grinning ear to ear, she cast a glance around the room. "Who says the guys get to have all the fun?"

Esther sagged against Annabeth, and a soft laugh slid free. Her adrenaline ebbed, and it was then that she heard the sirens outside and saw the strobing red and blue lights through the windows.

Faye walked over and opened the door to let the officers in.

"Do you need to sit down?" Annabeth asked quietly.

"Please." Annabeth's hold was likely the only reason she wasn't in a heap on the floor. It certainly wasn't her wobbly knees keeping her upright.

"Let's go this way, then." Annabeth led her to the side and to a dining chair, helping her ease into it.

"Thank you." Esther brushed a tendril of hair out of her eyes, then took in a trembly breath and looked at Lennox, who squirmed on the floor as the police filed inside. His words replayed through her mind, and her heart rate kicked up again. "Leah." She gripped Annabeth's wrist. "Did he get to her again?"

Annabeth's eyes widened. "I'm not sure." She turned. "Brooke."

The other woman looked over.

"Find out if Leah's safe."

A wicked smile crossed her face. "Gladly." She knelt onto Lennox's back again, making him howl. Bending low, she spoke to him.

"No." He tossed his head. "Goddammit, get off! I didn't touch her. I don't know where she is."

Brooke rose, then turned to Annabeth and Esther. "I'd say she's safe."

Esther rolled her eyes. "You've spent too much time with my sister."

Edie snorted. "She got *that* attitude from Ford."

"You're both wrong." Brooke smirked. "I was born with it."

Fifty-Five

Dear God, *please let them be okay.*

Asher repeated the prayer over and over in his head as Stroud turned onto Esther's street. They'd heard the all clear come over the radio, but little else.

Sirens still screamed through the cloudy afternoon skies from the patrol units parked haphazardly out front. Their light bounced off the front of the house. No one was outside. What did that mean?

Stroud came to a bone-jarring halt behind one of the cruisers. Asher was out of the car before the detective could tell him to wait. The front door was open, but he couldn't see inside.

"Esther!" He ran through the grass. Stroud called out behind him, but Asher ignored him. Bursting through the door, he paused, taking in the scene.

Conversation ceased at his appearance. Faye and Edie stood to his right, speaking with an officer. To his left, Lennox lay on the ground, a colorful scrap of fabric wrapped around his wrists, which one officer was attempting to remove and put handcuffs in its place. Brooke stood to Lennox's left, watching. Audra stood on the other side, speaking to a third officer.

Behind her, he saw the only thing that mattered, however. Esther sat at the table beside Annabeth.

Oh, thank God. The relief made his legs weak, but they were strong enough to carry him around Audra and the officer.

"Horn, I told you to... wait." Stroud stepped inside and took in the scene. "What the hell happened?"

Asher dropped to his knees in front of Esther, still ignoring the detective, and wrapped her in his arms. He breathed in her sweet scent, then lifted his head, gently cradling one side of her face. "Are you all right?"

"I'm fine. I'll probably be sorer later from being manhandled, but I'm okay."

"Manhandled?" Asher glanced over his shoulder to glare at Lennox. "What happened?"

"I'd like to know that too," Stroud said.

"The Lady Brigade happened," Faye said, grinning.

Edie chuckled. "Lady Brigade?"

"Badass Lady Brigade," Brooke said. She looked at Asher. "You guys aren't the only ones who get a cool nickname." She turned to Audra. "I think we did pretty good, don't you? Maybe I should make us some business cards and give Ford's little side business a run for its money."

Audra laughed. "No, I think we can leave the chaos to them. I'm quite looking forward to just running security for your hotel."

"None of that tells me what happened." Stroud raised a hand, the glower on his face telegraphing his exasperation clearly.

Brooke rolled her eyes. "Fine. We got back from the store and noticed the house was dark. With the clouds, we had a few lights on in the house, but they weren't on when we got back." She pointed up. "It's still cloudy, so why no lights? Anyway, Audra made us get out all quiet-like, and we snuck up to the house and peeked in the window. That's when we saw him holding a gun on Edie, Esther, and Faye." She pointed at Lennox, who now sported some shiny handcuffs instead of the colorful fabric.

Brooke noticed and pointed to the scarf on the floor beside the officer kneeling next to his prisoner. "Oh, that's mine."

He picked it up and held it out to her. Asher now recognized it as the scarf she'd had on earlier.

"That was some crazy knot." The officer gave a little head-shake. "Took me a minute to undo it."

"Thanks. I figured if it'll hold a shark, it'll hold a human."

The man frowned. "What?"

Asher's lips twitched.

Brooke waved a hand. "Nothing." She looked at Stroud. "Once we realized what was happening, we went around back, where we saw the busted windowpane in the back door, which was open."

"At that point, I suggested we attempt to flank them," Audra said. "So Brooke went in through the garage, while Annabeth and I crept in through the open back door."

"Which is when I saw them," Edie said. "When we walked out to the living room, I happened to glance over and saw Audra's face at the edge of the hallway. When I realized they'd returned and knew what was going on, I faked a stumble and told Mom to cause a distraction."

Faye scoffed. "That wasn't hard. I was already angry he was holding Esther hostage. And he tried to shoot Edie when she came in from checking the breaker box."

"From the power outage?" Asher asked.

"You knew about that?" Esther frowned.

"The alarm sends out what amounts to a Hail Mary when the power's cut. I got a message that the system was offline. Your text came in a few minutes later."

"What happened after you created the distraction, Mrs. Campbell?" Stroud sighed, shaking his head.

"They... descended on him. From all sides." She motioned to the others.

"I broke a potted plant over his head, then grabbed his gun hand," Audra said. "Edie pulled Esther away as Brooke came in through the garage door."

"She brought me a knife, and I jumped on him," Edie said.

"Is that where the blood came from?" Stroud asked.

"Yes. He didn't want to put his gun down, so I showed him I meant business."

"Crazy bitch, is what she is," Lennox muttered from the floor.

"Stockton, get him out of here." Stroud swept an arm toward the door.

"Yes, sir." The officer stood and rolled Lennox onto his side. "Come on."

"Make sure you have medical check his neck."

Stockton nodded once as he hauled Lennox to his feet, then helped him out the door.

"I'm sorry about your rug, Esther." Edie's nose wrinkled as she looked at the floor where Lennox had lain. "I really didn't want to mess it up."

"It's fine, Edie. We can probably get it out. Or I'll get a new rug." She looked at Asher. "It might be time for a change. Who knows?"

A slow smile spread over Asher's face. "It might be, yeah. A big one." At her happy smile, he stretched his neck to press a gentle kiss to her lips.

Fifty-Six

Light filtered in from the street outside and caressed Esther's skin, turning it a pale porcelain. Her dark red lashes rested against her cheeks, a sharp contrast to the paleness. Asher skimmed the back of his knuckles over her face as he watched her sleep.

After the police took their statements, a crime scene unit had shown up to process the house. While they worked, he'd noticed the ever-increasing droop to Esther's eyelids. As soon as they'd left, he'd whisked her upstairs and put her to bed.

She'd argued, of course, saying they hadn't even had dinner, that it was Halloween and she wanted to see the kids in their costumes. But her protests had been feeble. In minutes, she'd drifted off.

That was two hours ago. He'd laid beside her and just watched her rest, contemplating what their next steps were. The one thing he'd figured out for certain was he couldn't go back to Costa Rica without her. Not even to pack up his stuff and move here, if that was what she wanted. He'd wait until she could fly down with him. After nearly losing her twice, he planned to be glue. She'd get sick of him before he'd leave her alone.

Her head lolled to the side, and she made a soft mewling noise. Those dark copper lashes fluttered against her skin as she came awake. A sleepy smile brightened her face when her gaze landed on him. "Hey." She raised her arms over her head and stretched, wincing a bit as her abdominal muscles pulled.

"You okay?"

She brought her arms down and rolled to her side, wrapping them around his forearm and snuggling closer. "Yeah. I'll be glad when I can move and not be sore." A yawn overtook her, and she covered her mouth, then waved her hand. "Sorry."

"Do you want me to leave so you can go back to sleep?" He wanted to stay and keep up his vigil, but he'd go if she wanted to get more rest.

"No. Actually, I'm hungry, so I'd like to get up and eat. Did the tomato soup and grilled cheese Edie wanted ever get made?"

"I'm not sure. I think there were plans to order in. I don't know what they got, though. I've been up here with you."

Her eyebrows rose. "The entire time?" She lifted her head to look at the clock. "It's been two hours. Did you sleep too?"

"No. Just watched you. And did some thinking." He brushed her hair back and played with the ends, thinking some more.

"About what?"

"Us."

She hummed. "What about us?"

"What the future holds, mostly. I'm not going back to Costa Rica. Not without you."

Surprise flashed in her pretty blue eyes. "But your life—"

"Is wherever you are, Essy." He brushed his knuckles over her cheek. "What do you want? And before you say anything, you should know I intend to marry you. As soon as you can walk down the aisle."

That single eyebrow rose, reminding him of the look he'd gotten from her sister many times whenever he presumed something and she was about to school him. It made him smile.

"Who says I want to marry you?"

"You do."

"You're sure about that?"

"Yes." He stroked her cheek again. "You know how I know?"

A smile flirted with her lips. "How?"

"It's in your eyes. These beautiful, deep eyes of yours. You can see our future. The companionship and the passion. The silliness and the love. The children who will have your bright smile and my dark hair. And hopefully not yours or your sister's stubbornness."

She laughed. "I'd prefer that too. Although, if they're as tenacious as we are, I'll be happy. It's come in handy the last couple of weeks."

He agreed. Her tenacity—and Edie's—was why she was lying here with him and not in a coffin. "I'm sure God will look at our list and laugh, then throw the stubbornness in there, anyway." He grinned. "But we'll handle it. Because we have each other. Always each other." He ran his fingertip over her lips. "So, what do you say? Will you marry me?"

Again, she hummed. "As soon as I can walk down the aisle, huh? What if I want a lavish wedding?"

"Do you?"

She shrugged one shoulder. "I'd like the dress and the flowers. And to see you in a tux. Definitely more than a quickly planned weekend affair."

Asher sighed. "I suppose I can live with waiting long enough to plan that."

"Good. It'll give us time to move one of us."

A bit of the happiness in her smile died. Asher didn't have to ask to know what she preferred. She wanted to stay here.

"It will. Dismantling my lair will be a labor of love."

The frown that overtook her smile was swift. "What?" She popped up onto an elbow to stare at him.

"Essy, I can tell you don't want to move. You love your job. Your parents and grandparents are here. This is your home. Don't get me wrong, I love Costa Rica and the little house I have there. And I'll miss everyone, but *my* home is you."

Moisture gathered in her eyes. "You're sure?" she whispered.

"One hundred percent. I do have one request, though."

"What's that?"

"We need a bigger house."

"Just how many kids are you envisioning?" A playful smile appeared, reaching her eyes.

He chuckled. "It's not about that. Though I was thinking two or three. No, I'm not sure you understand just how many computers I have. They need a room of their own. Plus, we'll need a guest room, for when Edie comes to town."

"True. Probably more than one."

"Yep." He slid a hand up her arm and into her hair. "Plus room for all our babies."

Her eyelids fluttered, but not from sleep this time. "Mmm-hmm."

"So, what do you say?" His mouth hovered inches from hers.

"I say, I'll call my mom tomorrow and have her set us up with her realtor friend."

"Good deal." Asher swooped in and sealed his lips to hers.

∼

Thank you for reading *Asher's Assignment!* I hope you loved it! Want to see Max finally get his happily-ever-after? Check out *Max's Mission* on Amazon: *https://books2read.com/maxs-mission*

If you'd like to read more about Asher and Esther (and the other characters in this series), join my mailing list. Subscribers get a bonus chapter or scene after every book! You'll also get access to exclusive teasers, giveaways, and the occasional book recommendation, as well as sneak peeks into my world as I create my stories. Scan the QR code below to sign up and get your bonus scene!

Keep reading for a sneak peek at *Max's Mission...*

Max's Mission

Wagner Brigade

Book 6

CHAPTER ONE

It took everything Margot Gaultier had not to drop to the floor in a heap. Her hands shook, and she clenched the phone to her ear to stop the tremors. She rolled her lips inward, bringing a halt to their quivering.

One of her daughters squealed and waved her toy, showing off the "You did it!" message, telling her she'd matched all the shapes correctly.

Margot forced a smile, then turned so Emily couldn't see her face. The little girl didn't need to see her mother on the verge of a breakdown.

"I know this is a shock, but the sooner you can come, the better." The detective kept his voice soft and polite. Margot wanted to reach through the phone and shake him and ask him why his world wasn't tipped upside down too.

Instead, she forced herself to be civil. "I understand," she replied quietly. "It'll take me a day or so to get there."

"If you could keep me informed of your plans, that would be great. I want to stay available for when you arrive. Hopefully, we can make this process as quick and painless as possible."

"Me too." She closed her eyes, blinking back the moisture gathering there.

"All right. I'll see you soon, Mrs. Gaultier. I'm so sorry for your loss."

Margot wanted to scoff, but held back. She'd suffered the loss a long time ago. It was just permanent now. "Thank you. Goodbye." She hung up and squeezed her eyes shut. A single tear slid free. She swiftly wiped it away.

Emily squealed again, closer this time. A moment later, Margot felt a tug on her pant leg. She glanced down, forcing a smile. "Did you match them again?"

"I match!" Emily held the toy up.

"I see. Good job, sweetie. Do you want to try again?"

The little girl bobbed her head and sank to her butt, engrossed in her toy.

Margot inhaled a steadying breath. She needed a moment.

"Sweetie, you stay here with your sister. Mommy will be right back."

Emily didn't even look up. Margot glanced at Lily, who sat beside the desk with a box of giant crayons and a coloring book. Both girls were content for the moment.

Crossing the small room, Margot left her office, closing the door behind her, and went next door to Annabeth's office. She was thankful they were still in the building phase of their little clinic. Focusing on patient care would be nigh on impossible after that bombshell.

She rapped her knuckles on the wood as she stepped into the doorway. "Hey, do you have a minute?"

The smile of greeting on her friend's face swiftly died when she took in Margot's expression. "What's wrong? Sit. Where are the girls?"

"They're next door. I—" The sudden lump in her throat cut off her words. She swallowed and tried again. "A detective just called. From North Dakota. Tad's dead." She'd never expected to see her ex-husband again after the way he left, but knowing that was now a certainty brought out all the emotions she'd buried fourteen months ago.

"What?" Annabeth breathed. "What happened? And what was he doing in North Dakota?"

"They're not one hundred percent certain it's him, but they found a National Park Pass with the body and got his name from that. He—he asked if I could come up and help them identify the body. I guess they're not sure it's him."

"Oh my God." Annabeth stared at her with wide eyes. "I'm assuming they found his driver's license online, if they knew to call you. How are you supposed to ID him if they can't tell it's him from his license?"

"The detective wants me to look at the personal effects. He said there was a car key in his pocket that goes to a car they found months ago, abandoned. It was full of stuff. Like he'd been living in it. He also asked me to submit a DNA sample from the girls." She dropped her head into her hands. "Oh, God, Annabeth. I don't want to do this."

Annabeth got up, moving around to sit next to her. She laid a hand on Margot's shoulder. "I'm so sorry, Margot. What do you need from me? I can go with you. Or Dean can. We both could, if you want."

"Um..." Margot threaded her hands together and stared at them. Her mind swirled with a million thoughts, but one thought screamed louder than the others. She didn't want to take the girls with her. "Actually, could you and Dean watch the girls while I'm gone? Traveling with them is a nightmare, and they don't need to be exposed to the situation."

"Of course we can watch them. But you're not going up there by yourself, are you?"

Margot shrugged. She hadn't had time to figure out what she was doing.

"Take someone with you. Max would go, I'm sure."

A pair of lovely, silvery blue eyes popped into her mind. She knew Annabeth was right; he'd help her in a heartbeat. But he already did so much for her and the girls, she didn't want to impose more. That was the very reason she had the girls with her today after her sitter called and said she was sick. She'd become too reliant on Max and wanted to break the cycle. He wasn't her husband or her significant other. It wasn't his job to rescue her all the time. She was grateful he was her friend, but she didn't want him to think she only hung around for what he could do for her. She liked him for so much more than that.

"Don't." Annabeth aimed a finger at Margot's face.

Margot frowned. "Don't what?"

"Don't take the choice away from him. I know you think you're imposing, but Max would do anything for you. Let him help. You shouldn't do this alone. No one should."

A bang and a screech from next door propelled Margot to her feet. "I'll think about it." And she would, but she'd never ask him to go. It was one thing to ask him to babysit or to come fix something at her house. Flying to North Dakota on short notice was on a whole other level.

"Let me know when you need us," Annabeth called.

Margot raised a hand and gave her a thumbs up as she hurried out of the office. After she rescued her daughters from each other, she had a lot to think about.

Chapter Two

The deep-throated purr of Max's car engine cut abruptly as he shut the vehicle off in Margot's driveway, Annabeth's cryptic message still fresh in his mind.

Margot could use a distraction.

Like, what the hell did that mean? Were the girls extra ornery today? Had something happened? When he replied to ask why, she ghosted him.

So, here he was with a carton of Margot's favorite pineapple passionfruit gelato, hoping she wouldn't be pissed that he'd shown up unannounced when she'd had a rough day.

Pebbled gravel crunched under his flip-flops as he walked up the short path to her front door. The little pale-yellow bungalow with its pink front door could fit inside his living room, but Margot insisted it was fine for her and the twins. He and the others had tried to convince her the other house she looked at closer to his would be a better fit and give her and the girls more room, but she wouldn't be swayed. The neighborhood was nice, and she could literally step out her back door and yell for Annabeth, which, Max was sure, had been the deciding factor. He couldn't blame her for wanting to be near her friend. She'd moved thousands of miles from home to a foreign country after a major life change. It was probably comforting to have her best friend close by.

Through the wooden front door, he could hear Emily screeching. One side of his mouth lifted. That girl was hardly ever quiet. Usually only when she was asleep.

Raising a fist, he knocked on the door.

Thirty seconds passed with no answer, so he tried again. "Margot?"

When another thirty seconds went past and she still hadn't answered, he tried the door. It was unlocked.

Pushing the colorful door inward, he stepped inside. "Margot? It's Max." The small living room he walked into was empty, though it looked like a tornado tore through it. From the short hallway to the left, he heard splashing and Emily's shriek of joy. A moment later, Lily joined in. Now he understood why she hadn't answered. It was bath time.

With a few strides, he crossed the living room and rounded the corner to the hallway, looking right into the bathroom. Margot sat on her knees on the floor, water splotches all over her clothes. As he watched, she scooped a cup of water out of the bath and dumped it over Lily's soapy head.

"Margot."

She yelped and spun around. "Jesus!" She pressed a hand to her chest. "Max!" Closing her eyes for a moment, she inhaled a breath through her nose. "You scared me. I didn't hear you."

"I noticed. The door was open, so I let myself in. Need a hand?"

She spared a quick glance at the girls, who were busy pushing plastic fish through the water at each other. Em looked up and saw him. With a wide smile, she lifted her fish out of the water to show him, spraying her mother with soapsuds in the process.

Margot closed her eyes for a second and sighed. "Um... no. I think we're about done. What are you doing here?"

He held up the gelato carton. "Annabeth said you needed a distraction. Pineapple passionfruit gelato fixes everything."

Margot looked away, a hardness settling over her face that confused him. "I'll just bet she did," she mumbled.

"What?" He frowned.

"Nothing." She waved a hand, looking at him again. The smile she sent his way didn't reach her eyes. "As much as that sounds wonderful, I need to get these heathens to bed. I'm sorry you came all the way over here for nothing."

Max narrowed his eyes, sure now more than ever that something was wrong, and Annabeth was right to send him over. "I didn't. Put them to bed. The gelato—and I—will be waiting for you when you're done."

"Max—"

He ticked a finger. "No arguments. I don't know what you need a distraction from, but Annabeth was right that you do. I'll be out there when you're done." He tipped his head toward the kitchen and living room as he stepped back.

"I'm fine, really."

"Then we can enjoy our gelato and some light conversation before you go to bed."

She stared at him for a beat. "Anyone ever tell you you're pushy?"

"All the time, babe. All the time." Grinning, he faded into the hall and walked away before she could truly kick him out.

Entering the kitchen, he took one look at the sink full of dirty dishes and the mess on the island and put the gelato in the freezer. It could wait.

No wonder she hadn't wanted to relax after the girls were in bed. She couldn't.

He found a dish rag in a drawer and a clean sponge and set to work. Squirting dish soap in the sink, he turned on the faucet. While he waited for the sink to fill with hot, soapy water, he scraped the last bits of food from the girls' plates into the trash, then did the same with the skillet. All of it went into the pile of dirty dishes on the other side of the sink.

When the sink was full, he shut the water off, then cleaned the small island Margot used as a table. Once it was clean, he wiped out the girls' booster seats, then set about washing the dishes. He had them all done and in the drying rack by the time Margot emerged from the hallway. He'd also picked up the toys scattered around the living room and put the crayons back in their box, stowing them on a shelf with the coloring books.

Her reaction to him cleaning up was not what he expected, though. He'd thought she'd be surprised and thank him, or, considering her attitude in the bathroom, get a little defensive that he'd taken the chore off her plate.

Instead, she burst into tears.

Eyes wide and feeling more confused than ever, he crossed to her side. "Margot. Hey, what's wrong?" He put a gentle hand around her bicep and tugged, pulling her into his chest. When she didn't back away, he wrapped his arms around her and stroked the back of her head. The silky blonde hair under his fingers was cool to the touch and just slightly damp.

She clutched the sides of his shirt and buried her face in his neck. With a hiccup, she looked up. "I'm sorry. I'm—" Another sob choked off her words. She inhaled a breath, making a snort-snuffle sound.

Max took her hand and led her over to the couch, handing her some tissues from the box on the end table. "Take a breath. Tell me what's wrong."

She took the tissues and dabbed at her face. "Nothing."

"That's crap, and you know it. Tell me what's going on. Why did Annabeth say you need a distraction?"

"Annabeth has a big mouth." She sniffed and wiped her face again.

"She's worried about you."

Margot sighed. "I know."

"So, what's going on? Why are you so upset?"

"I'm not."

He snorted. "The tear tracks on your face tell me otherwise."

"I'm not upset. Just... overwhelmed."

"Because of the girls? What did Em do today?" That girl could try the Pope's patience.

She barked a short laugh. "It wasn't Emily."

"No?"

"No." She reached over him for more tissues, then blew her nose. When she finished, she stared at the wad of white in her hand.

"So, should I keep guessing?"

Margot lifted her head. There was a bleakness in her eyes that punched him in the gut. He hadn't seen that look since he'd first met her when her life was in total turmoil.

"I got a phone call today. From a detective in North Dakota." She rolled her lips in for a moment, then let them go on a slow exhale. "My ex-husband is dead."

Shock made him sit up straighter. He stared at her for several seconds, a frown forming as he mulled her words over. "You said a detective called? Not the medical examiner's office?"

"Yeah. I don't know many details. He didn't seem like he wanted to discuss it too much over the phone. Apparently, um..." She trailed off and rubbed at her temple. "Um, he was... decomposed, so they're not completely certain it's him."

"How did they know to call you, then? *Why* did they call you? You're divorced."

"They found a car key in his clothing that went to a car

they'd found abandoned months ago. I guess something in it gave them his name. The girls are his next-of-kin, which makes me his next-of-kin since they're so young. He doesn't have any other family except for a few distant cousins. The detective asked if I could submit a DNA sample from one of the twins." She looked away.

Max narrowed his eyes. The way her gaze darted away set off his inner radar. "There's more, isn't there?"

Her eyes met his, then she looked away again. "Stop reading me."

"It's not like I have to try, Margot. Your face is an open book. What else does the detective want?"

She sighed and muttered a soft curse under her breath before she met his gaze again, defiant. "He wants me to come up there and identify him from the things they found in his car. He's got questions too."

Like a lightbulb illuminating the darkness, Annabeth's reasons for sending him over became crystal clear. "You plan to go alone, don't you?"

"I don't have anyone else. Annabeth and Dean are watching the girls. I'm an only child to two elderly parents who didn't really want to be parents. I'm not even sure where they are right now."

Max's eyebrows met his hairline. "You realize you have a town full of people who would hop on a plane with you in a heartbeat, right? Any of us would go. All you have to do is ask."

She pushed to her feet and walked to the kitchen, throwing open the freezer to get to the gelato.

He got up and followed her. "Margot."

She sent a glare at him as she yanked open a drawer and withdrew an ice cream scoop.

He stayed by the island, not wanting to crowd her. Why she was so angry, he didn't understand. Her attitude didn't put him off of their discussion, though. If anything, he wanted to know more—wanted to understand why she was so surly.

She heaped gelato into two bowls. "I know I'm being unreasonable, but—" She flattened her lips, glancing away as she thought. When she met his gaze again, moisture shimmered there.

With a sniff, she grabbed a spoon, jabbing it into her gelato. "First, I'm not used to having help. Before Tad, I did everything alone. It's the curse of having parents who were in their forties when I was born and didn't really want me. They left me alone a lot. Even when they were home, I had a nanny. Second, you all have done so much for me already. What happened with Tad—it's my mess."

"Okay, I understand the alone thing. But how is this stuff with Tad your mess? The man left you with no notice." Max didn't know much about what happened with her ex. She never talked about him, but he knew that much.

"Something drove him away. Whether it was my drive to succeed or becoming parents unexpectedly—I'm not completely blameless."

He'd heard enough. Marching forward, he didn't stop until she was forced to look up to see his face. "He left you. No discussion, no expressing his concerns. He just up and left. Whether he didn't like something about you or the life you two had, it's not your fault. It's his. And as far as helping you goes, that's what friends do. Especially our group of friends. We're more than that. We're family."

"But I'm not. Not really. I'm just Annabeth's tagalong."

Max forced his hands to stay at his sides. He wanted to grab her and shake her at the same time he wanted to hold her close. This was a side of Margot he'd never seen. In all the time he'd known her, she'd been on the quieter side—except around her daughters and Annabeth—and it suddenly made sense as to why. She felt like she was on the outside looking in.

"No, Margot, you're not. The moment Dean brought you into the fold, you were part of the family. You and the girls." This was not a subject he was willing to debate, so he changed the subject.

"Have you booked a flight up there?"

She waved her spoon at him. "I know what you're doing, Max. Changing the subject won't make things magically change."

"No, but maybe by doing so, eventually you'll come to realize I'm right. Now answer my question."

She stabbed her gelato again. "No."

"Good. I'll book two flights. When do you want to leave?"

"Max..."

"Don't argue with me. Not on this. You need someone with you. I'll follow your lead, but I know we'd all be happier if you didn't go alone. You don't know what the cops are thinking, and you don't know what you'll be confronted with when you get there. Let me be the shoulder to prop you up? Please?"

She stuffed another bite in her mouth, the angry frown on her face turning slightly less belligerent and more thoughtful. Finally, she looked at him again. "This is hard for me. Accepting help. Annabeth badgered me into moving in with her when Tad left, otherwise, I'd still be in Texas trying to make my life work while I spent ninety hours a week at the hospital and the rest trying not to be a stranger to my children. She's the only person—other than Tad— I've ever truly trusted, and I need her now to watch my kids while I straighten this out. But you're right. I don't want to go alone. I'm dreading going at all."

"So, does that mean you won't protest if I tag along?" he asked when she paused.

Margot scooped up another bite of gelato and sighed. "I

suppose not." She narrowed her eyes at him. "But that doesn't mean I'll let you buy my ticket."

Max shoved a bite of his own gelato into his mouth, hiding the smirk. One way or another, he'd get his way. "How about you let me arrange all the travel? You can pay me back."

She snorted. "No. I know you. We'll end up in first class, which I can't afford."

He thought fast. "But I can. For both of us. How about this? I get the first-class seats, but you pay me for the cost of an economy ticket?"

Her frown returned. She opened her mouth to speak, but he cut her off.

"I don't want to sit in economy for a flight that long. I'm too tall, and I can afford not to be smushed. I also don't want you to sit alone. That's just dumb." Which was true, but if she pushed back too hard, he'd happily give in and suck it up so she didn't have to sit by herself. He hoped she didn't, though. They would both be much more comfortable in first class. "And it's not like an extra first-class ticket will break me. I'm not Brooke rich, but you know I'm far from poor."

She pursed her lips and blinked at him. Finally, her expression relaxed. "All right. You win. But can we not stay in a super fancy hotel? The local Holiday Inn is fine."

"I will see what they have there." And make sure they had all the space they needed.

～

Discover what happens and get your copy at
https://books2read.com/maxs-mission

About the Author

Ashley started writing in her teens and never stopped. Her first novel, Smoky Mountain Murder, came out in 2016, and she has since published two more series and has plans for more. When not writing, you can find her with her nose stuck in a book or watching some terrible disaster movie on SyFy. An avid baseball fan, she also enjoys crafting and cooking. She lives in Ohio with her husband, two kids, three cats, and one very wild shepherd mix.

Website: https://ashleyaquinn.com
Facebook Reader Group: facebook.com/groups/
349932159616427

goodreads.com/ashleyaquinn

amazon.com/Ashley-A-Quinn/e/B07HCT4QST

facebook.com/ashleyaquinn.writer

instagram.com/ashleyaquinn.writer

Wagner Brigade

Ford's Fight

Dean's Dilemma

Jordan's Journey

Sam's Salvation

Asher's Assignment

Max's Mission

www.ingramcontent.com/pod-product-compliance
Lightning Source LLC
Chambersburg PA
CBHW022302310726
48973CB00001B/177